GW00371209

SURREY

Overdue items may incur charges
as published in the current
Schedule of Charges.

L21

LEGENDS OF THE DARK MILLENNIUM

ULTRAMARINES

GAV THORPE, NICK KYME, GRAHAM McNEILL, JOSH REYNOLDS & STEVE LYONS

BLACK LIBRARY

A BLACK LIBRARY PUBLICATION

First published in 2015 by Games Workshop Ltd.
This edition published in Great Britain in 2016 by
Black Library,
Games Workshop Ltd.,
Willow Road,
Nottingham, NG7 2WS, UK.

10 9 8 7 6 5 4 3 2 1

Produced by Games Workshop in Nottingham.
Cover illustration by Raymond Swanland.

A CIP record for this book is available from the British Library.

UK ISBN 13: 978 1 78496 286 9
US ISBN 13: 978 1 78496 453 5

It is the 41st millennium. For more than a hundred centuries the Emperor has sat immobile on the Golden Throne of Earth. He is the master of mankind by the will of the gods, and master of a million worlds by the might of his inexhaustible armies. He is a rotting carcass writhing invisibly with power from the Dark Age of Technology. He is the Carrion Lord of the Imperium for whom a thousand souls are sacrificed every day, so that he may never truly die.

Yet even in his deathless state, the Emperor continues his eternal vigilance. Mighty battlefleets cross the daemon-infested miasma of the warp, the only route between distant stars, their way lit by the Astronomican, the psychic manifestation of the Emperor's will. Vast armies give battle in His name on uncounted worlds.

Greatest amongst his soldiers are the Adeptus Astartes, the Space Marines, bioengineered super-warriors. Their comrades in arms are legion: the Astra Militarum and countless planetary defence forces, the ever-vigilant Inquisition and the tech-priests of the Adeptus Mechanicus to name only a few. But for all their multitudes, they are barely enough to hold off the ever-present threat from aliens, heretics, mutants — and worse.

To be a man in such times is to be one amongst untold billions. It is to live in the cruellest and most bloody regime imaginable. These are the tales of those times. Forget the power of technology and science, for so much has been forgotten, never to be re-learned. Forget the promise of progress and understanding, for in the grim dark future there is only war. There is no peace amongst the stars, only an eternity of carnage and slaughter, and the laughter of thirsting gods.

CONTENTS

CATECHISM OF HATE

GAV THORPE

'The more I learn about these aliens, the more I come to understand what drives them, the more I hate them. I hate them for what they are and for what they may one day become. I hate them not because they hate us but because they are incapable of good, honest, human hatred.'

Inquisitor Agmar

PROLOGUE

If ever there were an abomination given form, it was the tyranid hive ship. Cassius could see it clearly through the armoured windows above the launch bays. Less than three hundred kilometres away, the hive ship was a blot against the bright orb of Argo Secundus's primary moon; an impossibly vast, half-coiled mass of chitin and flesh. The Chaplain could not see the damage wrought by the battle-barge's torpedoes and cannons but knew from experience that the alien creature's armoured form would be pocked and split from plasma blasts and shell detonations. Feeder tendrils, each dozens of kilometres long, trailed from the prow of the hive ship, and a miasma of frozen ichor surrounded the wounded craft.

Though injured, the hive ship was still a threat to the planet below. It was too close to Argo Secundus for further bombardment; if it had been further crippled the hive ship would disgorge its mycetic spores onto the world in a last, desperate detonation to despatch its cargo of bio-constructs. Long, hard experience had taught the Ultramarines this, so the commander of the battle-barge had known when to stop the attack, just short of that self-destructive orgy of seeding.

The next strike would be the riskiest. Cassius and his warriors would board the hive ship with virus charges and melta detonators, to cripple the synaptic corridors along its dorsal nerveways. With these pathways severed, the hive ship would not be able to launch its thousands of spores, trapping the creatures aboard. The strike force would withdraw and the Ultramarines flotilla would complete the hive ship's destruction.

It sounded simple, this breach-and-destroy mission. Like all Space Marine Chapters, the Ultramarines had perfected starship assault tactics over their long history, and in recent decades the Codex Astartes had expanded with the experience of fighting the tyranids.

In practice, it would be a tense, bloody action. The tyranids excelled at close quarters combat, even more so than the Adeptus Astartes, and the Ultramarines task force would literally be entering the heart of their nest-ship. Speed and precision would be vital.

Leaving the gantry, Chaplain Cassius made his way down to the launch bay below. His black-painted armour glowed with a dull, ruddy aura in the pre-launch lighting. In their blue livery, the seventy-two Space Marines of his command waited beside four boarding torpedoes, ready for the order to embark on the transport missiles. Cassius knew that in the neighbouring bay, three Thunderhawk gunships were readying to lift off, carrying another assault force that would conduct an initial strike against the energy cortex located in the underbelly of the hive ship.

Striding across the mesh decking, he opened a vox-channel to address his force. The Ultramarines turned in unison to face their venerable leader, raising bolters and heavy weapons in salute as he stopped at the top of the ramp leading up to the closest boarding torpedo.

'Hail the Emperor!' Cassius declared, the call echoed over the vox-net by his warriors. 'Praise the primarch! Today we go into battle against the worst kind of foe. We know this enemy well, for they came to our own world, to glorious Macragge. On the snowy tundra and the wind-swept plains, our brothers and forebears gave their lives to defeat the tyranid menace. This foe, this filthy xenos plague, brought our Chapter to the brink of annihilation, but we prevailed. It is our duty to protect mankind against such alien horror, but to face the tyranids is more than a duty. To destroy them is more than a matter of honour and glory. It is our right!

'There are countless foes that beset the worlds under our aegis, but it is for the tyranids that we must unleash our greatest hatred. The threat they pose is nigh immeasurable. Dozens of worlds we have lost to them. That would be reason enough to eradicate them, to seek them out at every turn and wipe them from existence. There is another, grander reason to be proud of their extinction. The foe we destroy today is a pitiless, unthinking devourer of worlds. It is an alien intelligence that is beyond our comprehension because it is incapable of any act other than destruction.

'We are the Emperor's Angels of Death, but in raining death upon our enemies we bring safety and prosperity to mankind. The tyranids are a malaise of galactic proportions that do not negotiate, do not barter or surrender. Only the utter annihilation of every tyranid organism will see this threat ended. Only with the most ruthless hatred will we prevail against them.

'It is not our battle-barges and bolters, our lascannons and melta bombs that will bring us victory. These are merely devices of destruction. It is our will to wield them without compromise, to unleash righteous devastation in the Emperor's name, which will bring us victory. Hate these foes! Hate them with every fibre of your being. Hate them in your hearts and despise them in your souls. Purge them with flamer and sword and rejoice at their deaths.

'There are some men, weak philosophers and cowards, who say that hatred clouds the judgement. They are wrong! Hatred gives us purity. Hatred gives us focus. Hatred gives us our purpose. Board now the vessels that will take us to the foe and make us the instruments of the Emperor's vengeance and listen to my words of hate. Bring your thoughts to bear on this tale as you prepare for battle against this noxious enemy.

'Let me tell you of the cleansing power of hatred. Listen to the story of Styxia and know that hatred is our most potent weapon.'

CHAPTER I

The bureaucrats of the Departmento Munitorum called it Phagolitic Xenos Threat Omega-seven-octa; the men and women tasked to fight the invading aliens simply called it Hive Swarm Gorgon. The first sign of the hive swarm's approach had been the encroachment of the so-called Shadow in the Warp over the Styxia star system. Blotting out astropathic communication, eclipsing the holy light of the Astronomican, the might of the tyranid hive mind had swathed Styxia and the surrounding systems with psychic darkness. Astropaths of the affected worlds had broadcast general alarms as the Shadow had enveloped the populated star systems to the galactic east of Styxia, where Hive Fleet Kraken had splintered after the great battle for Ichar IV.

The warp shuddered with the dream-messages of the astropaths. Attuned psykers within hundreds of light years were assailed by images of all-devouring maws and grasping claws. A filthy umbra tainted everything, creating a serpentine, coagulating mass of hysterical ravings and apocalyptic vistas that drove many astropaths to madness and suicide; their last words ranted warnings of a terrifying beast of the abyss arisen to consume the galaxy.

Then there had been silence, black and impenetrable.

The Chief Librarian of the Ultramarines, Tigurius, had felt these panicked waves through the warp and known well what they presaged, as had other astropaths on waystations and monitoring posts across the sector. The Ultramarines were not the only force to have heard the cries for help suddenly snuffed out by the all-consuming advance of the tyranids: the Imperial Navy and Imperial Guard were being mustered for battle at Styxia. The quietude that had followed the eclipsing of the beleaguered astropaths was filled by message and countermessage that commanded the raising of regiments and the redirection of fleets.

Knowing this, Tigurius relayed the matter of the unfolding situation to Marneus Calgar, his Chapter Master, aboard ship en route to a campaign against the orks rampaging through the Vortengard Spiral. The flotilla came together at Arensis, the first of several staging stops to keep the vessels together on the seven hundred light year journey to Vortengard. Knowing that further progress would take his warriors away from Styxia, the Chapter Master called a pause before the next warp translation and brought together his trusted advisors – members of the Librarius, his company captains and Chaplain Cassius, most venerable of the Chapter's warriors.

From across the fleet they gathered on the flagship, the *Octavius*.

* * *

They formed their quorum in Calgar's personal chambers, to discuss their response to Tigurius's communication. Their meeting took place in a small hall, lit by hanging rosettes that gleamed with golden light reflected from marble pillars flanking the chamber. The walls were painted with murals depicting famous scenes from across the realm of Ultramar: the pillared underground halls of Calth; Kronor's immense furnace-spire whose summit burned brighter than the local star; rugged mountains swept by lightning storms on Espandor; Guilliman's solace lodge amongst the forests of Iax; surf-cutters chasing a giant aquatic beast on Talassar.

The floor was made of heavy tiles of obsidian and granite, each inlaid with a gilded insignia in the shape of an inverted omega: the symbol of the Ultramarines. The council table stood at the centre of the room, also dark in colour, circular in shape and large enough for twenty Space Marines to be seated around it. Before each chair was a sigil carved into the top of the table and set with shining silver to mark the position of the council attendees: Master of the Fleet; Master of the Watch; Chief of the Librarium; Chancellor of Macragge; Master of Sanctity and many others. It was not often that every seat was filled, such were the many demands that split the Chapter across the Eastern Fringe. Today would not be such a day, though nearly a dozen captains and other high ranking officers would be in attendance.

The ceiling was decorated by tiny glass beads that formed a mosaic of the Seal of Macragge – a wreath-crowned eagle between scrolled insignia that had been the mark of Konor, foster father to the Ultramarines Primarch Roboute Guilliman. It had become the badge of office of every Chapter Master since the old Legion had been split – a mark that was now the privilege and the burden of Marneus Augustus Calgar.

Sitting on a heavy, high-backed chair, the Chapter Master of the Ultramarines waited patiently for his warriors to attend him and make their statements of allegiance and dedication. He accepted the liege-words of each warrior with a simple nod of the head. His hands, encased in the massive Gauntlets of Ultramar, lay in his lap unmoving, though his stillness of body was not matched by his eyes. These moved quickly, taking in the faces and expressions of all who came into the hall, reading their mood and intent by long experience and close companionship. Of the Chapter Master's disposition there was little sign, except perhaps tightness in the jaw and a slight downward curl of the mouth, that hinted at some disquiet.

Armoured in their full war panoply and accompanied by their entourages of servitors and serfs, the command council attended to the words of their Chapter Master. Each knelt and spoke words of fealty, flanked by banner bearers and helots carrying weapons and other relics appropriate to the rank and duties of their master, before taking their station at the large table that filled the centre of the hall.

Calgar's explanation of the situation was brief and to the point: the Ultramarines were already committed to the battles at Vortengard and other Imperial forces had responded to the menace at Styxia. It was his view that the Ultramarines should continue on their set course and defer the defence of Styxia to the Guard and Navy forces already being despatched.

'The matter seems to be in hand,' said Captain Ixion, commander of the Seventh Company.

'Styxia is an agri world, home to less than five million souls,' pointed out Captain Agemman, who held the title of Regent of Ultramar, second in authority only to Calgar. 'A thousand times that number are threatened at Vortengard. Our priorities are clear, we must not be distracted from our current course of action.'

'Had we rebuilt ourselves to our full complement from the devastation at Ichar Four, we might respond,' said Pulo Astersis, a veteran Techmarine who was the most senior member of the Armoury present in the fleet and hence de facto Master of the Forge. 'Still we await replacements to the vehicles and armour lost in that conflict.'

Cassius growled his displeasure and the eyes of all the Space Marines around the table turned in his direction. The Chaplain stood up and leaned forwards, resting the knuckles of his armoured gauntlets on the polished black marble of the table. Like the table, the Chaplain's armour was jet black, only his left shoulder pad painted in the blue of the Ultramarines. Skull devices adorned his armour amongst a welter of wax-sealed purity parchments, and at his hip was chained a copy of the *Liber Ultramar*: the roll of honour of the Ultramarines.

He was the oldest warrior of the Chapter, not including those who had been chosen for the honour of internment in a Dreadnought. Cassius's skin was thick and leathery, heavily scarred from centuries of fighting. His short-cropped hair was pure white. His right eye had been replaced by an augmetic substitute decades before, and the red lens of the bionic glittered in the lights of the hall.

'You wish to say something?' said Marneus Calgar, waving a hand to invite Cassius to speak.

'It is not my place to countermand the wishes of this

council, but I have words that need to be heard,' said the Chaplain. His voice was deep, his words spoken quickly but clearly. 'Who knows better than those seated here what devastation the tyranids can unleash? Who but the Ultramarines has the experience and the knowledge to defeat this threat? More than that, who above the Ultramarines do the people of the Imperium look to for salvation from this alien menace?'

'We cannot fight every foe, no matter how much we might desire it,' said Agemman. 'Always we must weigh up the price of action. Styxia cannot be considered a more important cause than the hive worlds and manufactories of the Vortengard Spiral.'

'In material terms, you are correct,' said Cassius, moving his gaze from one Space Marine to the next, until his eyes met those of Marneus Calgar. 'Yet it is not our place to make purely material judgements. We are the Ultramarines, Primogenitors of many hundreds of Chapters, spiritual leaders amongst the Adeptus Astartes. Our actions resonate across the galaxy, for good or ill. What are we to say if Styxia falls to the tyranids? That it was a battle not worthy of our attention?'

'You do not know that Styxia will fall,' said Agemman when Calgar offered no reply. 'Nor can you say for certain that our intervention is necessary to prevent its fall. Styxia is unremarkable.'

'Perhaps your detestation of the tyranids clouds your judgement, Cassius,' suggested Captain Ixion, his voice mellow despite the accusation behind the words. 'You seek retaliation in opposition to strategic necessity. Our judgement must be of sound military basis, not founded upon emotion and personal desire.'

'Yes, I detest the tyranids!' said Cassius, thumping a hand to the tabletop, causing the whole slab to shudder. 'It is no bad thing to hate our foes with passion and conviction. You speak at this council to provide rationale and strategy. I am your inferior in this regard and do not gainsay any statements that have been made. If we are to resolve ourselves entirely by cold logic and logistics, there is no argument.'

'Yet you have another view?' asked Ixion

'I am Master of Sanctity and it is for the honour and spirit of the Chapter that I speak,' said Cassius. 'If we do not fight at Styxia, then where would we do battle? If each action is weighed only on the merits of risk and reward, what of our reputation and the example we set?'

Cassius stepped away from the table and crossed the hall to where a broad bookcase stood beneath a tapestry showing the north facade of the Macragge senate house. The Chaplain took the first volume from the top shelf, a hefty tome the spine of which barely fit into his giant hand. Carrying the book, he moved around the table and placed it in front of Agemman.

'The Codex Astartes,' said Cassius, stroking the book with a reverent gesture. 'Penned by the primarch. Show me, Severus, where in the wisdom of Guilliman are we told to put logic before honour?'

Captain Agemman did not rise to the bait, but instead glanced at Calgar for support. None was immediately forthcoming, the Chapter Master seeming content to keep his thoughts to himself for the moment while his subordinates aired their differences of opinion. Whether he had made up his mind and was gauging the mettle of his officers, or was genuinely waiting for them to conclude their counsel, was not obvious.

'I can turn to the pages that tell us not to waste the lives of our warriors in the cause of vanity, if you like,' said Ixion, reaching across the table for the Codex.

Cassius's hand met the captain's just before Ixion grasped the book, fingers gripping the other Space Marine's wrist. The Chaplain locked his eyes to those of the other Space Marine, his expression stern rather than angered.

'I know the pages of which you speak,' said Cassius. 'It is not a fool's errand that we face. It is not vainglory to support the soldiers and ships of the Imperium.' The Chaplain released his grip, picked up the Codex Astartes and returned to his chair. 'If not Styxia, then where? There is always some other threat, some other world to be saved. You are correct: we cannot be everywhere at once. Yet we are expected to be. What world is important enough that we would always leap to its defence? Macragge? What if Terra were under threat, would we defend even Macragge? We do not weigh the lives of men by their numbers and we do not judge the worth of a world simply by its strategic significance.'

'To what advantage would we send our warriors into this campaign?' said Agemman. 'If not strategic, nor personal, what end do we serve if we were to respond to this call above all others?'

'We give hope,' Cassius said quietly. 'Ever has it been that the Space Marines are too few to conquer every threat. Yet the truth of our existence and the hope of our intervention steels the hearts of lesser warriors and lends strength to their conviction. They hold out against impossible odds and offer up prayers to the Emperor that the Angels of Death will come. They fight harder, knowing that if they do so we might intervene. Mankind believes our Emperor to be a god, and that is both foolish and blind. Yet they also believe the Adeptus Astartes to be the instrument of His will, and that is not so ignorant. I cannot say whether the Emperor answers prayers thrown up in desperation, but I do know that the Ultramarines reply to calls for aid if it is possible. To not answer that cry for help threatens to shatter something far more precious than ore worlds and hive factories: faith in the Space Marines.'

There was no word raised from the captains against the powerful argument spoken by the Master of Sanctity. Ixion shook his head slightly as Cassius looked directly at him, while Agemman lowered his eyes, unable to meet the Chaplain's gaze. The council turned to Marneus Calgar, who had remained attentive but dispassionate throughout the exchange.

'We cannot abandon our war against the orks,' he said, raising a hand as Cassius opened his mouth to offer argument, silencing the Chaplain. The Chapter Master looked at Cassius. 'Oaths have been sworn to defend the people of the Vortengard Spiral. However, it is not right that we abandon Styxia to the uncertain care of the Imperial Guard. Our expertise could prove vital in such a campaign.'

Calgar stood up and walked around the table to lay a hand on the shoulder plate of the Chaplain.

'Cassius will lead a task force to Styxia. Company strength, drawn from across the Chapter,' Calgar continued. 'One hundred Space Marines should be enough of a command to make the presence of the Ultramarines felt. Does that suit you?'

'It does,' said Cassius with a nod. 'I shall ask for volunteers.'

'No,' said Agemman. 'That would be unfair. There is not a battle-brother in the Chapter who would not follow you to war, and I would not have those who are not chosen feel that they have been judged against. We shall draw a force from amongst our companies sufficient for the task.'

'As I warned, materiel is scarce,' said Astersis. The Techmarine stroked his chin in thought. 'Some Rhinos and Razorbacks could be spared.'

'Take the strike cruiser *Fidelis* as transport,' said Calgar. 'It has sufficient berths and craft to effect a landing for one hundred warriors.'

'Your faith will be rewarded,' said Cassius. 'A hundred Space Marines is a force that will baulk any foe. The glory of the Ultramarines will be maintained, our honour upheld.'

'I will look unkindly upon unnecessary heroics,' said Calgar, his expression grim. 'We cannot afford heavy casualties at this time. I trust you not to spend the lives of the Chapter's warriors without good cause. Do not disappoint me.'

Feeling chastised, Cassius dropped to one knee and bowed his head to his Chapter Master.

'Your disappointment would be the most severe castigation I could suffer,' said the Chaplain. 'We will not fail.'

CHAPTER II

At first encounter, Cassius thought the defence of Styxia appeared shambolic. Once the *Fidelis* had transitioned back into realspace and gained full sensor reports, a more coherent pattern emerged and the Chaplain evaluated his assessment of his new allies.

Four hive ships had entered Styxia several weeks earlier. One had been destroyed by the great effort and sacrifice of the system defence ships and the first elements of the Imperial Navy flotilla that had been despatched. Two others had been intercepted and turned away from the most heavily populated world, Styxia Prime, though they remained dangerously close to gaining orbit over the world.

The fourth had not been stopped. It was dead now, a gigantic carcass with a slowly depleting orbit that looked like a small, shrivelled moon circling Styxia Prime. Its destruction had been too late, however, and a huge mass of tyranids had made planetfall.

Still ten days from Styxia, Cassius ordered the
Fidelis to approach at full speed, ignoring the ongoing
cat-and-mouse encounter between the Imperial vessels
and the two functioning hive ships. All attempts to separate the tyranid vessels from one another had failed,
and the battleship and two light cruisers tasked by the
Navy to halt the invasion simply did not have enough
firepower to take on both foes at once. Navy reinforcements were supposedly only days away, including two
battle cruisers, but there was a fear that Gorgon had not
yet revealed its whole strength and other hive ships might
appear at any time.

The first priority was to secure the main city of Plains
Fall, which formed the hub of the agri world's export-
ing capability. A city-sized starport, Plains Fall was the
only vaguely defensible position on the entire planet;
the rest of the population was spread thinly across the
farms that provided cereal and grox meat to hungry hive
worlds light years away.

Although the Imperial Navy had not fared too well in its
initial defence of the system, they had safely transported
two Imperial Guard regiments to the surface before the
tyranid landing: the Astcarian Fourth, a heavy infantry
formation which had been bolstered by a company of
Imperial storm troopers; and the Cadian 308th who had
been despatched from their home world on the other
side of the galaxy two years before, in response to the
battles against Hive Fleet Kraken in the build-up to the
war for Ichar IV.

In overall command of the Imperial defenders was
General Arka, who Cassius had met before in the aftermath of Ichar IV. This heartened the Chaplain a little, as

Arka was known as a capable commander and Cassius's own experience of the man had been positive. Three days from orbit, the two were able to hold a conference of sorts.

It was during this brief council of war that Cassius received further good news. Several Titans of the Legio Fortitudis had been brought to Styxia, including two massive Warlord-class machines. The only deficiency that Cassius could see was a lack of airpower and orbital supremacy. With the Imperial Navy unable to destroy the remaining hive ships for the time being, the troops on the ground were wary of further enemy planetfalls. Though the arrival of the *Fidelis* was a little boon in this regard, the strike cruiser was mainly fitted out for orbital assault rather than engaging other starships. The bulk of her space was taken up with launch bays and drop pod cascades, her weapons geared towards providing orbital bombardment of a dropsite prior to the Space Marines assault.

During their short conversation, Arka invited Cassius to join him at Plains Fall to assist in the defence of the city. The decision had been made to pull as many inhabitants as possible back to the city, sacrificing the fields and grox farms to the tyranid swarm. Crops could be re-seeded and herds restocked in a short space of time, but the massed orbital elevators and docking facilities at Plains Fall would take decades to rebuild if they were overrun and destroyed.

The city had grown around three gravity lifts that soared up into the clouds. Each metres-thick cable was still working, offloading the last harvests to cargo haulers waiting in orbit, the bulk carriers elevating thousands of tonnes of raw foodstuff every few minutes while empty carriages descended. Scores of warehouses the size of hangars encircled the lifters, supplied by a steady stream of crawlers that entered along the dozen roads radiating from the transit hub like spokes of a wheel. Each highway was lined with teetering tenements housing thousands of stevedores and teamsters, overlooked from an artificial mount by the white-walled palace of the Imperial Commander, Sevastin Goul.

Fourteen landing aprons were arrayed around the central complex, linked by a maze of elevated highways and railroads that teemed with trucks and locomotives. Steam and smoke and exhaust fumes billowed around the city, creating a hazy fog that drifted lazily into the cloudy sky.

As soon as the *Fidelis* had attained low orbit, Cassius took a Thunderhawk down to the city. As he descended towards the main dock, the forces and preparations of the Imperial Guard were evident all across Plains Fall.

Earthworks tens of metres high were being erected around the whole of Plains Fall. Prefabricated bunkers were shipped into position slung beneath enormous tetracopters. Engineer and pioneer teams hundreds-strong dug kilometres of trenchworks and excavated dozens of revetments for mortars and heavy weapons. At each of the twelve inroads, fortified bastions were growing up from the bare earth, studded with weapons turrets and firing ports, covering the open approaches into the city.

Storage sacks had been filled with dirt and sand to make bagged enclosures on the top of the flat-roofed buildings, manned by the Guardsmen under General Arka's command. Columns of Leman Russ tanks prowled further out along the highway, while at the limit of vision, squadrons of Sentinel walkers patrolled back and forth, waiting for the first approach of the tyranids.

The Titans of the Legio Fortitudis stood guard to the north and west: a Warlord Titan at each highway supported by smaller Warhound Titans and hundreds of Adeptus Mechanicus skitarii in Chimera transports and eight-wheeled armoured cars. The adepts of the Machine-God had brought with them batteries of strange-looking weapons mounted on four-legged walking machines. Cassius recognised some of the artillery – sonic cannons, plasma launchers, lightning generators and more mundane shell-firers – while others were a bewildering array of tubes, cables and dishes whose purpose was unknown to the Chaplain.

Imperial Navy forward ground officers and Departmento Munitorum quartermasters marshalled the effort, and it was from one of these that Cassius's pilot received confirmation that General Arka had made his headquarters in the Teamster Guildhouse near to landing pad quatros. Directions were given and the Thunderhawk touched down in a spume of plasma and smoke in the north-west of Plains Fall.

Striding down the Thunderhawk's ramp, Cassius found himself greeted by a contingent of Cadian officers in long coats and peaked caps. Their uniforms were dark grey mottled with ochre, and every one of the five men had at least half a dozen honour badges pinned to their breasts or stitched on the sides of their caps. No aristocratic officer class here, as was found in many Imperial regiments. These were Cadian commanders, raised on the most embattled world in the Imperium and promoted purely on merit and ability.

'I am Colonel Taulin,' one introduced himself: a short, wiry man with a thin, grey moustache and bright blue eyes. 'General Arka's aide-in-chief.'

Cassius nodded in greeting as the others stepped forwards and gave their names. Taulin waved to a half-track staff car parked at the side of the apron. Two gunners manned heavy stubbers in a compartment at the back, their weapons trained towards the sky.

'We have had sporadic gargoyle attacks for the last two days,' explained Taulin, noticing the object of Cassius's interest. 'No great numbers, just scouting forces we think.'

Without comment, Cassius followed the man to the vehicle and vaulted over the side into the space between the gunners, the half-track rocking on its axles from his weight. The officers sat down on the padded benches in front as the driver gunned the engine. Taulin twisted in his seat to continue the conversation.

'Sorry we couldn't find something a bit more dignified to convey you to the general, but all of the Chimeras are being used to ferry as many refugees as we can find into the city.'

Cassius tested a thick-sided ammo crate and found it sturdy enough to use as a seat. Still he towered over the other men as he looked down into the wood-panelled seating compartment.

'Do not bother yourself in that regard,' said the Chaplain. 'I expect to be treated with the minimum of ceremony and pomp. We are all soldiers of the Emperor here.'

'Of course,' said Taulin, stretching an arm along the back of the bench. 'General Arka would have met you himself, but we have just received word that contact was lost with a storm trooper patrol about eighty kilometres to the west. The general is coordinating our response.'

The staff car bumped off the apron access ramp onto a potholed roadway that headed west towards the edge of the city. To either side, doors and windows on the column-fronted grain stores were being barricaded, while more Guardsmen set up anti-air weapons atop silos and vast storage tanks.

'Arka is a man attentive to detail, if I remember him correctly,' said Cassius.

This raised an unexpected laugh from the cadre of officers.

'Yes, he is very keen on detail,' said one of the lieutenants. 'Arka would pick the target of every man and woman under his command if he were able!'

'I hope he realises that my force will operate with autonomy from the general command structure,' said Cassius. 'I will discuss strategy with him, but the operational implementation of our agreed plan will be my decision alone.'

'The general expected as much,' said Taulin. He pointed at a building a little way ahead with a wide portico at the front reached by a flight of shallow stone steps. Numerous communications masts and dishes had been set up on the roof. 'Our headquarters, Chaplain.'

A Leman Russ Demolisher was parked by the entrance, the short but wide barrel of its howitzer directed up the street. A platoon of storm troopers in heavy carapace armour coloured a deep red, hellguns held across their chests, stood guard at the top of the steps. Their faces were hidden behind the black visors of their helms, reflecting the front of the building opposite as they watched

the new arrivals disembarking from their vehicles. Their
lieutenant gave a shout and they came to attention, presenting their weapons amid the clash of booted feet.

Taulin gave a fly-swat of a salute in return as he took
the steps two at a time, trying to keep up with the long
stride of Cassius, the other command orderlies trailing
behind the pair. The Chaplain stopped and placed his
fist against the Imperial aquila emblazoned across the
gorget of his armour in a return gesture.

The interior was the same as Cassius had experienced
countless times before: a mess of people and equipment
that seemed to be teetering on the line between calm and
anarchy. The doors to the guildhouse opened onto a tiled
lobby, and through open archways to each side could be
seen groups of Guardsmen clustered around vox sets,
analytical cogitators, map tables and hololithic displays.

The soldiers of the Emperor were dressed in a variety
of uniforms. Amongst the grey-and-tan of the Cadians
were bright splashes of deep blue trench coats, which
Cassius presumed were the colours of the Astcarians.
Here and there, the sombre black of the commissars was
present, watching over everything with stern expressions
and hawk-like vigilance. Half-machine servitors babbled
streams of information from the vox traffic, while young
boys in tight overalls ran to and fro carrying messages
from one command staff to another. A few tech-priests
monitored the metriculators and sensor banks, their red
robes standing out amongst the darker fatigues of the
Guardsmen.

Taulin paid no attention to the throng, leading Cassius
to another flight of steps that swept up from the far end
of the lobby to the storey above. At the top, he turned

and walked around a mezzanine overlooking the foyer, taking the Chaplain to a broad set of double doors leading to a room above the entrance.

Inside was a stark contrast to the activity below. The chamber was obviously some kind of meeting hall for the guild – their badge of crossed cranes was emblazoned at one end behind a stage of dark wood, with worker team banners and plaques mounted to either side. Chairs, cabinets and other furniture had been carefully stacked in front of the long row of high windows overlooking the street, leaving only the light from a huge chandelier at the centre of the hall.

In the wide space, General Arka had set up two distinct areas. On the stage had been mounted a larger projector mechanism, attended by a pair of servitors and a junior lieutenant. On the sheet-like screen beneath the guild seal was displayed a map of Downland, the continent on which Plains Fall was situated. Under the direction of the lieutenant, the servitors interfaced with their device, overlaying runes and sigils onto the chart to represent Imperial positions and the possible locations of the tyranids.

Cassius had studied the topography of Styxia Prime whilst travelling through the warp on the way to the system. It had three major landmasses, the largest of which was Downland, covering nearly twenty-eight million square kilometres. Many thousands of years ago, sometime during the Dark Age of Technology, the first human settlers had come to this world and re-ordered the planet to their liking. Mountains had been levelled, seas filled in and rivers diverted to create a land of pastures and gentle uplands. At the heart of Downland were four artificial volcanoes, delved into the earth to bring forth nutrient-rich expulsions that were conveyed by land and water to the mega-farms.

The hills around these volcanoes had been seeded with fast-growing trees to provide hard timber, and it was from this dense wood that many of Styxia Prime's buildings were constructed, with only the largest and most important edifices, such as the starport and governor's palace, being supplemented with ferrocrete panels and ornamented with sandstone blocks quarried from the coastal cliffs.

Plains Fall was located to the east of the continent; its name derived from the thousands of square kilometres of flat fields that surrounded the city. The highways that converged on the city traversed the length and breadth of Downland, crossing hundreds of rivers and canals. For much of their length, the carriageways were raised up on enormous piles fifty metres above the ground, enabling crops and livestock to be grown beneath and allowing the highways to traverse irrigation waterways without interruption. The longest of these stretches, the so called Minoran Gradient, lifted one of the east-west roads to the central highlands, not touching the fertile earth for two and a half thousand kilometres.

A cursory glance at the strategic map confirmed to Cassius that General Arka was concentrating his forces to the west of the city. Sensor reports had shown that the majority of the tyranid spores from the dying hive ship had landed in the volcanic uplands. There was nothing to prevent them ravaging the lands further west – there being no settlement or natural feature upon which to form a defensive salient – and so Arka had rightly drawn a cordon across the highways leading from the highlands to Plains Fall, to intercept any swarm-broods advancing on the city. The rest of Downland would be sacrificed for the survival of the world's only major conurbation.

A much smaller, more primitive, map was mounted on a wooden easel in front of the stage, depicting Plains Fall itself. It was a mass of colour, showing defensive lines surrounding the city and the labyrinth of communication and supply lines linking the growing fortification complex together. Around this map were about a hundred seats arranged like an amphitheatre, empty at the moment with no briefing in progress.

Far from the stage was a communications area. Several vox sets were lined up on wooden trestle tables, manned by staff officers and attended by more youthful runners. A single cogitating machine stood close at hand, spewing mathematical reports on ribbons of paper, which were then passed to a waiting tech-priest to decode. The tech-priest's robes were marked with sigils that Cassius knew identified him as a lexmechanic – a statistical analyst who was expert at extrapolation and prediction. His hood was thrown back, showing the bulky metallic implants in the left side and rear of the tech-priest's skull, linked to the cogitator by three coiled cables. Processing the data-flow from scouting reports and orbital surveys, the lexmechanic translated this pure data into something comprehensible to a group of officers uniformed with the badges of the general's staff headquarters.

Not far from these aides was the commander himself, immediately recognised by Cassius. The general was a tall man, with narrow shoulders and a somewhat chubby face that looked too big for his body, made to look all the fatter by the thick bushes of his greying sideburns. He removed his forage cap and stroked a hand over his balding head, sweat gleaming in the artificial light. His drab uniform was crisply pressed, his left sleeve stitched with a long line of battle honours, his right breast coloured by the ribbons of more than twenty medals of heroic service. He moved slowly, with a stiffness that spoke of aging joints and old battle wounds, but his gestures were as neat and meticulous as his appearance, if somewhat laboured.

Arka was in conversation with a group of agitated-looking officers from the Astcarian Fourth, the gold frogging and gilded buttons of their dress uniforms a stark contrast to the general's nondescript battle fatigues. The general noticed the arrival of the Ultramarines Chaplain and dismissed his audience with a few words and a crisp nod of the head. A few seconds later, he was waving for Cassius to join him.

The general extended a hand in greeting, which Cassius shook gently, careful not to hurt the aging officer.

'It was with some pleasure that I learned the Ultramarines had heeded the call to arms,' said Arka. 'When I learned that it was the revered Chaplain Cassius in command, I thanked the Emperor profusely.'

'I was surprised that you were still on the Eastern Fringe, general,' said Cassius, releasing Arka's hand. 'Pleasantly surprised.'

'Thank you,' said Arka, nodding in acceptance of this rare praise. 'As we just missed out on the fighting at Ichar Four, I decided we should look for another war. This is our third encounter with the tyranids so far. I do not expect it to be our last.'

'I see that you have your strategy well in order, general.' Cassius waved a hand towards the briefing area. 'Do you have any request to make of me?'

'I do, I do,' said Arka. He gestured to Colonel Taulin, who had briefly conversed with the lexmechanic and his liaison officers. Cassius noticed that the general's knuckles were red and swollen, the skin thin over his fingers. Many a man in his position would have undergone anti-agapic therapy or other rejuvenat processes, but Arka was clearly determined to grow old and die within his natural duration. As long as this had no effect on his mental faculties, Cassius was content to accept this foible without comment.

'It seems our early predictions were correct, general,' said Taulin, handing a schematic to his commander. 'Storm trooper and Sentinel patrols have confirmed significant tyranid infestation in the sixth quadrant of the highlands. Vanguard organisms have been seen moving eastwards towards the city in the last two days. The closest was fifteen hundred kilometres, moving along the main highway.'

'I would like you and your warriors to take the forepoint position at the heart of the predicted line of attack, Chaplain,' said Arka. He handed the schematic to Cassius. 'Three rivers and the highway intersect at a staging post called Cordus Via, some seven hundred kilometres west of here. The topography will force the bulk of any attacking force to convene. If Cordus Via can hold for a few days, it will allow us to finish the defensive perimeter closer to the city. I expect it will be the hardest fighting. How strong is your force?'

'I have a total of one hundred Ultramarines,' said

Cassius. 'I concur with your plan. We will hold the lynch-pin at Cordus Via to stall any advance on the city.'

'You'll not be alone,' said Taulin. 'The Warlord Titans *Victorix* and *Dominatus Rex* are to be stationed in that quadrant too.'

'Even better,' said Cassius. 'I will have my warriors drop directly to Cordus Via and will meet them there. We will have the position secure within five hours.'

'Are you sure you want to land so soon?' asked Taulin. 'It will take the Titans at least twelve hours to reach their positions.'

'Then it is even more important that someone is ready to guard the crossing,' said Cassius. 'Unless your reports are woefully inaccurate, we should not expect any significant enemy force to arrive before the Titans. I know that General Arka prides himself on the quality of his intelligence, and so I expect to meet only minimal resistance, if any. We are quite capable of dealing with any tyranid advance until the Legio Fortitudis reach the line.'

'Are you sure you do not want any extra assistance?' said Arka. 'I could spare some storm troopers. Maybe move up some of the Astcarian self-propelled guns?'

'That will not be necessary, general,' said Cassius. 'We operate best when we have full autonomy. Having to guard your forces will only present extra complications.'

Taulin laughed at this, but his humour quickly wilted under the stare of Cassius.

'I shall provide you with all of the relevant logistical data, Chaplain,' said the colonel, looking away. 'Comm net frequencies, contact protocols and such.'

'Thank you, colonel.' Cassius gave a nod to Arka and Taulin. 'If I require anything else, I shall let you know.'

'The Emperor protects,' said Arka. 'May He watch over you, Chaplain.'

'You should have no fear in that regard,' said Cassius. 'We are the Ultramarines, the Emperor's chosen.'

CHAPTER III

Situated at the confluence of several fast-flowing rivers, Cordus Via was predominantly a long arc of the highway supported by spire-like struts that thrust up from the floor of the plains. It formed an intersection of several smaller elevated roadways that stretched hundreds of kilometres to the north and south, linking the mega-farms with the arterial route. The bulk of the settlement was made up of storage towers, a refuelling depot and thick-timbered accommodation blocks for passing convoy teamsters.

Just a hundred metres west of the waystation, three rivers joined at a mighty cataract, plunging some two hundred metres down a gorge. The roar of descending water sent constant vibrations through the settlement, an oppressive noise that blotted out all other sound.

The lead elements of Cassius's force – three tactical squads led by Sergeants Dacia, Heletis and Octanus – had made planetfall less than thirty minutes after the

Chaplain's conference with General Arka. They had reported the site empty of inhabitants, though over the following hours, three columns of refugees passed through while the task force's Thunderhawks had shuttled more forces from orbit. Questioning the fleeing farmers, the Ultramarines learned that the isolated farmsteads in the low hills to the west had been attacked by scattered tyranid broods some twenty hours earlier. The refugees had managed to fend off or escape the initial assaults for a short time, before abandoning their farms to head to Plains Fall.

Cassius's gunship arrived just as dusk was settling. The last Thunderhawk run was being completed, another of the strike cruiser's three gunships touching down beside the Chaplain's transport on the wide, black surface of the main highway. A devastator squad disembarked, their heavy weapons in hand, and were met by Sergeant Dacia – as the most senior sergeant in the force, he had been marshalling the defence in Cassius's absence.

Dacia's blue and white armour was covered with litany parchments and purity seals, testament to many battle honours. Along with his squad from the First Company, Dacia had been amongst a new generation of Space Marines promoted from the other companies to serve as veterans after the heavy casualties suffered against Hive Fleet Behemoth. They wore standard power armour for this engagement; the highly valued Tactical Dreadnought suits so closely associated with the First Company were in short supply too and had been taken with the Chapter Master for hive city-fighting in the Vortengard systems. The shortage of Terminator armour was a constant reminder to the veterans of the sacrifices made by their predecessors, and Cassius expected his First Company squad to be exemplars to the rest of his command.

Dacia acknowledged Cassius's arrival by raising his storm bolter in salute. The setting sun glinted from the weapon's gold casing as the sergeant lifted it to the brow of his white helm. Cassius responded to the gesture, bringing a fist up to his chest. As all Chaplains did, Cassius wore the black livery of purity, only his left shoulder pad remaining blue to signify his allegiance. Atop a golden *crux terminatus* badge – a legacy from Cassius's days in the First Company – the Chaplain bore the Ultramarines symbol fashioned from snow-white stone, hewn from the same quarry as the majestic pillars and halls of the Chapter's fortress-monastery on Macragge. The symbol was riveted to the left pauldron by bolts made from shards of the crozius arcanum wielded by the previous Master of Sanctity, Agai Paulus, who had fallen in battle against foul xenos warriors in the Halo Stars.

The Chaplain considered Paulus's fate a noble one, and was resigned to his own death at the hands of the tyranids some day in the future. A day long in coming, he was sure. Styxia would not be his last war.

Cassius had been in constant contact with his second-in-command throughout the deployment, and the sergeant's assessment of the position and his disposition of the Ultramarines force had been faultless, guided by the teachings of the Codex Astartes. While Dacia directed the devastators to their place in the defensive cordon, the two Thunderhawks lifted off – one to return to orbit for refuelling, the other to begin air patrols around Cordus Via. Dust and vapour billowed across the roadway from the plasma jets of the departing gunships, momentarily obscuring Cassius's vision. The autosenses of his armour switched to a thermal scan, the vents of the Space Marines power packs flaring brightly against a backdrop of reds and blues.

'Heletis and a combat squad are performing patrol two kilometres west,' Dacia reported as the cloud dissipated. Cassius joined the sergeant as his view reverted to a normal-spectrum image. Dacia turned towards the buildings of Cordus Via and pointed to each Ultramarines placement as he continued. 'From the roof of the dormitory building, two of the devastator squads cover the western and northern approaches. This third one will be at the fuel storage tanks of the waystation, providing support fire to the south. We have Corilinus's assault squad in mobile reserve at the power plant, and a full-strength cordon of tactical brethren patrolling in combat squads. There are three subterranean chambers located beneath the warehouses to the north, with gate access from the garage complex beside the highway off-ramp. I've had all but two sealed and set with plasma charges. The others we can use as sally ports if necessary, to encircle any tyranids that breach the inner compound.'

'Vehicle pool in the garage?' said Cassius. The two of them began to walk down the highway slip road, which turned a lazy circle down to the tightly-packed buildings.

'No,' said Dacia. 'Too difficult to defend, with the highway passing directly overhead. I have the Razorbacks at the roadway intersections to provide point support. The Rhinos are laagered two hundred metres south, should we require a withdrawal.'

'There will be no withdrawal, sergeant,' said Cassius. 'We will hold Cordus Via.'

The sergeant hesitated in his stride for a moment before continuing on towards the waystation.

'It was my understanding that we are to delay the tyranid attack only. I have read the Imperial Guard reports. The tyranids have landed in strength on this world. We do not have the resources to halt any advance completely.'

'Nevertheless, we will not be surrendering Cordus Via to the enemy. That is my command.'

'As you say, Brother-Chaplain,' said Dacia. 'We stand ready to lay down our lives in the defence of this place.'

Before Cassius could say anything further, a sharp noise echoed up from the buildings. It was the unmistakable crack of a bolter being fired, followed by several more shots.

'Brother Liades is down!' Sergeant Augustin barked over the comm. 'Tyranid infiltration organism in warehouse six, south-west corner. Pursuing.'

More firing erupted dully from the outskirt of the settlement as Dacia and Cassius broke into a run.

'All squads in the south-west sector to converge on Augustin's position,' snapped Cassius. 'South and west patrols increase perimeter to overlap with established routes of displacing squads.'

Affirmatives drifted back over the comm net. There were no more bolter shots until Cassius and Dacia had linked up with the sergeant's squad, who had been stationed where the slip road met the ferrocrete apron of the refuelling facility. This time the firing came from Cassius's left, to the north – the sound of several bolters being fired in unison.

'Another lictor here!' came the report from Sergeant Octanus. 'We discovered it before it had been able to hide. Enemy destroyed. No casualties. Continuing patrol.'

'I'll start a second sweep to the north,' said Dacia, signalling to his squad to move out.

'Yes, sergeant,' said Cassius. 'I will join the southern perimeter. I want a street-to-street, room-by-room search. When the main attack comes, we cannot afford any enemies to have secreted themselves behind us. Stay alert.'

With armoured boots pounding on the ferrocrete, the Chaplain ran down the street, heading to the main throughfare that cut across Cordus Via. He listened to the reports of the squads converging on the lictor's position in warehouse six. The building was already quarantined, each exit covered, but the tyranid creature could well have gone to ground to launch another surprise attack inside. Locating it would be perilous.

Though he was running fast, Cassius was still scanning every street, alley and building he passed. His eyes flicked across empty windows and shadowed doorways and passed over the roofs and balconies, missing nothing. His ears strained against the thunderous background noise of the cataract, his suit's autosenses doing their best to filter out the blanketing cacophony.

Cassius stopped suddenly, pulling free his bolt pistol with his left hand. With his right, he slid his crozius arcanum from his belt and pushed the activation stud. The winged skull-shaped head of the weapon shimmered with the red light of its power field as Cassius turned to his right and looked back at an alleyway he had just passed, his intuition telling him something was wrong. Examining the alleyway more closely, his gaze fell upon that which had sparked his subconscious: a line of darker patches leading across the alley to an external ladder that ran up the side of one of the warehouses. Magnifying his vision, the Chaplain's suspicions were proven correct. The dark patches were splashes of liquid.

One of the river banks was located less than fifty metres away from where he stood. None of his Space Marines had been into the water, so something else must have crossed the river, leaving the trail of drips in its wake.

'This is Cassius,' he said over the comm. His eyes roved over the facade of the warehouse, finding the identifying plate next to the wide doors. 'Possible sighting, warehouse three.'

'Squad Dacia will be with you in two minutes, Brother-Chaplain,' came the first reply.

'Negative, sergeant,' replied the Chaplain. 'Continue to sweep the north sector. I will call for assistance if required.'

Rather than follow the infiltrator up the ladder, where it might be lying in wait on the roof, Cassius entered the warehouse through a side door. It was dim inside, the open space lit only by a few narrow windows at ground level. Activating his thermal view, the Chaplain looked left and right, seeking any anomalous heat signatures. The warehouse floor was almost empty, only a few empty crates stacked along one wall. Metal steps ran up to the upper storey, ten metres above his head, where the clerks' offices would be located.

Still checking the shadows as he advanced, Cassius crossed the freight floor towards the stairway. He was aware of the loud thudding of his boots on the ferrocrete, but there was nothing he could do about that. Reaching the bottom of the steps, the Chaplain holstered his pistol and drew out a frag grenade from his belt.

'Ground floor clear,' he told his warriors. 'Continuing to upper level.'

Thumb poised over the primer rune of the grenade, he ascended quickly, taking the steps three at a time, the cavernous warehouse ringing with his heavy tread.

He stopped just a few steps from the top and tossed the grenade ahead, suspecting that the lictor might be poised to attack as he emerged from below. Two seconds later, the warehouse echoed again with the *crack* of its detonation, shrapnel clattering against the walls and floor, the top of the stairs illuminated by the flash of the blast.

Hurling himself up the last few steps, Cassius came out onto the upper floor with bolt pistol readied again, the glow of his crozius bouncing back from thin walls peppered with grenade shrapnel. Spinning on his heel, he checked the passageway behind him but saw nothing in the gloom. By the gleam of his weapon, Cassius navigated his way towards the north side of the building, glancing into cubicle windows as he passed, finding nothing. He came to a ladder leading up to a small access panel in the ceiling. As far as he could tell, the hatch had not been opened for some time. There was rust around the lock-bolt and undisturbed cobwebs on the ladder.

It did not mean for certain that the lictor was still on the roof, though it seemed increasingly likely. There could be other ways into the warehouse from above. Still on his guard, Cassius continued his circumnavigation of the offices, the outer wall on his right-hand side.

Coming to a place where another corridor met the outer walkway from the centre of the building, Cassius paused once more, checking each approach. As he glanced behind, he thought for a moment that he saw movement in the darkness – a smudge of deeper red amongst the mist of heat left by his armour.

Suddenly feeling that he was being observed, Cassius did not look back to verify what he had glimpsed, but instead stepped into the central corridor. He knew that the lictor would attack as soon as it thought it had been discovered, but until then would stalk its prey for the most opportune moment. At such close quarters, the Chaplain knew that the lictor would be able to strike him down in an instant if it had the chance to attack. Somehow he needed to gain the upper hand, to manoeuvre into a position from which he would be the hunter.

Stepping backwards at the same steady pace he had been walking before, Cassius moved away from the junction, pistol raised towards the outer passageway. He knew he would not get much warning of the impending attack. The lictor's skin was covered with chameleonic scales that blended with the environment, and its exoskeleton was capable of masking all but a small fraction of its body heat. Sound would be the best detector, but with the whole warehouse quietly thrumming with the pounding of the nearby cataract, it would be almost impossible to detect the scrape of a clawed foot on the floor or the rubbing together of chitinous plates, even with the Chaplain's superhuman hearing and the aid of his armour's autosenses.

Lictors had been evolved by the tyranids to be stealth incarnate, and their oversized claws made them experts at ambush attacks, slicing apart their victims before they even knew they were in danger. Such a being was a threat to even a power-armoured Space Marine, but it would be even more deadly if it remained undiscovered and was able to attack whilst the Ultramarines were dealing with the first wave of assault organisms that were surely following the pheromone trail it had left in its wake.

It is behind me again.

The thought came to Cassius from nowhere, a message sent to his reasoning mind from some animalistic, instinctual part of his brain.

He turned and fired without questioning the moment of intuition, the muzzle flare of the bolt pistol illuminating the monstrous form of the lictor as it stretched up to its full height, nearly a metre taller than the Space Marine. Its main attack claws were drawn back overhead, serrated edges glinting sharply in the blaze of light. Its face was barely two metres from Cassius, faceted black eyes gleaming with dozens of tiny reflections of the Chaplain. Its maw was a bundle of tendrils writhing like a serpents' nest, tasting the air. Hand-like claws flexed at the ends of its lower appendages, while sharply taloned feet were curling, digging into the stone of the floor to increase the beast's purchase for the killing blow.

The bolt hit the lictor in the left side of its abdomen, blowing out a hand-sized chunk of chitin and flesh.

Even as he fired a second shot, Cassius dived to his left, crashing through a flimsy door, a moment before the lictor's scythe-like claws flashed down in an instantaneous reaction to the Chaplain's attack. One claw smashed into the ferrocrete where Cassius had been standing; the other caught him a glancing blow on his right greave, scoring a jagged gash through the black armour, exposing the suspensors and stabilising gyros within.

Falling to his back, Cassius had his pistol pointed at the doorway within a double beat of his hearts, ready to fire again.

The doorway remained empty for several seconds, but Cassius knew better than to believe the lictor had fled. Its presence known, it was biologically programmed to finish the hunt, eliminating all witnesses to ensure it could disappear once more. Cassius had seen such attacks first hand on Macragge and Ichar IV and half a dozen other worlds, and read treatises detailing the same from others who had faced the tyranids. He would not be fooled by a few moments' pause.

Then the lictor came on, ripping a hole through the wall to Cassius's left rather than coming through the doorway, scattering chunks of plasterite across the room. The tyranid creature burst into the clerk's chamber at the heart of an expanding cloud of dust, jabbing wildly with its scythe-talons, ripping gashes across the floor.

Surging to his feet, Cassius narrowly avoided the next attack, the illuminator's desk behind him detonating in a shower of wooden splinters, coloured inks splashing across the floor and walls. The Chaplain swung his crozius, one wing tip of the powered mace's head burying itself into the wound opened by the Chaplain's first shot.

The lictor made no noise as it spasmed in pain, lashing out with its lower set of claws, tearing three lines across Cassius's right shoulder plate. Twisting the crozius arcanum deeper into the lictor's innards, the Chaplain pushed himself closer to his foe, underneath the deadly sweep of the beast's upper limbs. He brought up his pistol and fired into the cluster of feeder tentacles pawing at his helmet. The lictor's head split apart from within, spraying thick ichor and globules of brain matter across Cassius's armour.

Still off balance, Cassius found himself borne to the

ground by the weight of the dying lictor, the servos of his armour whining in protest for a moment before he crashed sideways into the bare ferrocrete. He lay there, pinned down by the lictor's corpse, the floor beneath him vibrating gently from the roar of the cataract while the creature above twitched and spasmed.

With a grunt, Cassius managed to heave himself onto his front, pushing the lictor's body aside. Gaining his feet, the Chaplain fired three more rounds into the creature, targeting the brain stem, secondary neuroprocessor at the base of the spine and the ventricle chambers within its abdominal cavity.

'Enemy destroyed,' he announced over the comm. 'Be vigilant. The first attack wave will not be far behind.'

CHAPTER IV

As day became night, a total of four lictors were discovered and destroyed inside the Cordus Via perimeter, though not before accounting for the death of two Ultramarines and the serious injury of three others. Brother-Apothecary Valion converted a floor of workers' dorms into a field surgery, located close to the centre of the settlement, but his ministrations were not enough to keep the wounded brethren battle-ready. The dead were relieved of their battle gear and ammunition and along with the wounded were taken by Thunderhawk back to the strike cruiser. Cassius marked the names of the fallen in his battle litanies that night, and reminded the rest of the strike force that there was no greater honour than to die in battle against the enemies of the Emperor.

With the sky swiftly darkening, Cassius faced a thorny decision: whether to bring the outer patrols closer to Cordus Via or not. The further the patrolling squads – three of them in total – were from the settlement, the more warning and information the main force would receive in the event of a tyranid assault. Counter to this, the likelihood of any patrol surviving such a first encounter was greatly reduced if they were beyond the range of swift support from their battle-brethren.

Cassius and Dacia discussed the matter in person. They met in a small outbuilding attached to the refuelling depot, which Cassius had dedicated as a battlefield chapelry. One of the Chapter's battle banners was laid over a cluster of tables and such small relics as Cassius had been able to bring with him were placed on this makeshift altar: a silver goblet that Roboute Guilliman had drunk from during his first meeting with the Emperor; the knife of Antonius Galeus, a much-revered Chapter Master of the Ultramarines; a second-revision copy of the Codex Astartes; and a claw from a tyranid hive tyrant, gilded and engraved by Cassius himself, taken as a token of the victory at Macragge.

The two of them stood on opposite sides of the altar, and addressed each other over their external speakers, not wishing to air their disagreement over the comm net. Cassius had granted audience to the veteran sergeant in recognition of his status as second-in-command, but had made it plain that he was all but set on keeping the patrols at long range.

'There is no advantage in keeping our patrols so far from assistance,' complained Dacia, leaning forwards onto the altar. 'If we are to keep Cordus Via from being overrun, every warrior must account for the highest toll of the enemy. Our patrols will be swiftly destroyed by any large tyranid force, for little advantage to our strategy.'

'We cannot risk the enemy coming upon us unseen,' countered Cassius. He was irked that Dacia was second-guessing his strategy in this way, though it was the role of a veteran sergeant to provide guidance and advice to his commanders. 'We also cannot afford the tyranids discovering some other route to Plains Fall – one that bypasses our position here.'

'So it is your intent that our patrols will be discovered, and in that way attract the tyranids to Cordus Via?' Dacia shook his head slightly and there was incredulity in the metal-tinged voice that came from his helm. 'You would use our battle-brothers as bait?'

'A harsh assessment, brother-sergeant,' replied Cassius. 'I have no intent to allow our patrols to be killed. They will withdraw immediately upon contacting the enemy, bringing the tyranids down the highway and into the strongest part of our defence.'

'I am not convinced that we could not achieve such an end in other ways, without the attendant risk to our patrol squads.'

'If you have a suggestion to make, sergeant, I will be prepared to give it audience.'

Before Dacia could voice his alternative plan, the comm crackled with a priority signal, cutting across the routine report transmissions that had been flowing back and forth between the Space Marine squads.

'Light source from the east, Brother-Chaplain,' said Sergeant Capilla. The sergeant led one of the devastator squads stationed atop the highest dormitory block. 'I estimate they are five kilometres away and approaching.'

'Understood, brother-sergeant,' said Cassius. 'Sergeant Dacia and I will join you shortly.'

The Chaplain walked around the altar and gestured for Dacia to follow.

'I believe we have a third option to resolve our difference of opinion,' said Cassius, switching back to external address. 'A lure that will ensure the tyranids attack here, but will not place our patrols in unnecessary danger.'

From their vantage point atop the tenement, the Ultramarines could clearly see the approaching Battle Titans. Beams from four massive searchlights blazed across the fields, mounted sixty metres above the ground atop the carapaces of the walking war engines. Smaller spotlights illuminated the windswept crops beneath the advancing behemoths, while the helmet-like command bridge of each Titan was lit from within, viewing canopies glaring like ruby eyes in the darkness.

With ponderous strides, the Warlords covered the ground effortlessly, stepping over walls and farmsteads without hesitation. Canals and irrigation ditches proved no obstacle either, bypassed by the massive legs of the Titans. The dull thump of each immense footfall could be heard more clearly, and silhouettes resolved into more detail, as the Warlords came closer.

Each was a humanoid metallic beast, hunched over beneath an armoured carapace of adamantium and plasteel. Two gigantic weapons were mounted upon the back of each Titan and hung from hardpoints either side of chamfered bodies where a man's arms would be. Triangular banners hung from these arm weapons, flapping and swaying with every stride, and another standard was slung on thick chains between the legs of each Titan.

The machine on the left, *Victorix*, was armed with two

multiple rockets launchers atop its carapace, each rocket held within the gigantic cylinders containing several dozen warheads capable of obliterating entire companies of infantry and smashing armoured vehicles. *Victorix*'s right arm was a squat, thick weapon surrounded by coiled pipes and bundles of cables: a plasma cannon powerful enough to level buildings. Its left was a multi-barrelled gatler that could spew forth a stream of titanium-tipped shells each several times larger than a Space Marine.

On the right, *Dominatus Rex* sported two such gatling cannons on its broad back. Beneath the crenellated carapace were slung two long-barrelled laser weapons that had been brought up into a locked position either side of the Titan's head-shaped cockpit. Known as volcano cannons, the fifteen-metre-long guns were designed to destroy enemy super-heavy machines, but would be equally useful searing through the massed broods of a tyranid swarm or vaporising the larger bio-constructs Styxia's defenders might expect to face.

Taller than the building on which Cassius stood, the Titans towered over Cordus Via. As well as the huge battle honour flags, each Warlord was strung with streamers and banners carrying the markings of the Cult Mechanicus. More than just weapons of war, these were idols of the Machine-God, wrought in sacred forge-factories to obliterate the enemies of Mars and its adepts.

Cassius had fought alongside Titans before, but had never encountered one of the metal beasts at such close hand. The thudding of their steps was loud even above the incessant sound of the cataract, every mighty tread causing the ground to shudder slightly, and with each stride came a symphony of growls, whines, hisses and clanking.

By the light of their own lamps, the red-and-black livery of the Legio Fortitudis was plain to see, painted in broad stripes across the upper carapace turrets and the armoured plates protecting the Titans' lower legs. Cog devices and half-skulls in bright metals marked the hard-angled surfaces of their bodies, gleaming in the reflected glow of the searchlights.

'Princeps Jasyn of the Legio Fortitudis.' The announcement was made over the strategic frequency chosen by General Arka for the disparate Imperial forces, the voice quiet, almost a whisper. *Victorix* raised its gatling cannon in salute, kill banner sweeping over a row of empty grain silos, its shadow passing across the tactical squad standing guard on the gantries around them.

'Princeps Perthion, pleased to make your acquaintance, Chaplain.' Perthion's voice was deeper, tainted with a hollow ring that reminded Cassius of the artificial voice boxes used by his Chapter's Dreadnoughts.

'Your presence is welcome,' replied Cassius.

'We are honoured to assist the Adeptus Astartes of the Ultramarines,' said Jasyn. 'Where would you like us to fight?'

Cassius had been considering this matter for some time, and in discussion with Dacia as they had made their way to the tenement block, had formulated a plan.

'I would have *Dominatus Rex* positioned on the highway, a kilometre to the west,' said the Chaplain. 'We have no weapons capable of covering the far side of the gorge to the north, but that will present little problem to you.'

'Understood, Chaplain,' said Perthion. 'I will protect your flank from encirclement.'

'And *Victorix*?' asked Jasyn. There was something about

the way the princeps used the name of his Titan, a familiar inflection, that made it sound to Cassius as if Jasyn were referring to himself.

'On the southern flank, overlooking the refuelling depot and highway would be appropriate, princeps. Your sensor arrays are more powerful than anything we possess and will provide warning of the enemy's approach.'

'We will be your eyes and ears, Chaplain,' said Perthion. A series of thunderous rattles preceded a drawn out, deafening hiss as the lock-bolts were released from *Dominatus Rex*'s volcano cannons. The immense weapons lowered into position with a creak and a clank. 'And your fists.'

'Blessed is the fist that strikes down the foes of mankind,' said Cassius. 'You will earn the gratitude of the Ultramarines for your actions.'

'Blessed indeed is the artifice of the Machine-God, that a humble man might lay low so many foes in the name of the Omnissiah,' came Perthion's reply.

Cassius watched as the Warlords split, swinging away to their appointed stations. He had no doubt that the open highway and fields would be a killing ground for the war machines. There was no intelligence to suggest that the tyranids had managed to land their largest constructs, bio-titans that would be the match of the Adeptus Mechanicus machines, and the Chaplain was confident the men of Legio Fortitudis would destroy many hundreds, if not thousands, of the enemy as they approached Cordus Via.

The streets of the main settlement were a different matter entirely, too tight for the Titans to operate. Despite horrendous casualties, the tyranids would come on and on, driven against their foes by their instinct to devour. No approach was one hundred per cent secure, and the Chaplain knew that despite his immense allies, it was likely the tyranids would eventually reach the buildings and the fighting would become close and deadly.

That would be when his Ultramarines would prove their worth.

'Sensor sweep detects multiple biological signals, four kilometres distant.' Princeps Perthion's warning was devoid of urgency, delivered in the same relaxed tone as his previously negative reports. 'Estimate two to three hundred life forms.'

Dawn was still three hours away, the darkness broken only by a faint glimmer of stars through the cloudy haze and the beams of the Titans' searchlights. The Ultramarines moved quickly into position, their autosenses allowing them to navigate the dark streets and alleys without hesitation. The thrum of powered armour, clump of boots, whine of power cells charging and click of magazines being checked sounded loud in the still night, echoing from empty buildings.

'Moving to engage,' announced Princeps Jasyn. *Victorix* shuddered into life, its weapons drawing up to the firing position. The ground trembled as the Warlord took two strides up the highway access ramp, the dazzling glare of the Titan's lamps lighting up the ferrocrete surface.

Cassius had been in the makeshift shrine room when he had heard the news. Walking swiftly – the distance to the enemy and the intervention of *Victorix* made it unnecessary to run – the Chaplain crossed the street to the main worker tenement and ascended the narrow stairwells, monitoring the reports of his warriors over the comm. The devastator squads had been in position since their arrival, while the tactical squads fell back to the settlement from their patrol routes, taking up guard stations in the outlying buildings to the west and north.

Cassius emerged onto the flat roof of the dormitory block as Sergeant Capilla and his devastators set themselves along the raised parapet at the roof's edge, overlooking the highway where it crossed the river confluence. Beyond them, *Victorix* was already several hundred metres along the carriageway, advancing at full speed.

'First enemy wave, three and a half kilometres,' reported the Titan's princeps. 'Enemy is dispersed along the highway and beneath, approaching at speed.'

To the south, on Cassius's left, the low roof of a storehouse lit up with the blue fire of plasma as a Thunderhawk gunship lifted from its makeshift landing site. It soared several hundred metres into the sky before turning west, accelerating towards the incoming tyranids. As the blue flares of its engines grew smaller in the gloom, another light broke the sky: a plume of fire from the carapace of *Victorix*.

Three blossoms of red surged from one of the Titan's missile launchers, streaking ahead of the Thunderhawk in a parabolic arc. Cassius almost lost their trail in the clouds, but picked them up again as the missiles descended. Each split into a fountain of white flashes as the warheads separated. A few seconds later, explosions erupted across a spread of ground around three kilometres away, creating a column of fire that blazed fiercely for several seconds, blotting out the Thunderhawk lights and Titan searchlamps. The crack of dozens of detonations rolled across Cordus Via a couple of seconds later.

'Good hit,' reported Sergeant Acheon from aboard the Thunderhawk. 'Enemy hit with all ordnance. Heavy casualties inflicted, formation disrupted. They are not stopping. Advancing at speed. Commencing attack run, do not fire.'

'Confirmed,' replied Princeps Jasyn. 'Weapons on hold.'

The blue sparks that highlighted the gunship's position rose briefly and then dived steeply. The cannon atop the Thunderhawk's dorsal mount blazed into life while wing tip heavy bolters blazed tracer rounds through the inky night and the lascannon in the craft's nose spat beams of white destruction. Cassius's autosenses dampened the flares of light, briefly turning the sky to a deep red, the weapons fire seen as pale yellow stars. Of the tyranids, nothing could be seen, though the commentary from Sergeant Acheon announced several dozen slain as the Thunderhawk swept over the enemy and then lifted away, plasma jets burning fiercely.

'Establish command feed, full aerial sweep,' Cassius ordered Acheon, and received the acknowledgement a few seconds later.

The Chaplain's helm display flickered with static for a moment as the link to the Thunderhawk's weapons surveyors established itself. When the image resolved, an inset in front of his right eye showed a grainy view from the circling gunship.

By the light of several pools of flickering plasma fire, obscured in places by patches of ashen cloud made of the bodies of the creatures that had been incinerated by the blasts, Cassius could see the tyranid foe. A sea of termagants was reforming, moving steadily towards the settlement. Each creature was smaller than a man, six-limbed and bent over. They scuttled forwards on their lower four limbs, their upper arms holding rifle-like organic weapons. Chitinous plates covered their backs and heads, long tails whipped back and forth as they ran.

Amongst the termagants were other creatures, with forelimbs composed of serrated blades, like smaller versions of the lictor's claw-scythes. The hormagaunts sprang and bounded quickly between the flames, crossing the scorched ground in long leaps, swiftly moving ahead of the termagant broods.

As the Thunderhawk continued its slow turn, it brought into view larger creatures: tyranid warriors. These stood taller even than a Space Marine, six-limbed like all tyranid creatures but walking on two legs. Twin upper arms merged into pairs of wicked-looking boneswords and grotesque guns with maws that dripped venomous ichor. Cassius knew from hard experience that while the warriors lived, projecting their psychic might onto the lesser creatures, the termagants and hormagaunts would fight to the death, driven on by the gestalt power of the tyranid hive mind.

The leading broods had reached the highway and were pouring onto the cracked ferrocrete by the score. Some split off from the main force, several dozen termagants and a brood of five warriors, heading beneath the causeway as it rose up from the plains, directly towards the river.

'Princeps Jasyn, another bombardment is required, four hundred metres short of last impact,' Cassius spoke calmly, assessing the situation as it was revealed by the Thunderhawk's artificial eyes.

'Sergeant Acheon, another attack run. Target tyranid warrior broods in the rear and eliminate. Squad Heletis, move to the dock area beneath the highway. Be prepared with flamer and bolters to counter any enemy emerging from the riverside. Squad Xathian, take up a supporting position to the north of Heletis.'

Satisfied with the orders he had given, Cassius cut the command link as the Thunderhawk dived groundwards for another attack run. Once more the night sky was torn apart by the barrage of its weapons. When the gunship had completed its pass, *Dominatus Rex* launched another barrage of missiles, bathing the highway and its surrounds with a welter of plasma detonations.

Cassius signalled to Sergeant Capilla, who broke away from his devastator squad to attend the Chaplain. His helm was hung on his belt, revealing a wide-cheeked face criss-crossed with scars.

'You have orders, Brother-Chaplain?' the sergeant asked, nodding his head as a sign of respect.

'It is imperative that the tyranids do not encroach upon Cordus Via, brother-sergeant. We cannot afford to fight a running battle through narrow streets and alleyways. Have your squad reposition to cover the quayside and be ready to open fire if Heletis and Xathian are forced to fall back.'

'We would be firing close to our brothers,' said the sergeant. 'Is that advisable?'

'Frag missiles and bolters pose little threat to our brethren but will reap a heavy toll of the enemy, sergeant. You have your orders.'

'Aye, Brother-Chaplain,' Capilla said, raising a fist in acknowledgement. 'We will cover the withdrawal of Heletis and Xathian.'

Cassius kept his gaze on Capilla as the sergeant returned to his squad. Like Dacia, he was a veteran of many decades' experience, and it was unlike Capilla to show hesitation when receiving a command. Cassius could not avoid the conclusion that Dacia and Capilla, and perhaps some of his other sergeants, were not wholly committed to the effort on Styxia. Perhaps Ixion or one of the other captains had issued instruction to the sergeants before they departed, regarding Master Calgar's edict not to sacrifice the force. If they showed similar reluctance in the heat of battle it could cost even more lives, and ultimately victory.

Feeling vexed by the situation, the Chaplain resolved to speak with his senior warriors when the threat of the initial tyranid wave had been dealt with. He could not afford for there to be any doubt in the minds of his brother Space Marines. They would defeat the tyranids on Styxia, and though Chapter Master Calgar had ordered that losses be minimised, Cassius would not sacrifice a world for the sake of a few lives. It was the fate of every Space Marine to die in battle; Cassius had long ago accepted such truth. If the battle for Styxia could be won, he would win it, even if he had to give his own life.

Dismissing such disturbed thoughts, Cassius returned to his shrine chamber to contemplate the fighting ahead. He reverently touched each of the relics upon the altar table, whispering a benediction to those who would give their lives in the coming battles. He lowered himself to his knees, head bowed in meditation, listening to the reports from his warriors over the comm.

Cassius was not wholly trusting of the Titans and their

princeps. They were powerful war machines, without equal on the ground, but their loyalties were to the Cult Mechanicus not the Ultramarines, and thus their agenda might change at a whim. If Arka or some other individual deemed them to be more useful elsewhere, Cassius would lose their support. It was best to plan for that eventuality; the Ultramarines were used to fighting on their own.

Such thoughts were interrupted by a communication over the command channel that had been assigned by Colonel Taulin. The Imperial Guard officer's voice was quiet, broken by the static of distance.

'Styxia command, seeking contact with Chaplain Cassius. Are you receiving our signal?'

'Signal received,' responded Cassius. He opened a panel in the sleeve of his armour and locked the command frequency. The back-and-forth messages from the Titans, Thunderhawk and patrolling squads reduced to a background whisper. 'Transmit.'

'Ah, good. General Arka has asked me to provide you with an update on the wider situation,' said the colonel.

'My strike cruiser has been monitoring all frequencies as well as ground movements,' replied Cassius. 'They will report if there is any matter that requires my attention.'

'I'm sure they will,' said Taulin. He coughed. 'That said, General Arka wants me to tell you that considerable tyranid attacks are falling upon outlying positions to the north and south of Cordus Via. They are being held back for the moment. He requests that your cruiser receives coordinates for orbital strikes, should our forces be required to withdraw. They are just out of range of our guns at Plains Fall, you see. It would be a boon if we could count on your support when we have to draw our men back to the next line.'

'"When" you have to, colonel? Do you not mean "if" you have to?' said Cassius. In the quiet before Taulin's reply, the Chaplain heard a report from Squad Heletis: tyranids sighted coming down the river bank.

'General Arka has created a collapsing perimeter, Chaplain. I thought he had explained that. We cannot hope to hold the furthest positions indefinitely. An orderly withdrawal is far more preferable to a rout in the face of attack, surely?' Taulin sucked in a breath, trying to hide his annoyance. 'Can General Arka send coordinates to your strike cruiser, Chaplain?'

'Yes, he can,' said Cassius, only half-listening to Taulin as more information about the attack along the river was transmitted amongst the Ultramarines. 'Liaise with Techmarine Pavorian aboard *Fidelis*. Tell him that command authorisation still resides with me.'

'Thank you, Chaplain. With your cooperation, I am certain we can defeat this threat.'

'Yes, we can and we will, colonel. Unless you have anything else you wish to discuss, I must attend to matters closer at hand.'

There was no immediate reply from Taulin, so Cassius cut the vox link. He stared at the relics on display for some time, ordering his thoughts. He was used to dealing with doubt, in others though never himself, and his current assignment on Styxia would prove no different. Those in command of the defenders would learn not to doubt the valour and determination of the Ultramarines, and those under his command would learn not to doubt the wisdom and fortitude of Chaplain Cassius.

CHAPTER V

A little before dawn, Cassius received a communication from the *Fidelis*, warning of a new sensor reading encroaching from the west. Passing on this news to the princeps of the Titans, the Chaplain started on a tour of Cordus Via, to check the position of his troops and see that all was in preparedness for any attack.

The latter hours of the night had passed without significant incident. The first wave of tyranids had been held back by the combined power of the *Dominatus Rex* and successive air patrols from the two Thunderhawks supporting Cassius's force. A few small broods of termagants and hormagaunts had made it as far as the stretches of river above the cataract, where they had been met by a counterattack of tactical and assault squads led by Sergeant Dacia and his First Company veterans. The Ultramarines had suffered no casualties, driving the smaller tyranid constructs into the swift-moving waters where they were easy targets for boltguns and missile launchers, or else were swept over the ninety metre drop of the cataract.

Cassius met with two combat squad patrols on their way back to the garrison in the main dorm block at the bottom of the Minoran Gradient access ramp. They had been north to check for tyranid forces that might have crossed the rivers farther west, but had seen nothing out of the ordinary. The Chaplain was about to wave the Space Marines on their way when his vox crackled into life, an ident-cipher in his helm display notifying him that Princeps Jasyn was hailing. Cassius activated the vox and motioned for the Space Marines to remain where they were.

'Revered Chaplain, I can confirm the sensor readings from your strike cruiser,' said Jasyn. 'We have aerial forces heading our way. Atmospheric distortion is increasing, but I would say four or five large creatures are en route to our position. We are also detecting a surge in land-based signals.'

'A second ground wave, supported by harridans and gargoyles,' replied Cassius.

'Harridans, Chaplain?' said Jasyn. 'I have heard of the gargoyles, winged versions of the creatures we have just been slaughtering. What are these harridans? What threat do they present?'

'Large constructs, princeps, thirty to fifty metres in length,' said Cassius. 'They act as long-range transportation for the gargoyle swarms, and are dangerous in the extreme.'

'Let us hope that they are heading for Plains Fall,' said the princeps. 'General Arka's anti-air batteries can take care of the problem.'

'A valid point, princeps. However, we must be prepared for an assault here.'

'We have some point-defence turrets in case the gargoyles try to swarm us, but other than that, neither *Victorix* nor *Dominatus Rex* are suitable for air defence. If the enemy land amongst you, our weapons will be useless.'

'I understand that, princeps. We will deal with the harridans and gargoyles as necessary. See to it that the second attack wave of ground forces does not intrude upon the proceedings.'

Jasyn signalled an acknowledgement. As Cassius made his way back to the main dormitory block to command the coming engagement, he felt the ground shuddering as the two Warlord Titans moved into position to forestall the coming ground attack. The Chaplain had reached the main thoroughfare when he received a signal from Sergeant Capilla.

'Airborne enemy sighted, Brother-Chaplain,' said the sergeant. 'Due west, three kilometres. Three harridans closing on our position.'

Cassius turned and looked into the cloudy skies to the west, magnifying his autosenses to full. He scanned the cloud layer and saw three dark spots approaching quickly, moving against the prevailing wind. The long-range visual equipment of the devastators was more accurate than the simple autosenses of the Chaplain's armour and Cassius had no doubt that the report was accurate. He signalled Sergeant Menaton, whose squad was aboard the Thunderhawk currently running air cover for the force.

'Sergeant Menaton, engage incoming targets at range. Keep distance to five hundred metres or more.'

'Understood, Brother-Chaplain,' Menaton replied. 'We will keep our distance. Lascannons and battle-cannon primed for attack.'

The Thunderhawk was currently on the northern leg of its perimeter sweep. It banked left and roared over the highway, arrowing directly towards the approaching tyranid flyers, gaining altitude as it did so. Menaton was experienced enough to know that the harridans were weakest from above, and would have to descend several thousand metres before they could release the flocks of gargoyles clinging to their undersides like horrific infants suckling at the breasts of their monstrous mother.

Cassius entered the tenement and took the elevator up to the roof where sergeants Capilla and Therotius had prepared their squads, a battery of lascannons, missile launchers and heavy bolters pointed skywards while the bolter-armed brethren created a defensive circle around the heavy-weapons armed warriors. Looking to the west, the Chaplain could see Sergeant Xathian's devastators doing the same on the gantries around the storage tanks in the depot.

Quickly reviewing the dispositions of his other force, Cassius made a few adjustments, moving some of the tactical squads south of the highway onto the roofs of the warehouses where they could be covered by the devastators of Therotius. Corilinus and his assault squad moved quickly up to the raised highway, their jump packs flaring in the dim light as they bounded up the slope. From there they would be able to cross easily to the roofs of the lower buildings to the north and south, in response to the tyranid attack.

Satisfied that all was well, Cassius recited a liturgy of

battle over the vox, preparing his warriors mentally for the fight to come. As he spoke the words of the second verse, a distinctive crack announced the firing of the Thunderhawk's main cannon. Directing his attention to the harridans, he judged the tyranids to be less than two kilometres away. Lascannon flashes seared across the grey skies as the Ultramarines targeted the lead beast, the pulses of white energy punching through the creature's immense leathery wings. Losing height, the wounded harridan turned sharply, dropping towards the ground. The Thunderhawk circled and fired again, this time striking the harridan in its rear quarters with a battle-cannon shell. Flesh and chitin rained down from the exploding wound, causing the harridan to contort madly, its wings spasming.

A flutter of smaller shapes spread from the beast's belly, scattering in the high altitude winds as the gargoyles detached from the mortally wounded harridan. Some were swept away immediately, disappearing into the clouds; the rest spiralled quickly groundwards, eventually gathering into a coherent mass as they descended into lighter winds.

The other two harridans were stooping into long dives, readying to disgorge their own living cargoes onto Cordus Via. The whine of power cells charging drifted across the rooftop from the devastators as Cassius finished the third verse of the litany and raised his crozius above his head, the gilded tyranid skull at its tip glowing from the power field generator concealed within. The tyranids were less than a kilometre away, swooping swiftly towards the rooftops.

'Let forth your righteous anger in the name of the Emperor!' bellowed Cassius.

Just as the words left his lips, the vox chimed in his ear, signalling a communication from Princeps Perthion.

'Revered Chaplain, sensor reports show excess of three thousand enemy heading our way,' said the Titan commander. 'Distance of two kilometres. We will destroy as many as we can, but we cannot guarantee total extermination.'

'Understood, princeps,' replied Cassius.

Two missiles streaked skywards from the launchers of Squad Xathian. Their contrails cut a converging path towards the closest of the two harridans. The beast's wings had ceased beating as it glided down on its attack course. At this range, Cassius could see the multitude of smaller creatures grappled to its underside: a swathe of quivering pale flesh and dark red chitin plates. As the missiles veered towards the harridan, the gargoyles stirred into life. Spreading bat-like wings, they dropped from the larger beast's underside in a cloud, scattering from the path of the incoming projectiles.

Both missiles struck the armoured head of the harridan, cracking thick chitinous plates and sending organic shrapnel flying but doing little real damage. Divested of its brood, the harridan plunged onwards. Cannon-like growths at the crooks of its wings spat forth a volley of living ammunition. As dark blurs, the projectiles flew towards Xathian's squad; Cassius watched their trajectory as the large slug-like bio-shells dipped across the highway.

Hitting the tops of the storage vats, the bio-cannon volley exploded with a cloud of organic acid, spraying several of the Space Marines with highly corrosive slime and razor-edged chitin shrapnel. Ceramite cracked and melted, the bio-acid searing through the armoured layers of the devastator's pauldrons and chestplates.

There was no time to consider potential casualties: the gargoyles from both harridans were now descending in a dark cloud while the grotesque mother-beasts beat their wings to regain height, turning towards the circling Thunderhawk.

More missiles converged on the incoming mass. Their time-activated fragmentation warheads detonated inside the cloud of creatures, scything through the winged creatures with loud cracks. As several gargoyles fluttered bloodily to the ground, the rest came on, heading straight for the highest building where Cassius and the others waited.

Heavy bolter fire greeted the descending swarm, joined a few seconds later by a fusillade from the rest of the squads' boltguns. Bodies exploded, spraying severed limbs and thick ichor into the wind. Undeterred, the gargoyles folded their wings and dived, approaching at incredible speed.

More bolt-rounds detonated through the flock, sending crumpled bodies down onto the highway. Cassius readied his pistol and took aim, fixing on the leering face of an onrushing gargoyle. A spiny crest jutted from the plate of chitin above its brow and its wings were edged with vicious claws. The creature had been created to spend its existence solely in the air. A barbed tail lashed back and forth, between two atrophied legs connected by wing flaps to the uppermost pair of limbs, acting like a rudder. Like the rest of the brood, the gargoyle's middle limbs were fused with a symbiotic weapon – a distinct species of its own integrated into the tyranid's bony hands.

The brood opened their mouths in unison, emitting a screeching wail. Cassius's ears buzzed as his autosenses filtered out the noise, the thunder of bolters and missiles suddenly muted. Beyond the swarm, the Chaplain caught a glance of a large shape following in the wake of the gargoyles – one of the harridans angling towards the tactical squads on top of the warehouses to the south.

Cassius fired when the gargoyle brood was thirty metres away, their shadows flitting across the Minoran Gradient. The shot hit the gargoyle in its right shoulder, tearing through ligaments and muscle. The tyranid's wing folded up immediately and it plunged down, crashing into one of the huge highway supports.

Aiming and firing again, Cassius's next shot passed through the wing of a gargoyle, the bolt-round punching a small hole through leathery skin but nothing more. And then the flock was on top of the Chaplain.

Plasma-like fire spewed from the mouths of the gargoyles, bathing the Ultramarines with green flame. Their bio-weapons spat volleys of beetles that rattled harmlessly against Cassius's armour, the spatter of their impacts obscuring his livery with thick ichor.

He swung his crozius back-handed, the blazing head connecting with the body of a gargoyle as it swept past. With a blast of light, the energy field tore through chitin and flesh, almost ripping the creature in half. A wing flap slapped across Cassius's helm as the dying beast speared into his shoulder, claws raking spasmodically across his shoulder plate in a welter of paint slivers and ceramite dust.

To Cassius's left, Sergeant Therotius was hacking through the gargoyles, the teeth of his chainsword hurling

gobbets of eviscerated flesh in all directions. The devastators used their weapons as clubs and struck out with
gauntlet-enclosed fists, sticky bio-plasma burning on
their armour where they had been struck. One of the
battle-brothers collapsed under the attack of four of the
creatures, falling to his side as bio-plasma ate away at his
armour seals and scrabbling claws punctured the joints
beneath his shoulders.

Cassius was at the beleaguered Space Marine's side in
five strides, swinging his crozius in a wide arc. The Chaplain's blow swept two of the gargoyles from the fallen
Space Marine, chitin and bones shattered by the impact.
The other two creatures clawed and bit in a frenzy, still
shrieking wildly, driven by instinct to keep slicing and
gouging until their prey was dead. The Ultramarine's
armour held up against the assault for another couple
of seconds, giving Cassius time to fire a shot into the
head of one of the attacking creatures. Its skull exploded,
sending the brow-horn spear-like into the side of the
remaining tyranid.

Something hit Cassius in the back before he could despatch the wounded creature. Warning icons blinked in
the Chaplain's helm display, and his ears were filled with
the scratch and thud of the gargoyle's claws slashing at his
backpack and helm. He turned quickly, trying to throw the
creature off his back, but it had sunk its wing-claw into a
heat exchange vent and would not be shaken free.

'Brother-Chaplain!' Cassius heard the warning over his
external pick-up rather than the vox and swung around to
see Sergeant Capilla with his bolter levelled at him. Cassius turned and dropped to one knee as a hooked claw
scratched against the right lens of his helm.

The bark of Capilla's bolter sounded over the screeching of the gargoyle; a shriek that ended abruptly with a wet spatter of ichor across Cassius's vision.

'Thank you, brother,' said Cassius, pushing himself back to both feet, looking for foes. Only a few gargoyles were still alive, wheeling up into the air above the devastators, spitting bio-plasma.

Cassius took aim but before he could fire, an immense shadow fell across him. Looking up, he saw the massive head of a harridan, long claws trailing from its lower limbs. The Chaplain hurled himself face first into the rooftop as the metres-long scythe swept overhead, missing Cassius by a metre or less. With their focus on the gargoyles, the devastators did not react so quickly.

Even as Cassius shouted a warning, two of the Space Marines were lifted from the rooftop, speared through their torsos by the elongated claws. Capilla fired at the immense beast as it passed over, the detonations of his bolt-rounds appearing as small sparks against the bulk of the harridan. The creature was followed by a downdraught of air that swept up grit and dust from the streets and buildings, swathing the Ultramarines in a thick cloud. Cassius's autosenses flicked to thermal in time to show the gargoyles dropping once more towards the devastators, hidden by the dust storm.

'Enemy above!' Cassius warned, but the cry was not needed. Therotius already had his squad prepared and the descending column of gargoyles were caught in a crossfire of heavy bolter-rounds and exploding frag missiles. The dust cloud churned with whirring bolts and ichor pattered down on Cassius like milky-white rain.

A shockwave rippled through the dust as the

Thunderhawk screamed past, its nose spitting las-bolts at the departing harridan, each shot tearing chunks from its ribbed underside. The gunship's main cannon boomed out, hitting the ascending tyranid on its dorsal plates, and then both were lost from view again.

'Casualty reports,' snapped Cassius. A wounded gargoyle flopped and flapped a few metres away. The Chaplain crossed the rooftop and brought his crozius down onto the creature's head, crushing its skull with one blow. 'All squads, report in.'

The devastators had not fared too badly: one Space Marine killed, three more too grievously wounded to continue fighting. Several had suffered minor injuries from bio-plasma and gargoyle claws but nothing that could not be ignored for the time being. The tactical squads stationed across the warehouses had suffered the wrath of the harridan and had lost five Space Marines to its bio-cannons and deadly claws before it had turned its attention towards the battle atop the dormitory building.

Apothecary Valion was already making his way from squad to squad in the southern outskirts, tending as best he could to those who had been injured. Sergeant Augustin was amongst those that had fallen, decapitated by the harridan as it had overflown his position. Cassius reviewed his mental list of the Space Marines under his command to find a suitable replacement.

'Brother Tyrius,' he announced over the vox.

'Yes, Brother-Chaplain?'

'You are now sergeant, Tyrius. We will speak the rites of promotion together when the current attack has been thwarted. Assist in the reorganisation of the tactical squads, brother-sergeant.'

'Thank you, Brother Cassius.'

'Do not thank me, Tyrius. Just do your duty. Service is its own reward.'

'Of course, Brother-Chaplain. I shall bear the honour of the Ultramarines without faltering.'

'Be sure that you do, sergeant.'

The wind was blowing away the dust cloud caused by the harridan's passage, revealing the creature turning northwards, pursued by the Thunderhawk. Cassius was aware that he had received several reports from the two Titan princeps whilst he had been watching the harridans and fighting the gargoyles. He reviewed his communications log, listening to the contacts on fast-recall.

The next tyranid wave was still heading towards Cordus Via. The Titans had reaped a heavy toll with their weapons, but the foe were too numerous to destroy utterly. Several broods of tyranid warriors and smaller organisms had made it past the Titans' bombardment and were heading down the highway and river.

The sun was barely above the horizon and the day would be filled with fighting.

CHAPTER VI

In the afternoon the clouds had burnt away, leaving Cordus Via baking beneath the hot sun. A haze of smoke drifted down the highway, the faltering winds bringing the smog from crop fields set ablaze by the guns of the Titans. Bounded to the north and south by the rivers, there was little danger of the fires spreading too far; in any case, it was no concern of Chaplain Cassius. He was not here to defend the cereal fields, but to ensure the safety of the people sheltering in Plains Fall.

In the settlement, the Ultramarines Rhinos were put to work clearing the tyranid corpses choking the streets. A mass of lesser creatures had tried to overwhelm the defenders with their numbers, and several hundred had survived the gauntlet of multiple rocket launchers, volcano cannons and gatling blasters to descend on Cordus Via throughout the morning, to be met by the unflinching fusillade of the Space Marines. With earthmoving blades, the armoured transports heaped the twisted and burnt bodies of termagants and hormagaunts into grisly barricades between the warehouses.

Cassius stood on the Minoran Gradient looking down at the aftermath of the morning's deadly work. Heat haze shimmered from the rockrete highway and fire flickered amongst the outbuildings as the combat squads of the Ultramarines moved through the settlement with flamers, seeking out surviving foes that had managed to get inside the buildings.

The cataract foamed pale green with alien fluids, the pool beneath the thundering fall of water choked with hundreds of tyranid corpses washed down the river. Sergeant Dacia and his veterans were using fragmentation grenades to dislodge the bodies acting as a dam across the river, blowing holes in the wall of dead piling up where the cataract narrowed to ensure Cordus Via did not flood.

The reports from orbit and the patrols of the Thunderhawks indicated that the tyranids had relented in their assault for the moment, pulling back more than ten kilometres. Cassius knew better than to think of them as mindless drones. The tyranids were driven by a compulsion to devour everything in their path, but they were not all simple beasts; alien intelligence directed their actions individually and as a swarm. Though their hive ship was destroyed, the tyranids that had landed were not an unending horde descending from orbit, and their strategy was still evolving. The Chaplain had fought this menace on more than a score of worlds, and they had never acted exactly the same, though there were predictable patterns, as with any foe.

Having tested the defenders at Cordus Via, and found them unbreaking, the mind guiding the tyranid assault was now seeking a means to circumnavigate the waystation. The Thunderhawks had reported flocks of gargoyles seeking passage to the north and south, but here the terrain was in the favour of the defenders, as Cassius and Arka had known it would be. The rivers were impassable further west of Cordus Via, except perhaps by the harridans and gargoyles and a few of the largest constructs.

If the mass of the tyranid swarm wanted to reach Plains Fall, it would either have to travel several hundred kilometres in a wide arc around the Ultramarines, or break through. There was little Cassius could do about the former strategy, and he was determined that the latter would fail.

The Chaplain received a communication from General Arka as he returned to the settlement along the highway access road. The Imperial Guard commander did not have good news.

'The orbital surveys from your strike cruiser show three distinct lines of advance by the enemy,' Arka told Cassius. The general's tone was quiet and determined, though Cassius's keen ears also detected an undercurrent of tension – a strain in Arka's voice that a normal man might not hear. 'To your north, the enemy have made progress along the Altaen Gradient and Messian Highway. I have reinforced the Astcarian infantry stationed at Nexus Via with several squadrons of Leman Russ tanks and Basilisk artillery guns, but they are being hard-pressed to contain the attack and I would not expect them to hold out more than a day.

'To the south, I have established a fortified line across

the Captian Highway at Matis Via, in anticipation of the tyranids finding a way across the river at the Serenin rapids. It's fast-moving but narrow, and I would not put it past these creatures to make a bridge of their bodies if needed.'

'In short, general, you cannot guarantee the security of either our northern or southern flanks,' said Cassius. It was a statement of fact, not an accusation, and Arka was experienced enough to take it as such.

'That is correct, revered Chaplain,' the general said with a heavy sigh. 'There is little point in reinforcing further at Matis Via or Nexus Via. I would just be lightening the defence on the city to send more men to their deaths.'

'I concur with your decision, general,' said Cassius.

He had memorised the topography between the highlands and Plains Fall and could understand the general's quandary. Once the tyranids had passed the outer line of defence, the highways arrowing directly towards the city would bring them together again in one mass, capable of overwhelming whatever fortifications were put in place. Matis Via and Nexus Via did not benefit from the terrain that offered Cordus Via protection from encirclement. Any man staying there against the full brunt of the tyranid assault would be on a one-way mission. Though sometimes such sacrifices were necessary, the chances of inflicting significant casualties, or creating a delay in the tyranid advance, were minimal.

'There is no need to endanger your troops further, general,' the Chaplain continued. 'It is clear to me that our flanks will be compromised at some point in the next twelve to fifteen hours, regardless of the efforts of your men and women. Withdraw your forward forces to the main line at Plains Fall and ensure the defence of the city is at its strongest possible.'

'I had considered the same, Chaplain, but I would not wish to leave you without any support. I am able to redirect some of those forces to Cordus Via.'

'That will not be necessary, general.' Cassius had reached ground level and turned towards his chapelry in the depot. Several tactical squads were reinforcing the buildings as much as they could with crates and containers from the warehouses, blocking up windows and doorways with heavy furniture taken from the administration buildings and dormitories. The depot, with its open ground and clear fields of fire, was to be the inner keep of Cordus Via's defences, and if necessary the Ultramarines would make their last stand there.

'In that case, might I suggest a withdrawal of your forces to the position I have created at Attan Terminus, about two hundred kilometres east along the Minoran Gradient? You'll be under the protection of our big guns at the city wall, plus I can move more of the Legio Fortitudis to support your defence.'

'That will also be unnecessary, general. The Ultramarines will halt the advance at Cordus Via.'

Cassius passed through the gate of the depot and glanced up at the devastators atop the silos to his left. He had noted the highly effective fire rained down by the squad during the last attack and resolved to mention the deed in his evening rites later.

'Chaplain Cassius, as much as I respect your skill and experience, I think it would be unwise for your force to remain in its current position. Your position will be defensively untenable within eighteen hours at most.

There is no shame in moving to a more secure position, and to stay at Cordus Via would be suicide.'

'Do not trouble yourself with the fate of my warriors, general, that is my concern alone,' snapped Cassius. 'I am not in the habit of throwing away the lives of Ultramarines, no matter what you might think of my stubbornness. When I arrived, you correctly identified Cordus Via as the lynchpin in your defensive strategy, and so it remains. We will not lightly surrender the advantages we have here.'

'Apologies, Chaplain, I did not mean any offence.'

'I am no more concerned with taking offence than I am with making a precipitous withdrawal, general. The Ultramarines have arrived at Styxia to ensure its protection, and that is what we will do, in the manner I best see fit. Unless you have anything else to tell me, I would prefer not to engage in further debate on the subject.'

'Of course, you are in command of your forces, not I,' said Arka. 'I will keep you informed as the situation develops. Arka out.'

The comm cut abruptly, static hissing in Cassius's ear for a moment before the connection was severed completely. The Chaplain grunted in irritation – he did not have the time or the inclination to deal with Arka's sensibilities. He was one of the best Imperial Guard commanders Cassius had known, but even bearing that in mind, he was still only human.

The tyranids came again in strength after nightfall, and as in the previous night the fire of rockets and blaze of lasers split the dark skies. Unlike the first assault, the wave of tyranids did not come as one in a large horde, but instead advanced along the line of the rivers and highway in smaller broods, perhaps seeking to avoid detection. Such a ruse was pointless; the sensoria of the Titans could pick up the encroaching aliens several kilometres distant, and each brood was destroyed in turn as it came into range of the Warlords' weapons.

Cassius was moving from squad to squad around the perimeter, ensuring not only that every warrior was alert, but also repeating his mantra that Cordus Via would not fall. As yet, the Ultramarines had not fired a shot in the latest battle, but there was no excuse for laxity. The vigil of the Titans was not perfect.

On the roof of a warehouse overlooking the cataract, the Chaplain met with Sergeant Dacia. His veterans waited in darkness, their eye lenses glowing in the gloom as they peered out across the starlit spume of the waterfall.

'Is all in order, sergeant?' said Cassius, stopping beside Dacia as he stood at the ledge bordering the flat roof.

'So far, Brother-Chaplain,' replied Dacia. 'Sergeant Octanus and his squad are mounting a patrol five hundred metres upriver, in case any lictors have passed the Titans.'

'And the spirits of your men, they are strong?'

Dacia looked at his squad, arranged like immobile statues gazing westward along the roof's edge, bolters, plasma guns and heavy bolter held at the ready.

'We are patient, brother,' said the sergeant. 'The enemy will come again, and we will be ready for them. There is no need to be hasty in our reprisal.'

Cassius sensed a slight rebuke in the sergeant's tone, his words hiding some other meaning.

'You believe that we should have withdrawn from Cordus Via, brother-sergeant?' Cassius asked.

'If you had consulted me, that would have been my

appraisal, Brother-Chaplain. The site itself is of no value other than its location. Abandoning it brings no dishonour if by doing so we continue to fight effectively. Now it is too late.'

'I do not understand your reticence, sergeant.' Cassius noticed that Dacia had not looked at him yet during their exchange. The Chaplain laid a hand on the sergeant's shoulder pad, and applied enough pressure to make the Space Marine turn. 'Be forthcoming in your reservations.'

'Our enemy knows what we know, brother,' said Dacia, his voice barely a whisper. Cassius could see nothing of the Space Marine's expression, but his voice was earnest. 'They will have us trapped here soon enough and will exterminate us at their leisure.'

Cassius frowned inside his helm.

'To hear you speak so, one would think we are already overwhelmed.'

'I have been thinking about the riddle their latest attack poses. What is to be gained by their attempt at subterfuge? It is quite obvious that our defence is not hampered by the fall of night. Why then, would they come at us with dregs, sending their forces forward in broods small enough to be easily despatched? They have tested us with a full assault and not found us wanting. There is no logic, no matter how alien, that suggests this desultory effort will be successful.'

The Chaplain pondered what the sergeant said, his frown deepening further, though now with consternation rather than anger.

'The enemy are keeping us occupied,' said Cassius, and Dacia nodded. 'Why have you only now brought this to my attention?'

'The answer has only just occurred to me also, Brother-Chaplain. As you were on your way here, I thought it better to speak to you in person rather than broadcast the fact over the vox-net.'

Turning away, Cassius took a few paces, his boots thumping loudly on the boards of the rooftop. He did not waste time chastising himself for his oversight, but focused immediately on a resolution. Before any was forthcoming, Dacia spoke again.

'There is also another reason for the piecemeal assault, brother,' said the sergeant, glancing back to the west. A blossom of fire spread across the farmlands, its glow shining over the desolated fields. 'It is a waste of the Titans' firepower to strike down only a dozen foes with each shot.'

'They expend our resources with their lives,' said Cassius, following the statement to its conclusion. 'While the princeps waste missiles and gatler rounds on termagants, tyranid warriors and carnifexes wait for their supplies to be exhausted.'

Cassius's first instinct was to order the Titans to cease firing, in order to conserve their ammunition. He ignored the impulse, because if the Titans curtailed their attacks, it would fall to the Ultramarines to take up the fight and their supplies would be depleted instead.

'It is a confounding situation, sergeant,' Cassius confessed, reaching no firm conclusion. 'At best, the Titans grant us more time, holding the mass attack at bay. While they still fire, the waiting horde is kept at arm's reach.'

'Yet with every passing minute, it is more likely that our Imperial Guard allies to the north and south will be overrun, brother. We will be attacked on three fronts, and we will not be able to hold Cordus Via. Should we begin to withdraw, I would stake my honour that the tyranids will know it and come at us hard, harrying us all of the way back to Attan Terminus.'

'We will not be so easily trapped!' snarled Cassius, his anger directed at himself for being too stubborn to foresee this outcome. 'Extend the cordon by five hundred metres and have the Rhinos and Razorbacks brought to the access ramp. I must speak with General Arka.'

Cassius strode away without waiting for Dacia's reply or the inevitable questions the Chaplain's orders prompted. He opened up a vox link to the command headquarters and as Cassius reached street level Colonel Taulin answered the communications request. The officer sounded tired, his voice a husky whisper.

'Yes, revered Chaplain, how can we help you?'

'I need to speak with the general now, Colonel Taulin,' said Cassius. He crossed under the Gradient and in the background heard Dacia issuing orders over the tactical frequency. 'It is imperative that I speak to Arka personally.'

'The general is not at headquarters at the moment, Chaplain. He is doing his rounds at the defence line. Is it urgent?'

'Of course it is urgent, colonel! Twelve Ultramarines have died in defence of this world so far, and unless I can speak to General Arka, their sacrifice and those to come will be in vain.'

'I understand. I will try to reach the general for you, Chaplain.'

The vox buzzed for some time as Cassius returned to his shrine room and began packing away his relics.

Touching them brought a sense of purpose and peace to the Chaplain's troubled thoughts, reminding him that the Ultramarines had faced countless perils and still they had endured for ten millennia. To be connected with that history, to be part of the legend of Macragge, was comforting. In turn, he picked up each relic and spoke words of devotion to his Chapter and primarch, and then he wrapped each in soft cloth and placed them in their metal containers, lining up the boxes against one wall.

Arka had still not contacted him by the time he had finished, so Cassius switched vox-channels to check on Dacia's progress.

'All transports are mobile, brother. I have arranged a collapsing cordon, devastators first, tactical squads second and the assault squad last, to fall back on the Rhinos and Razorbacks. If you would inform the Titans of our withdrawal, they will be able to cover us from the west. There is no sign of the enemy to the east, if we are swift we will reach Attan Terminus without encountering any foe.'

'You misunderstand my intent, brother-sergeant. Make ready to head westwards.'

'Westwards, Brother-Chaplain? That is towards the enemy landing sites.' As a Space Marine, Dacia could not feel fear but his voice betrayed confusion and consternation.

'I am aware of that, as you know, sergeant. We will not be withdrawing from Cordus Via. We will be attacking.'

CHAPTER VII

The two Warlord Titans had moved back towards Cordus Via, overlooking the highway with their immense guns and rocket launchers. True to their oaths of obedience, the Ultramarines did not question their Chaplain's command, but made an orderly withdrawal to their transports. A drizzling rain had started around midnight, droplets of water rattling from the hulls of the transports, reflected in the light of the Titan lamps. It pattered on Cassius's armour as he left his sanctuary to join his warriors at the accessway.

As Cassius's force readied to embark on the Rhinos and Razorbacks, Apothecary Valion appeared, accompanied by Sergeant Acheon.

'Brother-Chaplain, may I speak with you?' asked the Apothecary. Receiving a nod in reply, he continued. 'There are twelve wounded in my infirmary, brother. Though they cannot fight on here, if given proper attention they will make a full recovery and return to the Chapter whole.'

'You may take one Rhino, brother,' said Cassius, anticipating Valion's request.

'Brother-Chaplain, a Thunderhawk would be more suited,' said Acheon, who had obviously been brought along to lend weight to Valion's appeal. 'The road between here and Attan Terminus may be in enemy possession. Brother Caphon is fit enough to pilot if necessary, and a lift to orbit would not require any able-bodied brethren to provide protection.'

'You also misunderstand my personal intent, brother,' added Valion. 'The brethren have been stabilised and I can induce their sus-an membranes to keep them secure until they reach *Fidelis*. I will be accompanying the attack, brother. I am sure you will need me.'

Considering his options, Cassius concluded that the Apothecary and sergeant were correct. The Thunderhawks were one hour from changing their rotation and it would be no further burden for the wounded to be taken directly to the strike cruiser on board the gunship returning for re-armament.

'Very well,' he said. A thought occurred to him as he reviewed what Valion had told him. 'There are nineteen casualties under your care, Apothecary.'

'I will administer the Emperor's final mercy on three of the others, brother. If we are to leave, they will not survive being moved.'

'The last four want to stay here,' said Acheon. 'Each of them has suffered serious injuries and they will no longer be suitable for combat duties with the Chapter. They request that they surrender their armour for return to the Chapter and they will defend Cordus Via for as long as possible. Of those that have fallen already, we will conduct their bodies back to the *Fidelis* along with the living so that they are not consumed by the foe.'

Taken aback by this, Cassius had to consider his options carefully. The warriors he left behind would be slain, without question. His counterattack had already cost the lives of seven more Space Marines before it had begun. Yet such was the fate of a Space Marine, and Cassius hardened his heart to the decision. The tyranids had to be stopped, no matter the cost.

'Their names will be entered upon the roll of honour and their sacrifice spoken of to the Chapter. I will speak to them myself before we depart and will conduct the rites of the fallen upon those who will not survive to see us leave.'

'Thank you, brother,' said Valion. Acheon nodded his own appreciation and Cassius felt a moment of strange pride in his brothers, and not for the first time. He was being thanked for allowing them to lay down their lives in the defence of the Emperor's realm. Only the Adeptus Astartes could truly understand what an honour that entailed.

No sooner had Cassius finished dealing with Acheon and Valion when the vox link chimed in his ear.

'Taulin tells me you have something urgent to say, Chaplain,' said General Arka. 'Is everything all right there? I have to tell you, Matis Via has been abandoned. Sentinel sweeps indicate the tyranids have already reached the waystation there. Nexus Via is surrounded and will hold for no more than two more hours. I cannot give you any longer than that. If you plan to withdraw t–'

'We will not be withdrawing, General Arka.' Cassius manipulated his vox controls, bouncing his conversation with the general onto the Ultramarines tactical channel so that all of his warriors could hear what was said. 'It is my intent to strike back at the tyranids. Our initial assessment appears to be in error. The tyranids have far greater numbers than we expected from a single planetfall, and thus I am forced to conclude that amongst the creatures that made it to the surface is a norn queen – a breeder. This is not a battle that will be won by attrition, even by the Imperial Guard.'

'I would argue that point, Chaplain,' said Arka. 'We have a highly defensible position, massed tanks and artillery and tens of thousands of men. Plains Fall will hold for a generation if necessary.'

'We do not have the luxury of time, general. The other hive ships in the system are still active and it is possible that further tyranid ships will be brought to the system to reinforce the attack. I am sending the *Victorix* and *Dominatus Rex* back to Plains Fall to assist in the final defence.'

'A sane man would come with them,' said Arka. 'You cannot hope to destroy this horde by yourselves.'

'A sane man would retreat, it is true,' said Cassius, and these were the words he wanted his warriors to hear. 'Yet a sane man would not gladly march to battle, nor wake up every day of his life hoping that day will see him plunged into combat with a nightmare foe. Yet that is the truth of the Space Marines. We are not men, and you cannot judge us by the standards of men.

'The tyranids will grow stronger the longer we delay. I am sure of it. Once they have a grip on this world, you might fight for a generation, for ten generations, and never be free of the taint. This incursion is in its earliest stages, but I have seen planets where continents have been consumed and oceans drained dry by this many-headed beast. We have seen rocks scoured of all life by the tyranids, with not even bacteria or atmosphere left. Styxia is doomed to a slow, inexorable death if we cannot halt this attack in its infancy, and that is what I plan to do.'

'I still do not see how you can hope to achieve any meaningful objective,' said Arka. 'I am the first to laud the power of the Ultramarines, even when few in number, but the foe you face is of an order of magnitude higher than anything I would expect you to overcome.'

'And that is why I need you to promise support, general,' said Cassius. 'As a soldier of the Imperial Guard, you swore oaths to serve the Emperor. As commander of this force, you pledged alliance with the Ultramarines.'

'Have I given you reason to doubt my resolve now, Chaplain?' said Arka, sounding hurt by the notion. 'Have I not offered you support since the moment you arrived?'

'I need more than support, general. I need your faith – your faith in the Emperor, your faith in the Ultramarines, and your faith in me as the embodiment of both. We cannot hope to puncture this horde and survive on our own, but if your forces attack in support of our advance, we shall destroy the source of this threat and survive to tell of it.'

'You want me to abandon the defence of Plains Fall?' There was a long pause. 'You ask too much, Chaplain. You remind me of my oaths, but I must remind you that I also swore to protect the three million people sheltering behind my guns.'

'They are dead if we do not act,' Cassius told the general. 'It is better to strike now while the *Fidelis* has the upper hand in orbit than allow the tyranids free rein on the surface. If I show you it can be done, will you attack?'

'I will,' said Arka, the words slightly catching in his throat even as he made the promise. 'How will you do it?'

'All tyranid swarms are controlled by a hive tyrant,' Cassius said. 'They are the focus for the psychic connection that drives the creatures onwards. The Mechanicus refer to them as synapses: nodes of intelligence alongside the warriors and other larger creatures that instil the need of the hive mind into lesser beasts. We will slay the hive tyrant controlling the swarm on Styxia. The tyranids will be in disarray, for a while at least. If the Ultramarines can kill the hive tyrant, will the Imperial Guard leave their positions and attack?'

'If you can slay the hive tyrant, we will be ready to push the advantage,' said Arka. 'Are you positive there is no further assistance I can offer?'

'Just be ready to attack, general. That is all I ask.'

'Very well, Chaplain. The Emperor will guide you to victory.'

'By His truth and the wisdom of the primarch, we will prevail,' replied Cassius.

Caught up in his discussion with Arka, Cassius had not noticed a group of five sergeants had gathered close at hand: Dacia, Heletis, Capilla, Xathian and Acheon. They were all looking at Cassius, and though their expressions were hidden by their helms there was something in their demeanour that irked the ancient Chaplain. Dacia stepped forwards.

'Your plan is flawed, Brother-Chaplain,' said the veteran

sergeant. 'The tyranid swarm covers tens of thousands of square kilometres. Even with scanning from the *Fidelis*, we will not be able to locate the hive tyrant before the main enemy attack reaches Plains Fall. We have less than forty-eight hours to find and destroy the hive tyrant.'

'You have an alternative to suggest?' snapped Cassius, looking at the cabal of sergeants. How long had they been whispering to each other, perhaps voicing words of doubt over his ability to command? It was now that the Chaplain understood what had irritated him about their demeanour. Their stance, the way they grouped together, spoke of defiance.

'Brother-Chaplain, it is understandable that you wish to slay as many tyranids as possible, but your hatred of them clouds your judgement,' said Capilla, slightly apologetically. 'You are not thinking clearly.'

Wisdom tempered instinct again. If Cassius issued a direct order, they would obey. It was not only their duty, it was an act ingrained into their psyche from the moment that had been brought to the Chapter as youths. If the Chaplain spoke the right words, his warriors obeyed without question, like machines whose logic circuit had been activated.

Alternatively, Cassius could berate his subordinates for their craven behaviour. Their actions bordered on dissent, especially in the midst of a campaign. A verbal chastisement and threats of punitive action once they returned to the Chapter would be enough to bring the dissidents back into line.

Yet Cassius did not want to lead automatons into battle, nor to exert authority for the sake of it. For centuries he had looked into the eyes of warriors who had known they would die and were glad for it. He had come to know the minds and spirits of the Ultramarines, as a whole and as individuals. Dacia and his companions did not speak against Cassius out of disobedience, nor were they cowards. Such was an impossibility for the warriors of Macragge. The concerns they expressed were genuine, and their doubts had cause. Such concerns needed to be allayed, not crushed.

'It is an honour for us all to fight in such fine company as we have here,' said the Chaplain, keeping the force-wide channel open so that all could hear his speech. 'We shall be lauded as the warriors that saved Styxia. What we do in the next day will echo down the centuries, marked in the roll of honour for eternity. The people of Styxia will know the names of their saviours and they shall praise them for generations to come.

'But that is not why we will sally forth against this foe today. It is not for praise or recognition that we plunge into the tyranids as a dagger seeking their heart. It is not for glory or even honour that we attack rather than retreat. It is something far more than strategic necessity that leads us to place our lives in the way of harm rather than seek sanctuary.

'We will find the hive tyrant and we will slay it. We do this for the Emperor and the Chapter. We do this because we swore oaths to defend the worlds of the Emperor against all threats, xenos and human, from without and within. We will do this because we were created to be bright stars in the firmament of battle.

'We will not show doubt, we will not hesitate. How do I know this? Because we are Ultramarines! For ten thousand years our ideals have been the bastion upon which the survival of mankind has been founded. We are the exemplars, the bright beacon of war to whom all turn in darkness! It is our privilege to destroy these foes for the Emperor, and in His name we will cleanse the unholy stain from His realm. Our hate for this foe, our righteous loathing that brought us to this place, will be our sword and our shield, cutting down our foes and protecting us from fear.

'Do I hate this enemy? Yes! A thousand times, yes! I hate them with a passion that would scour worlds and extinguish stars. I hate them with a ferocity that breaches walls and topples towers. Yes, I hate the tyranids! I hate them because they slew millions who were under our protection. I hate them because they dared set their clawed alien feet on the sacred soil of Macragge, and defiled our home world with their spores and their beasts. I hate them because they killed my battle-brothers and brought Ultramar to its knees.

'All of these are reasons enough to hate with a fire that melts adamantium and scorches the heavens. Yet I have one more reason to hate these creatures, one more cause to despise them with every fibre of my soul and every cell of my body. I hate them because they humbled us, the greatest Space Marine Chapter in the Imperium. We came so close to being destroyed – we, the light of the Eastern Fringe, the heroes of Ultramar, the sons of Roboute Guilliman, protectors of the Codex. We are the first amongst a thousand in the minds of a trillion men and women and our light guttered and almost died – on our own world!

'We endured but there is a wound inside my soul that will not heal, and its pain is more bitter than any scar on my face and any puckered mark upon my body. It is an injury that cuts me to my core, virulent with the putrescence of failure that lights a fever in my heart. I hate the tyranids as water hates fire, and I would be the same and extinguish their presence with mine.

'To hold on in a glorious last stand is as equally pointless as retreat. A Space Marine owes it to the Emperor and the Imperium to give his life only at great cost to the enemy. To await one's fate, to accept a death without meaning would be cowardice. I know the tyranids well and know how to hurt them. The Ultramarines will attack!

'The task is daunting, but that is no reason not to attempt it. Remember this simple truth: Hatred finds a way. Where love for our brothers and Emperor might ultimately falter, hatred perseveres for eternity. It is the Emperor's greatest gift to us and we have nurtured it in our hearts these long years of disgrace. Set aside your doubts and know that hatred will see us revenged upon this foe.'

'Hail the Emperor!' roared Dacia, slamming his fist to his chest in salute. 'Praise the primarch! Honour the Chapter!'

The cry and salute were echoed by the other Ultramarines. There was a growl to the sergeant's voice as he stepped up close to Cassius. Dacia dropped to one knee. Behind him, the rest of the command followed suit, paying obeisance to their commander.

'Show us the foe and we will slay them for you, brother. Forgive us the doubts of these past days.'

'There will be no more doubt,' Cassius said, laying a hand on Dacia's bowed head, 'only death.'

CHAPTER VIII

The Ultramarines mounted up, full squads in the Rhinos, five-man combat squads in the heavily-armed Razorbacks. They headed slightly north of west, away from the Minoran Gradient, directly towards the volcanic uplands where the tyranids had made planetstrike. Behind the Ultramarines, Cordus Via was lit by the flicker of bolt-rounds and the blinding blast of the Titans' weapons as Ultramarines and Legio Fortitudis continued the pretence of defending the settlement, drawing the tyranids away from Cassius's line of advance.

Smothered by the dark, the engines of their transports growling, the Space Marines were kilometres away when Cassius received a final signal from Princeps Jasyn. The Titan commander's tone was hushed.

'No more defensive fire registering from Cordus Via, Chaplain. The last of your warriors have fallen. They took a heavy toll of their foes. We will honour their sacrifice.'

'They will be remembered,' replied the Chaplain. 'Join the defence of Plains Fall, princeps. You have the gratitude of the Ultramarines.'

'We will incinerate Cordus Via before we depart, to ensure the bodies of your dead are not defiled by these hideous creatures. We will re-arm and return. The Legio Fortitudis will lead the counterattack when Arka commands it and we will be reunited soon enough, Chaplain Cassius. May the spirits of your weapons stay true and may the Omnissiah grant you his divine knowledge to destroy this enemy.'

'*Ave Imperator dominus*,' Cassius said before closing the link.

He moved from the front of the Rhino to the main compartment, where Dacia and his squad were sat on the benches to either side; the seven surviving veterans were acting as honour guard to the Master of Sanctity. Cassius crossed to the rear door controls and lowered the ramp halfway. Above its rim could be seen the glow of Cordus Via burning on the horizon as *Dominatus Rex* turned its volcano cannons on the waystation. The depot ignited with a huge fireball that raced into the air, illuminating the gigantic war machines standing over the settlement.

'We will avenge.'

Cassius turned to find Dacia and his squad had stood up, kept steady by their power armour actuators as the Rhino bumped over the burnt earth. It was the sergeant who had spoken.

'We will avenge,' said Cassius.

Dawn saw the Ultramarines more than two hundred kilometres from Cordus Via. Standing at one of the fore hatches of the Rhino, its mounted storm bolter tilted to one side, Cassius surveyed the ground ahead. The land rose steadily into a series of steep foothills, before rising higher still as the volcanic peaks thrust up from the fields and orchards. A dark smudge swathed the distance, which Cassius took to be ash from recent eruptions. The highlands constantly spewed new life to the surface, the influx of nutrients more than compensating for thousands of hectares of crops lost to flash fires and lava flows.

Kilometre after kilometre of cereal fields stretched to either side of the column of vehicles, swaying in the ever-present winds. Not far ahead, less than a kilometre away, the grassy young stems were thrashing more violently. Beyond, in a swathe that was several kilometres wide, there was nothing but dark desolation stretching far into the distance.

At the front of the convoy, Cassius's Rhino was the first to come level with the tortured crops. From the vantage point of his cupola, by the light of the Rhino's headlamps and the rising sun, the Chaplain could see a carpet of snakelike creatures with bulbous heads and pronounced mandibles chewing their way through the crop. Known colloquially as rippers, they were the primary means for the swarm to take on biomass; other tyranids had vicious jaws and fangs, but did not feed on flesh. Anything slain was left for the rippers to consume and return to the norn queens for reprocessing into new tyranid bio-constructs. The ripper swarm was like a conveyor belt, moving forwards, consuming and breaking down everything on the surface, while a steady stream of full rippers slithered back towards the mountains.

'Our task has been set out for us,' Cassius signalled

his warriors. 'We need only to follow the swarm back to its source and we will discover the location of the norn queen.'

'The death of the creature will halt reinforcement, brother, but we promised Arka we would destroy the hive tyrant,' replied Dacia.

'I am confident, brother-sergeant, that if we threaten the norn queen, the hive tyrant will come to us.'

'A good plan, Brother-Chaplain,' said Dacia. 'The beast will be lured to its doom.'

'Squads Menaton, Heletis and Tyrius, use your flamers to set a blaze in the fields. We shall let the flames consume those beasts we cannot spare the time to destroy ourselves.'

Even as Cassius spoke these words, the Rhino reached the leading edge of the approaching swarm. Rippers hissed up at him from the ground as the transport's tracks crushed carapaces and fleshy bodies beneath plasteel treads. Those vehicles that were equipped with frontal blades lowered them, carving wounds through the near-continuous mass of creatures, until the hulls of the vehicles were encrusted with gore and chitin.

Behind the Ultramarines, the flames grew, spreading to the north and south as the winds fanned the growing blaze. From track, blade and fire, thousands of rippers were slain, yet Cassius knew it was but a drop in the ocean of alien filth that still stained Styxia.

It took two and a half hours to pass through the main part of the ripper host. The further the Ultramarines drove, the more desolate became the land they passed. They had not seen crops for a hundred kilometres, and seventy-five kilometres ago the half-eaten remains of grox and unfortunate farmers had disappeared also. Here, two hundred and fifty kilometres behind the leading rippers, the creatures were gnawing their way into the dirt itself, draining it of nutrients, viruses and bacteria, sucking every last vestige of life from the increasingly parched earth.

It also became clear to Cassius that the darkness that engulfed the highlands was not caused by a cloud of ash. In the far distance, their bases beyond the horizon, large spore chimneys were spewing swathes of gloom into the sky. Dark streamers of spores lay like tattered cloth on the wind, stretching for hundreds of kilometres to the south and east. The microorganisms carried across the continent would work in conjunction with the rippers, breaking down all biomass to make it easier to consume by the approaching swarm.

'Spore risk,' Cassius warned the column. 'Recheck ventilators and seals.'

Individual spores presented little danger to a person, especially a Space Marine, but an unarmoured human caught in a cloud would be slowly eaten away, skin first, then fat, then flesh, then bone, turned to a mushy pool of constituent elements. To breathe them in was agonising, even for a Space Marine, and the spores had a nasty trait of settling inside airways to replicate, choking their unfortunate host to death.

As at Cordus Via, the two Thunderhawks had been rotating combat air patrols around the column, ready to warn of any sizeable enemy force and engage distant targets if needed. On the ground, the spore cloud was still thin, but carried on volcanic updraughts into the upper atmosphere, the cloud was much, much thicker. The

Thunderhawk pilots reported the filters on their engine intakes were becoming clogged with the tiny creatures, threatening their ability to fly. Rather than risk losing one of the craft, Cassius had to concede to the concerns of the crews and ordered the Thunderhawks to return to *Fidelis* to fit new filters and await further command.

Onwards the Ultramarines pushed, into the heart of the wilderness, into the dead land left in the wake of the Great Devourer. Kilometre after kilometre passed by with monotonous regularity, the only features left being the mound of a hill or the empty buildings of a farmstead. All vegetation had been engulfed, the land stripped to rock.

Night fell as the column passed one thousand and forty kilometres from Cordus Via. With no desire for comfort, their armour protecting them from bumps and bangs inside their vehicles, the Space Marines were able to advance at speed, their transport slowing only to negotiate some of the larger drainage ditches and irrigation trenches. The drivers turned off their lights, not wishing to attract attention now that they were approaching the heart of the tyranid drop-zone.

Two hours after sunset, Cassius was studying the scanner reports from *Fidelis*. The ground ahead was uncertain; the strike cruiser's scans had been affected by the volcanic ash and the growing spore cloud, which acted as a blanketing shield against some of the vessel's sophisticated surveyors. The Ultramarines needed to head further north, where there seemed to be the largest concentration of organic matter. He could be wrong – it might be some forest hidden from the tyranids in an ancient caldera, but Cassius's instinct told him that combined with the heat register that had been detected, he would find the norn queen amongst the spore funnels three hundred kilometres north.

He was broken from his thoughts by a loud crack and a vibration that ran through the hull of the Rhino. He first looked to the sweeping scanner screen to his right, but all it showed were the haphazard heat registers of rippers returning to the spore funnels to throw themselves into the digestion pools surrounding the norn queen.

The driver, Brother Exeletus, cursed suddenly and brought the Rhino to a sliding stop as another resounding detonation shuddered the vehicle from front to rear. The vox-net filled with inquiries as the column slewed to a halt behind the Chaplain's vehicle.

'Hatches open, ready weapons for quadrant defence!' Sergeant Dacia's voice cut through the noise, silencing all chatter. 'Locate source of attack.'

'I saw something, a thermal flicker just before the impact,' said Exeletus.

'Where?' demanded Cassius. 'What sector?'

'That is the problem, Brother-Chaplain. It was right next to us. I think we must have...' Exeletus's voice drifted away and he leaned forwards, peering through the driver's vision slit. He glanced at Cassius. 'There is another one. Off to the right, thirty degrees.'

'I have it,' said Dacia. The veteran squad had opened the double doors of the armoured hatch above the troop compartment and were on firing steps, bolters and other weapons ready to repel any attack on the vehicle. The sergeant dropped down from the open hatchway, causing the Rhino to rock on its suspension for a few moments. He pointed his bolter to the right. 'Spore mines, Brother-Chaplain. Take a look for yourself.'

Cassius pulled himself up to the opening and looked in the direction Dacia had indicated, switching to thermal vision. Sure enough, several shapes resolved in his view. They appeared as bright red globes, trailing half a dozen tendrils of orange that faded to green. Increasing magnification, the Chaplain did a full sweep, turning around completely. He counted at least twenty spore mines within two hundred metres, and had seen the telltale glimmer of scores more further away. Focusing on one of the organic mines, he watched it drifting on the breeze, buoyed up by gases inside its spherical top. Its tentacles just touched the ground at their claw-like tips, so that it appeared to be walking, changing direction with flicks of its tendrils as its rudimentary sensory organs detected light, heat and sound.

It had started to head towards the convoy, drawn by the idling engines. Checking again, Cassius saw that several more were heading in the direction of the Ultramarines.

'Lights on, move forwards,' said the Chaplain. 'Batten hatches, remote weapons only.'

He let himself drop to the floor of the Rhino, boots clanging on the decking as the veteran squad lowered themselves around him. With a wheeze of hydraulic pistons the overhead hatch doors closed. Cassius moved back to his command seat beside the driver and quickly surveyed the screens laid out before him. He activated the controls for the remote storm bolter situated on the hull above his head and another screen flickered into life, relaying an image from the weapon's motion-pict. With steady movements of his fingers, the Chaplain brought the storm bolter to aim at a spore mine forty metres ahead. He thumbed the trigger button just as the Rhino lurched forwards and started to pick up speed. The mine exploded in a shower of hard carapace and acidic mist moments before the Rhino sped through the expanding cloud.

Elsewhere there were other detonations as the storm bolters of the other Rhinos and the assault cannons and heavy bolters of the Razorbacks shredded more of the drifting organic bombs. Directing the fire of his storm bolter ahead, Cassius ordered the Razorback gunners to cease their firing; it was best to conserve ammunition for more worthwhile targets they would surely encounter once the attack on the norn queen began.

Pressing on through the night and the spore mines, the column was sometimes slowed to a crawl by the weight of creatures in front, other times able to speed up the increasingly steep slopes. Despite the attention of the Rhino crews, it was impossible to spot every spore mine and destroy it if the column was to advance at any reasonable speed. Every few minutes a distinctive crack would sound as a Rhino or Razorback came too close to a spore mine.

Hunkered in their vehicles, the Space Marines were safe from harm, though the irregular detonations grated on Cassius's nerves and every time the column was forced to slow it was irritating in the extreme. For all that Cassius knew, the hive tyrant could be half a continent away, though it seemed unlikely. The sooner the attack on the norn queen could commence, the more swiftly the hive tyrant would be brought forth from the horde and destroyed, relieving the pressure on Plains Fall.

Most of the night had passed when Sergeant Octanus reported that his Razorback had thrown a track and been forced to a halt. The other vehicles quickly drew up in a laager around the stricken transport, weapons directed out towards the moving field of spore mines. Only when the position was secured did Cassius open the rear ramp of his Rhino and meet Octanus beside his vehicle.

Successive spore mine hits had gradually worn through the track links, every detonation splashing a little more acidic compound onto the vehicles, every explosion eating away another layer of metal. The transports looked in a sorry state, most of their livery eaten through by acid, their ceramite plates blistered with sworls of melted, cracked ceramite. Octanus's Razorback had been the first to succumb to the speedy advance and the constant erosion of the spore mine attacks, but most of the other vehicles were in much the same poor state. Some had perforated exhausts, others suffered from compromised tracks or damage to the road wheels concealed behind the slab sides of the vehicles and one of the Rhinos had acid damage to its running gear, making it hard to turn to the right.

Cassius ordered a full halt for repairs and replacements. It was necessary but frustrating – Cassius estimated they were perhaps only ten kilometres from the probable location of the norn queen. The sky above was swathed with dark clouds from the spore funnels, and what little starlight breached the fog of microscopic organisms showed the mountainous chimneys jutting in every direction.

Swinging lamps outwards and using the lights of their armour to augment their autosenses, the Ultramarines kept watch at the perimeter, but it was taxing work. Starting with Octanus's Razorback, one vehicle at a time was brought into the middle of the laager to be examined and have repairs effected by Brother Sesiphus, a member of Dacia's squad who served in the Armoury and would shortly be elevated to the ranks of the Techmarines.

The process was slow and laborious, but as the ever-increasing frequency of spore mine detonations at the perimeter indicated, there was no way to spare more warriors to effect the repairs. After two hours, only three of the twelve vehicles had been patched up by Sesiphus and the gunfire from the Ultramarines was ever more frequent. Through the strange web of the hive mind, the spore mines were being drawn in for kilometres in every direction; mindless, but driven towards this threat at their centre. Now, the heavy weapons troopers were having to expend lascannon shots and frag missiles to keep the crowding mass of explosive organisms at bay.

'We cannot hold this perimeter for another ten or more hours,' Dacia told Cassius. Along with Capilla, the veteran sergeant had been summoned by the Chaplain for a brief council of war. 'As it is, if we move on now it will still require considerable effort to clear a path ahead.'

'We cannot proceed on foot, that would be just as dangerous,' said Capilla. 'Speed was our best defence against this threat.'

'And speed is the greatest risk we now face,' concluded Cassius. 'If we push the vehicles too hard now, with the damage they have suffered, we could end up stranded again – perhaps in an even more compromised position.'

'The longer we stay here, the more mines will be drawn to us,' said Dacia. 'We need something else, a decoy to move them away.'

'What would you suggest we use as a decoy, brother?' said Capilla.

'My squad,' replied the veteran sergeant. 'There is room for the Master of Sanctity to travel with any of several other squads. We shall take our Rhino and draw the spore mines away from the perimeter, acting as a rod to lightning.'

The sergeant's tone made it clear that his mind was already made up, but Cassius needed to be sure that Dacia and his men understood what they were advocating.

'We will not be able to wait for your return, brother,' said the Chaplain. 'We must press on to the attack against the norn queen without further delays. Are you sure you wish to do this?'

'We are not only sure, we are adamant, Brother-Chaplain. Only a direct order from you would prevent us. It is not a fool's errand, nor a suicide mission.'

'There is considerable risk, brother,' countered Capilla. 'It is likely that you will perish. Perhaps one of the other squads should fulfil the role, rather than our prized warriors of the First Company.'

'To be the First is to be above all others, in regard and in risk,' said Dacia. 'I would no more send another squad to act in my place than you would keep safe your life rather than risk it in defence of your brothers. We are the veterans, who have seen this foe at close hand a dozen times and more. It is our right to do this, as well as our duty.'

'Head south and return to Plains Fall if you can,' Cassius told the veteran.

'Not before we have succeeded in freeing the column from this incessant menace,' said Dacia. 'Unless you have other objections, brothers, we will depart as soon as we are able.'

Dacia nodded and sent the two Space Marines back

to their squads. News quickly spread of Dacia's decision and the First Company warriors mounted their Rhino with their names being praised by their battle-brothers, even as the guns of the force turned north and blasted a corridor through the spore mines for the squad to follow.

After the frenetic barrage, the guns of the convoy fell silent. The sound of the Rhino's engines was loud in the sudden quiet. With no ceremony, the driver gunned the engine and left the safety of the laager, heading into the gap opened by the earlier torrent of fire. When the Rhino was two hundred metres away, disappearing into the night, it suddenly lit up with a blaze of muzzle flare. Top hatch open, the Rhino slowed to a crawl while the veterans opened fire sporadically, a source of harsh light and sharp sound and exhaust fumes for the spore mines to latch onto.

'It's working!' shouted one of Therotius's men.

'Quiet there!' Cassius snapped back. The Space Marine had been correct; the spore mines had halted in their inexorable glide towards the laager and were now slowly moving in the direction of the veterans.

'I will summon a Thunderhawk,' Cassius told Dacia over a command link. 'It might not be able to find you in the fume, but I will call for it anyway and they will search for as long as possible.'

'Thank you, brother, for your leadership, your faith and your devotion,' replied Dacia. 'I consider it one of my greatest honours to have served as your second-in-command. I will see you again in the Cathedral of Sanctity on Macragge.'

'You will, brother,' said Cassius. He saw the Rhino speeding up again and it was soon swallowed by the gloom of night and spores. 'The blood of the primarch is strong in you, Dacia. Fight hard and long.'

Another brief spark of light betrayed the presence of the Rhino another few hundred metres away, seeming tiny in the blackness. A thermal sweep confirmed to the Chaplain that the nearest spore mine was more than a hundred metres away and drifting after the departing Rhino. There were some that would still cross the laager, but the perimeter could be weakened and the Space Marines put to better use aiding in the repairs.

'No noise, let us get these repairs done quickly and quietly,' Cassius told his warriors. 'Honour their sacrifice with your diligence.'

CHAPTER IX

Once they had completed their repairs, thanks to the distraction offered by Sergeant Dacia and his veterans, the Ultramarines set off on their final thrust towards the spore funnels. Heading up into the volcanic highlands they encountered little resistance and by the time they were clear of the spore mine swarm, they were able to travel even faster, coming upon a handful of scattered broods; a few dozen hormagaunts and termagants without any synapse creatures to guide them.

Cassius travelled with Tyrius's squad, lending his experience and presence to the newly-promoted sergeant. The Chaplain knew Tyrius well, having inducted him into the Chapter as a neophyte, monitored his progress through the Scout Company and awarded him his colours upon becoming a full battle-brother – as he had done for hundreds of other Ultramarines. Tyrius was quiet and competent, calm when sometimes others would grow headstrong, which made him ideal for leadership of a tactical squad; all of which the Chaplain felt no embarrassment in telling Tyrius as the column delved into the heartlands of the tyranid landings.

'What if the Guard don't come?' Tyrius asked. 'Normal men are weak, cherishing their lives above honour.'

The question had occurred to Cassius, but it was not his concern any longer now that his force was committed to the strike on the norn queen. That Tyrius had asked it suggested the idea that the Ultramarines would be abandoned to the tyranid horde was in the minds of other warriors in the force too.

'Some men are weak, that is true,' said Cassius. 'Yet some men are strong. You and I were once normal boys, with the hearts of men. We were chosen because we were strong, because we had courage and honour. Not all men with courage and honour become Space Marines. Some die with their potential unfulfilled. Others find a way to serve the Emperor by other means, as missionaries or Imperial Guard officers. General Arka is a strong man, and his men are dedicated to him.'

'It is reassuring to know that our attack will have purpose,' said Tyrius. 'To expend our lives in completion of this mission and yet not ensure the protection of this world with our actions would be vanity.'

'We stay until we slay the hive tyrant, that is all we need to do,' Cassius replied. 'Our foes will take time to recover, with their synapse commander destroyed. With the pressure relieved at Plains Fall, Arka will feel confident that the Imperial Guard can launch their counter-offensive. Our focus must be upon the hive tyrant, unfettered by all other considerations.'

'Of course, Brother-Chaplain.' Tyrius's words professed understanding, but his tone betrayed an element of doubt.

'I know that it can be unsettling to rely so heavily upon a fragile and uncertain alliance, sergeant,' Cassius told Tyrius. He opened up a company-wide channel to address the rest of the force. 'Success, and our honour, must be placed in the hands of others at times. So it has been since the time of the Imperium's beginnings. The Ultramarines are a powerful force, but even when mobilised in its entirety, our Chapter numbers but a thousand warriors. A thousand Space Marines can accomplish many things, but they cannot achieve everything.

'There are perhaps one million Space Marines to defend the Imperium, and as old wisdom would have it, that is but one warrior per world that owes fealty to the Emperor. So has it been, from time immemorial to today, that the Space Marines must be the tip of the spear but the Imperial Guard are the weight of the haft behind it. We are the sabre that slashes, they are the hammer that smashes.

'This is as true in Vortengard, where our brothers fight, as on Styxia. The Ultramarines cannot win this war by themselves, but it is our task, our purpose of existence, to make it possible for the Imperial Guard to bring victory. If one does not believe in this idea, one must doubt the Chapter's duty to the Imperium as a whole.'

With these stern words ringing in their ears, the Ultramarines pressed on. When daylight came, Cassius mounted the cupola in the roof of the Rhino to examine the surroundings. The spore-fume was thick, blanketing the bare

rock and filling the air. The blue of the Rhinos and Razorbacks was hidden beneath a layer of the filth and Cassius
was forced to continually wipe the lenses of his helm as
the column sped on through the murk.

Despite the spore gloom, it was possible to see the
immense chimneys rising up ahead and to either side.
Like the volcanoes upon which they were erected, the
spore funnels were conical in shape, spewing out a steady
stream of blackness as an eruption vomits ash. Passing
close to the base of one such structure, which reached
up at least two hundred metres above Cassius, the Chaplain saw that it was still under construction.

The chimney was a mass of writhing biomatter:
grub-like growths and metre-long worms entangled
each other in a mass of slimy strands, while six-legged
crabs smaller than a thumbnail knitted together the hardening xeno-silk, followed by more larvae that excreted
processed organic matter in dribbling rivulets, encasing
the structure with a hardening outer covering.

Absorbed by his study of this activity, Cassius at first
did not notice the monstrous apparition looming out of
the spore fog in front of him. A warning from Sergeant
Menaton drew his attention forwards, where the column
was slowing to a halt.

The norn queen squatted amongst the spore chimneys,
equally as mountainous in its bulk. The flanks of the monstrous brood-mother were covered with a swarming layer
of rippers, hundreds of finger-sized larvae slipping from
cord-veined incubator tubes while engorged, full-grown
adults dragged themselves into puckered digestive tract
openings to be absorbed back into the genetic material
from which they had been spawned.

Intestinal tracts like thick cables hung between the norn queen and the surrounding funnels, dripping with alien fluids. Like perverse celebration decorations, amniotic sacs hung from these organic chains, each foetal pendulum swaying with a life of its own. Four stunted limbs tipped with claws hugged the creature's upper body, which was covered in segmented plates that expanded and contracted slowly as other organs half-concealed within contorted and spasmed.

Ovipositor tubes spat out streams of fist-sized, mucus-covered eggs that were manoeuvred into piles around the norn queen's haunches by hundreds of fibrous vestigial tentacles. Here they were tended to by flat-bottomed slug-like nurturers that arranged the eggs into neat rows, their slime trails soaking nutrients into the nascent creatures within the leathery casings.

At the summit of this fleshy hill was a small head, no larger than that of a tyranid warrior, with six plates at its crest and black eyes. Slowly the head turned towards Cassius and his convoy. Glancing to his left and right, the Chaplain saw immature termagants and hormagaunts emerging from ichor-encrusted cocoons, while clusters of the fully grown creatures lurked in shadowed tunnels woven into the fabric of the spore chimneys.

Cassius had never seen the like of this horrific vision. The norn queens usually kept aboard the hive ships, and fed upon a devoured planet through massive capillary towers lowered from orbit. The plight of the hive ship had obviously forced the tyranids on board to eject in their entirety, and the norn queen had somehow survived the descent to Styxia's surface. Adapting to this harsh environment, the brood creator had manufactured new organisms to cope with life on the surface.

'How are we to destroy such an abomination?' asked Sergeant Xathian.

Along with his devastators, the sergeant had disembarked from his Rhino, their heavy weapons trained upon the massive norn queen. Around them several tactical squads had drawn up a defensive perimeter, though as yet the termagants and hormagaunts had not attacked.

'We are equipped with beacons to assist in teleportation operations,' said Cassius. 'Their signal can penetrate the spore-fug and reach the *Fidelis*, which can recalibrate her weapons augurs to the teleport signal and fire through the cloud with accuracy. Sergeant Therotius, begin a survey of the area to calculate the most suitable impact sights for orbital bombardment. I want the queen and as many funnels destroyed as possible.'

'One cyclotronic torpedo would level this whole region, Chaplain,' replied Therotius.

'And render a hundred thousand hectares of farms barren for centuries, sergeant,' Cassius said. 'There is no point in protecting Styxia if we are to destroy its infrastructure. Bombardment cannon only.'

'Affirmative, brother. I will assess the attack zone,' said the sergeant.

A bolter shot rang out to the left as one of Squad Heletis opened fire on the lurking termagants. In response, several of the creatures charged into view, their weapons spitting a hail of gnawing grubs that cracked into the armour of the Space Marines.

'Squad Octanus, provide close support to Sergeant Therotius,' snapped Cassius. More bolt shots sounded as the Ultramarines engaged the emerging tyranids. 'Knives, fists and swords! Conserve ammunition, brothers, there will be deadlier foes to face before we are victorious today.'

For two hours the Ultramarines fought back the increasing numbers of attackers, the buzz of chainswords and wet impacts of fists on flesh becoming a monotonous backdrop to the Space Marines work. Under the guidance of Therotius, six teleport homing devices were placed, three of them close to the norn queen itself, three more at structurally weak points on the half-finished spore towers around the beast. The norn queen seemed oblivious to their intent, unable to comprehend the importance of the knee-high transmitters with their signal arrays and blinking lights.

Cassius was in contact with the crew of the *Fidelis* throughout the operation, bringing the strike cruiser into position above the highlands and ensuring the weapons sensors were locked on to the correct signals. When all was prepared, the Ultramarines boarded their transports for the withdrawal.

Before the lead vehicle had travelled more than a few metres, the vox-net was alive with warnings as the vehicles' auspexes detected a massive surge in readings. Concealed by the organic thatch-work nature of the spore chimneys, hundreds of beasts had been able to approach the Space Marines undetected. Cassius put it down to coincidence rather than design that they had chosen this moment to launch their attack, pinning the Ultramarines in place and so preventing *Fidelis* from opening fire.

Ordering the breakout, Cassius took hold of the Rhino's storm bolter and laid down a curtain of fire to the left, gunning down the first waves of lesser creatures as they boiled up from subterranean tunnels criss-crossing the whole landing site. The auspex in the cabin below him was pinging wildly, registering heat sources and movement all around. Cassius swung the storm bolter in a half circle and cleared the passage entrances on the other side as the driver slammed the Rhino into motion, running over a cluster of hormagaunts that had been preparing to leap onto the front of the vehicle.

The column roared out with the fume of exhausts billowing in their wake and the thunder of bolter fire rebounding from the spore funnels. A red and white mass of creatures converged on the Ultramarines from every direction, and the crack of spike rifles and fleshborers engulfed the convoy. Heavier venom cannons smashed the armour of the vehicles, splashing highly corrosive acid into the interiors to melt through gear chains and control cables.

Half a kilometre from the norn queen, Cassius was forced to call a halt when Squad Capilla's Rhino suffered a catastrophic malfunction. Flames and smoke burst from its transmission system, sending the transport crashing into one of the boulders scattered along the side of the volcano. At a word from the Chaplain, the rest of the column came to a stop, forming a perimeter of fire to allow the stricken Space Marines to disperse into the other vehicles.

The delay almost proved costly, as more and more of the larger tyranid constructs closed with the Ultramarines. A hulking carnifex, as large as the transports, stormed from one of the cavernous openings in the chimney foundations, bellowing bio-plasma at Squad

Heletis's Razorback. The twin lascannons in the vehicle's turret spat back two stabs of white light as the carnifex lumbered into a charge, its claws ready to rip apart the transport. Striking the beast in the abdomen, the lascannon beams seared through its armoured plates and reinforced endoskeleton, severing a leg. More fire converged from the other vehicles, turning the fallen carnifex into an exploding mass of flesh and ichor.

Down the flank of the volcano sped the column, almost reckless in their haste to get to the minimum safe distance. They were still two kilometres short, a flock of gargoyles not far behind, when Cassius signalled *Fidelis*.

'This is Chaplain Cassius. Authorisation is given to initiate planetary bombardment. Target coordinates as established. One round at each signal.'

It took a few seconds for the command to reach orbit and the reply to return. Cassius could barely make out the words over the roaring of the Rhino's engine and the thundering of the storm bolter in his grip.

'Please confirm, Chaplain. Our sensors indicate that you may still be in the blast zone.'

'Open fire, in the name of the Emperor!' bellowed Cassius. 'Annihilate everything on that mountain!'

More than a minute passed before Cassius saw the first streak of white against the black fume of the spore cloud. Descending from orbit, the bombardment shell was little more than a directed meteorite weighing eight tonnes. Its ablative entry shielding burned off, flaring like a second sun for several seconds, and then it disappeared. Cassius picked up the dark blur twenty seconds later a few kilometres above the spore funnels.

The shell needed no high explosive. The kinetic energy

of its descent from orbit was enough to generate a blast that ripped open the flank of the spore chimney it struck. Punching through the tyranid edifice into the rock below, the bombardment shell created a shockwave that rippled along the mountainside, toppling the spore funnel.

Twenty seconds later the second shell hit, on the other side of the norn queen. And then the third struck, and the fourth. Pounded from above, the volcano was breached, its outer layer of rock smashed apart, newly created fumaroles belching forth hot lava.

The fifth shot ripped through the norn queen, shredding its bulbous form from within, sending splinters of carapace hundreds of metres into the air. Around their brood-mother, the tyranids died in their hundreds as the sixth and final shot slammed into the ground, igniting gases gouting from the dead breeder-construct so that flames roared into the heaving sky, mingling with the ash and magma of the volcano's eruption.

Borne upon the detonation's shockwave, an avalanche of smoke, spores and flame spilled down the volcano, rushing after the Ultramarines in a towering wall. Cassius gave the order to close hatches scant seconds before the wave hit. It engulfed the convoy in a swirling mass of debris and fire, blotting out sensor signals, clogging engines and swamping tracks. Shuddering to a halt, the column was half-buried with dust and grit in seconds.

As the gloom dispersed, Cassius opened up the cupola hatch again and surveyed the damage. Several transports had been upended by impacts, tossed like stones across the mountainside. He called for a casualty report and was saddened and angered to hear that three battle-brothers had died; the main door on their Razorback had jammed, allowing them to be engulfed by red-hot ash that baked them to death despite their armour's environment systems. Of Squad Heletis, only two Space Marines had survived. Manning their cupola weapons, they had been able to leap clear as their Rhino had been swept into a gorge by the volcanic tide.

It was clear that the convoy would be going no further. Every vehicle was bogged down, and even those still working churned their tracks uselessly through the drifts of ash, unable to gain purchase enough to pull themselves free of massive chunks of chimney wall, solidifying lava and hurled boulders.

To the south and east, the spore cloud was already dispersing across the plains, but the sight they revealed was no comfort to the Ultramarines. As far as the eye could see stretched a tyranid horde: countless enemies converging on the devastation at their landing site.

'See, my brothers?' shouted Cassius, pointing towards the coalescing swarm no more than two kilometres away. 'We draw their bite from Plains Fall.'

The pattern of the attack was familiar to all – the smaller creatures coming on in a vast wave, buying time for the larger beasts to approach. The tumult of the volcanic eruption had left the convoy scattered, so it was around the five operational Rhinos and one Razorback that the Ultramarines rallied.

Cassius knew their number: sixty-two warriors, including himself. He did not think it too few for the task at hand.

'Remember, save your shots for the largest creatures!' he commanded. He lifted up his crozius and its head lit up with the gleam of the power field. 'They will come and we shall slay them.'

With the vehicles acting as strongpoints in the line, the Ultramarines formed up to await the living tide that now surged up the mountainside towards them. Missiles and lascannon blasts streaked out over the horde, as the devastators targeted their weapons at the broods of tyranid warriors and carnifexes striding up the slope. Before these beasts came a surging, undulating mass of red chitin and pale flesh, scores of termagants and hormagaunts rushing heedlessly towards the Ultramarines, urged on by the presence of the synapse beasts.

'What is it to be a Space Marine?' asked Cassius, reciting the first line of the Macragge Catechism of Hate. He had penned the catechism himself after the defeat of Hive Fleet Behemoth and the words had been taught to the Chapter during numerous sermons since.

'It is to be death!' came the reply from the throats of his warriors.

To the left and right, chainswords screeched into life and knives were drawn from sheaths. Fists were clenched in readiness to greet the wall of tyranids streaming towards the Ultramarines position.

'What is it to be death?'

'It is to be the destroyer, the end of all things.'

'What is it to end life?'

'It is an honour, to be the executioners of the Emperor.'

Cassius loosened his grip on the haft of his crozius as the lead broods of the swarm converged on his position at the centre of the line. Around him, bio-ammunition exploded on the armour of his warriors but he paid the fusillade no heed – his entire focus was on the creatures in front of him. Beyond the mass of small tyranids he spied his target, a looming monstrosity thrice his own height, with an enormous crest and jutting dorsal spines: the hive tyrant.

The Chaplain took a step forwards and swung his crozius, crushing the skull of the first hormagaunt to leap at him. Around him, the Ultramarines advanced a pace, their weapons tearing through the first wave of tyranids.

'Why do we fight?' roared Cassius, the sentiment of every question and answer burning through the core of his being.

'To protect the Imperium and deliver mankind from the evil of the xenos, the mutant and the heretic!'

'What is the xenos?'

'A blight to be purged!'

'What is the mutant?'

'A cancer to be excised!'

'What is the heretic?'

'A shame to be expunged!'

Striking out left and right, Cassius advanced, the tip of the spearpoint driving towards the heart of the tyranid swarm. To his left, the jump packs of Squad Corilinus flared as the sergeant led his warriors on a charge against a brood of tyranid warriors. To the right, the devastators took up position again and opened fire with their heavy weapons, while a constant barrage of heavy bolter, storm bolter and assault cannon fire flew overhead from the cordon of vehicles, punching a hole in the tyranid mass ahead of Cassius.

'What is the bolter, the flamer, the missile?'

'The incarnation of destruction, by which we bring about the death of the Emperor's foes!'

'What is the armour, the helm and the shield?'

'The embodiment of our faith, our determination given form.'

The squads were firing their bolters now, cutting down the tyranids by the score, ripping into the enemy like a blade plunged into an unprotected gut. Here and there along the line a battle-brother fell, slain by the claws and fangs of the enemy or killed by the venom cannon of the hive tyrant or the bio-plasma of carnifexes, but still the advance did not falter. As a single entity, the Ultramarines pushed further into the foe, united by their hatred, bound to their fate by the words of their Chaplain.

'Who is the primarch?'

'Our father, our guide, our king!'

'Who is the Chapter Master?'

'The primarch's regent, to whom we swore oaths, the voice of the Emperor in the mortal world.'

'What are our oaths?'

'The steel that binds our lives to the Emperor.'

'What did we swear?'

'Our lives are as nought in the vision of the Emperor, save that by them we shall destroy all foes.'

Erupting beasts of flailing, hooked tentacles appeared amongst the Space Marines, fired by the barbed stranglers of the enemy. The ground ruptured in fountains of dirt and rock as tunnelling raveners burst from below to swallow Space Marines in their gaping maws. The roar of bolters reached its climax as Cassius's catechism came to its own crescendo, his voice a bellow above the din of weapons and screech of dying tyranids.

'What is the fate of all foes?'

'To perish in the fire of battle and be cleansed from the galaxy.'

'Who will prevail against the darkness?'

'The Ultramarines!'

'Who are the swords of the Emperor?'

'The Ultramarines!'

'Who are the sons of Macragge?'

'The Ultramarines!'

This last shout came not just from the external speakers of the Space Marines, but entered Cassius's ear over the comm. A row of explosions tore through the tyranids as missiles streaked down from the skies, followed a moment later by the white-hot stab of lascannons and the bloody eruptions of heavy bolter fire.

Plasma jets screaming, the two Thunderhawks of the *Fidelis* raked across the enemy, leaving swathes of dead aliens in the wake of their guns. The two converging lines of fire met around the hive tyrant. Cassius watched as the synapse creature straightened, turning its venom cannon towards one of the approaching gunships. A las-blast punched through its chest a second before heavy bolter-rounds stitched a row of cracks along its armoured plates. The fusillade culminated in two titanic blasts within moments of each other, as the gunships' dorsal cannons both fired, eradicating the hive tyrant in an incendiary detonation.

The destruction of the hive tyrant was greeted by Cassius with a triumphant shout.

'For the Emperor and the primarch! Death! Bring death to our foes!'

EPILOGUE

The Thunderhawks and boarding torpedoes of the Ultramarines blazed across the firmament, heading towards the crippled hive ship. In the lead torpedo, Cassius hunched in his seat, strapped across his chest by the massive bulk of the safety harness. His hands were fists upon his thighs and inside his helm his lips were drawn back in a snarl as he remembered the battle of Styxia.

General Arka had not only held to his oath, he had exceeded his promise. No sooner had the Ultramarines set out on their search for the hive tyrant than the Imperial Guard had sallied forth from Plains Fall, their commander showing utter faith in the Ultramarines. The lead elements of Arka's army had joined up with Cassius's force only three hours after the bombardment of the landing site.

Styxia had been cleansed after a further seven days of hard fighting, but Cassius had known from the moment the hive tyrant had fallen that victory was assured. Of the Space Marines who had travelled to Styxia, forty-three returned to the Chapter uninjured, and a further twenty-six would fight again for the Lords of Macragge. Sergeant Dacia had briefly been made captain of the Ninth Company, but after only three more battles had fallen against the orks of Vortengard.

Cassius turned his head to look out of the tiny viewing port in the nose of the torpedo. The sight of the hive ship filled him with disgust. There would be no respite until the tyranids were annihilated, no peace amongst the stars whilst the inhuman menace remained. Their destruction had become his purpose, and he gloried in the execution of that particular duty more than any other.

Activating the command vox, Cassius stared with hatred at the hive ship and asked a simple question.

'What is it to be a Space Marine?'

VEIL OF DARKNESS

NICK KYME

'I am the Undying. I am doom incarnate...'

It towered over me, this monster of living metal. It wore a crown with a red gemstone, torcs banded its mechanised arms and an azure pectoral hung around its neck. These were royal trappings. Here I fought a king of the dead, a robotic anachronism of an old and conceited culture, full of darkest anima.

Necrons, they were called. Its regal status only spurred me on.

'We are the slayers of kings!' I declared, spitting the words in anger at the gilded monster before me.

We fought alone, the monster and I. None interfered. I had drawn only my sword. For my victory to have any meaning, this was how it had to be. Even terms, its crackling war-scythe matched against my venerable Tempest Blade. But in the end, it was not my sword that was found wanting...

After a savage duel, it cut me deeply. No foe had ever done that before. And with blood filling my mouth, I fell. I, Cato Sicarius, Master of the Watch, Knight Champion of Macragge, Grand Duke of Talassar and High Suzerain of Ultramar, fell.

And as the veil of darkness wrapped around me like a funerary shroud, I heard the monster's words again...

'I am doom.'

I came around coughing up amniotic fluid, spraying the inside of the revivification casket. I roared, thundering my fist against the glass, my muscles and nerves suddenly aflame.

'Release me!' I spat, half-choking.

Locking clamps around the casket disengaged, admitting me back to the world of the living. I arrived breathing hard, sitting in a half-capsule of briny, viscous liquid and murderously staring down my Apothecary.

'Welcome back, brother-captain.'

Lathered in gelatinous filth, I scowled. 'Venatio.'

My Apothecary had the good grace to nod.

He was wearing his full armour-plate, white to identify his vocation as a medic rather than the ubiquitous Ultramarine-blue of our Chapter, but he went without a helmet. An ageing veteran of my command squad, Venatio's hair was fair, closely cropped, and he had dark green eyes that had seen too much of death.

It was dark in the apothecarion, shadows suggesting the shape of various machines and devices the Chapter medics employed in the service of preserving life. The air reeked of counterseptic and a fine mist clouded the floor. It was clean, cold; a desolate place. How many had come through these halls bloody and broken? How many had arrived and never left? Always too many.

I made to rise but Venatio lifted a gauntleted hand to stop me.

'Don't presume you can keep me from climbing out of this casket,' I warned him.

The hand gesture became placatory. 'Let me at least run a full bio-scan first.'

Venatio had the device in his other hand and was already conducting his test, so I endured the amniotic filth a little longer. When he was done, I refused his proffered hand and extricated myself without his help. My side ached. Once I was out of the casket and standing on the tiled floor, I looked down and saw why. An angry scar puckered my flesh from where the Undying's war-scythe had cleaved me.

'It's remarkable you are even alive, let alone walking, brother-captain,' the Apothecary said, consulting biometric data from his scanner.

'I'll do more than walk,' I promised vengefully, but realised I had no knowledge of what had happened after I had collapsed. 'What of Damnos? Were the Second victorious?'

Venatio's already severe expression darkened, pinching together the age lines of his face.

'After your defeat, Agrippen and Lord Tigurius rallied the men. But we had badly underestimated the enemy and were forced to evacuate. Damnos is lost.' He lowered his voice. 'So too Venerable Agrippen.'

I clenched my fist so hard that the knuckles cracked. It was a sparse chamber we occupied; much of the apothecarion's equipment was situated at its periphery with only my amniotic casket within striking distance. I hit it hard, putting a fissure in the glass. Had I my Tempest Blade at hand, I might have cut it apart. Galling was not the word.

I was about to ask Venatio to tell me more when another voice from the shadows, a presence I hadn't noticed in my recently revived state, interrupted.

'I had to see it for myself...'

A son of Ultramar, *the* son of Ultramar, if some amongst the Chapter were to be believed, stepped into the light. He too was fully clad, his plumed helmet sitting in the crook of his left arm, a ceremonial gladius strapped to his left leg. Gilt-edged shoulder guards and breast-plate shone in the lambent lumen-strip above us, and his war-plate was festooned with the laurels of his many years of vaunted service.

'Severus.' I bowed my head out of respect for the veteran, but his stern expression, hardened further by his scars and the platinum studs embedded in his bald forehead, suggested he came here with ill news.

'Cato.'

I hated the fact he used my given name, though I knew he hated me for doing so first. We were rivals, he and I. Severus Agemman was my predecessor as Captain of the Second. He in turn succeeded Saul Invictus after the great hero fell at Macragge. Now he stood as Calgar's right hand, and I beneath him. We were rivals because our war philosophy was very different. Agemman was a blunt but effective adherent to the Codex Astartes, whereas I *interpreted* our primarch's teachings and was less predictable. Some have said reckless. Only Agemman has ever said so to my face.

He smiled, but it was a cold, pitiless gesture.

Out with it then.

'I wish I could I report I was here merely to see the dead brought back to life...' Agemman gestured to the formidable scar raking my side. The smile faded to the thin, hard line of his mouth. 'But, I cannot. You are to stand before Lord Calgar. The Chapter Master would have knowledge of what happened on Damnos and why we returned to the empire in ignominious defeat.'

My eyes narrowed, but I held my temper. An argument here, now, with Venatio looking on, would serve no good purpose.

'And am I to be held responsible for this defeat? I know that whilst I yet stood, the warriors of the Second were not routed.'

Agemman refused to be baited. He was rigid, and a pain in the arse for that.

'You have six hours to prepare your testimony.'

'My *testimony*? Am I to be judged then?'

My opponent betrayed no emotion, though I refuse to believe he did not take some petty pleasure in all of this.

'The events on Damnos were disastrous. Questions must be asked.'

I began to walk towards the chamber door, still dripping.

'Then let us go now. I have nothing to hide and don't need six hours to realise that.'

Agemman put his armoured bulk in my path.

'Cease this wanton disregard for orders, Sicarius! Your reckless behaviour is what has brought you to this point.' He calmed down, though it took some effort to reassert the mask of control he had been wearing ever since addressing me from the shadows. 'It seems you have yet to learn that.'

'Don't speak to me like a neophyte, Agemman,' I warned. 'As they have on countless occasions, my swift actions prevented an earlier defeat. I prefer to win hard battles, not easy campaigns and reap the hollow glory. Next time you behold my banner on the field, look at the victories upon it and then look to your own.'

I goaded him out of a desire to return the disrespect he had just afforded me. I vaunted the First, and their captain. They were some of the bravest and most capable warriors in the Chapter, but that didn't mean I had to like them.

Agemman had every right to strike me. To my irritation, he resisted, but as he spoke through clenched teeth I knew he'd come close.

'Six hours.'

Agemman left the apothecarion without another word. He'd be saving them for my trial, no doubt.

To his credit, Venatio said nothing. He merely gave his professional report.

'You are fit to resume your duties, brother-captain.'

At a command from the Apothecary, a serf entered the room from a side chamber and began scraping the remaining amniotic gel from my skin.

Still seething after Agemman's exit, I nodded to Venatio.

'Tell me, Brother-Apothecary. Where are my armour and weapons?'

'The Techmarines have been repairing them. I understand there was much damage to the war-plate in particular. You'll find them in the armourium. East wing.'

Dismissing the serf, I grunted a word of gratitude to Venatio and left for the weapon workshops. Something in the penumbra around the apothecarion had set me on edge and I desired the return of my war trappings as soon as possible.

The Fortress of Hera is a vast and near-impregnable bastion. It is the noble seat of Macragge, the slab-sided barrack house of the Ultramarines Chapter, and has always been so. Its armouriums, battle cages and shrines are many. We all worship at them in our own way, these temples of violence and honour. I found Techmarine Vantor easily enough.

Like the apothecarion, the armourium was dark, but far from cold. It radiated heat that prickled the air and raked my nostrils. There was smoke and flame, ash and the taste of metal. Great engines tended by serf-engineers and cyberorganic servitors pummelled iron and steel. Here, the artefacts of war were repaired and manufactured. On a metal dais, a Rhino armoured transport lay gutted, whilst incense was burned and canticles of function were invoked. At a great anvil, blades were tempered and honed by hammer-armed servitors. Workshops were arrayed in multitudes with their rows of dark iron benches and churning machineries.

All of this fell into insignificance, however. For nearest to me was a servo-armed Techmarine, stooped over a suit of magnificent power armour.

It was good to see it again. It would feel even better to don it.

'Brother...' I announced my presence at the armourium's door, which had slid open to admit me into the expansive workshop.

Vantor turned at the sound of my voice, his bionics grinding noisily as he moved.

He bowed slightly. 'Captain Sicarius, I have almost finished my ministrations to your armour.' Spoken through the vox-grille covering his mouth, the Techmarine's voice was as mechanised as his right arm and leg. 'I'm sure you'll be pleased to learn that, like you, it yet lives.'

I always found it curious, the way the adherents of the Cult Mechanicus regarded inanimate adamantium and ceramite. Vantor had not only been repairing my armour, but also had been soothing its machine-spirit too. As a Techmarine, Vantor wore not the blue of the Ultramarines but the red of the Martian world where he had received his clandestine training. Only his shoulder pad remained the blue of Ultramar as a concession to his dual fealty.

'Indeed I am, brother. I long to wear it again, and feel the grip of my Tempest Blade in my–' I stopped abruptly, my eye drawn to a work-team of servitors labouring at the back of the chamber.

I could not disguise my anger. 'What in Terra's name is that?'

Beyond the honest industry of the armourium, beyond the slow beaten battleplate and forged blades, the tanks and engines, was an abomination.

Vantor turned, incredulous.

'Frag, shrapnel. They are what remnants of the enemy we managed to salvage before the evacuation.'

Ranked up, steadily being logged and categorized, examined and tested, were pieces of the necron. Heads, fingers, limbs, even broken portions of their weaponry, were under heavy scrutiny by the Techmarine's lobotomised serfs. I counted over twenty different benches of the material.

The urge to grasp my sword deepened.

'They are inactive, I take it?'

Vantor nodded. 'Of course, but by studying even the inert pieces of necron technology we can develop our knowledge of them.'

The fact that the Techmarine could neither see nor appreciate the danger in bringing this flotsam into our fortress-monastery only served to show the gulf between us in sharper relief.

I walked through the workshop, Vantor following, and approached one of the work benches where a servitor was toiling over an array of limbs, heads, even torso sections. I reached out to touch one of the silver skulls, its rictus grin mocking me even in destruction, but fell just short of touching it.

'How are they even here? I am no expert on the necron, but aren't they supposed to disappear when destroyed?'

Vantor came to stand beside me. A blurt of binaric dismissed the servitor and set it to another task.

'Apparently, the Damnosian natives found a way to retard that ability through magnetism.'

I frowned at Vantor. 'Really? A human colony with rudimentary engineering ability, using only electromagnets and a theory, achieves what the Mechanicus couldn't?'

'I was similarly unconvinced, and yet...' He gestured to the workshop full of deactivated components.

'I would not have sanctioned this research,' I declared. My gaze lingered on one skull in particular. There was something strangely familiar about it.

He blinked, his very human eyes like flashes of burned umber.

'Lord Calgar agrees that our knowledge of this enemy is of paramount importance if we are to fight it effectively.'

'We fought effectively enough,' I replied, my manner absent-minded as I drew closer to the skull. Like a siren it seemed to call to me, beckoning, reminding...

I felt the darkness close, the veil around me tightening and suffocating. Vantor's next words were lost in this fog as was my response. All I could see was the skull, the eyes aglow and its rictus grin. I reached for my blade but grasped air, neither hilt nor scabbard. Legs buckling, unable to hold my weight, I fell to my knees and gasped. The air would not come. I was drowning with no ocean for miles, save the one of oil and blackness devouring me. Everything surrendered to the dark: Vantor, the armourium, the serfs, my armour – all was consumed. Only I remained, staring down the lidless orbs of that gilded, grinning skull.

'*I am doom...*'

The last of my breath ghosted the air as an icy chill came over me. I felt ice underfoot, though I was still inside the fortress-monastery, and a low rumbling tremor in its frigid depths...

I breathed and the darkness crowding my vision bled away at once like ink dispersed in water. The ice melted and I resurfaced. The necron skull was in my hands, grasped tight. Its eyes were lifeless, dead in their sockets, a rusty patina weathering cheeks, pate and temples of gunmetal grey. Not gold. Not the king. Not here.

Vantor was gone – only the servitors were left and I assumed he had let me stay here to peruse the battlefield relics as if I alone could unlock some secret by merely looking at him. He hadn't realised I had become lost in a dream.

The wound in my side flared anew and I grimaced to keep the pain at bay.

My armour was waiting for me, a gift from Vantor.

I took it, eager to leave the armourium and the unquiet resonance it had stirred inside me. I needed to ease my mind. It had been never so pure and focused as when in combat. I headed at once for the battle cages.

I found an old comrade in the lonely arena.

Daceus was the only warrior sparring that night and I crossed a gloomy threshold of empty cages, their servitors dormant and inactive within, to reach him.

'Brother-sergeant,' I called up to him, having to raise my voice above the punishing din of his sword blade striking the vital kill-points of the combat servitor he had chosen to pit himself against. It was a grossly uneven contest, of course. Daceus could have wrecked the machine many times over but was here to practise his form and test his stamina, not incur the wrath of the Techmarines by needlessly dismantling servitors.

'Pause routine,' he uttered breathlessly and looked down at me, his face mildly beaded with sweat. Daceus saluted, sword in front of his body. 'Brother-captain, I am glad to see you returned to us.'

'I hoped to bless the reunion with honest combat.'

Ever the martial exemplar, Daceus stepped aside and hammered the icon which opened the cage door with his fist.

'Then let us see what benedictions you might offer.'

Already, he was measuring my combat efficacy, observing, strategising. My brother-sergeant wanted to know how sharp my fighting edge was. So did I.

Using the Tempest Blade in the battle cage would dishonour the weapon and put me at an unfair advantage, so I selected a training gladius from the rack to match the one wielded by my opponent. The balance was good, the blade straight and sharp despite the many hours of practice bouts it must have endured. It was no master-crafted weapon, but it was a worthy one.

'Helmets on or off, brother?' asked Daceus. Here in the cages, once blades were drawn, rank ceased to have meaning.

'Off. I want to be able to breathe and use my senses without hindrance.'

'Agreed. No strikes above the neck then. First to three hits?'

I nodded, taking up a fighting stance in my power armour. Vantor would be annoyed if I scratched it so soon, but I believed war-plate needed scars before going into battle proper.

'Begin.'

Daceus's first thrust was quick and aimed at my torso. I barely parried it before a second lunge caught me off guard and took a chip out of my plastron.

We paused and returned to our initial engagement positions.

'First hit is yours, brother.' I tried, and failed, to hide my annoyance. 'Again.'

Daceus chopped downwards, high to low, and I managed a hasty block in response. Stepping back, I invited him to advance, which he did with a swift back to forehand slash. I used a hilt guard to protect myself and forged a jab of my own, but Daceus deflected it easily and used the kinetic momentum to rotate his blade into a half circling up and over slash that smashed against my clavicle and put me down on one knee.

I was sweating, but Daceus returned to the initial engagement position and did not dishonour me by offering me a hand up.

'That's two,' he said with the barest hint of a smile.

Now I was burning with shameful anger. Returning to position, I adopted a ready stance. 'Again.'

This time I swept in low, beneath the crossways slash crafted by my opponent and went in under Daceus's guard. He stabbed downwards, a makeshift block, and our blades clashed. But the force pushed his sword hand outwards and I used the weakness to hammer my shoulder into his solar plexus. Daceus reeled, staggering back to regain footing, but I pressed my attack, first using an overhead slash to break open his flailing guard, then delivering a diagonal uppercut that put a groove in his plastron and pulled him to the ground.

We went again, this time exchanging a flurry of blows, feints and blocks. Our blades became a blur of clashing steel and I began to feel like my old self again. After a brutal riposte, I swapped hands mid sword flourish and smacked the flat of my gladius against Daceus's gorget.

He gasped as the blade came close to his neck: a foul stroke.

I ignored his slight shock and returned to position.

'Evens, two hits apiece. Again.'

As I moved through the blade disciplines, the finely crafted sword strokes, I felt a background pulse directly behind my eyes. It was like an intense headache, a drum inside my skull, pounding in time with my heartbeat.

Shadows flooded the arena that housed the battle cages; it had been this way since I had entered. But now, the darkness began to coalesce and I felt it close around me like a slow clenching fist. A silent predator lying in wait, it crouched at the edge of my vision and from somewhere distant I felt a chill enter my bones.

It was snowing, the battle cage far away and forgotten as an arctic tundra overwhelmed it in my senses. At the edge of a frost-encrusted ruin, the veil of darkness persisted. Through the black fog, an enemy emerged.

'I am doom...'

Beneath my feet, the ice trembled like the beating of some immense heart.

The king had returned, in all his gilded and terrible majesty.

We clashed, I with the Tempest Blade crackling in my gauntleted fist, the primarch's name on my lips like an unsheathed sword.

The king swung his war-scythe around, the great reaping edge like a crescent moon cut from the bleakest night and fashioned into a weapon. Our blades struck together in a cascade of sparks and we broke apart. I took a moment's respite but the necron king needed none, his anima fuelled by some ancient will and driven by the machine he had surrendered his mortal flesh to become. Massive, overpowering, he loomed over me in seconds.

'Not again!' I roared. 'I am a Lion of Macragge, I am Master of the Watch. A slayer of kings!' With fury born of desperation and hate, I hurled myself at the necron. His scythe haft shattered, sheared in two by my blade and I battered his weary defence as he threw up his arms in surrender.

'No mercy for you,' I vowed, raining down blows until my shoulder ached and my lungs were fit to burst.

Breath did not come. I was drowning again and the veil

of darkness crept into my field of vision, smothering and denying me my prey.

'No! I will not be cheated of my victory. Not again, not–'

As I collapsed, retching what I thought was fluid from my chest but bringing up only air, I saw Daceus.

His gladius was broken, split along the blade. His vambraces were hacked apart, his face awash with shock and anger.

'My brother...' I struggled to gasp, falling. Daceus, despite my wounding of him, rose up to catch me.

At the doleful clang of our power armour meeting, I resurfaced from the dream and the pool of dark imaginings that choked me.

'Brother-captain...' He sounded panicked. I waved his concern away, and stood up unaided.

'I am all right. And you?' I asked, gesturing to his battered war-plate.

'A scratch,' he lied, then frowned. 'What happened?'

I saw no sense in hiding the truth, so I told him of what I had seen, of my slayer reborn, of the duel I thought I was fighting against *him*.

'I could have killed you, Daceus.'

'But you did not.'

But I could have. I almost did.

A remnant from Damnos, some revenant I had brought with me, lingered. I felt the chill of it in the air around me and the dull pain in my side. I saw it in the shadows, the veil of darkness which harboured monsters of cold steel and viridian fire.

Something in the gloom around us caught my attention and I seized the Tempest Blade, throwing a fresh sword from the rack to Daceus at the same time.

'What is it?' The sergeant caught the blade easily and swung around, trying to follow my gaze.

I whispered, 'Are we alone?'

Daceus nodded slowly and I eased open the door to the cage.

'Not any more...' I told him.

Together, we crept from the battle cage and spread out. My eyes never left the exact spot where I had seen movement, and I battle-signed the enclosing manoeuvre to the sergeant.

As well as the battle cages themselves, the arena had a servitor rack. It was an automated station where deactivated combat-servitors yet to be invested with sparring protocols would wait until called upon. Some sixty of the automata were currently in the rack in three rows of twenty, one surmounting the other.

More machines. More cold steel.

In the dingy arena hall, they did not look so dissimilar from the necrons displaced around the east wing armourium.

Daceus and I closed on the servitors' dormant forms. One in particular had drawn my eye. On Damnos we had seen necrons that clothed themselves in the rancid flesh of the dead, using their skins as a crude and scarcely effective form of camouflage.

I could almost swear the eye sockets of this one were aglow...

Not waiting for Daceus, I thrust with my blade, releasing an actinic blur of fused steel and energised brutality.

Impaled on my sword, I wrenched the interloper from the servitor rack and with a grunt threw it down for us to finish off.

Daceus stopped me.

'Brother-captain...' He sounded concerned, but was looking at me and not our enemy. 'It is just a servitor. Not even active.'

'Strength of Guilliman...' I breathed, before letting the Tempest Blade sag down by my side. He was right. It was just an automaton. Nothing more. No assassin clothed in flesh. 'Perhaps I left the care of Brother Venatio too soon.'

To his credit, Daceus tried to reassure me.

'You were in a suspended animation coma, brother-captain. Some... side-effects are to be expected.'

I grunted, the equivalent of a vocal shrug, and heard the chime of choral bells echo throughout the arena.

'Has it been that long?'

Daceus's eyes narrowed in confusion. 'Long for what?'

'I am to stand before Lord Calgar and be judged for my command on Damnos. I had thought I had longer to prepare.'

'It would be my honour to accompany you to the Hall of Ultramar, my lord.'

'Aye. Agreed.' I clapped Daceus on the shoulder. He was as good and loyal a soldier as any captain had a right to have in his service. 'Gratitude, brother.'

We left for the Hall of Ultramar and an audience with its regent and most august lord.

Replete in his war panoply, the Lord of Macragge was seated upon a throne like a battle king of old, and my heart both swelled with pride and trembled with awe at the sight of him. He wore his formal battleplate, a ceremonial suit festooned with laurels and awards. A pair of hefty power gloves clothed his hands, which he rested regally on the throne arms. His hair was white as hoar-frost, and he glowered at me through one organic eye. The other eye was a bionic, and even less welcoming.

'Brother-captain,' he said, radiating authority. 'Come forward.'

Here in the Hall of Ultramar, the great and noble were personified in statue form and shadowed me as I walked the long processional to a place before my lord. I saw Invictus, Helveticus and Galatan, Titus, all measuring my worth with the weight of their marble stares. I would not be found wanting.

Daceus had come with me as far as the great bronze doors, and there I had bid him stay, despite his offer to the contrary. I didn't want him caught up in this. Any judgement would be my burden to carry.

As I walked, I passed under great looming archways and saw again the shadows within the chamber's lofty vaults. I tried to avert my gaze, turning my mind to the matter at hand, but when my eyes alighted on Lord Calgar I saw a strange halo encircle his head. At first I continued with the slightest break in step, aware of not only Calgar's eyes upon me but Severus Agemman's too and the honour guard of Macragge. Then, as I drew closer, I realised that what I believed to be a trick of the light was an actual glow. No, not merely a glow, a *mark*. It was viridian green, and I saw a fraction too late what it portended.

'Get down!'

Agemman reacted first to my warning, putting himself between me, as I ran down the processional, and Calgar, who was at the other end of it. He thought I had lost all sense and was preparing to knock some back into me. I had drawn my pistol, prompting the honour guard to draw arms also. Five bolt weapons were trained on my chest in an instant. My gaze went to the eaves above us, the shadows in the vaulted roof, and I pointed to get my brothers' attention and stop them from executing me.

'Up there!'

Agemman saw it too, crouched like an iron gargoyle, the darkness as its cloak. A single eye betrayed its position, but we would be far too late to prevent it achieving its goal. In truth, the optic was a targeting matrix and Lord Calgar was in its crosshairs.

A long, slim rifle slid into its grasp. I watched it shoulder the weapon and aim it. Reality slowed, as if the assassin were chronologically a few seconds ahead of us and functioning in a different time stream.

A plume of viridian gas expelled from the rifle's vents like a breath. There was no recoil, only the expulsion of a missile that raked through the air. I followed the missile's trajectory in my peripheral vision, triggering my pistol in the same moment and setting the vaults alight with a pulse of energised plasma. The others had seen the danger now and were discharging their own weapons into the time-shifted assassin above us.

Calgar grunted, the sound someone makes when they're gut punched and the air is blasted from their lungs. Having got to his feet when the interloper had been discovered, he fell back and clattered into and then out of his throne, half rolling down the steps that led up to his seat.

We destroyed the archway where the assassin had made his nest, ripping up the shadows with streaks of blinding muzzle flash and plasma and bringing down a cascade of debris. This was the Hall of Ultramar and we had wrecked it like a band of careless thieves.

Time resumed, our weapons fell silent again, but the quarry was gone, slipped back into whatever darkness had spawned it. The assassin hadn't merely escaped, it simply wasn't there anymore, phased out like the necrons too badly damaged to self-repair. Only we hadn't destroyed it. Not even close.

With the immediate danger passed for now, Agemman was at Lord Calgar's side. The honour guard closed around them protectively like an armoured cocoon.

'Stay with the Chapter Master...' I was running back down the processional, the vaunted marble heroes urging my every step. Every footfall I took was punctuated by a glance above me, back into the shadowed roof and searching for my enemy.

Bursting through the bronze doors, I met Daceus.

The brother-sergeant was armed, having clearly heard the gunfire from within.

'What's happened?'

I didn't linger, but kept on down the corridor, intent on reaching the east wing of the armourium where I knew an answer would be waiting. Daceus kept step.

'Our enemy is in the Fortress of Hera,' I told him. 'They have just tried to assassinate Lord Calgar.'

'Blood of Guilliman! Is he–'

I spared the brother-sergeant a stern glance. 'He lives. He *will* live.'

Daceus would chastise himself for his doubt later; now we had to reach the armourium.

I was about to raise Vantor on the vox to get a warning to the Techmarine when the shrieking alert sirens told me I was too late. Light from the lumens and glow-globes shrank to an amber wash that overlaid the halls of the fortress-monastery in sickly monochrome.

I activated the vox in my gorget. 'Agemman.'

His reply was a few seconds late in coming.

'We're headed for the apothecarion. Brother Venatio awaits us.'

'The alert?'

'Is coming from the armourium in the east wing.'

All my fears suddenly crystallised. The memory of the necron 'corpses' returned, those that were too badly damaged to self-repair but unable to phase out. Only they weren't damaged. It was a ruse and in our ignorance we had invited them into our bastion, our home.

I wanted to hit something, but instead I bit back my anger and answered Agemman.

'Sergeant Daceus and I are on our way there now.'

I cut the link – the First Captain had enough to deal with.

As we entered the east wing, the corridors strangely abandoned, I saw the veil of darkness. Something writhed within it, something of cold steel with viridian eyes like balefires.

'Am I imagining that?'

Shaking his head, Daceus racked his bolter slide and took aim at the mechanised horrors emerging from the shadows.

The Tempest Blade is a relic of Talassar, and I am a descendent of that world's noblest household. I honoured my ancestors by bringing its fury to my enemies. A necron exoskeleton is formidable but no match for a power sword such as this. They were warrior-caste, the foot soldiery of their darkling empire. The first I vaporised with a ball of incandescent plasma, the second I beheaded. My armour was impervious to their beam weapons and I was barely slowed as I hacked the arm off a third and then bifurcated its torso. Three necrons phased out in a cascade of howling energy.

Daceus neutralised three more with precise burst-fire from his bolter. Even when one of the mechanoids was a handspan from his face, the sergeant was unflinching and maintained strict fire discipline. He tore the thing apart almost point-blank and let the frag pepper his armoured form.

When we were done and the necrons vanquished, we waded into the darkness looking for more but the veil was thinning by then and disappeared entirely in a few more seconds.

Daceus scowled. 'How many of these things are we dealing with?'

'Judging by what I saw dissected in Vantor's workshop, dozens.'

'Could they gain a foothold here, a means of bringing greater forces directly into the fortress?'

I clapped my sergeant's shoulder guard to reassure him.

'We won't let that happen, brother.'

Ahead of us, the east wing of the armourium beckoned. Its entry gate was open and a flickering light from within threw syncopated flashes into the gloom.

Inside, the armourium was a charnel house. Blood streaked the walls and machineries. It mingled with oil from the drones. Every serf, servitor and enginseer was dead. Their bodies lay strewn about the workshop, eviscerated and impaled. The luminator rig above had been damaged during the commotion and threw sporadic light across the grisly scene. Every flash revealed a fresh horror: faces frozen in terror and death. But there was no sign of the necron, none at all. The limbs, torsos, skulls and weaponry were all gone.

Then I saw Vantor, and my grief redoubled.

The Techmarine was dead, split from groin to neck by an energised blade. It had cut through his artificer armour like tin. Biological entrails entwined with cables and wires as all that comprised Euclidese Vantor was vented out and strewn like offal. It was no way for my brother to meet his end. His murderers had robbed him of glory.

I placed my gauntleted hand upon his face to close his still-staring gaze. Even the dishonoured dead should be allowed eternal sleep. Such was the damage done, even his gene-seed could not be recovered.

For a moment I shut my eyes, marshalling my anger, turning it into something useful.

The sensation of drowning came back, and the darkness in my mind's eye returned with it. I fought it down, clenching a fist to stay focused. Whatever trauma I was experiencing would have to wait. I was determined to master it.

I addressed Daceus.

'A deadly enemy is at large in these halls, brother. It has already laid low our Chapter Master and now it seeks to end us into the bargain.' I gritted my teeth. 'We will not yield to it. We must rouse our battle-brothers, hunt this menace down and exterminate it.'

Daceus nodded grimly and we left the armourium as we had found it. No time to mourn or bury the dead.

More caskets would line the Fortress of Hera's funerary chambers if we did not act.

'Brother-captain!' Daceus stabbed out a finger, and was already raising up his bolter as the veil of darkness returned. It was real this time, not a shadow creeping across my subconscious.

I fed a surge of energy down the Tempest Blade and it crackled into an azure beacon.

It was the assassin, his cyclopean eye aglow.

'By Guilliman's blood,' I swore. 'I will have that bastard's head...'

But he wasn't alone, as three bulky warriors stomped up alongside him bearing twin-barrelled cannons. A trio of muzzle flares roared into being.

I got off a single shot, and took the one-eyed assassin directly in his glowing orb. Unprepared to engage his chronometric defences, his head exploded in a pulse of scorching plasma. As the corridor lit up with the flare of a necron cannonade I had the satisfaction of seeing Calgar's shooter crumple and phase out.

Resurrect from that.

'Move!' I grabbed Daceus and we dove back inside the armourium as the corridor where we'd been standing was stitched with viridian beams.

Hunkered down, our backs against the wall as our enemy advanced down the corridor spewing fire, Daceus handed me a primed charge.

'Here...'

I glanced at him quizzically.

'One can never be too prepared.'

'Even in the fortress-monastery?'

He shrugged. In my hand, I held a krak grenade.

I leaned out into the corridor, squeezing off a snapshot and clipping one of the bulky cannon-wielders. The necron was heavily armoured but the plasma bolt tore off its right shoulder and most of its arm. Unable to heft its weapon, it stumbled and collapsed against the corridor wall. But it was far from finished, as its self-repair protocols activated.

Behind the first wave, three more immortal warriors lumbered into view.

'There are too many.'

Daceus fired off a bolter burst one-handed, the two of us alternating our snap-fire in an attempt to slow down our enemy. It wasn't working.

'Agreed,' said the sergeant.

A plan formed. I thumbed the krak grenade's detonator, and primed it for a six-second timer.

'Give me some covering fire.'

Daceus triggered a three-round burst as I leaned out with him a fraction later and clamped the krak grenade to the wall.

'Back, now!'

We ducked back inside the armourium as a firestorm ripped through the corridor, bringing most of the ceiling down and sealing it off.

Daceus and I were back on our feet a moment later. Outside the armourium, the dust was still settling. Chunks of debris fell from the ceiling, and where internal circuitry was exposed, wires spat and fizzed.

Our enemies were trapped, but already the veil of darkness was beginning to coalesce again.

Daceus raised his bolter but I seized his arm and urged him away from the rubble.

'Come on. We need to gather reinforcements.'

We had scarcely taken a few steps when the vox crack-led again.

'Sicarius...' It was Agemman. His voice was strained and I heard the distinctive sounds of combat in the back-ground. *'We are under attack. The necrons have laid siege to the apothecarion. Lord Calgar is in danger. I don't know how much longer we can–'*

The link was severed in a blurt of hostile static. Agem-man was gone and no amount of attempts was going to raise him again.

Like smoke on the wind, the darkness abated. It was headed elsewhere, possessed of a singular purpose.

Grim-faced, Daceus and I set off for the apothecarion. I hoped to Guilliman we would not be too late.

Despite the wailing alert sirens, the warning strobes and its call to arms, the Fortress of Hera was eerily empty.

It had unnerved Daceus. 'Where are our battle-brothers?'

I shook my head, hurrying down the ghost-like hall-ways as my vox hails were met with forbidding silence.

'Engaged against the necrons.'

'With no word, no warning or attempt to coordinate defences?'

Daceus was unconvinced.

So was I.

'There is no other explanation, brother-sergeant.'

That too was a lie. I could think of one, so could Daceus, but neither of us would speak it.

There were no further encounters with the necrons before we reached the apothecarion. Standing at the end of the short hallway to the chamber's entrance, I realised why.

There was no entrance. It had been entirely consumed by the veil of darkness.

As if sentient and reacting to our sudden presence, the tendrils of night began to whip and eddy as if borne by an ethereal breeze. Twisting and uncoiling, unfurling like a ragged black cloak, the darkness came for us.

Within its depths were the necrons.

Three armoured warriors stomped towards us, coffin-shaped shields locked together in the manner of some ancient empire. Unlike the other necrons we had faced, these carried energised khopesh blades and were emblazoned with dynastic symbols. I knew a warrior elite when I saw it. I also knew who they were protecting.

A one-eyed necron, not an assassin but more a vizier, cowered behind this trio of formidable guardians. Stone like lapis lazuli accented his mechanised body in long strips and a gilded beard clasp protruded from his chin. In one metal-fingered hand he carried a staff; the other clutched the tethers of the veil. Here was the architect of darkness. And it was through him we would have to go if we were to reach our stricken Chapter Master.

As his guardians marched towards us, the vizier extended a talon in our direction.

His voice echoed with the resonance of ages.

'Defilers. Infidels. You are an inferior species, lesser in every way to the Necrontyr. Behold what your arrogance has wrought. You will have all eternity to regret it.'

I glanced to Daceus. His bolter was aimed and ready.

'Bold words. Sounds like a challenge.'

My brother-sergeant snarled. 'Which I gladly answer.'

Daceus unleashed an unceasing storm of fire from his bolter. The heavy shells hammered the necron shield

wall, battering the guardians back and breaking their
defence. It ended with the hard *thunk* of the bolter's
empty magazine. Daceus dropped it, unholstering his
sidearm in one hand and drawing his gladius with the
other.

I saluted our opponents with the Tempest Blade, hilt
raised up to my eyes.

'In the name of Ultramar, you will not stand between
us and our Chapter Master.'

Two of the vizier's guardians yet lived. I brought my
sword down preparing to engage them, when Daceus
stopped me.

'No, brother-captain. Kill that thing,' he nodded towards
the vizier. 'Save Lord Calgar.'

After a moment's hesitation and knowing the fate my
sergeant had condemned himself to, I ran down the
corridor.

One of the guardians stepped into my path but I parried its khopesh blade and thundered a kick into its
lowered shield, smashing the necron aside. Hearing
Daceus engage them both, and not stopping to see how
he fared, I leapt at the vizier.

The ancient necron recoiled, brandishing his staff
defensively as vortices of shadow swirled around him.
I watched the darkness retreat, like mist before the sun,
carrying the vizier with it, clinging on like some infernal
passenger. I vaulted into the air, the sword of Talassar
held aloft in a two-handed grip. As the blade descended,
the vizier was already fading. Cruel laughter echoed
around me as I scythed through nothing, embedding
my sword in the deck-plate underfoot with a resounding *clang*.

But I would not be denied, and gave chase into the apothecarion. Behind me, Daceus was fighting for his life. I could not stop, or his sacrifice would mean nothing.

With the scent of my fleeing enemy still on me, I hurried through the gaping doorway.

The vizier had not run far, for inside the apothecarion the veil of darkness howled like a captured thunderhead. It bleached all vitality from the room and its occupants as if their very life forces were being surrendered to sustain it.

At the eye of this storm, I saw Agemman and the survivors of Calgar's honour guard. Two were dead already, slumped against the medi-slab where the Lord of Ultramar lay supine and unconscious.

Venatio was nearest to him, but far from ministering to our wounded Chapter Master, he was fighting hard against a score of necrons. Like the creatures we had fought on Damnos, they wore the skins of the dead like mantles or trophies, and carried no weapons as such except for their dagger-length talons. The Damnosians had taken to calling them *flayed ones*.

One turned as I entered the apothecarion, alerted to my presence by the vizier who was skulking in the background, half-smothered by shadow.

It sprang at me, this flesh-draped horror.

I weaved away from its reaching claws and cut its midriff, parting abdomen and torso through its spinal column. I didn't wait to see it dissipate – more were coming.

I shot one with my swiftly drawn plasma pistol. The burst took it in the chest, arresting its mad leap and blasting it into the ether. I aimed at a second but one of the flayed ones slashed my forearm, tearing up the vambrace and disarming me. Sweeping the Tempest Blade, I decapitated it. A third I impaled through the chest, staggering a fourth with a heavy punch. It was dazed, or rather I had forced a system reboot, and it took a few seconds for it to adjust. Long enough for me to cleave it open diagonally from shoulder to hip. It phased out in a flurry of sparks.

My efforts had got me as far as the medi-slab.

Calgar's recumbent form looked frighteningly still and I tried to tell myself he yet drew breath.

Some eighteen necrons had been struck down around us. Several had phased out, but the rest were currently self-repairing. In the encroaching veil of darkness, I saw more viridian balefires flicker into life as the vizier summoned yet more warriors.

For Agemman's benefit, I aimed my sword at the vizier.

'We need to end that thing.'

The other defenders' bolters had run dry of ammunition long before and the First Captain had taken up one of the fallen Ultramarines' relic blades in preference to his ceremonial gladius. The remaining honour guard wielded power axes, whilst Apothecary Venatio had his chainsword.

'How do you propose we do that?' Agemman gestured to the necron horde that had just redoubled in size. A ring of steel stood between us and the vizier.

There was but a few seconds' respite to form a strategy before the flayed ones would be on us again.

'With courage and honour, Severus. He won't escape this time. Make me a breach with your warriors, and I'll pierce whatever passes for a heart in this thing.'

'What of Lord Calgar?'

Venatio spoke up. 'I'll stay by the Chapter Master's side.'

Agemman glanced back at me.

'If this fails, you'll be overwhelmed.'

I nodded. 'Aye, but you always said I was reckless.'

I heard the smirk in his response. He summoned the honour guard and prepared to open the gap I needed.

Self-repairing, several of the necrons jerked back to their feet. Their jaws clacked as if laughing, and they sliced their talons against one another in anticipation of the kill. For machines, they displayed an unnerving awareness of malice.

I lowered my sword, looking down the blade as I adopted a ready stance.

'Cut deep...'

Leading the honour guard, Agemman charged the necrons.

The sudden attack briefly stunned the horde and for a few seconds they reeled against the First Captain's fury. Agemman used his bulk and strength to break the flayed ones apart, ignoring the claws that raked his armour.

He roared, cutting a necron down with every sweep of his borrowed relic blade.

'Courage and honour!'

Through the flurry of power axes, I saw mechanised limbs fall in a metal rain. Torsos were hacked apart, heads cleaved. Like their captain, the honour guard were brutal. Relentless. My warrior's heart thundered with pride to witness such unstinting determination and bravery.

Like a speartip they had driven deep into the flayed ones, forcing a channel that thrust all the way to vizier. Embattled on every side, Agemman cried out and with one last effort made the breach I needed.

'Do it, Sicarius... Now!'

The distance was short, my passage blocked only by broken necrons underfoot.

I fixed the singular orb of the vizier with a glare that promised retribution.

'For Ultramar!' I declared, my fury unstoppable. 'Here you die!'

As I reached my enemy, I sprang into a shallow leap using it to gain loft and additional momentum. Holding nothing back, I struck down one-handed putting every iota of strength I possessed into the blow. My Tempest Blade cut the staff in half and carried on without pause into the vizier's skull. I split him down the middle, bifurcating his cyclopean eye, and did not stop until I had sheared him clean through. Both halves collapsed in a frenzy of flashing sparks and thrashing wires. The vizier phased out before they even hit the ground.

Triumphant, I turned to Agemman.

The darkness was receding, my plan had succeed–

Agemman was down, parted from his relic blade. The three honour guard were strewn around him, slain. Venatio lay sprawled on his back. The Apothecary was unmoving.

Calgar was alone, unconscious and undefended on the medi-slab.

As I saw the thing that loomed above him, I realised it would be his mortuary slab instead.

My sword felt loose and heavy in my grasp. I scarcely had breath to speak.

'No...'

An old enemy turned to regard me and in its fathomless gaze I saw the fall of empires and the terrible entropy of ages.

It had returned. The gilded king, my nemesis, the Undying of Damnos.

'I am doom.'

As the darkness closed in around me and I drowned again, I saw its war-scythe held over Calgar in an executioner's grip. There was no pity in his eyes, no mercy, not even malice, just a deep abiding ennui that presaged an end to all things.

The ice came back, crusting the ground and shawling my body in a sudden snowfall. Beneath it, I heard the beating heart that quaked the very earth.

I gasped, but breath wouldn't come. Black spots flecked my sight, converging at the edge of my vision. I raged but knew I was dying. My gauntleted fingers slipped from the sword's hilt and I heard it clatter uselessly to the ground.

I fell to one knee, then all fours.

Crawling, still defiant, I felt the scrape of talons pinning me as the flayed ones swarmed over me, swallowing me in a sea of cold metal. Something seized my face and then a hand clamped around my neck. A blade pierced my shoulder, another in my back and I was steadily transfixed.

Powerless, I could only watch as the war-scythe descended...

As the veil of darkness claimed me, I heard far away voices but dismissed them as nostalgic memory. I had died on Damnos and come back, but there was no returning from this.

A dense ball of white heat flared in my side prompting a gout of hot fluid to erupt from my throat, spewing up over my lips in a coppery wash. I spat it out, retching up the blood–

No... it wasn't blood. It was the briny, amniotic soup of the revivification casket I could taste in my mouth.

I opened my eyes and found I was cocooned by a viscous recuperating gel.

Had I survived? Were the voices I heard real after all? Did Daceus yet live and muster reinforcements?

My mind overloaded with uncertainty, and with my senses restored I hammered a fist against the inside of the casket. My rebreather had come loose and I was drowning in this filth.

The locking mechanism disengaged and I fell forwards onto the apothecarion floor as the revivification casket opened with a blurted warning chime.

On my knees, coughing up the amniotic brine that had saved my life and kept it tethered to the world, I looked up into the eyes of my Apothecary.

I could scarcely believe what they were telling me.

'Venatio?'

He nodded respectfully, fashioning a warm smile. 'Brother-captain. Welcome back to the world of the–'

'You're alive...' Staggering, I got to my feet. I was sweating with the intense biological rigours my body had just undertaken and was still a little unsteady. Venatio went to assist me but I held him back with my outstretched palm.

'And so are you, Sicarius. You were badly injured and have only just–'

I interrupted for a second time. 'Injured where? Here, in the fortress-monastery?'

Something wasn't right. An odd sense of recollection, a very mortal experience described as *dèja vu*, that which is 'seen already', was affecting me. I remembered the chronometric device utilised by the assassin, how it had blurred time and I wondered if I was somehow trapped in it.

'Damnos.' Venatio's eyes narrowed. He was already consulting his bio-scanner, as if their readers could provide some clue to my sudden distemper. 'You were struck down on Damnos, several weeks ago in fact. You have just this moment come back to consciousness.'

I gazed around the apothecarion, at the shadows at its periphery, but saw no veil of darkness, no hidden foes this time.

'I was drowning...'

Venatio bowed his head, abruptly contrite. 'Apologies, brother-captain. Your rebreather came loose towards the end of suspended animation. You appeared to be experiencing some form of nightmare. It's not uncommon. So close to revival, I couldn't interrupt the process to wake you or replace the rebreather. It was inactive for but a few seconds.'

I was shaking my head.

'But this is... it's impossible.'

The Apothecary showed his hands in a placatory gesture. 'You are here. You are back with us. What is your name?'

I frowned, incredulous. 'My name?'

'Yes. What is it?'

'Cato Sicarius. I am master of my senses, Venatio.'

'You do not seem it.' Agemman stepped from the shadows, just as he had before.

'Severus...' Another apparition. 'I saw you fall.'

The First Captain opened his arms as physical testament to his veracity. 'I am standing before you now, Cato.' He disengaged the locking clamps on his battle-helm and removed it, placing it in the crook of his arm. 'Brother.' He came over and put his hand on my shoulder. This scarred veteran of the Tyrannic Wars, hair shorn close to his scalp, service studs gleaming in his brow, was trying to reassure me as one battle-brother to another.

I began to realise the truth and it stirred an even greater concern within me.

'You are here to summon me before Lord Calgar, are you not?'

Nonplussed, Agemman let go of my shoulder. 'I am, yes. How did you know?'

I didn't answer and turned to Venatio instead.

'Apothecary, tell me – did we bring anything back from Damnos, anything from the necron?'

Venatio nodded slowly. 'Yes, but–'

'And is it under Techmarine Vantor's custody in the east wing armourium?'

Agemman answered. 'It is. What is this about, Sicarius?'

I met his questioning gaze with one of certainty and urgency. 'Do you have a sidearm you can lend me?'

Agemman nodded, not understanding but beginning to trust my instincts. He unholstered his bolt pistol and handed it over.

Appreciating the grip of the weapon, I regarded them both.

'We have to get there at once – the Fortress of Hera has been breached.'

Daceus had been on his way to the apothecarion when we met in the corridor.

I quickly explained the situation and together the four

of us made all haste to the armourium in the east wing of the fortress-monastery.

Both Agemman and Daceus had their bolters, whilst Venatio and I held pistols. I hoped it would be enough for whatever awaited us in Vantor's workshop.

'Should we invoke a fortress-wide alarm?' asked Daceus on the way.

Agemman shook his head. 'Let's see what's in there first.' He had donned his battle-helm again, so I couldn't see his face, but I knew he doubted my assertion that the fortress was in danger and I suspect he didn't want to create needless panic.

I saw him exchange a glance with Venatio. The Apothecary hid his concern poorly, but I took no heed. We had arrived at the armourium.

We had not voxed ahead. I was insistent on this. Whatever awareness the dormant necrons in the workshop possessed, I didn't want to risk my warning activating them prematurely.

I hammered the icon for the door release and stepped first into the armourium.

It was much as I remembered: a hive of industry and labour, serfs and engineers hurrying back and forth, servitors engaged in their menial tasks, arms and armour in various conditions of repair and restoration. And there, at the back of the expansive workshop, tended by a small army of menials, was the salvage from Damnos.

Vantor turned as I entered. He was just finishing working up my armour-plate. I saw the Tempest Blade and my plasma pistol on a separate rack nearby.

'Brother-captain, your timing is impeccable.'

'I do hope so.'

The Techmarine's expression changed from warm greeting to slight confusion as Agemman, Daceus and Venatio filed in after me.

'Is there a problem I am unaware of, brothers?'

My gaze was fixed on the back of the workshop.

'Evacuate your labourers.'

Vantor looked to Agemman for confirmation.

'Do as he asks, brother.'

Like ants returning to the nest, the horde of serfs, enginseers and servitors removed themselves from the armourium. None questioned their orders, but some looked worryingly askance at the Ultramarines in their midst as they departed.

'With me.' I advanced into the workshop, indicating a perimeter around the necron salvage where I then came to a halt.

Vantor joined the others as they fell in beside me.

'This is illogical, Captain Sicarius. What are you trying to–'

Dozens of viridian eyes flaring into life in the gloomy armourium arrested the Techmarine's question and had him instinctively reaching for his plasma carbine instead.

'They are self-repairing...'

I raised Agemman's bolt pistol. My battle-brothers readied their weapons in unison with me.

I scowled as the necron host began to reassemble itself.

'Not for long.'

Roaring muzzle flare and a hail of fire broke the tension as the five of us unleashed our weapons, engulfing the back of the workshop in explosive annihilation and destroying everything in it.

Only when we had emptied our clips did we stop firing.

Even Vantor exhausted the power cell in his plasma carbine.

When it was over, the back of the workshop was a scorched, half-destroyed ruin. It was as if a battle had just ended. In truth it had. We had won.

Agemman slammed a fresh clip into his bolter, ever the prepared soldier.

'Whatever is left, incinerate it.'

Daceus and I were sifting through the wreckage, making sure we had cleansed the room thoroughly.

I lowered my borrowed bolt pistol, and signalled to my sergeant to stand down.

'There's nothing left. The threat has been neutralised.'

Across the workshop, Venatio caught my eye. He gestured to the carnage around us.

'How did you know?'

I had no good answer for him, so I told the Apothecary the only thing that made any sense.

'I saw a darkness in my dreams and vowed I would not see it come to pass.'

Agemman was more pragmatic. 'Whatever the cause of your prescience, I for one am glad of it.' He bowed his head. 'Gratitude, Sicarius. But Lord Calgar yet awaits.'

Agemman insisted I be cleaned and wearing my armour before my audience with the Lord Calgar. As I had seen in my half-remembered dream, I walked the processional of the Hall of Ultramar with the statues of heroes measuring my every step.

And as before, I knew I would not be found wanting under their gaze.

Lord Calgar waited for me, seated upon a throne, his

banners describing a legacy of war and glory behind him. Agemman was by his side.

I stopped at a respectful distance and saluted.

With a huge, power-gloved hand, Calgar beckoned me to approach. 'Come forth, Cato.'

I obeyed, masking any surprise at such informality, and took a knee before the Lord of Ultramar.

I bowed my head solemnly. 'I stand in judgement.'

'Rise. You are not being judged this day, though I had reviewed the engagement on Damnos.'

My eyes narrowed in confusion as I came to my feet.

'My lord?'

Agemman maintained his studied silence as Calgar explained.

'Damnos wounded us all, but you and the Second suffered more grievously than most.'

'It is a stain on my honour.'

'One I would see removed, Cato. I will not have this go unchallenged.'

I frowned again, not quite grasping Calgar's meaning.

'Permission to speak freely, my lord.'

'Granted.'

'What exactly are you saying?'

Calgar's eyes were like chips of steel. 'In your unconscious visions, you saw the ice? You heard the beating of its heart?'

My voice almost caught in my throat at this revelation. 'Yes.'

'It is the necron, mocking us. I feel it in my bones, Cato. Whether it be one year or fifty, we are not done with Damnos, and it is not done with us.'

A nerve tremor in my cheek didn't quite manifest into

a smile. And it would not until the stain against my honour was removed and Damnos reconquered.

'I shall count the days until our return, my lord. This isn't over.'

CATO SICARIUS: MASTER OF THE WATCH

NICK KYME

There was life in this place once.

Once.

Before the skies grew dark, before the warp fell silent, before the Great Devourer began its feast of worlds.

Now there was barren rock, a desert where there used to be a forest, a husk where once stood a city. Here, the alien tyranid had left its mark and no survivors.

Save one.

Cato Sicarius walked alone in a wasteland. Injured, he dragged his left leg where a spur of metal had pierced it during the crash. His battle-helm had split in half and been discarded. Bareheaded, there was no way to mask the smell, the reek of dust and emptiness.

The broken drop pod was far behind him, as were the corpses of the Vanguard veterans he had been accompanying. Agemman would have something to say about that. He would bring up the ice world again.

Even Daceus had advised Sicarius not to go, especially without his Lions, but the sergeant went unheeded. Damnos had made Sicarius reckless, more so than before. When he had looked into his sergeant's eyes, Sicarius suspected Daceus thought the same. It had not changed his mind. Sicarius had to know if he still had his edge. The Lions would stay with the main army and maintain a command presence, whilst he would infiltrate with a small squad. Their mission: assassinate the node creature that maintained the link to the hive. That plan had gone awry when a spore mine had exploded in their airspace during insertion, even if the means to enact that plan had not.

The device was still hooked to his weapons belt, a dull orb about the size of his fist. Praise the Throne *that* was still intact.

The rest was all fire, smoke and blood.

At least without his trappings, he was light. He wore stripped down power armour, not his Mantle of the Suzerain. Such finery did not befit this kind of work, and Sicarius was glad of it. Even his Tempest Blade was absent, a sheathed gladius strapped to his hip instead. He kept his plasma pistol, which sat snug in its holster and was, as of yet, unused. But as Sicarius approached the ghostly ruin of a settlement, that fact was about to change.

Shadows lurked here. They also *chittered*, perhaps in some crude approximation of speech. To the Master of the Watch, it sounded like laughter.

They had been drawn to him, these hunter-slayers, drawn to his living biology. A need drove them that went beyond hunger. Consumption was to the tyranid as war was to a Space Marine. The two could not be separated.

By Sicarius's reckoning, the farthest Ultramarine outpost was still several kilometres away. He would have to fight through the husk of the dead city, and its new xenos tenants, if he were to reach his brothers.

He made for the ruins, mindful as the shadows drew closer with his every step and began to grow claws.

Sicarius had barely crossed the threshold of some former municipal district, its lonely barricades and toothless defences still standing but empty, when the first of the hunter-slayers emerged from darkness.

Slipping the plasma pistol from his holster, he aimed and fired. The tyranid was vaporised by the superheated bolt, but Sicarius's triumph only lasted until the moment his sidearm red-lined and refused to function.

'Guilliman's blood...' he said beneath his breath, cursing the crash that had obviously damaged the pistol.

Now there were more hunter-slayers, drawn by the demise of their brood-mate, and cautiously scenting easy prey.

Sicarius spat, 'Ugly little bastards,' as the ochre-skinned, canine-like aliens began to scurry towards him. He had made it far enough that he could peel off the main concourse and head down one of the lifeless streets. Limping badly, Sicarius grimaced and cursed with every step, but was determined not to submit. He needed a better vantage, somewhere the diminutive aliens' numerical superiority would count for less.

He found a lexographer's office. Kicking in the door, ignoring the pain from his leg, he found a small chamber with a narrow corridor leading off into an even smaller domicile at the back.

Sicarius was heading for the corridor when the

hunter-slayers burst through the doorway. Savage teeth sank into his back, armour screeching as razor-sharp incisors bit hard. With a roar, he shrugged the creature off and heard it strike the wall. A second clamped to his wounded leg. Now he screamed. Agony gave way to wrath, as Sicarius wrenched out his gladius and pierced the tyranid through its skull. It squealed once and fell limp.

Three more barrelled into him, their combined weight nearby taking over him. The close confines of the clerk's office made for a tight battlefield. Using his forearm, Sicarius crushed one alien against the wall, the second he stomped using the foot of his good leg, the third he decapitated.

Gore washed over his face and torso. It burned a little, and he smelled his own seared skin.

More were coming. He could hear them further down the street, chattering like jackals. The spilled blood of their kin had drawn them.

His own blood leaking from a dozen minor wounds, Sicarius headed down the corridor as he had originally intended, but instead of looking for a place to make a stand he sought an exit as a fresh strategy superseded his previous plan – escape and get to higher ground. With a decent vantage point, he could chart a route through this ghost city and possibly signal his company.

Damnos returned again, taunting him with its bitter memory. Failure was no easy pill for Sicarius to swallow. Even here, wounded and outnumbered, Sicarius refused to yield.

'I still have the edge,' he snarled through clenched teeth as he found what he was looking for.

A ladder in the rear domicile led to the roof. He took it, the metal groaning against his power armoured weight. Punching through the hatch, he emerged into dismal half-light and onto the roof.

It was a good vantage point. Higher up, he looked out across the city...

...and beheld a horde.

Emerging from drains and sewer pipes, from every crack and alcove, were hundreds of tyranids. The hunter-slayers were in the numerical ascendency but there were larger forms too that scuttled, stomped and champed.

It was impossible, even for one such as he.

'No way through...' Sicarius almost laughed at the senselessness of it all as he unclipped the fist-sized orb at his belt. Pride had brought him to this place. Not here, in this city, but this moment. It was a little late for a realisation, though. Resolve forced him into a different direction, the recognition and acceptance of a final duty.

The vortex grenade was intended for the node creature, but Sicarius would have to settle for a host of its minions instead. It wasn't the end he had imagined for himself. Fate had dealt him a cruel hand with that crash. It was merely chance... or was it?

Sicarius had the grenade out in front of him. It was ready, primed and only needed to be activated.

'Fortune favours the bold... Perhaps I have become too bold.'

Ever since Damnos. Ever since he fell. He had been trying to prove something... To his Chapter, to himself.

Such thoughts were the province of fools. Until now, Sicarius had never considered himself amongst such men.

Creeping towards him, the sea of tooth, claw and chitin reached the edge of the building.

One hand on the vortex grenade, the other clamped around his gladius, Sicarius prepared for his duty to finally end. He was about to shout a challenge when something stopped him.

There, at the edge of the ruins, a pale mist was rolling in. It came on fast, thick, and engulfed the horde in a matter of seconds. As if reacting to a threat, the aliens began to snarl and snap at each other. Soon even that was lost to the mist.

Sicarius's grip on his weapons tightened as an unearthly chill went through him like a jolt of electricity.

To his left a muzzle flash erupted, partially smothered by the mist. Then another, and another until the pale obfuscating cloud was awash with weapons fire. He heard blades, first unsheathed and then cutting. The alien screams came next. He half-glimpsed a figure moving in the white miasma below. It looked familiar, definitely Adeptus Astartes, but belonging to no Chapter Sicarius had ever encountered. At first he thought they might be Deathwatch – an operation on this world would suit their tactical predilections – but the warriors in the mist moved too fast to be Space Marines. No warrior in power armour could move like that.

Sicarius had no time to wonder further. In a few minutes, silence returned, the mist evaporated as swiftly as it had appeared and nothing else remained. Nothing. Not even the dead.

Reattaching the vortex grenade and sheathing his sword, Sicarius rubbed his eyes. He *was* wounded. Perhaps the blood loss... no, he dismissed that as he heard a low thrum overhead become a dull roar. It had been there for a while but Sicarius put the throbbing down to his injuries. It was actually a turbo-fan.

Overhead, the bulky outline of an Ultramarines Storm-raven loomed.

As the gunship drew close, its assault cannons cycling down when no targets presented themselves, it turned. Standing on the rear ramp, Daceus waved his captain aboard.

'When we found the downed drop pod, we thought you might be dead,' said the sergeant.

'I nearly was,' said Sicarius.

'This area is crawling with xeno-forms. How did you avoid them?' Daceus sounded genuinely incredulous.

'I didn't.'

Daceus cocked his head asking an unspoken question.

'I did have help though,' Sicarius answered.

'From whom?'

'An unexpected quarter.' Sicarius said nothing further on the subject.

Daceus called behind him, 'Apothecary.'

'No,' said Sicarius, holding up a hand and prompting the medic to shrink back into the gloom. 'Bring me my armour. This war is far from over, but I suspect the scales have been tipped in our favour.'

Daceus didn't ask, for Sicarius showed no sign of providing an answer.

In truth, he couldn't but knew that he was right.

The ramp closed, the gunship peeled away, headed back to the Ultramarines lines.

In the darkness of the hold, Sicarius remembered the mist and the warriors within it. He remembered something else too, a detail of their war-plate. Bone, it was bone. They were covered in it.

A debt was owed, his life preserved for some greater fate, and Sicarius wondered when it would have to be paid.

EYE OF VENGEANCE

GRAHAM McNEILL

It was the smell of Quintarn that hit you first, a gut-punch mix of turned earth, gaseous discharge from the domed agri-cities and the planet-wide reek of synthetic fertiliser. One of the bread basket worlds of Ultramar, its arid surface was hot and dusty, but no amount of desert wind could mask the pungent stench that wormed its way through even the most advanced air scrubber.

Deserts of red and gold covered much of the planet's surface, making it an odd choice for an agri-world, though it was one of the most productive in the Imperium. Hundreds of sprawling agri-cities covered the planet's surface, and each one contained millions of acres of arable land beneath its protective domes. In the normal run of things, Quintarn, along with its sister worlds of Tarentus and Masali were quiet, industrious and peaceful worlds.

But these were not normal times.

An invading army had descended upon the Three Worlds, a bastard host of murderous corsairs, war machines and diabolical priests of the Dark Mechanicus. They called themselves the Bloodborn, and they fought under the command of a nightmarish creature known as Votheer Tark. Little more than a filthy scrap of ravaged meat and neuro-synaptic tissue suspended in an amniotic vat, Votheer Tark's legions of battle engines came not to conquer or enslave.

They came to destroy, but they would not find Quintarn lacking in defenders.

The 5th and 6th Companies of the Ultramarines stood against the Bloodborn, and their victories were legend, their names bywords for courage and honour. Quintarn itself boasted an impressive defence auxilia, thousands of men and women under arms and sworn to the defence their homeworld.

But the fate of Quintarn would not be decided by massed ranks of soldiers or the battle companies of the Adeptus Astartes.

It would be decided by a single warrior.

His name was Torias Telion.

Situated at the confluence of three rivers, the dome-shielded city of Idrisia rose like a cluster of sun-kissed blisters from the arid plains. Beyond its shimmering perimeter, a heat-hazed desert spread to the horizon, and sand drifted at the base of its armaglas structures. The planet's star burned hot and white in the sky, like a metal disc heated in an armourer's forge. Little could survive in the parched landscape, but beneath the city's incredible domes, the landscape was rich with life.

Ten thousand soldiers of the Quintarn defence auxilia were billeted within the city, their myriad tents and vehicle parks crushing flat field after field of crops grown to feed the Imperium's hungry mouths. Despite the auxilia's best efforts, the Bloodborn had broken through the northern bulwarks, and the soldiers' sky-blue uniforms were bloody after the retreat from Castra Mondus. Now, with the routes to the southern hydroponics cities wide open, Idrisia was sure to feel the Bloodborn's wrath next.

But a force of warriors of far greater prowess now stood ready to face Votheer Tark's demented war machines and blood-hungry army. The Ultramarines occupied the heart of Idrisia, and modular barrack buildings of gleaming azure jostled for space alongside temporary fortifications and the ancillary battlefield structures that came with the Adeptus Astartes at war. In the heart of the Ultramarines deployment sat an octagonal command structure with an arched roof that bristled with vox antennae, rotating auspex dishes and integral void shields.

Moisture formed on the gold-winged eagles stamped upon the breastplates of the ten Ultramarines stationed around the perimeter of the command tower. It dripped from their boltguns and their shoulder guards, five trimmed in iron black, the others in brilliant gold, and hissed on the hot vents of their armour's power packs. All ten warriors stood as still as statues, immobile guardians of the captains within. To protect the army's commanders was a singular honour, and only the best warriors from each company had been selected for so vital a duty.

Within its walls, banks of battlefield cogitators hummed with power, digesting information gathered from after action reports, vox-thievery, surveyor sweeps and inloads from the few remaining orbital auspex.

The picture they painted was one of a world on the brink of falling to the enemy.

Tech-priests moved in circular sweeps around the darkened chamber, pausing to burble a short burst of binaric prayer or minister to a piece of equipment. Aides and scrivener servitors kept to the shadows, ready to stand forward at their masters' behest at a moment's notice.

The four warriors tasked with defending Quintarn gathered around a central plotting table fixing the ghostly topographical image with piercing stares, as though force of will alone could alter the bleak strategic situation before them.

Captain Galenus of the 5th Company was the first to speak.

'Idrisia,' he said. 'It's the key. Lose it and we lose the war.'

'You think I don't see that?' asked his fellow commander. Captain Epathus of the 6th folded his arms and leaned on the raised lip of the plotting table. 'It's the gateway to the southern cities, but it's not strong enough to withstand an assault. Not yet.'

Antaro Chronus spoke next, his voice a throaty grumble, so like the engines of the tanks he commanded. 'I can hold them for a time,' he said, jabbing a fist at the projected map. 'Here. At the edge of the Upashid Scar. With the armour units from the defence auxilia, I have enough vehicles to keep the bastards at bay for a time.'

'How long?' asked Epathus.

'Long enough for you to fortify this damn place,' replied Chronus. 'I'll kill a great many, but they are too numerous to hold forever.'

The fourth member of the command group nodded, his face obscured by a grim skull-faced helmet. Chaplain Ortan Cassius wore armour black as night, embossed with gold and blue, with a repeating skull motif worked into every trim and plate. Though none could see his disfigured face, they all felt the grim purpose of his gaze.

'Votheer Tark's Bloodborn make war like the Great Devourer,' he said, his voice a wet rasp of damaged vocal chords that no amount of augmetic surgery could repair. 'His Dark Mechanicum consume the iron bones of fallen machines and remake them to swell their numbers. Every piece of equipment and forge we lose is cannibalised to create more war machines for the Bloodborn.'

'A bleak assessment, Chaplain,' said Galenus.

'An honest one,' replied Cassius.

'How do you fight an enemy that grows stronger with every battle?' asked Epathus.

'I think I can help with that,' said a voice from the shadows above.

Every warrior in the command tower spun toward the speaker, and weapons were pulled from holsters with Adeptus Astartes speed. A half-glimpsed figure sat upon a structural rafter, an elongated bolter rested casually across his lap.

'Security!' barked Galenus, trying to fix on the indistinct form.

The warrior swung down from the darkness and dropped lightly to the decking of the command tower. The spectral half-light of the plotting table seemed not to touch him, leaving his spare frame shrouded in shadows where no shadows should be. His dusty fatigues were coated in ochre dust, and the blue of his armour was scratched and worn by wind-blown sand. A face tanned the colour of baked leather from the light of a thousand suns was framed by a neatly trimmed beard of silver, and regarded the assembled commanders with a faintly disapproving grin.

'Telion? Is that you?' said Epathus. 'How in Guilliman's name did you get in here?'

'You know I'll not tell you that,' said Torias Telion, foremost Scout of the Ultramarines.

'When did you get to Quintarn?' demanded Galenus. 'And why was I not informed of your arrival?'

Telion ignored Galenus. 'My Scouts were on Quintarn long before you got here. Did you think the Bloodborn forges on the Kodian Uplands simply destroyed themselves?'

'That was you?' asked Chronus.

Telion nodded. 'It was.'

'Damn it, Telion,' snapped Galenus. 'You can't fight alongside our companies without attaching yourself to the order of battle. How can we formulate strategy when we don't know what assets we have in the field?'

Telion shook his head. 'You have a more pressing concern than my omission from the order of battle, Galenus.'

'And what's that?'

'Your security,' said Telion, gesturing to the roof space with a single upraised finger.

Galenus and his fellow commanders looked up.

Five scouts perched on the rafters, each with a weapon trained on the commanders below.

Telion waved his finger in admonishment. 'If we had been the enemy, you'd all be dead now. Think about that while we re-arm and resupply.'

* * *

It had been a long, hard run from the Uplands, a fast dash from mayhem with the enemy's hunters dogging their footsteps through broken hinterlands between the burning ridge and the southern plains. The enemy had some capable hunters, and only forty-three of his sixty warriors had returned from the arid desert.

But none of the Bloodborn had the guile and skill of Torias Telion.

He had served under three different Chapter Masters, and earned more battle honours than any other Scout in Ultramarines history. No scrappy, half-trained machine-fused seeker was going to catch *him* in a pursuit.

He was tired, but did not let it show as he led his Scout squads through the familiar layout of the Ultramarines position. Everything was laid out as decreed in the Codex Astartes, regularly, precisely and... predictably.

This unannounced arrival at Idrisia wasn't the first time Telion had bent the tenets of his primarch's teachings at war, but it was certainly the most obvious. He knew of at least one captain who had been banished from the Chapter for such breaches of the Codex's teachings, so kept his own little heresies out of sight of any command ranks that might object.

Telion saw Ultramarines warriors staring at his Scouts, and couldn't suppress a flush of pride at the respectful nods he saw. His reputation within the Chapter was well known, and these warriors knew that with Torias Telion and his Scouts watching over them, they had guardian angels in place. The battle-brothers of the 5th and 6th Companies welcomed their arrival, even if Captain Galenus did not.

He heard steps behind him, knowing from the length

of stride and weight of the footfall that it was Draco. The youngster was a hellion with the missile launcher he carried slung on his back, a dead-eye shot who could send a warhead up the exhaust port of a skimmer's engine at five hundred metres.

'Are we joining the battle companies, brother-sergeant?' asked the boy.

'For a Scout trained in stealth and evasion you're remarkably obvious in your questions, Draco,' replied Telion.

'Just want to know what we're about, sergeant,' said Draco. 'I don't like the idea of making this a straight up fight.'

'Then put your mind at ease,' said Telion. 'We're not attaching ourselves to the companies. We're just here to resupply.'

Draco nodded and Telion suppressed a smile as the boy rejoined his squad. The snipers, Zeno and Dareios, seemed pleased with the news, though Agathon, their newest member, clearly didn't share their enthusiasm.

'That won't please Captain Galenus,' said Sergeant Kaetan. Though Telion had attached himself to Kaetan's squad, the sergeant had naturally stepped aside to allow the veteran Scout to take command. No-one among the 10th Company, save perhaps Captain Antilochus, would expect Torias Telion to serve under them.

'I don't much care what Galenus thinks,' said Telion.

'He's right though, we *should* attach to the order of battle.'

'That's not how we'll be most effective, Kaetan, and you know it,' said Telion.

Kaetan nodded and said, 'I know that, but disregarding the wishes of a captain is a sure-fire way to get yourself sent on a Death Oath.'

Kaetan was a dark-skinned veteran of Masali, a hard taskmaster and thorough teacher. Telion respected his ways, and believed him to be one of the best sergeants the 10th Company had seen in decades.

Telion checked to see that none of the Scouts were listening and whispered, 'Perhaps you're right, but I see the anger he harbours towards Lord Calgar, even if no one else can. He blames the Chapter Master for the deaths of his men on the *Indomitable*.'

Kaetan's fingers flickered in the Scout sign for *Enemy Observing* and Telion fell silent. He had heard the approaching footsteps, but had spoken anyway, knowing who came near. Chaplain Cassius marched across the plaza towards the Scouts, the spiked head of his crozius maul jutting out behind his left shoulder guard.

'Chaplain,' said Telion. He gave a short bow of respect to the venerable warrior.

'Kaetan, Torias,' said Cassius, one of the few individuals with the authority to call any warrior in the Chapter by his first name. 'I came to wish you good hunting.'

'Gratitude, Chaplain,' said Telion, touching the Ultramarines symbol embossed on his Stalker-pattern bolter. 'It's not often you come to see the hunters loosed.'

'You suspect me of an ulterior motive?'

Telion smiled warily. 'I wouldn't word it *quite* like that, but yes.'

'Always a Scout, eh, Torias?'

'Until the day I die.'

'Then I will be as blunt,' said Cassius. 'You would do

well not to antagonise Galenus. It is not wise to wound the pride of a battle captain.'

Anger touched Telion. 'He sends you here on his behalf?' he said.

'You know he does not,' said Cassius. 'And your belligerence does you no credit.'

Telion sighed, knowing the Chaplain was right. 'I apologise, Chaplain. It has been a long campaign for us. The abominable things we saw in the Uplands were beyond imagining. It makes me forget my manners.'

Cassius waved away his clumsy apology. 'Galenus will get over a little wounded pride. The loss of half his company aboard the *Indomitable* has left a blight on his soul and he lashes out when he should look to his warriors that remain.'

Telion nodded and made to turn away, but Cassius stopped him with a firm hand upon his shoulder. Armoured in full battleplate, the Chaplain was a head taller than the Scout-sergeant, and it was impossible not to feel the threat and strength in his armoured form.

'You take a great many risks,' said Cassius. 'Be careful you do not overstep your reach. Others who have done so have suffered greatly.'

'I always watch my step, Chaplain. It's what I do best,' he promised.

'Be sure that you do, Torias,' said Cassius, lowering his voice so that only Telion could hear him. 'When this war is over there will be many wounds that must be healed, and not all of them can be treated in an apothecarion. Suspicion and mistrust have taken root in our Chapter, and we will need to purge ourselves of their poisonous taint. Your voice is much respected within the Chapter, and if you show disrespect, others will hear of it and take heed. Think on that before you are so brazen with your reckless disregard for the chain of command.'

Cassius turned away, and Telion waited until he was out of sight before leading his Scouts onwards. The Chaplain's words had angered him, but he didn't know whether it was the deeper truth that had touched a nerve or the fact that he was being admonished for his behaviour. Truth be told, either explanation sat ill with him.

What had Cassius meant by suspicion and mistrust? A Scout lived or died by the awareness of his surroundings, and it galled Telion that he was ignorant of the subtler happenings within the Chapter. But these were questions for another time. He couldn't let thoughts beyond his immediate concerns distract him from their mission.

The ammo stores were housed within a modular construction built against a solid structure that had once served as an administrative centre for Idrisia. The quartermaster was a Techmarine from the 6th Company, and Telion was more than a little surprised to find that Captain Galenus's authorisation for the release of ammunition and supplies had already been communicated to the quartermaster.

The Scouts picked out what they required from the stores with the efficiency of looters, but took no more than they required, knowing through experience what they would need in the field and what was unnecessary weight. Within ten minutes, the Scouts were fully equipped and ready for combat operations again.

Telion gathered Kaetan's Scouts in a small square with a stag-headed satyr at its centre – a holdover of Quintarn's ancient beliefs from the days before the Imperium.

A number of marble statues of wild animals surrounded this figure, sitting around him like the audience of a storyteller.

'We're heading north,' he said without preamble. 'Our brothers and the defence auxilia need time to fortify Idrisia for attack, so Antaro Chronus is leading an armoured formation north to fight the Bloodborn's battle engines at the Upashid Scar. We're going to lend a hand.'

'What kind of enemy are we looking at?' asked Dareios.

'Armoured,' said Telion. 'Battle engines, transports, mobile artillery, that sort of thing.'

He was pleased by the absence of fear in his Scouts. In their lighter armour and without heavy support, they would be achingly vulnerable, but they had Torias Telion to lead them, and their faith in him was a potent force in itself.

'We help out where we can, but this isn't our fight,' said Telion 'We have another mission, and I don't want us dragged into an armoured brawl, understand?'

A hand went up.

'Draco?' said Telion.

'If we're not engaging fully, then what's our mission?'

'It's a dangerous one,' said Telion. 'One that only the best damn Scouts of the Adeptus Astartes can take on. We're going to take out the enemy forge at the Maidens of Nestor and win the war for Quintarn in one fell swoop.'

The Scouts set off within the hour, each squad taking its own route to separate targets as Antaro Chronus's armoured strikeforce assembled. Telion led Kaetan's squad through the cracked red gold deserts, skirting the plains and keeping to the rocky uplands wherever possible. They moved swiftly, but silently, hugging the few shadows on this arid world and leaving no trace of their passing.

Telion watched the squad as it moved through the hot, dusty environment, offering advice and instructional pointers as they went. It was a strong squad, already bound as brothers and eager to prove their worth.

Dareios was the taciturn killer, a sniper of methodical skill and calculating intelligence. He had mastered the intricacies of the long-range kill with ease, yet there was no flair to him. The lad would make a fine warrior, but Telion suspected he would never have the passion to become more than a line officer.

In contrast, the squad's second sniper was rash, but a quick learner. Zeno had natural talent, yet lacked the focus to be the patient hunter. Younger than Dareios by a year, he had time yet to master his temperament.

Draco's worth had already been proved, and he'd be a natural fit within the Devastators upon his elevation to battle-brother.

The squad's most recent addition was Agathon, a devoted youngster from the forest world of Espandor. Over the centuries, his family had sent two previous sons to the Ultramarines, and Telion remembered them both. They were dead now, slain on Tarsis Ultra and Ichar IV, both victims of the Great Devourer.

After ten hours of swift march, Kaetan called a halt to rest and re-hydrate as a vicious wind blew down from the mountains, wreathing the parched deserts of Quintarn in a scouring haze of dust particles.

They took shelter in a jagged crevice in the rock, and while Dareios kept watch, the rest of the squad rested in preparation for the next push. The Imperial armoured units would be following the Scouts, and Telion wanted to get into position before they arrived.

Agathon took a drink from a canvas-wrapped canteen and wiped his chin with the back of his hand. The young Scout's bolter was cradled easily in his arms, like a mother holding a newborn babe. Telion was pleased to note that even with the dust and hot winds scouring Quintarn, the weapon was as pristine as one fresh from the crate.

'Can I ask you something, Sergeant Telion?' asked Agathon.

'What is it, lad?'

'Do you really think this mission will win the war?' asked the youngster.

Telion grinned as he saw the other Scouts turn to hear what he had to say.

'I wouldn't have said it if I didn't think so,' he said. 'But let me turn it around and ask you a question. Why are we losing this war?'

Zeno ventured an answer. 'Because the enemy outnumber us?'

Telion shook his head. 'No. These Bloodborn are chaff, a host of bastardised war machines led by a warlord who wouldn't know strategy if came up and bit his metal arse.'

'It's because the Bloodborn don't care about losses,' said Dareios. 'Any war machine they lose or capture is reforged into some other weapon.'

'Exactly,' said Telion, 'but their leader has made the mistake of relying on that to win him this war. That makes him vulnerable. Take it away and he's got nothing.'

'And the forge-temple at the Maidens of Nestor is his vulnerability?' asked Zeno.

'Exactly,' replied Telion. 'The other forges we destroyed were important, certainly, but they were just processing hubs. The forge-temple at the Maidens of Nestor is where the enemy creates its most lethal battle engines. They turn crop sprayers into flame-tanks, threshing machines into flesh tearers, harvester leviathans into battle fortresses. We take this forge out and the Bloodborn are just another ragamuffin host of corsairs and renegades.'

Draco patted the missile launcher propped up beside him and said, 'Just show me where to shoot, Sergeant Telion.'

They laughed at Draco's bravado. Sergeant Kaetan stood and shook the dust from his camo-cape.

'If Sergeant Telion has finished dispensing his pearls of wisdom, we need to move if we're going to play any part in the battles to come. On your feet!'

The Scouts responded instantly, and minutes later, they were on the move, all sign that they had stopped obscured by the howling winds.

Flames from burning vehicles lit the underside of the clouds, and strobing bursts of gunfire lit the craggy surface of the Upashid Scar. A tectonic flatland of shallow canyons, teetering mesas and glassy riverbeds, it was a bleak patch of striated desert that stretched from coast to coast. Booming traceries of artillery pounded the southern ridges as Bloodborn tanks fought through the winding gullies or hauled their bloated bulk over vitrified dunes on clanking, multi-jointed legs.

Explosions shook the ground as a volley of shells

slammed down in the midst of the Bloodborn, master-fully guided in by Sergeant Vorean's spotters. A dozen vehicles were vaporised in the pounding barrage, and only a single survivor crawled from the wreckage on fire-blackened stumps.

As impressive as such destructive power was, it was a drop in the ocean against the Bloodborn host. Telion counted at least a thousand enemy vehicles, a creeping horde of diabolical war machines crafted by degenerate minds twisted in ways too terrible to imagine.

No two were alike, and each was a horror of blasphe-mous mechanised arts, abortions of brazen iron and flesh. Giant crawlers crushed the earth beneath their bulk, moving like blood-fat leeches across the sandy rock and leaving a trail of stinking engine fluids in their wake. Tanks with pulsating hulls that glistened like flayed muscle fired hideously organic cannons and blazed with weaponry that seemed grown rather than attached.

Juggernauts of bloodstained steel stamped forward on piston-driven legs, braying their war cries from loath-somely organic horns. Shattered glass carapaces shawled them, flapping at their weapon mounts with the sound of a million windows breaking at once.

Others resembled giant insect creatures, bulbous and glossy, with lethal antennae that spat fire and lances of destructive energy. From a distance, the battle engines of Votheer Tark resembled escapees from a madman's workshop, but Telion did not allow their bizarre appear-ance fool him as to their capabilities.

Facing the monstrous horde was a glorious host of tanks in the azure of the Ultramarines and the blue and white of the defence auxila. Though outnumbered by nearly three to one, the Imperial forces had angels on their shoulders.

Telion took the first kill with his Stalker-pattern bolter, putting a burst of fire through the fuel lines of a chittering vehicle that resembled a low-slung spider with mechanised legs and a bulbous turret that spat torrents of lasfire. Blazing fuel emptied into its hull, and the machine buckled as its crew died and the vehicle collapsed to the sand.

Draco took out tank after tank with missiles fired through the weaker top armour of more conventionally designed tanks. Zeno and Dareios guided each other's sniper fire to take out exposed commanders, ammo feeds and fuel lines. With Telion's expert guidance, no shot was wasted, and Zeno put a kill shot through a cracked vision slit in the turret of a battle engine that might once have been a Baneblade, but which now resembled a mobile fortress of blades and gibbets. Whatever had commanded that monstrous vehicle died with that shot, and it was easy prey for the tank-killer vehicles of Antaro Chronus.

With each kill, the Scouts moved on, each squad firing only once from any position within the Scar, taking advantage of the natural cover and speed to evade any return fire. The machine intelligences of Votheer Tark's battle engines were cunning, and it took all of Telion's superlative skill to stay one step beyond their reach.

'Spider tank, ten o'clock,' shouted Zeno, tracking a vehicle through the scope of his sniper rifle. 'Range, six hundred metres.'

'Engaging!' said Draco, dialling in the range to his launcher as a missile fed itself into the breech. Telion watched the young Scout as he led the vehicle, depressing the firing trigger with a soft squeeze.

The missile leapt from the launcher, arcing up into the sky like a star shell before turning the seeker head back towards it target. It streaked back down to earth, a blur of phosphorent light that slammed into the spider tank's topside. The warhead blew and a searing plasma jet punched into the vehicle, instantly incinerating its crew and blowing the turret ten metres into the air.

'A fine shot, Draco,' said Telion, slapping the Scout on the shoulder guard.

'Target of opportunity!' cried Dareios, his eye fixed to the scope of his rifle. 'Dead ahead, a thousand metres.'

Telion knew they should displace, but crouched next to the Scout and pressed his own sighted bolter to his eye, scanning the ground before him. He had seen armoured clashes before, but was rarely this close to a tank fight. Scouts paved the way for the battle companies or harried the enemy from the flanks and rear, they didn't usually get this close to a tank fight.

'We've lingered here too long,' warned Kaetan. 'We should move to another position.'

'I know,' said Telion. 'But Dareios rarely offers up targets without good reason.'

Kaetan scowled, but nodded. 'What do you have, Dareios?'

'Command walker by the looks of it,' replied the Scout. 'Looks vulnerable.'

Telion had to agree.

Superficially, it resembled the defence auxila's Sentinels in that it was a two-legged war machine that supported a pilot's armoured compartment. But where the Imperial walker was a practical response to the needs of war, this seemed a ludicrous folly. Instead of an armoured cockpit, the reverse jointed legs supported a sphere of blackened glass in which frothing amniotic fluid sloshed back and forth with the machine's bow-legged gait. Dozens of whipping aerials protruded from its rear section and Telion saw something fleshy and foetal floating in the viscous suspension. Jagged runes were branded into its sides, and the embellishment in its workings convinced Telion that Dareios was right to call it in.

'Take it out,' he ordered.

'Engaging,' said Dareios.

The Scout took a breath and let the air ease from his lungs rather then expelling it with a force that might upset his aim. His rifle fed him wind velocities, ambient temperatures, local gravitational fields and myriad other variables that would affect his shot.

The rifle snapped as it fired, and Telion watched the walker as the blackened glass sphere hazed where Dareios's shot struck. Cracks spread out from the point of impact, and less than a second later, Zeno's shot took the kill. The glass broke like a blister and steaming liquid poured from the ruptured interior. Arcs of electrical energy blazed from the wreckage as a scrap of deformed meat and distended bone flopped out onto the sand, trailing a forest of copper wires and crackling input plugs.

Telion didn't waste time by wondering what vile flesh-alchemy had wrought such a by-blow, and said, 'Up! Good kills, but it's time we were going.'

The Scouts scooted back from the edge of the ridge and followed Telion as he ran low through a shallow gully, taking turns apparently at random. Explosions burst overhead and the deafening, percussive force of shell-fire and impacts rolled over them. Roaring engine noise echoed weirdly around the gully and streams of gunfire disintegrated its upper edges. Stone fragments fell like rain, but Telion kept going. A thunderous impact on the ground made them all stumble, and Telion held up a fist. He pushed himself back against the stone walls of the gully as the ground shook once again with a pounding reverberation. A shadow filled their hiding place as something enormous passed overhead, its mass large enough to traverse the gully without effort.

'What in Hera's name was that?' breathed Draco.

Telion silenced him with a glare. He darted across the gully and sprang onto an embedded boulder, peering through a cleft in the rock to see what had passed them by. He saw it in fragments, but pieced enough together in those glimpses to identify the war engine.

The Imperial designation was Stormlord, a monstrously heavy tank bristling with weapons, any one of which could wipe out the Scouts with barely a moment's pause. A hellishly large bolter cannon was mounted on the turret, and a plethora of powerful weapons jutted from bladed turrets and blister-like sponsons: rotary machine guns and promethium jets. Its hull was a corroded rust colour, and a figure in rubberised overalls and a bestial-moulded gasmask stood arrogantly in the upper hatch. He waved a bloodstained flag, like he rode in a triumphal parade instead of in a battle.

'That's just asking to get a bullet in the head,' said Telion.

'Would that they were all that stupid,' agreed Kaetan, coming alongside him.

'Stormlord,' said Telion, dropping back into the gully. 'Nasty.'

'Let it go,' warned Kaetan, seeing the glint in Telion's eye.

Telion shook his head, and scrambled onto the upper edges of the gully. The Scouts followed him, keeping close to the jagged edges so as not to silhouette themselves.

The Stormlord rolled over the rocky terrain with a teeth-loosening rumble, moving far too fast for so heavy a machine. The cannon on its turret swung around as a pair of defence auxila Chimeras rounded a leaning arch of rock. Fire blitzed from the chugging barrels as a hurricane of solid shot shredded the light armour of the Imperial tanks. Both transports skidded to a halt, wounded and bloody soldiers spilling from their blazing interiors. The Stormlord lurched forward and a spurting tongue of flame played over the survivors.

The screams were mercifully short-lived as the monstrous tank's guns finished the job of murder.

'Come on, Torias,' said Kaetan. 'It's a super-heavy. We don't have the weapons to take it out.'

'At least let's take out that cocky bastard in the turret,' replied Telion. 'One shot and we're like ghosts.'

'Don't even think about it,' said Kaetan. 'We have a mission.'

Telion sighed and nodded. 'You're right, but it would have made an impressive notch on the Stalker.'

Too late, Telion saw Zeno aim his sniper rifle towards the Stormlord's commander, frowning as his sights returned nonsensical information with every pulse of the range finder.

'Don't!' hissed Telion, but the damage was done.

The turret swivelled toward the hidden Scouts, like a prey creature suddenly catching the scent of a hunter. Its weapons clattered as the tank's loaders prepared to fire.

'Emperor's blood!' hissed Kaetan. 'It's onto us.'

'Everyone down!' shouted Telion as the sky lit up with pyrotechnic fury. Metre deep gouges tore through the lip of the gully and craters punched deep into the opposite wall of rock. The noise was deafening and Telion heard at least one of the squad cry out as ricocheting shrapnel sliced through light armour.

Dust and grit choked the gully, and even Telion's gen-hanced vision could see nothing though the billowing clouds. The echoes of the barrage had barely begun to fade when he heard the heavy rumble of the Stormlord drawing near.

'Move!' he yelled. 'Get out any way you can and we'll rally a kilometre to the north! Go!'

Telion ran as fast as he could, looking for an escape route through the choking dust clouds. Stone crashed down behind him as a portion of the gully collapsed under the super-heavy's tracks. Telion risked a glance over his shoulder and saw the tank's guns depressing to fire along the gully.

An Imperial tank commander would never have wasted such a powerful vehicle's energy and ammunition on so few infantry, but the Stormlord had the scent of blood in its nostrils. The kill was all that mattered, not any grand strategy of its master. It had their scent and wasn't about to let go until it had taken their corpses to mount on its track guards.

Volcanic fire blazed down the gully, filling its width

with a blitzing storm of shells. Telion threw himself down a side passage, feeling the air being sucked from his lungs by the supersonic jetwash of the Stormlord's fire. He rolled onto his front, letting his secondary lung sift the reduced oxygen content of the air, crawling away from the main passage of the gully on his belly.

A column of hot dust billowed through the passages of the gully, and he changed direction often, moving on his hands and knees for greater speed. Telion heard the angry roar of the super-heavy behind him. It was circling, looking to confirm its kills, and he caught sight of its jagged outline through the clouds of smoke thrown up by its gunfire. A few desultory muzzle flashes lit up the smoke, a sniper rifle and a bolter.

A good Scout knew when to fight and when to escape, and Telion forged a path onwards through the dust-filled gully, knowing he could do nothing against so powerful a foe. Zeno's foolishness had cost them dear, and Telion hoped enough of the squad had survived to continue the mission.

Thirty minutes later, Telion regrouped with his Scouts. He was grateful to see that the entire squad had survived, though Dareios and Agathon had taken shrapnel wounds from the exploding rock, and everyone else was covered in dust and bruises. The mood was ugly, and the focus of the Scouts' anger was directed at one of their number in particular.

'You could have killed us all,' hissed Kaetan.

Zeno had the good sense to look contrite, but the sergeant wasn't finished. 'It is disrespectful to aim your rifle and not take the shot.'

Telion raised a hand to stem Kaetan's tirade.

'It *was* foolish, Kaetan,' he said. 'But we still have a mission to accomplish. Punish Zeno when we return to Idrisia.'

'His mistake could have killed us all,' protested Dareios.

'Aye, lad, it could have, but it didn't,' said Telion. 'Let that be enough for now.'

Dareios nodded curtly and turned away. Telion saw the anger in his face, but let him go. A methodical killer, Dareios did not take kindly to his fellows making mistakes.

As the Scouts prepared to head off once more, Kaetan approached Telion and said, 'You are getting soft in your old age, Torias. Time was you'd have flayed that boy alive for a mistake like that.'

'I know,' agreed Telion. 'But we yet live, and the lad won't do it again. Call it a hard won lesson. They're the kind that stick.'

Kaetan shrugged, 'Perhaps,' he said, 'but we should get on with the mission.'

'Absolutely. We'll assume ingress positions by twenty-one hundred hours local in the foothills of the Maidens, a kilometre from the forge-temple.'

Kaetan consulted his chronometer. 'That doesn't leave us much time.'

'Then we'd best move fast,' said Telion.

Kaetan's squad made their way from the armoured clash at battle pace, leaving Antaro Chronus and the vehicles of the defence auxilia to continue the fight without them. Kaetan was right, they *didn't* have much time, so Telion drove the Scouts hard, setting a murderous pace that tested even his fully developed Adeptus Astartes physique.

They did not stop to rest or rehydrate, but kept pushing up the craggy haunches of the mountains. As darkness drew in, the Scouts reached the end of a shadowed valley that cut a ragged path towards the Maidens of Nestor. And there, atop a vast shelf of rock that was all that remained of a mountain planed flat, was the forge-temple of Votheer Tark.

The Maidens of Nestor were all that remained of Quintarn's tallest mountain. Named for the thousand priestesses who had hurled themselves from its cliffs rather than be taken prisoner by greenskin reavers, it had been razed flat by an orbital barrage and the molten rock sculpted into a monument to their sacrifice. Around the circular plateau, a thousand toothed fangs of glassy basalt reared up like a sharpened fang, one for each of the lost maidens.

In the centre of the vast stump of the mountain, a churning mechanical edifice thundered like the engine of the most colossal starship imaginable. More machine than structure, its chaotic assembly was a nightmare of thundering pistons, fire-belching stacks, geysering overflows and arcing electrical towers. Streaming banners flapped in the nightmare thermals billowing around the mountain, and hellish runes of blasphemous entities were stamped on every piece of blood-soaked iron that had gone into the forge's construction.

A constant stream of heavy mass-carriers bore thousands of tonnes of captured machinery into the blackened forge, feeding the dark adepts within the raw materials with which to craft the battle engines of the Bloodborn warlord. Acrid smoke hugged the ground, a ready-made smokescreen.

Telion halted the squad in the shadow of one of the Maidens and reached up to touch the smooth stone.

'Maidens of Nestor, grant me a measure of your courage,' he whispered. He felt eyes upon him and turned to see Kaetan watching him.

'For luck,' he said.

'I didn't think the great Telion needed luck,' said Kaetan.

'The more I fight, the luckier I get, but it never hurts to have a little spare.'

Telion attuned his senses to the myriad noise patterns among the clanking acoustic mess surrounding the forge-temple. Even amid so horrific a place, there was rhythm and pattern. This forge was the domain of the Dark Mechanicus, twisted machine priests who melded the power of the immaterium with that of their blasphemous mechanical creations. And such abominations worked to the beat of artificial hearts. Beneath the cacophony of sound echoing from the mountainsides, Telion heard the regular booming crash of giant forge hammers, working in time with heaving presses and ore furnaces.

He scanned the side of the temple, seeking an entry point. He found what he was looking for fifteen metres above the plateau, an intake flue that drew great gulps of polluted air to feed the furnaces within. A web of pipework snaked across the flanks of the structure like corroded vines, and they would be easy to climb.

'Be ready,' said Telion. 'Move when I move and keep low.'

He counted along with the percussive sounds of the forge, waiting until the crash of metal hammers echoed over the mountains before breaking cover and sprinting through the reeking vapours. Almost instantly he was running blind as the temple spewed a poisonous breath and screamed with every one of its exhaust vents. These were birth cries. The forge was howling its pleasure and pain at the monstrous by-blows taking shape within its mechanised guts.

Telion heard revving engines and the heavy footfalls of ironclad machines. He saw blurred outlines of hideously altered servitors and brain-cut labour brutes, slave creatures formed from random machine parts and organic debris.

They ignored the Scouts, and Telion returned the favour.

The soaring iron cliff-face of the forge loomed out of the noxious yellow fog, and Telion leapt onto the pipework. Hand over hand, he climbed to the flue and peered within. A slowly rotating fan filled the circular pipe, around two metres in diameter. Telion swung around the edge of the pipe, ducking beneath the slowly rotating blades, and ran towards a grilled vent.

Shouldering his bolter as he ran, Telion fired four shots, one to each corner of the vent, and kicked it free of its mountings without breaking step. Behind the vent was a bizarre machine, part sucking compressor, part pumping mechanism fashioned from the upper torsos of steel-clad creatures that might once have been men.

Behind the machine was mesh grille through which spilled a hellish red light and the thundering sounds of heavy industry. As Telion crouched at the grille, the rest of the squad emerged into the pumping chamber, immediately taking up defensive positions.

'Through there,' said Telion, tapping the grille with the barrel of his gun.

Using their combat blades, Telion and Kaetan removed it from its mountings and set it aside. The Scouts slipped through the hole in the wall, dropping onto a tangled mass of ductwork. Pushing forward on his belly, Telion eased his way onto a corroded junction box and peered down into the hellish workings of the forge-temple.

Orange light filled the cavernous space, a fane to a ruinous parody of the Machine God. Glowing ore vats bubbled like volcanic pits along the edges of the colossal chamber, and giant cauldrons of brazen iron suspended on iron chains drooled blood into each pool of molten metal. Hundreds of chanting priests in dark robes consecrated it with scrapcode prayers of impossible binary, and the stench of burned metal and scorched flesh caught at the back of Telion's throat.

Streams of molten bloodmetal were drawn along grooved channels towards hellish forge machines that rolled, pressed and shaped weapons of war. Foremost amongst those machines was a vast furnace that growled and hammered with animal hunger. And tending to this black altar of hellish creation was a towering abomination of steel and fire.

'Emperor's teeth,' said Telion. 'What in Guilliman's name is that?'

It had once been a Warhound Titan, but it had been brutally augmented with so many loathsome additions that its original builders would have wept to see it so degraded. The battle engine towered over the attendants that surrounded it, though it was hunched over like a bent-backed scribe. A complex arrangement of mechanised arms that were an indivisible mix of weapons and machine tools depended from its carapace.

'A high priest?' suggested Kaetan.

'I think you might be right,' said Telion. 'I need to get down there.'

'I just *knew* you were going to say that...' sighed Kaetan.

The Scouts gathered around Telion, and he outlined his plan of action with succinct clarity. Ambiguity would see them all dead. Worse, it would see the mission fail. Satisfied everyone in the squad understood their role, Telion moved off, finding a trunk-line of cabling that led to the floor of the temple. Blasts of superheated steam gusted from brass-rimmed vents, and Telion waited for a particularly thick cloud to drift past before sliding over the edge of the ducting to shimmy down to the ground.

The heat on the floor of the forge was like the hottest desert Telion had ever known. The fumes from the bloodmetal pits sucked the moisture from the air and made it painful to take a breath.

A Scout was proficient at creating havoc behind enemy lines, but Torias Telion was the master of mayhem. He had already identified the most vulnerable parts of the forge from the ductwork above, and knew exactly where to place his melta bombs. He moved swiftly and carefully through the chamber, keeping to the shadows where possible and making the most of the industrial cover.

None of the black-robed priests ever saw him as they made their ritual circuits of the bloodmetal pits. With calm surety of purpose, Telion picked his way through the chamber, planting his melta charges behind junction boxes, buried within cable nodes or on the reverse of pressure gauges.

The battle engine moved through the chamber with booming footsteps, devotional squalls of scrapcode burbling from augmitters mounted upon its carapace. Each static outburst was greeted with answering spurts of faulty machine noise from the priests. Telion could understand nothing of the noise, but registered no hostility or sense that he'd been discovered in the tonality of the sound.

With only two charges remaining to be set, Telion moved towards the giant machine at the end of the chamber. Even as he drew close to the seething, hammering, machine, he knew something was wrong. Seething vents pulsed with fiery light, like windows into some hellish inferno. Though he knew it was ridiculous, Telion felt as though the machine was watching him, regarding his intrusion with a mixture of amused curiosity and irritation.

He dismissed the thought, but the nagging suspicion that something was amiss would not leave him. Telion paused. He had not lived this long without trusting his instincts, and right now they were screaming at him that something was very wrong.

'What's wrong?' said Kaetan's voice over the vox-bead in his ear.

'I'm not sure,' said Telion. 'Any change in the enemy?'

'None I can see,' replied Kaetan. 'Wait... Telion! Get out of there!'

Though he could see no obvious threat, Telion obeyed Kaetan's warning without hesitation. He turned away from the great furnace and swiftly retraced his path through the forge-temple as a towering bellow of machine noise filled the temple, like a million vox-servitors screaming in unison. The bloodmetal pits spurted geysers of blazing ore in a raucous bellow of volcanic anger.

Stealth would avail him nothing now, and Telion sprinted through the temple with his bolter pulled tight to his shoulder, the muzzle moving to match each motion of his eyes. Three of the robed priests appeared before him, wielding jagged trident-like weapons that buzzed with electrical fire. Telion put a bolt-round through the chests of the first and second as a sniper round from above pulped the skull of the third. He didn't break stride and vaulted the corpses before they'd even hit the ground.

'Go right,' ordered Zeno in his ear.

Telion obeyed and darted around a tangled webwork of pipes. Three more of the machine priests came toward him, but a missile impact blew them from their feet, leaving a searing afterimage on Telion's retinas. Draco's aim was as sharp as ever. Even over the howling, mechanical rage of the forge-temple, Telion heard the distinctive snap of sniper fire, punctuated by the deeper report of Agathon and Kaetan's bolter fire.

'Start blowing the charges!' ordered Telion, shooting down another dark machine priest.

'You're still in the kill box,' Kaetan pointed out.

'Blow them or I'll never leave it,' snapped Telion.

A pulse from Kaetan's vox triggered the first of the melta charges, and a section of the metal plating surrounding one of the bloodmetal pits vanished in a searing column of incandescent fire. The pool of liquid metal poured out, like tidal flood through a disintegrating levee. Moving with viscous slowness, it oozed onto the floor of the forge-temple, spreading further with each passing second. Another charge detonated and yet more magma-hot metal surged from its confinement. A third and a fourth blew, and fires erupted all through the temple as pipes melted in the heat and sprayed flammable liquids and gasses in blazing arcs. Telion blasted a path through the disintegrating temple, ducking behind a rising nexus of cables and pipes as a rattling hail of bullets sprayed the ground before him.

The machine priests had triangulated his position, and were closing the net on him. He rose from cover and sent a snap shot through the face of a robed priest that clattered through the temple on multiple legs like a mechanised spider.

Twin bursts of fire drove him back to cover, and a ricocheting fragment of metal scored his cheek. Blood welled in the cut, then clotted almost instantly.

'Clear me a path!' ordered Telion.

'We don't have a shot,' replied Kaetan.

'Why not?' demanded Telion, but the answer was soon revealed.

Emerging from a rising wall of flames and smoke was the battle engine, its hideous bulk silhouetted in the glare of the temple's dissolution. The towering machine's carapace was daubed with dripping runes of blood, its head worked in the image of a grinning daemon. Its armour was studded with bladed spikes and corpses hung from its trophy racks.

The cockpit glass shone red, and its weapon arms clattered as autoloaders slotted home magazine hoppers capable of holding thousands of heavy calibre rounds. Telion threw himself flat as the battle engine's weapons unleashed their fury and a blitzing hurricane of shells tore a metre-deep trench in the metal floor of the temple.

Telion sprinted through the furious storm of the battle engine's wrath, hearing the booming thunder of its footfalls behind him. He fired without aiming, hearing the shots impact the titan's voids with a bray of electrical discharge. The engine let out a keening screech as it came for him through the smoke. Telion knew he couldn't outrun the machine and made the only choice he had left to him.

He turned and ran towards it, firing as he went. Every shot struck the titan with sparks of void flare, but did nothing more. Its weapon arms depressed, the barrels shrieking as they spooled up to fire.

Telion dived forward as the guns opened up, but he was within their minimum range and the weapons tore collimated trenches behind him. The machine halted, as though confused as to why its target was not destroyed. Telion rolled to his feet and slung his bolter as he leapt for the titan's right leg. A blade sliced the armour at his shoulder as he gripped the leprously oily body of the battle engine, taking hold of its rivets, bolts and lubricant pipes to haul himself up.

The engine spun, sensing the insect crawling over its body and Telion hung on for dear life as the machine crashed back and forth. Choking clouds of toxic smoke billowed around the engine as it thrashed to dislodge him. Shapes moved in the smoke, and Telion caught flashes of the robed priests crushed beneath the engine's stomping feet.

By the time he'd climbed halfway up the titan's leg, Telion's hands were bloody and torn, his armour battered and pierced. The engine slammed into an iron column, sending an arcing blaze of energy skyward as its voids buckled and blew out on its right side. The flash of its collapsing voids almost blinded Telion and the thunderclap of energy scorched his armour black. The underside of the princep's compartment was almost within reach and Telion wrapped his arm around a hissing coolant feed line that throbbed with a repulsive peristaltic motion. He wedged his foot in a gap between armoured plates and drew his combat blade.

Telion sliced along the length of the feed line and a disgusting, viscous substance spurted from the wound. Oily and reeking of rancid meat, it drenched Telion's armour and he gagged, tasting the loathsome biological make-up of the fluid as it spilled down his face. The machine howled and swung around with such violence that Telion's grip slipped and his blade spun away into the smoke.

With his free hand, Telion reached down and plucked one of his last melta charges from his belt and rammed it into the ruptured feed line. A second followed, but before he could arm them, the battle engine smashed its body on the edge of a bloodmetal pool with a last, desperate heave.

This time Telion couldn't hold on, and he tumbled through the air to land with a bone-crunching impact on the lip of the pool. Lava heat burned his armour and burned the skin beneath the canvas of his fatigues. He fell away from the molten metal and kept rolling until he was clear of the madly thrashing battle engine. Its foot slammed down on the spot where he had landed, cracking the ground, and he rose to his feet with a grimace of pain.

'Go forward ten metres!' shouted Kaetan. The vox was

lousy with static, but Telion obeyed as he heard the
machine's auto-loaders once again. Telion saw the cable
run he'd climbed down and leapt onto it, shimmying up
like a vine-creeping cudbear until he'd reached the level
of the twisting ductwork.

Kaetan's Scouts were spread throughout the structural members, firing down into the gathered masses
of machine priests. Bullet impacts on the wall behind
them, and scorched patches where electro-throwers had
struck testified to the ferocity of the overwatching battle they had fought.

Telion jerked his thumb at Draco and shouted, 'The
voids on its right flank are down! I jammed two charges
on its underside. The junction of its legs and princep's
compartment.'

Draco understood immediately, and worked another
missile into his weapon's loading breech. With the missile launcher slung over his back, he slid down the pipes
towards the ground. The battle engine let out a triumphant roar as its infernal detection gear finally pinpointed
its prey. Its footsteps shook the temple as it loped toward
them, and the whine of its guns cut through the air like
a bloody knife.

'Spread out!' ordered Telion.

He pulled his bolter tight into his shoulder and fired
three quick bursts of fire at the titan's unshielded flank,
each shot exploding against the armoured carapace without effect. Sniper rounds blew off trophies and bulbous
extrusions that might have been sensor arrays, but did
little else.

The machine's upper body swivelled, its guns ratcheting
up as they prepared to obliterate them in a hellstorm of

shells. Time slowed to a crawl. Telion saw the firing arms pumping shell after shell into the spinning barrels. Before any of those shells were fired, Telion heard the whoosh of a missile launch, followed an instant later by a deafening bang of superheated air as two melta bombs exploded.

Spun around by the force of the blast, the battle engine's guns tore an arc of white-hot fire through the central columns of the temple. The machine lurched backwards like a punch-drunk fist-fighter, and gobbets of molten metal dribbled from its underside, like wax from the candles in the company chapel. Spurts of flaming oil and engine fluid sprayed in jetting arcs. The titan took a broken step forward. Metal squealed, and the machine stumbled as its wounded leg finally gave way. Off balance, the battle engine crashed to the ground with a thunderous howl of buckled metal and mechanised anger.

It thrashed like a dying animal, its one remaining leg churning the air as it fought to right itself. Sparking cables flopped from the wound and iridescent bio-fluids pooled around its shattered carapace. The machine's binaric death-screams echoed throughout the forge-temple, a gurgling rasp of agony and hatred that hurt to hear and left bitter taste in the back of the throat.

Telion let out his breath as the red light faded from the slit windows of its daemonic head.

The forge-temple loosed a cry of loss and hatred, each one of the black-robed priests falling to the ground and convulsing as the scrapcode backwash of the engine's death blew out portions of their cognitive architecture.

Explosions flared all through the forge-temple as systems controlled by the engine began to fail. The destruction wrought by Telion's bombs, combined with the death of the temple's high priest, was causing a cat-astrophic chain-reaction of destruction. Klaxons blared, binaric warnings screeched from roof-mounted loud-speakers and a cascade effect of collapse was marching through the forge-temple.

'We need to go!' shouted Kaetan. 'Right now!'

Telion nodded and keyed the vox-mic. 'Draco!' he shouted. 'Get back here now! Immediate exfiltration!'

He received no response and desperately looked for any sign of the lad. Blazing fires and expanding lakes of bloodmetal hazed the air with smoke and choking fumes, making it next to impossible to see anything clearly. Kaetan led the rest of the squad back through the vent shaft that had brought them inside the forge-temple, and Telion knew he would have to join them soon.

'Draco!' repeated Telion. 'Respond, damn it!'

The smoke parted for an instant, and Telion's gaze fell upon an Adeptus Astartes pattern missile launcher slowly melting in a sinuous river of lava-like steel. Draco would never abandon his battle gear, and with sinking heart, Telion knew the Scout had perished saving their lives.

'Guilliman watch over you, lad,' said Telion, turning and making his way to safety. A titanic explosion tore the end of the forge apart as he reached the vent, and Telion gripped the edge of the opening as he took one last look around the collapsing temple for any sign that Draco might somehow still be alive.

There was nothing, and Telion ducked into the shaft as the forge-temple tore itself apart.

They watched its final collapse from a rocky ledge two kilometres from the Maidens of Nestor. The entire plateau was a glowed haloed in sunset orange as tears of molten metal wept down the mountain's flanks. Each glassy monolith reflected the glow of the forge-temple's destruction, standing proud amid the devastation.

No more would the Bloodborn craft engines of war to slaughter the defenders of Quintarn. No more would they be able to replenish their losses with impunity. Now the battlefields would be places of attrition to them, and Votheer Tark's lack of ability as a warlord would be hideously exposed.

Now the Ultramarines were in the ascendancy.

Telion ran a hand across his shaven scalp before making the sign of the aquila over his heart. Behind him, Kaetan, Dareios, Zeno and Agathon did the same, honouring their fallen brother.

'I shouldn't have lost him,' said Telion.

'You didn't,' said Kaetan. 'The war took him.'

'The war?' replied Telion, shaking his head. 'No, I let him down, and now the Chapter has been deprived of a fine Scout, a son of Ultramar who never had the chance to be the warrior it was his right to become.'

Kaetan put his hand on Telion's shoulder and said, 'Think on it this way. Draco's sacrifice saved all our lives. And how many lives will *we* go on to save?'

'One life for many? Is that what you are saying?'

'It is, and you know I'm right,' said Kaetan. 'I too grieve for Draco's loss, but if his death allows us to win the war for Quintarn, then I believe it was a price worth paying.'

Telion nodded. 'I know you are right, old friend, but to see those in their prime cut down while an old warhorse like me endures feels very wrong.'

'Nonsense,' said Kaetan. 'You are Torias Telion, the Eye of Vengeance, and you will live forever.'

Telion did not answer him, and turned towards home.

And behind him, a mountain burned.

TWO KINDS OF FOOL

GRAHAM McNEILL

Practical. That was how they'd once done things. Back in the days of the Legion. He'd read the picts of the most ancient pages of the Codex Astartes in the timbered Arcanium, looking back to a time when the kinds of missions he was known for were the norm. Back when the Ultramarines had, so the flickering image of yellowed parchment claimed, ruled hundreds of worlds.

There were few among the Chapter who would ever describe him or his methods as practical. Reckless, perhaps. Successful, certainly, but practical? Unlikely.

Yet with the ending of the war against the Bloodborn, the Chapter was renewing itself. Why shouldn't he?

A faded aphorism within the pages of the Codex Astartes spoke of two kinds of fool, those who *could* not change and those who *would* not change.

Cato Sicarius would be neither.

* * *

Final Absolution was an inhuman agglomeration of void-wrecks and spatial debris. A ghost ship passing down through the galactic plane, it had breached Ultramarian space fifteen days ago. Its mass and residual bio-signs had triggered the deep augurs of the Kryptman line, bringing *Valin's Revenge* and its escorts surging from the graving docks over Talassar on an intercept course.

Even without the Kryptman line, the presence of tyrannic organisms within *Final Absolution* was clear. Vast resinous plates crusted its hull armour and mucus-like accretions enveloped its dorsal surfaces like cancerous blooms of coral.

Three loathsomely organic bio-ships accompanied *Final Absolution*, smaller than the hulk, but still vast and grotesque in their resemblance to the nautilus beasts of Talassar's deep ocean. Waving tentacles, kilometres-long, probed the void from cavernous maws and frills of undulant flesh rippled upon their cliff-like flanks.

Another ten days would bring this splinter fleet within striking distance of Talassarian system space. Sicarius's birthworld had suffered the touch of the Thrice-Born's daemon-wrought. He had sworn a mighty oath upon his Tempest Blade that its people would not know the horror of the Great Devourer.

Valin's Revenge was a ship of the Second Company, but Severus Agemman had named the hulk, as was his right as senior captain. Three squads drawn from First Company's finest warriors had been added to Sicarius's order of battle. Their inclusion came at the behest of Lord Calgar, but Sicarius sensed the hand of Varro Tigurius in its origin. The mind of the Chapter's Chief Librarian was an ever-shifting labyrinth that looked in a thousand directions for threats to the Chapter and the means to counter them. If he and Lord Calgar had decided the warriors of the First were needed, then Sicarius was not about to gainsay them.

Killing tyranids aboard space hulks was what Terminators did best, but the warriors of the Second would be first in the fight.

The lightless axial corridor was thick with beasts, scores of leaping, screeching killers of the *hormagaunt* genus. Sicarius's command squad cut them down with disciplined volleys of mass-reactives. Explosions lit the way onward with strobing muzzle flare.

At the head of the Lions of Macragge, Sicarius met the tyranid charge head on. He went low, ducking under a slashing claw the length of a scythe, and he thrust his Tempest Blade into the creature's thorax and twisted its energised edge. Molten flesh and black-red ichor frothed over his gauntlet.

He kicked the dying beast clear and shoulder-barged the press of aliens behind it. Bodies broke before his bulk. He stamped down on chitinous limbs, breaking arcs of bone and crushing hard shells. A jaw snapped on his left wrist, razored fangs scoring the artificer-forged plate.

Gaius Prabian took the creature's head with a decapitating sweep of his power blade as Malcian unleashed a roaring blast of promethium from his flamer. A dozen monsters shrieked as superheated gel compounds burned them to bloody vapour.

Sicarius moved into the gap, the jaws of the disembodied head still gnawing at his wrist. The black orbs of its skull rolled over to white. Sicarius smashed it to bony splinters against the bulkhead and fired his plasma pistol. The searing beam burned out the chest of a dead-eyed horror of talons and teeth, penetrating a molten core through half a dozen more.

Vandius, Daceus and Venatio advanced with him, bolters locked to their shoulders. With flawless target prioritisation, they pumped shot after shot into the heaving mass of alien flesh.

Sicarius and Prabian led the charge, both warriors supremely gifted champions of the blade. Sicarius fought with the skill of a duellist, his sword arm trained since birth by the greatest fencing masters of Talassar. Prabian owned no such finesse. His blade arm was a killing tool, his shield a battering ram.

Malcian's flamer unleashed another burning stream, lighting the axial with the glow of a furnace. Alien bodies burned with a curious snapping sound, like fresh kindling on a bonfire. Bolter shells detonated hormagaunts like chitinous bladders, their noxious blood spattering the wall in vast quantities.

Sicarius saw something larger than a gaunt lope down the corridor, wreathed in the play of fire and shadow. Even hunched over, its bulk was impressive, ridged and bony, with sharp chitin-hooks running the length of its spine. Its skull was a bulbous horror of ridged, overlapping plates.

'Warrior genus,' said Prabian. 'A big one too.'

'Too big?' said Sicarius.

'Big enough that we ought to take it together.'

'Agreed.'

The tyranid warrior's alien lips peeled back from its elongated jaw to reveal long, yellowed fangs. Hissing saliva drooled, and a black tongue coiled from its red-raw gullet. The creature barrelled forward on monstrously powerful legs, trampling its smaller kin in its hunger to reach Sicarius.

Twin blades of acid-edged bone unfurled from folds in its upper limbs.

Sicarius pressed himself against the shielding protrusion of a corroded stanchion and said, 'Brother Malcian, give me some light.'

Malcian took a braced stance and a stream of liquid fire played over the creature. Its flesh ignited and it screeched in pain. Bolter shells detonated against its armour.

It left chunks of corpse-white flesh in its wake.

Prabian stepped from cover and swung his power sword in his favoured decapitating strike. A killing move, but one that could leave a warrior dangerously exposed. A flesh-wrought sword flashed up to block the blow, a second thrusting for the champion's midriff.

Prabian rammed his shield into the bonesword, cracking the bio-weapon in two. At the sound of the blade snapping, Sicarius swung low and rammed his plasma pistol into the side of the alien's reverse-jointed leg.

He pulled the trigger and the creature's knee vanished in an explosion of molten bone and flesh. The monster crashed to the metalled deck and Sicarius spun, reversing his Tempest Blade to ram it down, one-handed through the back of the fallen beast's skull.

Its agonised thrashing ceased instantly.

Sicarius left the sword embedded as the hormagaunts screeched in sudden abandonment, reeling in animal confusion. Sicarius knew the signs well enough; until another brood-leader imposed its dominance the tyranids were easy prey.

'Kill them all,' he said.

The Lions of Macragge advanced in a line to carry out their captain's orders.

Leaving the slaughter of the 'gaunts behind, Sicarius and his command squad pushed towards the bridge. In a normal boarding action, that location would be heavily defended, but the swarm creatures counted no particular region of the ship – save for the nests of the hive lords – as more important than another.

Sicarius climbed the processional steps towards the bridge. The walls were a mixture of resinous excretions and scorched metal. Glossy veneers of pulsing organic tubes pierced acid-burned bulkheads.

'Sergeant Ixion,' said Sicarius. 'Report.'

'*Moving up sub-deck seven-six-alpha. Heavy resistance.*'

Sicarius nodded; he'd planned for this. The larger, more aggressive forces of Ixion and Manorian were drawing the greater concentrations of tyrannic warrior creatures.

Leaving the path to the bridge relatively undefended.

Relatively. Already he heard scratching claws behind the walls and beneath the deck plates. The grunts, brays and screeches of incoming ravager packs were getting louder.

'Do you require assistance, sergeant?'

'*Macragge's Avengers need no help to kill tyranids, sire,*' replied Ixion, with the precise mix of arrogance and respect Sicarius cultivated in all his warriors.

'Good work, sergeant. Keep pushing them hard, draw in as many as you can. And be ready for the withdrawal order.'

'*Understood. Ixion out.*'

Sicarius switched vox-channels.

'Manorian,' he said. 'Time to objective?'

'*Current rate of advance puts us at sub-junction sigma-three-three in four minutes.*'

Bolter fire, muted by the vox, and the wet smack of cold steel into alien flesh echoed in Sicarius's helm. The tactical overlay on his visor put the sub-junction five hundred metres from the sergeant's current position. Hard to believe Praxor Manorian would take so long to reach an objective.

'Make it three, and the company banner's yours to lift when we return to Macragge.'

'*We'll be there in two,*' promised Manorian.

Severus Agemman's eyes darted over the updating engagement sigils on the battle-logisters of *Valin's Revenge*. The Lions of Macragge had secured the location the Techmarines had divined to be main engine control. Already the *Revenge*'s augurs showed heat blooms in *Final Absolution*'s engineering decks.

Within the hour, the corrupted hulk would be diverted from its current path, taking it and the hideous xenos threat within beyond the eastern fringe.

'Your plan is working, Cato,' said Agemman, hating the grating, artificial wheeze he now heard in his voice.

An all but mortal wound sustained at the claws of the thrice-born daemon lord had almost ended him on in the keep of Castra Tanagra. Only a cybernetically rebuilt chest cavity and an indomitable will to survive had kept his name from being added to the Temple of Correction's walls.

'Are you surprised?' asked Librarian Felix Carthalo, a brooding presence at his side. 'Did you expect it to fail?'

Agemman shook his head, wondering if the prescient powers of the Librarian read more than just his tone. In any engagement with tyrannic foes, the psychic might of a Librarian was a boon, but Agemman never relished fighting alongside the Chapter's warrior mystics.

'Far from it, Brother Carthalo,' said Agemman. 'That Cato's plan is working surprises me not in the least.'

'Your tone suggests otherwise,' replied Carthalo. 'Did you hope it might falter, necessitating a combat deployment for the First?'

Hearing the echo of his own desire to be unleashed in the Librarian's voice, Agemman said, 'The First Company live for war, Brother Carthalo. It is what we are bred for, but Captain Sicarius's strategy is a good one. If all goes to plan, our strength will not be needed.'

'Then perhaps the fates will present us an opportunity even amid Cato's success,' said the Librarian with the ghost of a smile playing around his thin lips.

Agemman turned from the battle-logister to face his senior squad sergeants, Tirusus, Gaius and Solinas. The three warriors were encased in bulked plates of tactical Dreadnought armour painted the cobalt-blue and pearlescent white of First Company.

Each was a hero of the Chapter, warriors whose names were known throughout Ultramar and beyond. Their faces were patchwork tapestries of scars earned in the thousand years of service to the Emperor shared between them and carved into their skin. These men had carried his mortally wounded body from Castra Tanagra in the dying moments of the battle against the daemon lord's host.

Brothers was too small a word for the bond they shared.

Sicarius's plan cast Agemman's warriors in the role of a quick-reaction force, a teleport reserve to smash any enemy counter-attack.

A vital role, certainly, but not one that suited First Company temperaments. Despite his diplomatic words, Agemman saw the hope in each sergeant's eye that he had seen a flaw in Sicarius's plan.

'Don't let Cato's past reputation fool you,' said Agemman, wincing as the cybernetics grafted to his chest sent a spasm of pain through him. 'Yes, some past stratagems of my brother-captain may have appeared reckless at face value, but they were never without a sound tactical basis.'

'Even though they might have taken victory to see it,' said Solinas, ever the quickest to find fault with Second Company's captain.

'Victory requires no explanation,' quoted Gaius.

That gave them a smile.

Agemman nodded, 'Very true, Gaius, but my surprise stems from seeing this plan's roots so firmly entrenched in the teachings of the Codex Astartes.'

Tirusus nodded. 'Perhaps the fighting on Espandor has given Sicarius–'

'*Captain* Sicarius,' Agemman reminded him.

'Apologies,' said Tirusus. 'Perhaps the fighting on Espandor has given Captain Sicarius a newfound respect for the primarch's teachings.'

'Or that he scents change in the wind,' said Solinas.

Agemman chose to ignore this last comment, seeing a flurry of intense bio-sign appear in the hulk's engine spaces. He had fought the swarms of the Great Devourer often enough to recognise the spoor of high-function synapse beasts when he saw it.

'The masters of the hive awaken,' said Carthalo, a shimmer-sheen of light hazing the crystalline hood of his armour.

Agemman instantly processed this new information.

Thus far, the xenos had fought in a purely reactive manner, like white blood cells attacking an invading bacteria. Simplistic, territorial behaviour, their instinctual patterns were what had allowed Sicarius's strike to penetrate so far and so quickly.

The awakening of the Overmind negated that advantage.

'Sergeants, muster your squads at the teleporter arrays,' said Agemman, turning to Librarian Carthalo. 'It appears the fates have provided. First Company is going to war.'

What was left of the bridge was a smashed ruin of machinery torn apart by solid rounds, hacking talons and bio-acids. But just enough remained of its control mechanisms to fire the engines.

'How long?' asked Sicarius, looming over Techmarine Orian, whose servitors interfaced with a dozen opened terminals.

'The reactors buried in the depths of this hulk are still functional, but their hearts are cold,' explained Orian, his servo-harness working in the exposed guts of three nearby banks of machinery. 'The rites of awakening are long and intricate, but I believe I may be able to coax their wrath sooner rather than later.'

'Give me something specific, Orian.'

'The spirits of dormant reactors don't do specific, captain,' said Orian. 'Best guess is that I'll have them at a level to push the hulk from Ultramar in around two hours.'

'Hard to believe they're functional at all,' said Daceus, his augmetic eye blink-clicking the damage.

'The resilience of blessed standard template constructs,' said Orian.

'Can't you just overload the reactors?' said Dacean. 'Blow this whole hulk and its escorts to debris?'

Orian chuckled. 'Hark at him,' he said. 'Spends a month detailed to forge protection and thinks he's an adept of Mars now.'

'Don't mock me, Orian,' warned Daceus.

'Then don't ask foolish questions,' snapped the Techmarine.

'Give him an answer, Orian,' said Sicarius, forestalling Daceus's anger. 'The question was honestly asked.'

Orian sighed and said, 'These reactors have been stilled for centuries and the power of any explosion will be insufficient to reach more than a few hundred kilometres from its outer limits. Not enough to be do more than scrape a layer of chitin from those escorts unless they pull in close.'

'Then why didn't you just say that?' grumbled Dacean.

Sicarius left the Techmarine to his labours, making a circuit of the bridge. Its bulkheads and supports were bare iron, encrusted with ice and hung with fleshy stalactites. It groaned as deep structures shifted in the temperature differentials, the noise a mournful, drawn-out prayer for an end to its suffering.

Numerous holes punctured the walls of the bridge, ancient ingress points ripped by attacking bio-organisms. Sicarius had gunners stationed at each one, together with a warrior trained in void-hulk auspex reading.

He inspected each defence point, passing words with

each man and lauding their conduct. His words were sincere and they knew it.

Sicarius moved to where Gaius Prabian stood at the head of the processional stairs. The vast doors to the bridge were jammed open, their mechanisms choked with resinous secretions harder than quick-setting plascrete.

'What does Orian say?' asked the champion.

'Around two hours until the reactors are ready to fire.'

'While we are static, we are vulnerable.'

'I know,' said Sicarius, 'but it is what it is, Gaius.'

The sub-deck was knee deep in reeking bio-excretions, digestive acids and liquefied metal. Its high vaulted ceiling was a pulsing network of peristaltic motion. Coiled intestinal tracts secreted waste products from the glacially slow digestion process that was slowly devouring the hulk from within.

Grub-like creatures wriggled in the ooze, and packs of larger, hunched things hung from the walls, drooling ropes of viscous slime. Submerged things with glossed and bulbous skulls sifted the waste for any residual traces of useable bio-matter.

A whipcrack of blue lightning arced between the sagging spars of a corroded gantry and fretwork-carved pilasters that depicted hooded tech-priests and eroded icons of the Adeptus Mechanicus. The creatures within the chamber looked up, hissing at this unknown intrusion.

The web of teleport energies coalesced in the heart of the chamber and exploded outward with a thunderous bang of displaced air.

The pool boiled in the sudden eruption of energy and

a circular bow wave surged from the circle of warriors who now stood in the centre of the chamber.

Seven Terminators in the livery of the Ultramarines stood in an outward-facing circle, wreathed in flickering corposant. Agemman stood at the head of the First Company veterans, flanked by Sergeant Tirusus and Librarian Carthalo.

Agemman blinked as his sensorium realigned with the physical world. He processed his surroundings in an instant, marking targets and registering the squad's route of advance.

A monster erupted from the pool, a worm-like beast with serrated fangs and a rippling underbelly of sucking tubes. Agemman's storm bolter roared and the thing exploded into wet scraps of meat and chitinous exo-armour.

The walls erupted with movement as the hunched creatures reacted to the threat in their midst. Scores of screeching beasts dropped to the pool or simply hurled themselves at the Terminators from the chamber's upper reaches.

Agemman waded through the filth towards a raised area of deck, blowing apart targets with every step. Squad Tirusus and Carthalo moved with him in perfect synchrony, their weapons reaping a fearsome tally among the aliens.

Deadly accurate storm bolter fire blazed. The squad assault cannon detonated dozens of creatures in mid-air. Forking blasts of elemental energies from Carthalo's obsidian-bladed force sword burned countless others to ash. A rain of burning blood and ruptured chitin splashed into the pool.

'Chamber is secure,' said Sergeant Tirusus as Agemman stepped onto the raised deck, his armour awash with stinking fluids.

'That won't last,' said Agemman, consulting the tactical overlay on his visor. 'All squads, report.'

'*Squad Gaius insertion on target point. Advancing to hive-nest objective.*'

'*Squad Solinas insertion point one hundred metres aft of target. Assuming battle pace to objective.*'

'The swarms are already converging on our position,' said Carthalo, his voice strained with effort and his crystalline hood pulsing with psychic resonance. 'Motile bio-sign increasing at exponential rates. Genestealers.'

'Then let's get moving,' said Agemman.

The information on his sensorium was undeniable, yet Sicarius still found it hard to credit. It showed incoming teleport signatures on three separate vectors of attack within the engineering deck.

'Severus?' said Sicarius. 'What are you doing?'

'*Reacting to a developing situation.*'

'What situation?' asked Sicarius, hearing the roar of assault cannon fire mixed with the thudding, echoing bangs of massed bolter fire.

'*Check your auspex feed from the* Revenge.'

Sicarius did so and instantly saw what Agemman meant. All three hive ships were drawing closer to the *Final Absolution*. The void glittered with tens of thousands of tyrannic organisms ejected from the bio-ships and swimming through space towards the hulk. Hundreds were already cutting their way in, like scavenger ants on the carcass of a land leviathan.

'Why did you board?'

'*The masters of the swarm are wakening in the deeps,*' said Agemman. '*I saw a chance to stir the pot and draw the swarm together.*'

'That wasn't part of the plan.'

'*Plans change, Cato,*' said Agemman. '*You know that better than anyone.*'

The vox crackled as Agemman's signal cut off.

'Orian!' yelled Sicarius. 'Change of plan.'

Beyond the vaulted digestion chamber, the route through the lightless depths of the hulk grew narrower and ever more constrictive. The way forward twisted like the path through a maze, lit by constant flashes of gunfire.

This deep, the vessel was unrecognisable as something wrought by the hands of man. Every wall was glutinous with secretions and ribbed chitin, the floor a spongy mass of cloying tissue. The temperature was searing, furnace heat escaping from spore vents and the nearby reactors as their molten hearts were roused to wakefulness.

Agemman led the way, his storm bolter blasting a path through hundreds of beetle-carapaced creatures. Genestealers, lethally fast killers with claws easily capable of tearing through even the thickest armour plates. They screeched and hissed, jamming the corridor with their bodies. He fought through them, crushing broken alien limbs like refuse beneath his boot.

'A righteous tide of alien blood!' yelled Carthalo, sweeping his sword through four beasts at once. His hood crackled with lambent energies, and his blade was a beacon of flaming illumination.

'These are vanguard organisms,' said Agemman, ripping

a leaping genestealer from his chest with his powerfist and smashing it into the wall. 'The larger monsters will be waking and gathering around the master of the hive.'

Attacks came from every single vector: in front, the sides, above and behind. Even below. Sucking orifices opened in the floor, gurgling organic chasms descending to Emperor-alone knew where.

Hundreds of genestealers retched from their brood pits. They dropped from sphincter openings in the ceiling or rushed along the passageway at their rear. Carthalo's prescient warnings alerted the Terminators to every danger.

Storm bolters fired never-ending hails of mass-reactives as Agemman led them deeper into the sickeningly organic heart of the hulk. They followed constricting passageways hung with frond-like growths that quested for their necks like living hangman's rope, and traversed chambers filled with hissing acid pools that stripped the paint from their armour. They waded through rivers of frothed matter, and burned clutches of leathery ovoid egg-sacs with flamers. Every step of their advance felt like plunging deeper into the rancid guts of a diseased plague-carrier.

They took their first casualty when a portion of the ceiling collapsed in a deluge of acids. Brother Meridax staggered, and a flailing creature erupted from a floor pit to envelop him. Its body was a segmented snake-like horror of rending claws and snapping fangs. Twin chitin hooks carved open his armour as the beast's weight drove him to the deck. Secondary limbs tore into Meridax's exposed flesh like the blades of a threshing machine. Its enormous jaws snapped shut on his helmet, swallowing it whole.

With a flick of its coiled tail, the creature sprang at Carthalo. It moved with blinding speed, but the Librarian made a quarter turn and cut it in half at the thorax with a mighty two-handed blow. The remains fell in a hissing, spitting heap before him. Carthalo stamped down on the fringed plates of its armoured skull and its thrashing ceased instantly.

'Mark our fallen brother,' said Agemman. 'We press on.'

What had once been a space devoted to the ritual circulation of coolant fluids had been transformed into a vast gestation chamber. Hundreds of metres high and a full kilometre in length, the walls were curved, rib-like vaults of bio-organic polymers, the floor a cratered wasteland of digestion pools, birthing pods and flesh-sculpting.

Innumerable swarm organisms filled the vast chamber, some still dormant in hibernation, but increasing numbers were tearing through membranous cauls of hibernation sacs. Packs of genestealers and hormagaunts moved in flocking patterns through the chamber, but now Agemman saw the larger brood strains – tyrannic warriors in all their myriad weaponised bio-forms.

'Guilliman's Oath,' said Sergeant Tirusus.

The pattern of their distribution was immediately obvious.

A towering beast, easily the equal of an Imperial Knight in scale, squatted in a pool of viscous bio-matter. The tyrant of this fleet was a gnarled leviathan, slick with drizzled fluids and bowed by monstrously thick plates of chitinous armour. Its body was ancient, a primordial creature birthed centuries, perhaps even millennia, ago in a far distant galaxy.

Its jaws could swallow a Rhino whole. Its claws could carve the leg from a Titan. It bared its fangs, dripping yellow tusks the thickness of a Dreadnought's fist.

'That's the beast,' said Agemman. 'Courage and honour!'

'For Macragge!' bellowed Carthalo.

They advanced in the wake of interlocking mass-reactives and assault cannon fire. Pinpoint volleys cleared a route through the chamber. Tyranid organisms surrounded them, hurling themselves at the Terminators with furious abandon. Heedless of pain, the implacable will of the Overmind drove them into the teeth of the Terminators' guns without fear of death.

Only genestealers weathered the storm of explosive rounds, but even they were pulped by powerfists or carved asunder by chainfists as the Terminators advanced with relentless, unstoppable hatred of their kind.

Yet even as the Ultramarines advance began to slow, squads Gaius and Solinas breached the chamber. A three-pronged assault now pushed into the nest, and the guarding swarms were forced to divide.

Agemman took heart from the sight of his warriors and drove himself into the fray with ever-greater resolve.

The pace of the assault renewed.

The lord of the broods loosed a bellow that shook the walls of the chamber, and Agemman met its alien gaze. Its eyes were ancient, marbled orbs the size of his fist, and Agemman saw the silence between the galaxies in their empty, soulless voids. He felt sudden, agonising pressure within his skull, the presence of something invasive and hideously alien pressing against the surface of his mind.

And in that instant of connection he was once again in Castra Tanagra as the daemon lord towering above him, its warp-sheathed claws poised to end his life. He felt the numbing horror of that moment again, paralysed by knowing there was absolutely nothing he could do to save himself.

Fear was alien to Severus Agemman, but the psychic scarring of the instant he had faced death was all too real. The hive lord's inhumanly powerful mind dredged deeply and amplified that pain and horror a thousandfold.

A hulking tyrannic warrior charged him, but Agemman lowered his powerfist and relaxed his trigger finger. The beast screeched in triumph and fibrous whips of muscle tendon lashed from cavities in its exoskeletal structure. They entangled his arms and pulled him off-balance. With him pulled in close, the beast vomited a spray of bio-plasmic fluids onto his helmet. Agemman's vision fogged with static.

The corrosive slime ate into his helm's grille and Agemman gagged at its foulness. The neuroglottis at the back of his throat rebelled at the stench, somewhere between a greenskin midden and necrotic flesh.

Mantis-blade arms scythed towards his head. A black-bladed sword intercepted them and a return stroke clove the creature's forelimbs from its body.

'Fight it, Severus!' yelled Carthalo, and Agemman felt the blistering heat radiating from the Librarian's psychic hood.

He felt the hive lord's fury as its hold was broken, and let out a shuddering breath as the nightmare of Castra Tanagra bled from his thoughts like a sickness.

Carthalo thrust his gauntlet at Agemman's attacker. A blaze of blue fire shrieked from his splayed fingers, instantly searing the meat from the creature's unnatural skeleton.

Agemman could barely see. The bio-acid had dissolved most of the front of his helmet. He ripped it clear, and the heat and stench of the cavern struck him like a physical assault. Memory made his chest a knot of agony where the organic scraps of his heart and lungs meshed with his internal augmetics.

Sergeant Tirusus's squad formed a wedge around him as Carthalo swept the torrent of his psychic fire over the alien host. That fire burned hotter and brighter than any natural blaze and the creatures shrieked as the Librarian burned a path towards the hive lord.

'Are you wounded, brother-captain?' asked Sergeant Tirusus.

Agemman shook his head, swallowing back a bilious mouthful of revulsion. Without the insulation of his helmet, the foulness of this alien nest was almost too much to bear.

'I am not,' he said, masking his horror at the lingering trace of the hive lord's mind by spitting on the molten bones of the beast Carthalo had slain.

Tirusus nodded and Agemman was grateful he turned away.

The first captain's transhuman body was mighty, but the daemon lord's claws had cut him to the quick of his life. Not even the combined skill of the Chapter's masters of the Forge and apothecarion could undo such mortal hurts entirely.

Agemman swallowed his pain and forged a path to Carthalo's side. Even as the Librarian fired his storm bolter and cut through packs of tyranid creatures, his hood blazed with the intensity of his unseen battle with the tyrant's mind.

What supreme skill must it take to wage war in both the physical and spiritual realm? To see a warrior fight with such mastery was humbling and inspiring.

Faced with furious assaults from three directions, the hive lord retreated into its pool, loosing a braying screech of animal desperation. Agemman was no psychic, but even he recognised a base creature's cry for help.

The monstrous creature spasmed in the pool, sending a wave of stinking fluids over the undulating deck. Its swollen belly bloated with hideous tumorous growths, like a thousand eggs in pustulant sacs suddenly brought to the surface.

Scores ruptured, spilling a froth of grotesque, foetal scraps onto the chamber's floor. They writhed like unclenching fists and knots of maggot-like termagants scrabbled to their clawed feet.

'Too little, too late,' said Agemman.

The First Company Terminators cut through them all, implacable, unstoppable and utterly without mercy as they closed the noose.

Once again, Agemman met the gaze of the hive lord.

This time all he saw was the reflection of his own implacable will to see the beast dead.

'Kill it,' he said.

The first explosion opened a seam along *Final Absolution*'s starboard flank. A volcanic flare of light boiled from its pitted surface, spilling out in neon-bright traceries of plasma fire.

The hive ships hung suspended alongside the dying hulk, bound to its doom by a crippling sense of emptiness and confusion. Vast quantities of radiation boiled into space, peeling the leathery void-hides from their bones like cinders in a firestorm.

The slaying of the hive lord had thrown the gestalt xeno-consciousness of the tyranids into a paroxysm of conflicting drives. By the time the most powerful minds achieved dominance of the trillions of other interlinked creatures, it was already too late to escape.

One hive ship had fought its way clear of the doomed hive lord's ship, but its wretched, dying mass was easy prey for the guns of *Valin's Revenge*. Its gutted carcass was already drifting off into wilderness space.

Secondary and tertiary detonations, minutes old, climbed to the hulk's surface and reticulated lines of fire shone through its crazed hull as though it contained a newborn supernova.

Sicarius watched the *Final Absolution*'s death with a hollow mix of satisfaction and victory denied. By any definition, this was a heroic action, one to be entered into the victory rolls with pride and honour.

'You surprised me today, Severus,' he said at last.

'I could say the same thing, Cato,' replied Agemman.

'How so?'

'It's no secret our interpretations of the Codex Astartes have always differed.'

'True. Diplomatic of you, but true. What's your point?'

'Today you cleaved to the teachings of the Codex Astartes as I have always done.'

'So why do I feel second guessed?'

'I saw the opportunity and I took it,' said Agemman. 'There is little else to say. Had our roles been reversed, you would have done the same.'

'Perhaps,' allowed Sicarius.

Agemman was correct in his assessment, but for one critical fact. Only Terminators could have fought their way through to the hive lord's nest.

'There is no *perhaps*, Cato,' said Agemman. 'You are a great warrior, perhaps one of the greatest Ultramar has seen in millennia, but I am not yet too old to surprise you.'

Sicarius smiled. 'Evidently not.'

'I am the master of First Company, the Regent of Ultramar and I'm not too set in my ways to change when I need to.'

'Nor am I,' said Sicarius.

SHADOW OF THE LEVIATHAN

JOSH REYNOLDS

The enemy burst out of the smoky darkness with a raucous, insectile clatter. The swarm of hormagaunts loped towards their prey, talons gleaming in the light of fading luminal panels, driven forward by the pulsing will of monstrous overseers. There were hundreds of them, a seething mass of ravenous jaws and twitching limbs, determined to devour every scrap of bio-matter in the hive-city.

Ghaurkal Hive was the last of the great Kantipuran Hollow Mountains, and soon it, like the others, would be claimed by the ravenous servants of Hive Fleet Leviathan. The work of centuries and generations without number would be undone in hours, as the once-prosperous world of Kantipur was stripped barren and rendered down to lifeless rock by the star-borne abominations – the hive-ships of the Leviathan – which even now hung bloated and foul in the upper reaches of the world's atmosphere.

The tyranids pelted through the battle-scarred streets of the hab-block, towards the curved rings of the broad marble steps, many metres across, which led from the cavernous hive to the broad, statue-lined avenue, then out of the mountain-hive and into the open air plateau occupied by the Rana Space port. In better times, hundreds of thousands of travellers would have moved up and down those vast steps, coming and going. Now, they were pockmarked by craters and stained by the blood of humans and monsters alike.

They were crowded with the shattered remnants of a once proud people making all haste for the dubious safety of the stars. It was these bloodied refugees that had drawn the tyranids, but as the creatures swarmed out of the darkness with ravenous intent, other, larger shapes moved out of the mass of panicked humanity to interpose themselves between predator and prey.

'As per the established stratagem, brothers,' Varro Tigurius, Chief Librarian of the Ultramarines, said to the blue-armoured shapes of his battle-brothers as they spread out in formation around him, moving to protect the screaming evacuees. 'Kill the synapse creatures first. We must be quick. Time is not on our side in this endeavour.'

'*Thank you for the reminder, Chief Librarian. In the heat of battle I might have forgotten standing orders,*' the vox crackled in response.

Tigurius smiled thinly. 'Merely doing my duty, sergeant. As are we all. Proceed at your leisure.' Clad in azure power armour, his bald, scarred head covered by the ornately engraved psychic hood that was both a sign of his office as well as protection for his body and mind, Tigurius made for an imposing figure, even amongst the finest warriors of his Chapter. Scrolls, parchments of incalculable age and purity seals hung from his battleplate, and he clutched an ornate force staff in one hand as his other rested on the butt of the master-crafted bolt pistol holstered on his hip.

'*Proceeding.*'

The response was curt, but then he hadn't expected it to be otherwise. The Sternguard were not men to waste words, and their sergeant, Ricimer, was taciturn even for one of that elite group. He was stolid, efficient and unmoveable – in other words, the perfect choice to command the Sternguard. The sons of Dorn would have been proud to call him one of their own had he the fortune to wear the colours of the Imperial Fists rather than the Ultramarines.

A moment later, bolters began to fire in a staccato rhythm, one after the other. Hellfire rounds thudded into the wide, armour-plated skulls of the tyranid warriors, delivering their deadly payload. The creatures staggered, slewing awkwardly through the swarm of their lesser brethren. One toppled backwards, yellowish smoke rising from its crumpled skull. Another stumbled forward a few paces, the tips of its bone swords dragging along the street, before it sank down and flopped over, twitching. The last ploughed on, ignoring the oozing craters that pockmarked its skull.

'*Reinforced cranial structure,*' Ricimer said.

'Yes,' Tigurius said. He stalked down the steps. 'I shall deal with it. Hold position.' He focused his attentions on the tyranid warrior and formed a killing thought in his mind – a thought of sharp edges and deadly speed, honed to a murderous point in the fires of his righteous anger. He sent it hurtling out with a gesture and felt it strike home as if it had been a physical blow. The tyranid swayed, reared back and shrieked.

He extended his hand as if to gather the tangled strands of the thought and made a swift, twisting motion. The tyranid's bestial frame gave a spasm, and a gout of superheated steam burst from its jaws. It sank down with a shrill wail, limbs twitching. The tide of hormagaunts stampeded around and over it, following its last command with mindless ferocity.

'*Fall back, Chief Librarian.*'

'No, I think not,' Tigurius said, facing the tide. 'I have fought these beasts before and I know how to send them scurrying for their holes. Hold position. Deal with any that get past me. I shall break them here.' He spread his arms and exhaled slowly. The sutras of strength and endurance unspooled in his mind. He brought his hands together, catching his staff between them. The air seemed to congeal about him as he lifted the staff, ramming the end of it down. The pavement cracked and split, venting steam and dust. A ripple of destruction spread outwards, tearing the street apart. A building, weakened by alien growths, collapsed atop the rear of the swarm, burying many of the skittering hormagaunts. The rest continued on, undeterred, plunging through the dust cloud to surge towards him.

'Come then,' he murmured. 'Come and die, little bugs.' Even as he spoke, he could feel the acidic heat of the hive mind bearing down on him from behind the eyes of every scuttling shape. It was an abominable weight on his mind and soul, but he bore it gladly.

Once, perhaps, his soul might have shrunk from that great, black shadow in the warp, but now he knew its secrets. And in knowing them, he could exploit them. Through such contact, he had come to know its wants, its drives and, more importantly, its weaknesses. He could sense the patterns of control and instinct which drove the servants of the hive mind, and disrupt them with ease.

In moments he was surrounded on all sides, the hormagaunts bounding towards him and talons scything through the air. Tigurius drew his bolt pistol. He fired swiftly, placing the shots where the leaping gaunts would be, rather than where they were. The creatures fell, skulls shattered. He pivoted, sweeping his staff out in a wide arc, to smash a third xenos from the air. The reinforced length of the staff, powered by genetically enhanced muscle, pulverised the creature's spiny shell, and dropped it to the ground in a twitching heap.

As the rest of the brood boiled towards him, Tigurius set his staff as if it were a standard, and let his fury flower to its fullest. The air before him ionised and, with a whip-crack of sound loud enough to shatter those few windows remaining in the closest buildings, his will slipped its leash. Leaping 'gaunts were obliterated, their bodies crushed beyond recognition as the cannonade of pure force hammered into their ranks. Ichor soon drenched the walls of the hab-units and street, and those who escaped the carnage scuttled back the way they had come.

Tigurius could feel the frayed pulse of primal fear that overwhelmed the creatures' natural ravenous inclinations. Without any of the larger synapse creatures to force them on, the broods were reduced to mere animals, with an animal's instinct towards self-preservation. He smiled in satisfaction. It was no longer a challenge to break the back of such swarms. He watched the last of them vanish into the darkness and turned back towards the steps.

'They're regrouping,' he said.

Ricimer didn't reply. The Sternguard sergeant began to issue orders, and Ultramarines moved to obey with crisp precision. Ten of the thirty who had accompanied Tigurius into Ghaurkal Hive moved to aid the evacuees in their efforts to reach safety. The rest split up into combat squads and moved out into the hab-block which extended out around the entryway to the space port. They would fan out and report any contact with the enemy.

Tigurius heard a rumble and looked up, through the shattered remnants of the immense stained-glass canopy that had covered the avenue to the space port. He watched as one of the vessels pressed into service for the evacuation lunged skyward on oscillating columns of flame. *Fly swiftly, fly true,* he thought.

Overhead, swirling clouds of tyranid gargoyles swooped and eddied. From a distance, the aliens looked like birds, moving with an instinctive synchronicity that eluded bipeds. They flew through the heavy, grey clouds and shot through with strands of sickly purple that obscured the sky. The vessel plunged into clouds and gargoyle swarms, rising steadily upwards and leaving the doomed world behind.

Outside of the hive, the air was thick with the black toxicity spewing from the thousands of fuming spore chimneys which had sprouted from the ground. The very stuff of the once-vibrant world was being broken down and reduced to its component parts for ease of alien digestion. Fuel for a fire that might yet claim Ultima Segmentum, unless some stroke of fortune snuffed it out.

Even here, in the last stronghold of humanity on this world, monstrous alien growths had begun to creep in and coil about the battle-scarred ruins. Many-limbed shadows moved through the upper reaches of the hive, scuttling amongst the networks of pipes and cabling which carried power, air and water to every hab-block and Administratum zone. The warble of the tyranid feeder-beasts slithered down from the upper spires, and the ululation of hormagaunts and still worse things rose from the underhive, combining to create a monstrous background cacophony.

And through it all, he felt the grotesque, singular pulse of the hive mind, watching, in hungry anticipation.

That was all it was, Tigurius knew. There was no true intelligence to be found there, only the avid hunger of an insect colony, bloated into something vast and far-reaching. The hive fleets were not enemies so much as storms to be weathered, or infestations to be exterminated. And such would be his pleasure, when the time came.

A number of other detachments of the same size and composition as the one he had led to Kantipur were engaged in similar evacuation efforts across the Gohla sub-sector. Indeed, the stratagem had been of his devising, after examining the skeins of fate and chance, and sifting through the premonitions which were his burden and his gift in equal measure. The Leviathan grew stronger with every world it devoured, and so, the Ultramarines had set out to deny this tendril of the hive fleet its provender, if possible. Starve the beast, rob it of strength and make it easy prey for the slaughter.

Exterminatus would have been easier, and had been suggested by others, with the Master of Sanctity, Ortan Cassius, among them. Burn the targeted worlds to cinders and let the swarm starve or devour itself. He knew the Blood Angels and their successor chapters were employing similar tactics in the Cryptus System. Tigurius doubted the long-term viability of such a strategy, however, and not simply because his premonitions had shown him glimpses of its ultimate futility. No, the Leviathan could be beaten, even as the Kraken had been, and the Behemoth. And if they sacrificed the very people whom they were sworn to protect, then what was the point?

Tigurius could feel the heat of every human soul still in Ghaurkal Hive in his mind. Each and every human – young or old, man, woman or child – had a tiny ember of flame within the chambers of their single heart... a flame which could burn as brightly as a sun. They were changeable things, humans, and capable of greatness, if given the opportunity. And for that reason, more than any other, Tigurius intended to make his stand and deny the Leviathan.

The Emperor made us to defend his chosen people, he thought, *and that is what the sons of Guilliman will do, or we will die in the attempt.*

He turned suddenly, looking out into the dark of the hab-block, and the hive-city beyond. He'd felt... something. It stirred in the dark, like an unseen shape sliding through black waters. A ripple of psychic disturbance which leeched his certainties away.

He had fought the mind-predators of the hive fleets before, and recognised their psychic spoor when he sensed it. Mind and body tense, he set his thoughts flying out over the cramped quarters of the hab-block, searching, hunting for any sign of it. The hive-city was full of swarms, mostly feeder-beasts, but worse things as well. Brute-simple warrior-broods and cunning infiltrator-species prowled the access tunnels and lower levels, in search of bio-matter to devour.

Tigurius stiffened as a lance of pain stabbed into his cerebral cortex. Even as he had been searching, so had something else – and it had found him first. He staggered, one hand pressed to his temple. A sound filled his head, swelling as if to drive out all thought and sanity. It was a scream, shrill and inhuman, and he dug his fingers into his skull, trying to marshal some defence against it. It was stronger than anything he'd yet encountered in his struggles with the hive mind.

'*Contact,*' the vox-feed crackled abruptly, and Tigurius stiffened. He recognised the voice of Geta, one of Ricimer's subordinates. He heard the stolid *crack-crack-crack* of bolter fire as well. Tigurius heard Ricimer speaking swiftly into the vox, making contact with the other squads.

'Estimate?' Tigurius asked into the vox.

'*Many,*' came the terse reply.

'Care to elaborate, brother?' Tigurius asked.

'*Too many.*'

'Thank you,' Tigurius said. 'Break contact and withdraw.' Geta didn't reply. Tigurius hoped that meant he was already falling back with the other members of his squad. Given the situation, he might not be able to.

Tigurius frowned and looked at Ricimer, who'd joined him before the steps. Ricimer was a bullet-headed veteran of the Ultramarines First Company. He held his helmet beneath his arm, and the majority of his blunt, chiselled features were hidden beneath the rim of the armoured collar of his Mark VIII armour. The pale furrows of old scars rose across his scalp from his cheek, a reminder of a previous conflict with the scuttling hordes of the hive mind.

'How long do we have, brother?' Tigurius asked, without preamble.

'There are still a few hundred left in the avenue. They're beginning to panic,' Ricimer said. He hefted his helmet and set it over his head, locking it in place with a hiss of pneumatic seals. 'We need to buy time, so the crew can finish getting them aboard.'

'Suggestions?'

'Offhand, I'd suggest shooting the tyranids,' Ricimer said. 'I've taken the liberty of ordering Metellus and the others to fall back. Stormravens are already en route. As soon as the last human is aboard and the transports are away, we can leave as well. We just need to hold until then.'

'And can we?' Tigurius asked.

'Emperor willing,' Ricimer said. He glanced at the shattered gates that marked the entrance to the avenue. 'Ten of us can hold that entry point, if they come in force. Less, if Metellus and Oriches get back here with the heavy flamers.' He turned and pointed through the gates, towards the avenue. 'Three possible strongpoints there, there and there, giving overlapping fields of fire for the gateway, allowing for withdrawal. Two more potential strongpoints at the avenue's mid-point. Even factoring in heavy losses, a fighting withdrawal should be possible.'

Tigurius smiled. Ricimer had his faults, but a lack of tactical acumen was not one of them. 'I'll defer to you then, brother. Arrange our withdrawal as you see fit.' The vox crackled again, loudly, in his ear. A garbled voice floundered in a wash of interference and then fell silent. The sound of bolter fire echoed up from the hab-block.

Ricimer cocked his head. 'Geta... report,' he said, hesitating. 'Metellus, Oriches, sound off.' Voices crackled over the vox, and Tigurius turned to see one of the combat squads hurrying towards them. 'Metellus,' Ricimer said.

'There's Oriches,' Tigurius said, gesturing with his staff. The second of the three squads came into view, firing behind them as they moved. One of the Space Marines, clutching the bulky shape of a heavy bolter, stopped and turned, levelling the weapon at some unseen enemy. The heavy bolter roared, and Tigurius heard the high-pitched cries of dying tyranid beasts.

'They're massing. Something's driving them forward again,' Oriches shouted, as he climbed the steps. His armour, as well as that of his men, was scorched and scored by blistering venom and alien claws. 'It's big, whatever it is.'

'One of the command-caste, perhaps,' Ricimer said.

'No,' Tigurius said. The echo of the scream was still in his head like an ache. 'It's something else. I can feel it.' He looked out into the dark. 'Geta?' he asked, looking up at Ricimer. Ricimer said nothing. He stared out into the ruins of the block. Tigurius could tell from the sudden flickering of his aura that the other Ultramarine was concerned. Geta should have fallen back with the others. If he hadn't, that meant his squad had engaged the enemy. The sound of bolter fire ratcheted through the still air.

Tigurius looked at Ricimer. 'Fall back into the space

port, as planned. If I have not returned by the time of extraction, you are to follow standing orders. Evacuate and turn this planet to ashes from orbit.'

'Where are you going?' Ricimer asked.

'I shall meet the enemy in the field, as is my right and privilege,' Tigurius said. 'Someone must remind them that the sons of Guilliman are not a meal that agrees with them.' *And I want to know what that was that I felt,* he thought. If the hive fleets had given birth to some new monstrosity, he wanted to know about it and test its might if possible. Knowledge was power.

'One of us should come with you,' Ricimer said.

'Geta will serve in that capacity,' Tigurius said, over his shoulder. 'When you see us, know that the enemy will not be far behind.'

'I don't need to be Chief Librarian to know that, brother,' Ricimer called.

Tigurius chuckled, but didn't reply. He moved quickly, gathering his strength as he did so. Something, some flicker of foresight, told him he would need it. He broke into a run, sprinting into the labyrinthine confines of the hab-block. He trusted in his senses, physical and otherwise, to lead him to Geta and the others.

As he continued on, the sound of bolter fire grew steadily louder, drawing closer. Geta and his brothers were hard-pressed, Tigurius suspected. Then, if what he'd felt were any indication, they might soon be a good deal worse than that. He'd never felt such raw power, not from any alien psyker he'd ever encountered. He hurtled along a broad avenue, moving smoothly, until a flash of movement caught his attention. He smelled the acrid tang of fear, mingled with blood, as he slid to a stop.

A group of ragged figures stumbled out of a side-street. He raised his staff, then lowered it as two of his battle-brothers came into view just behind them. He recognised them both – Valens and Appius – as members of Geta's squad.

'Chief Librarian,' Valens said, smashing a fist against his chestplate in a hasty salute.

Several of the humans wore the battle-tattered remnants of the uniform of the local defence forces. The rest were clad in Administratum robes. All were wounded, some worse than others. They looked at Tigurius dully, exhausted and drained of emotion.

'We found them holed up in a signatorium,' Valens said. 'We almost missed them, but one of them managed to signal us.' He gestured back the way they had come. 'Geta and Castus stayed behind, to give us time to get the humans clear. The enemy were right behind us – swarms of them, 'gaunts and more besides.'

'Forgive me, brother, but I am more concerned about what might be behind the chaff,' Tigurius said. He could feel something coming closer, like the rumble of distant thunder. He tapped Valens on the shoulder-plate with his staff. 'I need you to follow your orders. Go. I will find the others.'

Valens hesitated. 'But...'

Tigurius reeled as a sudden flare of pain seared his mind. The humans screamed and staggered, one falling to the ground, her eyes rolling to the whites, and blood pouring from her nose and mouth. Valens and Appius felt it as well, the former shaking his head like a stunned bovid. 'What in Guilliman's name...?' he croaked.

Tigurius didn't reply. A bolter roared close by, and he

saw Geta stumble out into view from the same side-street that Valens and the others had come from, shoving another battle-brother ahead of him. Their armour was scorched black where the bare ceramite wasn't showing, and it was wreathed in smoke. As the wounded Space Marine stumbled, Geta whirled about, his bolter rising. Something pale and radiating a sickly luminescence stretched out towards him. The wriggling ectoplasmic tendrils briefly fluttered over the Space Marine's head. His helmet burst asunder in a welter of blood, bone and brain matter.

Tigurius's eyes widened as Geta's body sank to its knees, and slowly toppled over, covering the form of his wounded brother.

'Castus,' Valens began, starting forward. Tigurius caught his arm. He could feel a cold scrabbling at the edges of his mind, as if something were trying to pry back his thoughts, in the wake of that searing scream. Whatever had killed Geta was more dangerous than any mind-beast he'd encountered before.

'I'll go. Withdraw, get the humans to safety,' he said.

Valens hesitated, but only for the briefest of moments. Then he and Appius were moving swiftly, following orders, falling in around the small group of bedraggled soldiers and civilians. Quickly, the Ultramarines scooped up those humans who were too injured to walk by themselves, or bent so that the latter could climb onto their backs. Valens held a small child cradled to his chest, the girl's mother clinging to his neck. Tigurius felt a flicker of pride at the sight. *Let them bestride the galaxy like the gods of old, sheltering mankind from destruction at the hands of an uncaring universe,* he thought. A line from the Codex Astartes, and a good one.

That was what it meant to be a Space Marine. That was what it meant to bear the colours of the Chapter into war. Theirs was not merely to bring death to the enemies of mankind, but to preserve life, where they could. They were the shield, as well as the sword, of humanity, and Tigurius did not intend to falter in that duty. *Emperor guide my hand,* he thought, letting his mind reach out towards the distant, flickering star that was the holy Astronomican.

As he did so, however, he recoiled in disgust. An intrusive, creeping miasma spread across his thoughts, plucking at his senses. It felt like acid splashed on flesh, and he staggered, his hand flying to his head. Pain flooded his nerves, and he fought to regain control of himself. It was worse even than the scream had been. He turned, teeth gritted, and saw Geta's killer stride into sight.

It was a centaur of sorts, moving forward on four thick limbs, but possessing a barrel torso, topped by a heavy, pulsing braincase and two long, deadly looking talons. Cruel spikes rose from its segmented carapace, and the squirming meat of its mind pulsed wetly, filling the air with a diseased radiance. The world turned soft around it, and he could feel the terrible weight of its regard as it turned its eyeless skull towards him. Its fang-studded jaws champed eagerly as it stalked towards him.

Tigurius did not recognise the beast, but he knew what it was, regardless. It was all the horror and fear that flowed in the wake of the hive fleets made manifest, and its servants bounded past it, screeching in predatory anticipation.

Tigurius tore his eyes from the larger creature and sent

a killing thought smashing into the scuttling hormagaunts. Even as they died, he wrenched his gaze back to
the thing that had killed Geta. Whatever it was, it would
die, as easily as all the rest. He sent a bolt of shimmering psychic force thundering towards it.

The sixfold mind-nodes which clustered on its skull
flexed unpleasantly, and the bolt washed harmlessly
across the shimmering barrier that had suddenly formed
about the beast. Tigurius stepped back, readying another
bolt, but his enemy was quick to take advantage of his
moment of hesitation.

Its jaws opened soundlessly, as energy speared from its
sightless cranium. The psychic scream carved through
his defences, obliterating the sutras that guarded his
thoughts from the vast, alien mindscape that pressed
down on his psyche. His skull felt as if it were swelling
within the envelope of his flesh, and he clutched at his
head. Streamers of vibrant agony ran up and down his
spine, and he could taste blood and bile. The alien mind
bore down on him, like a wrestler pressing an opponent
to the ground. He sank down beneath its pressure until
one knee touched the ground.

Tigurius drove the end of his staff into the broken pavement, as if it might anchor him in place. His
thoughts clung to the intricate designs, finding strength
in the millennia-old patterns. He had found it beneath
the Great Bastion on Andraxas, and it was said, by the
artificer-scribes of Corinth, that the staff might once have
belonged to Malcador the Sigillite, First Lord of Terra.
Sometimes, in moments of great stress, moments like
this, he thought he could hear the rasp of a voice out
of antiquity. A ghost of a memory of the man who had

once fought to defend the Imperium, even as Tigurius himself now did.

He focused on that dry, rustling murmur, and strove to block out the pain that sought to drown his mind. He reached up and clamped his free hand around the staff. Grasping it in both hands, he hauled himself to his feet.

The creature loped towards him, its four legs pumping like pistons. Its great talons swept out, and he only narrowly dodged aside. He rolled away, drawing his bolt pistol as he came to his feet, and fired. The tyranid shrieked as bilious ichor spurted from its flesh. It turned swiftly, and the tip of one talon scored a line across his chestplate, sending bits of ancient parchment fluttering to the ground. He fired again, ignoring the growing ache in his head, trusting in his mental shields to hold against the creature as its mind-nodes pulsed. That trust, however, was in vain. Smoke boiled from the circuitry that lined the interior of his psychic hood as its synaptic connectors burned out one by one.

Tigurius staggered. His staff and bolt pistol slipped from numb fingers. The creature hissed and slunk around him. He could feel it prying at the gates of his mind, scrabbling about in the shadows of his consciousness. His limbs felt heavy and awkward, and he sank down once more, borne under by the enormity of its will. The world gave a spasm, like a faulty pict-feed. He smelled rancid meat, and heard a riotous murmur that overwhelmed his thoughts, smashing them aside. He felt heat, and hunger... a terrible hunger.

That hunger tore through Tigurius, smashing aside his certainties and assurances, his confidence and surety, in a way it had never done before. All of it, all of his training, his skill, his power as Chief Librarian, was as nothing before that inhuman ache, and he realised with a growing horror that he had never truly faced the hive mind before – that this hunger was a roaring inferno compared to the flickering spark he had touched previously.

It was a hunger such as a fire might feel, enormous and unending. A hunger which would never know appeasement and would never abate, not even when the last sun had flickered and died, leaving the galaxy a cold, barren void at last. Even then, the hunger would not end, even then the hive mind would hunt, feeding on itself until, at last, the surviving shard of its intelligence withered and starved, alone in the dark and quiet.

But before that, it would feed on every world. It would batten on every star, and strip every system and sector of life. The Imperium would fall to it. There would be no salvation, no last minute reprieve. The murmurs grew in volume, and he clutched uselessly at his head, trying to block them out.

As Tigurius fought, trying to shutter the gates of his mind, scraps of sound and memory burned across the horizon of his thoughts. He saw flickering images, as if he were seeing through the eyes of the hive mind as it spread out to consume Ultima Segmentum. He heard the slow scrape of the monster's claws as it advanced towards him, across the street. But he could not rise to confront it, could not stifle the images which overwhelmed his mind with thoughts and memories not his own.

They were flashes only, brief moments of time, crystallised and vivid.

He saw Sisters of Battle fighting back-to-back with Militarum Tempestus Scions as a tidal wave of chitin and

talons loomed over them, ready to sweep them aside.
He felt their fear and pain as the image burst like a bubble, parting to reveal a Terminator, clad in the crimson
heraldry of the Blood Angels Chapter, grappling with a
multi-limbed broodlord in the burning ruins of an Imperial palace. As the broodlord swiped its cruel claws across
his brother Space Marine's chestplate, Tigurius clutched
at his own chest, feeling the pain of the blow as if he'd
taken it himself.

His mind reeled as the scene wavered and tore, revealing the sleek void-craft of the eldar, locked in battle with
a swarm of flying horrors birthed by the hive fleet. He
felt the ground tremble beneath him as the beast drew
closer. The alien stink of it was thick in his nostrils, but
he could not focus, could not even see it.

The images came faster and faster, overwhelming him
with their intensity. Some small part of his mind knew
that the creature was using them to batter him, to weaken
him, even as Tigurius himself had used his powers so
many times to weaken the tyranid swarms – to make
them easy prey. His head felt full to bursting. He saw a
warrior of the Grey Knights, trapped between the gib-
bering filth of the warp and a horde of hormagaunts.
Even as the Grey Knight moved to confront his foes, the
image came apart like sand in the tide, and suddenly,
Tigurius was caught in stultifying darkness. He saw green
lights, and heard the squeal of ancient machinery coming to life, but too late. The steel-limbed necron warriors
awoke from the slumber of ages as the tyranids flooded
the tomb, smashing the automata down as they rose.

He smelled and tasted blood. Blood Angels and Flesh
Tearers fought against overwhelming hordes beneath

a red star, and he felt their rage and madness as if it were his own. It threatened to overwhelm him, and he cried out. The image shattered and he was smashed to the ground by a heavy blow. Another blow caught him across the back and he felt his armour rupture. He rolled over with a groan, mind sluggish, body barely responding. Hoses popped and seals burst in his armour as its weight settled on him, driving his wounded back against the street.

Its featureless skull loomed over him as he struggled uselessly against it. Blossoms of ectoplasm sprouted on its head, unfurling and growing, becoming tendrils like the ones which had been the cause of Geta's death. The tendrils quivered, and then stiffened and shot towards him. Something cold touched him and darkness invaded him. It was stronger than the scream, impossible to resist.

His thoughts were ground under the relentless clamour of an alien intelligence far older and crueller than he had ever suspected – this intelligence was nothing like the others; the Leviathan was stronger than the Behemoth, and more dangerous than the Kraken. Worse, he'd been wrong. There was a mind there, amidst the hunger, a true mind, a fierce self-awareness that put the torch to every assumption and scrap of knowledge about the tyranids that he'd possessed.

And that mind hated him. It wanted vengeance. It wanted him. For the first time, Varro Tigurius felt the first stirrings of fear. Such a thing could not be defeated. His will was as nothing next to that of the hive mind. It would devour him, and then Kantipur, and after that, the sub-sector. It could not be stopped. Even Holy Terra would fall.

No!

Even as the thought filled his mind, he refused it. Terra would not – *could* not – fall. He focused, looking past the horror that held him, and up into the darkness beyond it. He could still hear the voice of the staff, even though it was out of reach. It whispered to him and he closed his eyes, trying to focus on it rather than the horror reaching out to engulf him. He could feel the heat and light of the Astronomican, he could hear its song, swelling in his mind, dimly at first, and then more loudly.

Tigurius reached out, even as he drowned in that cold, hungry darkness, and felt the light of the Emperor's grace, just at the tips of his fingers. Was it the same light that Malcador had felt, the day he took the Emperor's place on the Golden Throne? Had the Sigillite felt the light of the Astronomican on him, the day he'd sacrificed his life for the good of the Imperium? The whispers grew in strength, filling his mind, driving out doubt and hesitation. Malcador had died for the Imperium – could he do any less?

He grabbed hold of the light with all of his strength, and sent it pulsing outward, against the dark. There was a scream, like that of a startled animal, as the shadow in the warp met the blinding light of humanity's guiding star, and then the weight was gone and he could breathe again. His eyes popped open and he saw the xenos monster stumble away, shaking its head. Greasy smoke rose from its brain-case, and could smell the stench of rancid, burning meat. He lunged to his feet.

Acting on instinct, he snatched up his bolt pistol and flung himself at the monster. He caught hold of its carapace and swung himself up. It heaved, trying to buck him off, but to no avail. He shoved the barrel of his bolt pistol against the meat of its mind, and emptied the clip. The great body convulsed, and it took a faltering step. Then, with a sibilant whine, it toppled, slamming into the street hard enough to crack the pavement. Tigurius rolled clear.

He came to his feet and retrieved his staff. As his fingers tightened about it, he spun and extended it towards the twitching hulk, ready for it to spring to life once more. Thankfully, it did not. It sagged, and the acidic bile that passed for its blood began to eat its way free of the armoured shell.

Weary, his mind awash in pain, Tigurius turned towards Geta's body. He could hear the sound of tyranids scuttling in the dark, and knew that they would come again, and again and again, until Kantipur was theirs. They knew neither defeat nor victory, only hunger. And when this world had fallen, they would hurtle into the void, in search of another. Unless they were stopped, once and for all. Emperor willing, Tigurius would be there when it was accomplished. Even if it meant his death.

But for now, his fight was done, and it was time to leave. He dragged Geta's body up, and slung it awkwardly over his shoulder. He would not let the hive fleet have it.

The other Ultramarine, Castus, groaned. Tigurius bent low and hooked his arm. 'Up, brother,' Tigurius said, dragging Castus to his feet. 'It is time to go. Kantipur is lost. But there are worlds yet that might be saved.'

TORIAS TELION:
EYE OF VENGEANCE

GRAHAM McNEILL

Macragge City's coast sweated under a bone-white sky and a sun like a heated bronze disc. It wasn't Quintarn hot, which was something to be thankful for, but it wasn't far off.

Torias Telion nodded to Sergeant Kaetan, and they pulled a chromed ammo case from the back of the Cargo-6 parked next to the two idling Thunderhawks on the Evanestus platforms.

'Careful now,' said Telion as they carried the heavy crate into the gunship. 'These are custom-made stalker shells.'

'I'm not one of your bloody neophytes,' snapped Kaetan, nodding towards the squad of Scouts seated along the fuselage. 'And this isn't the first time I've loaded a Thunderhawk.'

'These are delicate, precision-made kill rounds that don't take kindly to your rough handling,' said Telion as they set it down in a recessed stowage bay in the deck.

Kaetan's fingers moved in Scout sign.

'Careful,' grinned Telion as they went back for the last crate. 'Language like that and I could cite you for conduct unbecoming.'

The platforms were thick with shouting voices, machine noise and hot fumes. Orbit-capable ships came and went in rigorously controlled schedules, and the backwash of atmospheric jets filled the air with light and noise. A pair of translifters from the Helion demi-plate were one platform over, offloading a host of blinking pilgrims. Other ships were spread further afield, bringing yet more pilgrims, workers and hopeful aspirants to Macragge.

Armed provosts in blue frock-coats escorted them all, guides and security combined. They would see them to the culmination of their pilgrimage at the Temple of Correction. Some pilgrims carried sling bags filled with their few worldly possessions, but most arrived on Macragge with nothing but the clothes on their back.

'Loading a gunship yourself, Telion?' asked Captain Fabian, standing at the ramp of a Third Company Thunderhawk. '*Accipiter* won't wait for us.'

Just the sort of thing a captain would say to an officer inferior to him in rank, but whose depth of experience far outweighed his own. Telion's eyes met Kaetan's and the younger sergeant looked away to hide his smirk.

'Get them to do it and let's be on our way,' said Fabian, gesturing to the brutish servitors, with their over-muscled torsos and piston-augmented limbs.

'If it's all the same, sir, I'd rather not trust my load-out to their clumsy hands.'

'I won't be delayed because you're getting all precious

about your ammo,' said Fabian. 'Get it loaded and get airborne.'

Telion nodded as the assault ramp of Fabian's gunship lifted with a pneumatic whine. Its engines spooled up to launch power. Kaetan opened his mouth to say something, but Telion beat him to it.

'Don't say a word,' Telion warned Kaetan. 'He's still a captain, and we're both sergeants.'

Kaetan nodded and they turned back to the Cargo-6. Telion took hold of the last crate, but paused as something caught his eye from the opposite platform. Something out of place.

Around six hundred pilgrims were in the process of being formed up for the long march towards the gates of the Servian Wall and into the mountains.

'You heard the captain,' said Kaetan, when Telion didn't lift. 'Let's get this on board.'

Telion stared at the people on the opposite platform. The pilgrims' faces were filled with wonderment at the sight of Ultramar's heart, staring up at the glittering might of the Fortress of Hera, the crenellated majesty of the Castrum, the Senatorial Halls and the great relic of the Residency. Telion's eye fixed on one man in particular.

Shaven head, narrow features. Borderline malnourished.

Nothing unusual for someone who'd travelled a mendicant's path to Macragge, but something about him raised Telion's hackles. He followed the man's eye-line.

Telion snapped his fingers and made the Scout sign for *enemy sighted*.

Kaetan's body language changed instantly.

Where?

North. One hundred metres, shaven head.

Acquired.

Telion eased his way around Cargo-6, lifting his Stalker from the running board and silently working a round into the chamber. He kept the vehicle between him and the pilgrim, never once losing line of sight.

Kaetan moved in the opposite direction.

Target threat?

'He's spent the last year or so in pilgrimage,' said Telion, activating his sub-vocal vox-bead. 'He's just arrived on Macragge, but *doesn't* look up at the Fortress of Hera? No, he's looking for someone.'

'Who?'

Telion scanned the platform.

'Him,' he said, spotting a man dressed in the oil-stained overalls of a stevedore. He was moving against the crowd towards the pilgrim, a heavy kitbag over his shoulder.

Two potential targets. No time to request backup.

'Lock him,' said Telion.

'Done,' said Kaetan. 'Risky shots.'

Telion shook his head. 'No shots at all. Could be wrong.'

Kaetan looked at him in askance.

'Since when?'

Kaetan was right. Telion's instincts were almost never wrong, but he wasn't about to shoot a potentially innocent man without being sure he was dangerous.

'They're closing,' said Kaetan, as Fabian's Thunderhawk lifted into the air on a screaming column of jetwash.

The stevedore put down his kitbag and two men came together, embracing like long lost friends. Telion saw the pilgrim pass something to the stevedore. Something metallic from beneath his robes. A piece of machinery?

A weapon? A relic of the Pilgrim Trail brought to Macragge for an old friend?

It was just about credible that the two men knew one another, but Telion doubted it. They moved like soldiers. Again, nothing unusual in Ultramar, where every civilian received training.

The stevedore bent to his kitbag. The pilgrim's face shone.

Telion's heart sank. He'd seen this before: the joyous release of tension, a job almost finished, the shimmer sweat of zealots.

No, not zealots.

Martyrs.

The pieces fell into place. Bloodborn posing as pilgrims, bringing a disassembled weapon to the surface, piece by piece so as not to trigger the chem-auspex or rad-counters.

And this was the last piece.

'Drop them,' he said, bringing his bolter to his shoulder.

Kaetan's pistol was on target a heartbeat later.

Telion centred the curve of the pilgrim's scalp in the scope and squeezed the trigger. The bolt carved a valley through the top of his skull without exploding. A kill shot, but one aimed high enough to not detonate the mass-reactive warhead and harm innocent people nearby.

The second man fell with Kaetan's pistol round ripping his arm off at the shoulder. Screams of panic erupted from the pilgrims, who scattered from the epicentre of the bolter impacts.

Provosts yelled at people to move. Defence Auxilia at muster points ran to the source of the shooting.

Telion saw the stevedore slumped over his kitbag. Half his side was missing from the torso up to his shoulder. A crudely assembled device sat exposed in the kitbag, all crudely-wrapped wiring and improvised components. The stevedore's other hand held a primitive trigger mechanism.

Telion fired again, putting a round through the man's wrist and sending his hand flying.

He and Kaetan ran over to the two dead men, weapons scanning for threats as yelling provosts corralled the pilgrims back aboard their vessels.

Telion knelt beside the kitbag. He'd built enough battlefield explosives in his time behind enemy lines to recognise what he was seeing.

'Tactical atomic,' said Kaetan.

Telion nodded. Something didn't feel right.

'This won't be the only one,' he said.

A second later, he was proved right as a blinding flash threw Telion's shadow out before him. He shielded his eyes and turned to see a miniature mushroom cloud of detonation claw its way into the horizon.

'One of the littoral platforms,' said Kaetan. 'Socus?'

'Too far,' said Telion. 'It's Lysis Macar.'

The rumbling blast wave billowed over the coastline, but the saw-toothed peaks of the Evanestus peninsula directed most of it out to sea. The ground shook and the fire of the expanding cloud rolled in on itself to spread dark tendrils of smoke in all directions.

'Damn,' said Kaetan, looking out to sea.

Captain Fabian's Thunderhawk plunged towards the ocean, its engines trailing smoke and flames.

'E-mag pulse,' said Telion. 'Must have blown out its avionics and engine controls.'

The Thunderhawk slammed down into the ocean, and came apart in an explosion of debris. Nor was it alone. A transloader fell out of the sky, its pilots helpless to keep it in the air as every machine aboard was overloaded and blown out by the devastating pulse. Dozens more aircraft were spinning down to the sea.

Warning sirens blew from the Servian Wall and multi-spectral lightning flared overhead as citywide voids were lit. Alert aircraft scrambled airborne from blast-hardened shelters.

Macro-cannon batteries unmasked and every aircraft currently still flying was warned off and directed out to sea.

'What is this?' asked Kaetan. 'A precursor to another attack? An invasion?'

'No,' said Telion, making safe his bolter. 'This is just spite. This is the Bloodborn showing us that even though we beat them, they can still hurt us.'

KNIGHT OF TALASSAR

STEVE LYONS

It seemed, at first, as if one of the stars had exploded.

A blue light flared above the all-too-close horizon, and a rumble like thunder shuddered through the moon's thin atmosphere.

Kenjari was on his way to the mine when it happened. It was early in the morning, although day and night were just divisions on a chrono face here. He stood with a pickaxe slung uselessly over his shoulder, a rebreather clamped to his face, his feet rooted to the barren ground as something – something huge and dark and oddly symmetrical – came hurtling out of the sky towards him.

It was only when his workmates panicked and ran that he thought to do the same. He wasn't ready to die; at least, not this way.

Kenjari was meant to die in the service of the Emperor, his body but not his spirit broken by the effort of hewing materials from the ground: vital metals to be forge into weapons and armour and vehicles for the Emperor's glorious armies.

His days of life had been numbered since his transfer to this remote facility.

The truth was that few men ever saw out their two-year postings here. The moon's atmosphere was toxic, even inside the billet huts since half the oxygen scrubbers had broken down. Almost as many miners were killed by minor rebreather failures as they were by tunnel collapses or simple exhaustion.

Every time he woke up on his lumpy mattress, Kenjari checked that his facemask was in place and wondered if this new morning would be his last.

After twenty months of wondering, he had just begun to feel, to hope, that he might be one of the lucky few. He had begun to think he might even see his home and his children on Agides Primus again.

Kenjari was a worker, not a soldier. He had always imagined that death would steal up on him slowly, through the shadows of a blocked mine tunnel or across the filthy floor of a medicae hut. Not this way. *Not this way!*

He hadn't run like this in twenty years. His lungs, clogged with rock dust as they were, reacted violently to the sudden demand placed upon them, and Kenjari coughed up a mouthful of phlegm and stumbled badly. Another bright blue flash cast his shadow, long and thin, across the small, raised landing pad ahead of him and, instinctively, foolishly, he turned his head to look.

The plummeting object blotted out the stars now; it wasn't a ship as he had briefly imagined – it was bigger, far bigger than any ship – nor was it a meteorite, it was clearly a man-made structure. It was something the likes of which he had never seen before, something that made no sense to his fear-addled brain.

It was wreathed in half-formed energy tendrils, clawing at its sides as if they were straining to hold it back. They didn't succeed. It crashed through the towering pit head and splintered its plasteel struts like matchsticks. The winding wheel was completely demolished, stranding hundreds of miners underground.

The leading edge of the object – or perhaps just one of its tendrils – hit the ground and filled Kenjari's head with a sound like every piece of metal in the world being tortured; and a cloud of dust and debris, the size of a hab-block and equally as impenetrable, crashed over him like a tidal wave.

He couldn't see his workmates, his friends, around him any longer or the ground beneath his feet. He knew that running was futile; still, he ran for as long as he could manage, until he stumbled again and finally fell. Then he lay on his stomach with his hands clasped over his head and a desperate appeal for the Emperor's mercy straining to escape his choked throat.

It was some time before he dared open his eyes again, before he realised that the all-pervading noise around him had given way to a silence that rang almost as loudly in his ears. His silent prayers must have been heard and he was alive. He was coated in rock dust; it sloughed from him as, gingerly, he tested each of his limbs in turn, relieved to find no broken bones. He discovered a body, half-buried, alongside him. Its head had been pulverised by a substantial hunk of debris, leaving him no means of identifying it. He had been lucky, that was all. Had his blind flight carried him an inch to the left or the right, he would likely have died too. He *should* have died.

Kenjari scrambled to his feet. A black cloud of terror hung over him, but for now shock was keeping it at arm's length and he only felt numb. The workers' billet huts had been shredded, their remnants strewn across the jagged landscape. The same fate had befallen the dark, tubular towers of the smelting plant. He couldn't tell where he was standing, which way he was facing, because every landmark to which he had become accustomed had been razed.

Only one thing, one structure, reached above the surface now. It nestled, lopsidedly, in a crater of its own making, impossibly intact although sections of its walls had fallen and black wisps of smoke curled lazily upwards from its bowels. Kenjari thought about the miners in the tunnels beneath it. He knew they must have been crushed; the black cloud descended closer towards him.

In that moment, he felt death stealing up on him through the shadows and he thought, for the first time, that he would rather not have seen it coming. *I should have died like the others*, he thought. *That would have been the true mercy.*

Kenjari was a worker, not a soldier. He had always expected it would be his work that killed him. He had never imagined anything like this.

He hadn't expected – of all things – a castle to fall out of the sky on top of him.

CHAPTER I

As usual, Captain Sicarius was the first to emerge from the Thunderhawk.

He stepped off the forward ramp onto earth that was cold and unyielding, even to his considerable armoured weight. He glanced up at strange patterns of stars, freckling the black sky. The captain wondered – as he had during every mission in the scant years since his rise to that rank – how many battle-brothers he would lose here.

They poured out of the transport ship behind him: thirty of the Emperor's finest, resplendent in blue power armour with gold and white trappings, the U-symbol of their Chapter emblazoned upon their left shoulders. They had donned their helmets, forewarned that the air was poisonous, so the only way to tell them apart was by their battle honours.

More gunships – Thunderhawks and Stormravens – were in the process of landing beside them, easing themselves down onto cushions of noxious exhaust gases. They disgorged the remainder of the Ultramarines strikeforce onto this, their latest battlefield. At the same time, more Thunderhawks – modified to carry vehicles in place of passengers – swooped in to deposit their cargos of Predator Destructor and Vindicator tanks.

The operation was executed with the utmost efficiency. Where, a few minutes earlier, this low plateau had been devoid of any life – or of anything that life may have created – now it teemed with proud blue juggernauts, and not a moment too soon, as the captain quickly apprehended.

His auto-senses picked up the dull cracks of shell fire, even over the aircraft engines, before he could get his bearings. He stepped to the plateau's edge and looked over a virtual labyrinth of trenches and foxholes. He could make out figures scurrying through those trenches: the soldiers of the Astra Militarum – a Death Korps of Krieg regiment, he recalled – whose reports had brought him to this tiny, unnamed moon.

His gaze, however, strayed beyond them – to the object of the Ultramarines' mission here. The horizon was closer than Sicarius was accustomed to, no more than three kilometres ahead of him to the east. Squatting there upon it, like some ancient, mythical monster, was the *Indestructible*.

It was the size of a small city, but had the look of a cathedral with its gothic spires and towers and covered walkways. It was a multi-layered, stepped structure, symmetrical, with four arms extending from the diamond-shaped basilica at its centre. It had once, evidently, been a burnished gold in colour, but its walls were soot-blackened, flaking and beginning to crumble.

It was a Ramilies-class star fort: a giant mobile base of operations assembled in the Imperium's own forges. It shouldn't have been here. It should have been out in space somewhere, proudly standing sentry over one of the Emperor's worlds; not crippled and stranded like this, held captive by the inexorable force of gravity.

The Ramilies was its own arsenal. Its towers bristled with gun emplacements, while torpedo tubes glowered warningly through its outer walls. Its cavernous launch bays could each easily contain a cruiser or multiple flights of smaller ships.

Four aircraft were rising from one of those launch bays now, from the Ramilies's far quadrant. Like the fort itself, they had seen better days – though possibly not much better. They were crudely constructed, with heavy guns grafted haphazardly onto their patched-together hulls. They looked too ungainly to fly, yet fly they did, as if keeping themselves in the air by sheer obduracy alone.

Ork technology; there was no mistaking it.

The shells that Sicarius had heard had been fired by the Guardsmen in the trenches, shot from Earthshaker cannons. The Earthshakers were siege guns, slow to reload and cumbersome to aim; they were built for breaking through walls, not for bringing down aerial combatants. So far, they had failed to score a direct hit on any of their four targets, only buffeting them with explosive blast waves.

One of the ork craft was thrown into a clumsy barrel roll, careening away from the rest of its flight. As Sicarius watched, however – against all odds, against all sense – its pilot managed to wrestle it back under control. All four ships were sweeping over the trenches, he realised, without deigning to return their occupants' fire. They were bearing down on the plateau on which he stood.

He bellowed an order to the Space Marines behind him: 'Scatter!'

The first ork craft roared over Sicarius's head, its bomb bay doors yawning open. Three rocket-shaped casings dropped out of its belly, one by one. Forewarned, the majority of Sicarius's brothers leapt out of harm's way; their vehicles, however, were virtual sitting ducks.

The first bomb smacked into the prow of a Predator Destructor, its gunner barely managing to duck back into his turret before it struck. The ensuing explosion lifted the vehicle off its tracks and set its engine ablaze, forcing its crew to evacuate.

The remaining two bombs took longer to choose their targets, and Sicarius realised that they had some form of guiding intelligence. One of them swooped low over the roof of the disabled Predator, and then began to climb again. It streaked towards a bright blue Thunderhawk which had been coming in to land; two Vindicator tanks were attached to the ship's underside, dangling helplessly.

Fortunately for their crews – not to mention the Thunderhawk's pilot – the bomb's controller had overreached itself. Its limited propulsion unit sputtered out and it faltered a good way short of its objective. It spiralled back to earth, some half a kilometre away, where it burst harmlessly.

'Let them come,' a familiar voice bellowed, defiantly. 'I will not cower from any stinking greenskins. Let them try to shift me from this spot.'

Brother Ultracius had not sought cover like the others.

He had been an Ultramarines sergeant once – but now, he was a walking tank himself, what little remained of his physical form interred inside a Dreadnought casing.

Standing at almost twice the height of his brothers, he had made himself an irresistible target. As the third and final bomb came around and dived towards him, Ultracius let rip at it with his massive twin-linked heavy bolter: a prodigious weapon that jutted from his right elbow in place of a forearm.

The bomb flew unerringly through a hail of bolt-rounds towards him, close enough to Sicarius now for him to see that machine-spirits didn't drive it as he had expected. It had a pilot: a gretchin, a member of a stunted orkoid subspecies. It was shorter – much shorter – and punier than a typical ork; still, it couldn't have fit easily into the bomb's casing, not unless its legs had been amputated.

Its squat body was hunched over a tiny control stick, its pointed ears trembling with malevolent laughter.

One of Ultracius's bolts had found its mark, and the guided bomb exploded barely a metre in front of the aquila symbol on the Dreadnought's chassis. A fraction of a second later and it would have hit him squarely, cracking even his armour plating. As it was, he weathered the blast, though it forced him onto his back foot and almost made his knee joints buckle.

The gretchin pilot perished in flames.

Less than three seconds had passed since the bombs had dropped.

In that time, however, the vox-net had exploded with urgent chatter. The pilots of the grounded Thunderhawks were hauling them back into the air; while those still carrying tanks and other vital equipment were flying evasive manoeuvres, looking for a chance to set down their heavy burdens.

The second and third ork bombers, delayed by the Earthshakers' covering fire, were intercepted before they could reach the plateau. One of them was crippled almost instantly, holed by an explosive punch from a Thunderhawk's battle cannon; the other craft put up a better fight. Its hull may have seemed less than aerodynamic, but it was tough enough to shrug off a fusillade from four twin-linked heavy bolters.

The bomber fought back. Its pilot was a fully-grown ork, looking somewhat out of place behind a glacis, a pair of goggles perched ridiculously on its green snout. Its primary weapons were a pair of automatic ballistic guns slung underneath its wings. Like most ork 'shootas', they were noisier than they were accurate.

In a one-on-one dogfight, the clumsy ork craft was probably outmatched. That didn't mean it wasn't a threat, however.

The fourth bomber – the one the Earthshaker cannons had sent into a spin – was finally coming up on the plateau; while the first – the one that had made one bombing run already – was coming around to make another. They found that the Ultramarines had three more gunships in the air, waiting for them.

We should have set down further behind the lines, Sicarius thought. His eagerness for battle and inexperience of command had made him incautious. He blamed himself, but, stuck on the ground as he was now, there wasn't much he could do to put things right. He could only watch as the opposing flights circled each other, spitting at each other venomously.

'The Emperor is with you,' he encouraged his pilots by vox, but resisted the urge to bellow instructions at them. They knew what they had to do and how to do it. They wouldn't have been sitting in those cockpits if their instincts weren't as finely honed as they could be.

He ordered his tanks to advance, separating as they did. They were moving targets now, grinding their way down the broad, winding trails that led to the plateau's base; still, moving all the same. In addition, the Stormravens had closed ranks to keep their enemies at bay, and were beginning to drive them back.

Nevertheless, one of the bombers opened its bay to eject two guided casings, but their intended targets were beyond their limited range. They detonated on the ground, and claimed no casualties other than their own hapless occupants.

Another ork bomber was fatally holed and sent screaming, nose over tail, out of Sicarius's sight. A moment later, a fiery cloud blossomed over the horizon to the north, reassuring him that the threat had been dealt with. In its turn a Stormraven gunship had also been damaged, smoke belching out of one of its engines; the pilot, however, sounded confident that he could make an emergency landing.

Sicarius stepped off the edge of the plateau. The drop was short enough for his armour to completely absorb the impact of his landing. He voxed his battle-brothers: 'Form up on me.' The first of the tanks was already pulling up behind him, while the situation in the sky seemed to be under control.

Then, a pilot's voice rasped urgently through his earpiece: 'The last ork, captain – it's coming right at you...

gambling everything on a suicide dive...' He could hear the rattling of patched-together engines growing in volume above him.

Sicarius wasn't worried. Three Stormravens had already dropped onto the bomber's tail, with their lascannons flaring. It wouldn't get close to him.

The inevitable explosion, when it came, made it seem as if a new sun was blazing in the sky, turning night into day for just a moment. The light glinted off blue ceramite and plasteel, and cast the shadows of a hundred armoured warriors and their powerful engines ahead of them. It was in that light that the Ultramarines strike-force began their march across the small moon's barren surface; a spectacle that would surely have caused their enemies to quail, had any of them only seen it.

The Ultramarines were marching to war.

CHAPTER II

A knot of figures emerged from the trenches to meet them.

They were wrapped from neck to boots in thick black greatcoats; their shoulder flashes revealed them to be members of the 319th Krieg Regiment of the Imperial Guard. Sergeant Lucien had never met a Krieg Korpsman before, but others had spoken highly of their courage and commitment.

Like the Ultramarines, they didn't show their faces. Thick rubber tubes snaked from the gasmasks they wore to rebreather units in battered leather casings slung from their webbing. The only features of the masks were pairs of opaque, round lenses, which gave the wearers a blank-eyed, expressionless look.

The masks were crowned by steel helmets, stamped with the image of the Imperial aquila; all but for one of them, who wore a commissar's peaked cap. It was he who headed the welcoming committee: a barrel-chested man with a long, assured stride. Marching a step behind him was a shorter, wirier figure, who wore a captain's rank insignia but, unusually, displayed no medals or other decorations.

The Krieg captain halted and saluted smartly, and Sicarius returned the gesture. The commissar began to extend a hand towards him, noticed the size of the Space Marine's gauntlets and thought again. He introduced himself as Dast, but named none of the rest of his party. Even the captain he identified only by his rank.

Dast, with his captain, led the way down a flight of shallow steps, chiselled out of the hard ground. Only Sicarius and his command squad, which included Lucien as the captain's second-in-command, followed them. They left the bulk of the strikeforce behind with their vehicles to await further orders.

Ultracius was left behind too. The trenches were a tight enough squeeze for an ordinary Space Marine, so the Dreadnought would have struggled to negotiate them.

The remaining members of the squad included the captain's standard bearer, his Apothecary and the Company Champion. They were joined by a Techmarine called Renius. While a loyal battle-brother, in some ways he seemed to stand apart from the other Ultramarines, in power armour the rust-red of the Adeptus Mechanicus.

Some recent rain had left the trenches spotted with puddles of water: stagnant, foul-smelling and, according to Lucien's auto-senses, mildly acidic. Improvised walkways of corrugated metal sheets spanned the largest of the trenches; more than one snapped, however, as the Ultramarines trampled over it.

Passing a Termite burrowing vehicle, parked in a small, muddy enclosure of its own, they could hear the Death Korps' guns still firing ahead of them, but the sound of aircraft engines had faded away.

Commissar Dast had noticed it too, his eyes searching the sky to confirm the evidence of his ears. 'I thought you might have kept the Thunderhawks on station,' he said over his shoulder as they walked. 'We could certainly use them.'

Sicarius's only response was a grunt of acknowledgement. 'I, ah, feel I must apologise for the reception you encountered,' Dast persevered. He was slightly in awe of the armoured giants behind him – in Lucien's experience men always were – though the commissar hid it better than most. 'Before today, we had only seen two ork fighter-bombers, and we thought we had crippled one of them.'

'It isn't like the orks to hold back resources,' said Renius.

'No,' agreed Sicarius, thoughtfully. 'Not like most greenskins.'

'We know they're in there,' said Dast, 'inside the star fort. They've made a few bombing runs, sent out the occasional raiding party, but they haven't attacked us en masse. We know they have a leader, a warboss, by the name of Khargask.'

Lucien clenched his teeth. The name was familiar to him.

'Obviously, he over-reacted when you arrived,' said Dast, 'and hoped to destroy the equipment you were bringing with you. Otherwise, for the most part, he has been sitting tight behind his shields and ramparts. The orks we have encountered, we believe, have slipped out against his orders.'

'You've been briefed on the *Indestructible* itself?' asked Sicarius.

'We know about the, ah, incident,' said Dast.

'The Imperial Navy would like its property back – intact, if that is at all possible.'

Dast looked at Sicarius as if surprised, though it was difficult to tell with his face covered. 'You do know the *Indestructible* is ancient? Thousands of years old. It had been damaged and was under repair apart when Khargask took it – and as we have seen, he couldn't keep it aloft for long.'

'I have my orders,' said Sicarius.

The commissar nodded his acceptance.

'Well, fortunately, perhaps,' he reported, 'the *Indestructible* still lives up to its name. We've been bombarding it for weeks, but–'

The Krieg captain interrupted him, speaking for the first time. His voice was low and husky, muffled by his facemask. 'But no structure is impregnable,' he growled.

'There is another matter that concerns us,' ventured Dast.

At that moment, however, they reached the sunken entranceway to a dugout. The Krieg captain disappeared through it, followed by his aides. Dast paused, eyeing up his armoured guests. 'Unfortunately, space is, ah, severely limited down here.'

Sicarius nodded. He asked Renius to join him inside the dugout, the others to wait outside. Lucien couldn't help but feel a little slighted. He hadn't yet been given the opportunity to earn the Knight of Talassar's trust and, at this rate, he never would.

Even Dast had to duck to fit through the square

opening, so the two Space Marines were forced to bend almost double, but the claw arm on the Techmarine's servo-harness still caught on a support beam and almost tore it down.

Lucien decided to take a tour of the earthworks. It behoved him to learn about the resources available here, and the men alongside whom he would be fighting. The latter he began to encounter almost immediately.

Following the sounds of shelling, he found his path teeming with Krieg Guardsmen in their hundreds, like industrious ants scuttling around a giant nest. Many of them carried digging equipment and were busy extending the already-expansive trench network. They moved aside for Lucien to pass, but always returned to their work as soon as he had. They never spoke to him.

The Earthshakers, he discerned, had been placed as far apart as possible, the better to protect them from enemy bombs. He made for the nearest emplacement. The trench he was following eventually opened up into a large, square pit. There were four Korpsmen here: two of them stood on the cannon's firing platform, behind its plasteel shield, while two more handed them shells from a pyramid-shaped stack.

The gun itself was anchored to an X-form base, with four broad feet stretching to the pit's four corners. It was broader than the passageways that led here, and so must have been lowered into its current position.

The long barrel was set at a thirty-degree angle, peering over the emplacement's edge. When Lucien lifted his head, he could see the towers of the Ramilies-class star fort, far closer and looming even larger now than before. He could also see tangles of razor wire, with several bloodied ork corpses caught up in it.

'When was the last attack?' he asked.

One of the Krieg men answered him, even as he hefted another shell up to his comrades on the platform. 'It happened sixteen hours ago, my lord. An ork mob came at us across no-man's-land. Most of them were slowed by the wire, enough for our lasguns to put them down before they could reach us.'

'And the rest?'

'The captain ordered a bayonet charge.'

Lucien was surprised. 'You went over the top? Why didn't you use the cannons? If the greenskins were struggling with the wire, they'd have made easy targets. You could have simply blasted them to shreds.'

No trace of emotion inflected the Krieg man's voice as he answered, 'Artillery shells are valuable.'

Lucien had heard that Krieg men never showed emotion. He had heard that they never removed their masks in front of outsiders, even where the atmosphere was breathable. He was starting to believe it.

This Krieg man was an officer, he realised. His coat was spattered with dry mud, which had obscured his stripes. This one – just like his captain, earlier – seemed especially deferential.

'How many casualties, lieutenant?' asked Lucien. He had encountered some orks in his time that were almost – not quite – a match for a Space Marine. They could probably have snapped a Death Korpsman's fragile neck with one flex of their clumsy fingers, especially when worked into a frenzy.

'Eighty-three Korpsmen were expended in the battle,'

the lieutenant answered, 'but the threat of the orks was neutralised, so those lives were worthwhile.'

Lucien found the man's attitude unusually pragmatic for a human.

One of the Krieg men on the platform had loaded the Earthshaker. The other sighted along its long barrel – though it would have been hard for him to miss his massive target – and fired. The recoil made the Earthshaker judder fiercely, but its heavy feet kept it in position.

Lucien followed the shell with his eyes as it hurtled across the black sky like a comet. Almost six seconds passed before it struck one of the star fort's towers; their size had made them seem closer than they were. There was a fierce, though distant, eruption of light and sound. However, when the smoke of the explosion cleared, the tower showed no signs of damage.

The star fort had prodigious shields, of course, reinforcing its robust construction. A concentrated bombardment might have broken through both, in time – shield generators could eventually be overloaded – but it wouldn't happen quickly.

No structure is impregnable.

Three more shells streaked over no-man's-land, from different parts of the trench network. The Krieg officer had already gone back to work, helping the rest of his crew to reload their weapon, regardless of his rank. How long had they been going through these motions, Lucien wondered? *Weeks,* the commissar had said, and yet still they performed their duties patiently, efficiently, like automata.

A more pressing question was why their enemies were taking it? Orks, quite literally, thrived on constant battle.

If they were hunkering down in their shielded bunker, ignoring the cannons that threatened to blast its walls asunder, then that had to be for a reason. A Ramilies-class star fort had powerful weapons too, and vast ammunition stores, so why weren't they returning fire?

Or was it simply that their leader was smarter than the typical ork? He had taken the *Indestructible*, after all, and dealt the Imperium a major embarrassment in the process. Did he have some cunning, longer-term scheme in mind?

For that matter, why had Khargask come to the Agides System? It contained no worlds of any particular value. And why was the Adeptus Mechanicus so keen to recover his plunder, anyway?

Lucien wished he could have attended the meeting in the dugout. He knew it was not his place to question; he would do as he was ordered, he didn't have to know the reason. He couldn't help but wonder, all the same, what he and his battle-brothers – perhaps even Sicarius himself – had not been told about their latest mission.

What exactly was happening inside the *Indestructible* – and what made it so important to the orks and to the Imperium alike?

CHAPTER III

The dugout contained no more than a few sticks of furniture.

The Krieg men folded up canvas chairs to give their visitors room to stand. Sicarius squeezed himself into one corner of the underground chamber. His helmet scraped the ceiling, causing dirt to rain on his neck and shoulders.

A collapsible table was strewn with data-slates containing tactical maps of their surroundings – onto which the Krieg trenches had been stencilled like contour lines. There were also old-fashioned paper maps, chipped and yellowing despite their plastek coatings, bearing detailed but faded schematics of the Ramilies-class star forts. These included internal layouts; though, given the age of the *Indestructible*, they were unlikely to be especially accurate.

A smaller, rickety trestle table supported a holo-projector, which one of the Krieg captain's aides had just activated. A translucent shape flared brightly an inch or so above the big table: the *Indestructible* – the upper part of it, at least, the part that could be seen from inside the trenches – picked out in beads of light.

There was something wrong with the hololith, however; it was shot through with purple and green flares, distorting the picture. Sicarius's eyes narrowed as he realised what he was looking at: a vid rather than a still image; the flares were a part of the recording, not a glitch as he had assumed.

'We recorded this six days ago,' explained Dast, 'but we witnessed the phenomenon three times before that and once more since. As near as we can tell, the flares are being generated by the star fort itself. At first, we thought they were the product of some weapon, but they're simply too random, unfocused.'

A weapon under construction, perhaps, Sicarius thought, *one that the orks have not yet perfected, but when they do...* He turned to the Techmarine to see if he had anything to say, but Renius was keeping his own counsel.

'The flare-ups, when they come, are accompanied by an unholy racket,' the commissar continued. 'It rises from the bowels of the earth, like the groaning of tortured machine-spirits. We lack the equipment to capture that sound, unfortunately, and our tech-priests, frankly, can't explain it.'

'How long do these episodes last?' Sicarius asked.

'No more than twenty seconds, or sometimes less, before the flares – and the sounds – die down again,' the commissar told him.

'We have an ork prisoner,' the Krieg captain spoke up. 'It was part of a mob that attacked us a couple of weeks ago,' said Dast. 'It made it all the way into the trenches before we finally put it down. It has certain, ah, augmentations that might bear closer scrutiny. I thought, perhaps, with the resources available to you, you might wish to–'

'Let me see this creature,' said Sicarius.

Dast led the way back out of the dugout, round several tight corners in quick succession and then some way along a northward-running trench.

Sicarius's standard bearer fell into step behind him. The rest of his command squad had found ways to make themselves useful: mostly routine maintenance work to their armour and weapons or praying. Sicarius kept Renius close to him.

They negotiated one more turn then, four strides to the east, they reached a small, open-topped enclosure, guarded by two Korpsmen. The prisoner knelt inside it, almost filling it. It was wrapped in chains, tight enough to prevent it from standing or sitting comfortably, and shackled to four wooden stakes driven into the ground.

It looked like any ork to Sicarius, with its jutting brow, lower-jaw tusks and flat nose, its shoulders broader but its legs stumpier than those of a man. On a second look, however, he saw that its right arm was metallic and that its eyepieces, which he had mistaken for pilot's goggles, were fused into the flesh of its face.

He had heard the ork howling and struggling violently as his party had neared the enclosure. Its chest was scarred with lasgun burns and bayonet wounds, and the lenses of its mechanical eyes had been shattered. It had been tortured.

The ork spat at its two armoured visitors – evidently, it could see them well enough – and bellowed angrily at them in its ugly native tongue. Among the unfamiliar words, Sicarius made out the name 'Khargask'.

'The prisoner was also in possession of a weapon, captain,' Dast volunteered. 'Quite unlike any we have seen before. It–'

Renius interrupted him. 'Ork bionics are nothing new. This merely confirms what we suspected.'

'That Khargask is no ordinary warboss,' Sicarius agreed, 'but rather what the greenskins call a "big mek" or a "mek boss".' He explained for the benefit of the Krieg men, who may have lacked his Chapter's extensive knowledge of the subject: 'Orks seem to have an instinct for making things, but that's all it is: an instinct. Few of them have the intellect to actually know what they're doing.'

'It's unusual for a more intelligent ork to gain power,' said Renius, 'in a culture that values strength and savagery above all else, but it can happen.'

'If the ork is smart *and* strong and savage,' Sicarius muttered.

'This brute here is not smart. If it were, it would have reined in its primitive bloodlust and remained inside the *Indestructible* as it was told. I doubt we will learn anything useful by studying it – or its equipment.'

'I assume we have no one who can speak its language?' said Sicarius.

'Even if we had,' said Renius, 'it's unlikely that Khargask would have taken it into his confidence – or that it would have understood him if he had.'

'We tried to find out how many orks are inside the

star fort,' explained Dast, 'but as you say, there is a language barrier. It also seems that the prisoner can count no higher than five, maybe, so, ah...'

'The ork is no use to us, captain,' insisted Renius. 'We should execute it and be done with it.'

He was probably right. It struck Sicarius, however, that he had been too keen to speak up, to see the captive ork dead, to preclude any possible further investigations. The thought – and its likely implications – rankled with him. He was sorely tempted to gainsay the Techmarine, if only to gauge his reaction.

He decided to bide his time. He gave a grunt of assent, then turned smartly and marched away. Renius followed him gladly.

Behind them, the Krieg captain issued an order to one of his sentries. They heard the distinctive crack of a lasgun being fired, followed by another bellow of injured rage, a fierce rattling of chains and the sound of at least one heavy wooden stake being shattered.

It took another two las-beams to penetrate the prisoner's dense hide and silence it at last. The Krieg captain had taken the Ultramarine's suggestion as an order. He hadn't questioned it, hadn't tried to advance an opinion of his own despite his greater experience here.

Renius was silent again as they made their way back to the command dugout. Sicarius opened a private vox-channel to the Dreadnought.

'You were right,' he told Ultracius. 'I only suspected it before, but now I'm certain. The Techmarine is keeping something from us.'

* * *

In the dugout, Sicarius studied the data-slates and ancient papers more closely, but they told him little that he hadn't already known.

'This moon was a mining colony, yes?' he barked. 'I need a plan of the mine tunnels.' The Krieg captain immediately despatched an aide to fetch one.

'Ah, most of the tunnels in this sector collapsed,' Commissar Dast pointed out, apologetically, 'when the *Indestructible* landed on top of them.'

Sicarius nodded curtly. 'Of course they did. It's a miracle the star fort itself wasn't disintegrated upon impact, shields or no shields.'

He threw a pointed glance at Renius, who didn't take the bait. 'Are the Ramilies' guns operational?' asked the Techmarine.

'Most of them,' said Dast, 'but Khargask employs them sparingly: a few warning shots when we venture too close to him, that's all.'

'He's conserving ammunition,' Sicarius deduced, 'the same as with the fighter-bombers. He didn't plan on getting into trouble out here. He didn't plan on his star fort falling out of the sky. His stores are probably depleted and he has no supply lines. He isn't trying to win this battle, just prolong it long enough for... what?'

'For reinforcements to arrive,' Dast suggested.

'Perhaps, yes. It would have required a fleet of tug ships to drag the Ramilies through the warp to this system, more than can be hiding in its bays. What happened to the rest of them? You've found no other crash sites?'

The commissar confirmed that they had not.

'Do we keep up the shelling, captain?' the Krieg captain asked.

'And step it up,' Sicarius confirmed. 'I will add my personnel and armour – my Predator and Vindicator tanks – to your own. We will concentrate our attack upon the most damaged quadrant, here.' He tapped a piece of paper. 'Once the shields are down, however, and the ramparts have been breached, we hold our fire.'

The basilica was the Ramilies' heart, he thought. So long as that remained relatively undamaged, then the Adeptus Mechanicus ought to be satisfied.

Renius spoke up: 'Captain. It is possible that, when Khargask sees he is beaten, he might destroy the Ramilies himself rather than allow it to be recaptured.'

'I had thought of that,' said Sicarius.

The Krieg captain's aide had returned with another data-slate, which the Ultramarine took from him. The slate seemed fragile in his massive gauntleted hand, and he held it carefully. 'The bombardment will serve primarily as a distraction. There are hundreds, perhaps thousands of pairs of eyes inside the *Indestructible* – I want them looking this way. If we can tempt a few more orks out here, all the better. Otherwise, I want them defending the ramparts, manning their weapon emplacements, anything to keep them busy.'

He plugged the data-slate into the interface jacks on his right gauntlet and loaded its contents into his armour. 'In the meantime, I will lead a combat squad through the mine tunnels – yes, commissar, what remains of them – and attack the *Indestructible* from below.'

'Permission to join that squad, captain,' Renius requested immediately.

Sicarius said nothing, only nodded. 'The star fort's base will have taken the brunt of the crash,' he continued aloud. 'If we're lucky, it might already have been holed. Either way, that's where it will be most vulnerable. With the Emperor's grace, we can climb up right inside the basilica itself.'

'We have tried that, captain,' Dast cautioned. 'We used a Termite to bypass the blocked tunnels, but the green-skins heard us coming and were ready for us. They laid ambushes for us underground. They set traps for us. We couldn't get through their defences, couldn't even get close to our objective.'

'We lost close to two hundred soldiers in the attempt,' the Krieg captain mumbled. His tone was rueful.

Sicarius smiled grimly beneath his helmet. So, there *was* a route through the mine tunnels to the star fort, he thought; the orks' presence down there proved it. 'With all due respect, captain, commissar,' he said, 'you sent two hundred men into those tunnels – Imperial Guards-men, perhaps, but just ordinary men all the same.

'Five veteran Ultramarines are a different matter.'

CHAPTER IV

Kenjari bent his knees.

He lifted another shell off the pile and onto his shoulder. It was heavy, but no heavier than the loads he was used to lifting. The repetitive nature of the work was also something he was used to, and it gave him some comfort.

He straightened up. He turned and took three steps across the earthen enclosure. He waited for the loader up on the platform to turn towards him. He hefted the shell into his arms and turned away. Three steps took him back to the pile of shells. He bent his knees again. He didn't have to think too hard about what he was doing.

Kenjari heard the blast of the Earthshaker cannon behind him. Once, he had thought he would never get used to that noise, but now he barely noticed it. He thought he might be losing his hearing, for want of ear protectors.

This wasn't too different to working the mines, he told

himself, to swinging his pickaxe at an unyielding wall of rock. Except that, if he dropped one of these shells, it could kill him. *And an accident in the mines couldn't?*

Working the mines had been different.

Kenjari had known how he would likely die, then, and had resigned himself to face it. His future, now, was uncertain and terrifying to him. He had seen the xenos that lived inside the castle – the one that had fallen from the sky – tearing soldiers apart. Others, he had seen cut down by the xenos' guns or shredded by their bombs.

The soldiers were supposed to have rescued him. He remembered the flutter of hope he had felt upon seeing their ships, new stars shooting across the firmament.

He didn't know how long he had survived, waiting for them, waiting for the Emperor to send someone. Days had passed, but he had had no way to count them.

He had taken rebreathers from the broken corpses of his workmates, when the filters in his own had become rotten. He had taken their food and water too, though it hadn't been enough. He had buried himself in the debris of the mine workings, to shelter from the moon's acidic rainstorms.

He had seen them, occasionally: the xenos, green-skinned and heavy-browed, on the ramparts of their fortress. He had kept his head down and hoped not to be seen in return. Sometimes, the xenos had spilled out across the moon, apparently in search of salvage, and he had been forced to hide from them.

They had found a survivor, once. They had dragged him from underneath the wreckage and slaughtered him for sport, making noises that sounded like barks of laughter. Kenjari had told himself it was a mercy; the man was crippled and dehydrated. He felt guilty, all the same, because he might have been able to help him.

He had thought about searching for other survivors like him, but he had lacked the courage. He had stayed in hiding, except for when he needed new filters or when hunger and thirst overwhelmed him. He had kept on waiting.

The ships had vanished over the horizon. They must have landed, but some distance away from the castle. Kenjari had waited another day, perhaps two, for the occupants of the ships to come and find him. Then, he had plucked up the nerve and marshalled the last of his strength to go and look for them.

He couldn't remember what had happened next. He could only surmise that fatigue had finally claimed him and he had collapsed.

He had woken in a hospital tent, with something heavy on his chest and a faceless figure hovering over him like an angel of death.

The figure had been wearing a mask, he had realised; he was wearing one too, in place of his smaller rebreather. The weight on his chest was a mechanical unit, connected to the mask by rubber hoses. Kenjari's cuts had been dressed and his broken shoulder set. God-Emperor be praised, he had been saved!

Less than an hour later, he had had a pickaxe in his hand again.

He had been given a tube of nutrient paste, a mug of water and thirty seconds to ingest both. He had been issued with combat fatigues and a heavy black coat and told to dress in them. A pair of aides had attached flak armour to his shoulders, legs and chest; it was torn and bloodied, leaving no doubt as to the fates of its previous wearers. Heavy belts and holsters and a bulging ruck-sack had been added to his burden. A helmet, too small for him, had been jammed onto his head.

Kenjari had been taken out onto the moon's surface and ordered to dig.

He had been surrounded by hundreds of other men with axes and shovels, doing the same. He hadn't been introduced to any of them and none had spoken to him; few would even meet his gaze. They were intent upon their work. With their eyes, their faces, shrouded, they hardly seemed human. He was dressed the same as they were, he had realised; he must have seemed as inhu-man to them.

His new co-workers were nothing if not efficient. They had soon dug a trench, a metre and a half deep and sev-eral kilometres wide, out of the obdurate black ground. Dropping down into it they had begun to extend tunnels from it, leading eastward towards the xenos' castle. He was inching his way back towards the one place he had been desperate to avoid.

Kenjari hadn't known that his helmet contained a comm-bead until a voice sounded in his ear, informing him that his work shift was over. He followed the others' lead, waiting for someone to take his axe from him before he joined the throng clambering out of the trenches and returning to their campsite.

The voice had spoken again, requiring a Trooper 3117-Delta to report to a Commissar Dast. Kenjari had recalled being given a number and, fumbling for his dog tags, had found it. He had had to ask where Dast could be found, and was pointed towards an eagle-shaped drop ship, one of several on the ground.

Dast had turned the ship's passenger compartment into his temporary quarters and office. He had been the first – and was still the only – soldier here who seemed to have a name; inside his air-conditioned sanctum, he had taken off his mask too.

The commissar had heavy jowls, pasty skin and an unnerving, narrow-eyed stare. He was also possessed of a brusque, impatient manner. He had asked Kenjari his name, age, occupation, height, weight, birthplace and medical history, while an aide tapped his answers into a data-slate.

There were no ships available to take him home, Dast told him. Nor could the Astra Militarum afford to feed a useless mouth. Kenjari had hurried to assure him that he would earn his keep. Dast had nodded, grimly, brought a stamp down hard on top of a sheaf of forms, thrust the forms across his desk towards Kenjari and informed him that now he belonged to the 319th Krieg Siege Regiment.

He was told to report to the quartermaster to be issued with arms and ammunition. Kenjari had felt his throat drying up. He had tried to explain that he hadn't been trained to fight, but Dast had dismissed him sharply. He had stepped out of the drop ship's hatchway in a daze. Suddenly, he was a soldier.

He had grown to hate Dast almost as much as he feared him.

His was a constant, interfering presence in the newly-dug trenches; with the drop ships returned to their orbiting cruiser, he wore his mask at all times, but was recognisable by his broad frame and commissar's cap.

It was the commissar's job to enforce discipline, though it seemed to Kenjari that few of the Krieg men needed it. In contrast, Dast could always find fault with Kenjari's conduct: he wasn't working quickly enough, hadn't cleaned his lasgun thoroughly enough or saluted the commissar smartly enough.

He had threatened to have Kenjari flogged or shot.

Once, Dast had pressed his bolt pistol up against a Guardsman's temple and squeezed the trigger. The safety catch had been on; the commissar had called it a warning. Kenjari had learned later that his victim was another non-Krieg citizen, another Agides miner, one whose name he vaguely recalled. He too had escaped the crash of the xenos castle relatively unscathed, to find himself enlisted.

At last, he had thought, someone he could talk to, someone who might understand.

By the time his shift had ended, however, the other man had faded into a crowd of black greatcoats and blank-eyed masks, and Kenjari couldn't find him again.

He had longed for the sound of conversation, to begin with, if only to break up the monotonous rhythm of the cannons. He had come to appreciate that rhythm, however, and to fear the sounds that disturbed it: the occasional answering crumps from the turrets of the castle; the drones of xenos bombers overhead; or an officer's voice, coldly feeding life-and-death instructions through his earpiece.

Thus far, Kenjari had been lucky. He hadn't been sent over the top of the trenches yet. He hadn't had to draw the gun that sat so uncomfortably at his hip. When the xenos – 'orks', the voices in his earpiece called them – had attacked, he had been left to man his Earthshaker cannon against them from a comfortable distance.

The closest he had come to the sudden, explosive death he so feared had been when a shadow had passed over his head and his failing ears had thrummed with the roar of aircraft engines. He had dived, instinctively, for cover. His sergeant had hauled him to his feet, screaming in his face – Dast hadn't been present, fortunately for him – but Kenjari hadn't been able to hear the reprimand.

The bomb that had been meant for their emplacement exploded on its lip instead, lighting up the sky and showering them with dirt and shrapnel.

Kenjari, still shaken, had been thrust back into work. The Earthshaker had been loaded and its barrel cranked skyward, waiting for the enemy to make another pass.

Instead, the xenos bomber had wheeled around and flown back towards the castle, venting black smoke from an engine pod. It must have been hit by one of the other cannons. Kenjari's heart had been beating like a hammer, and his face had been drenched in cold sweat behind his mask.

An hour later, he had been digging again: not a trench this time, but a pit, a mass grave for those who had been less fortunate than he had; rather, for their bloody, dismembered limbs and mangled heads and torsos.

These past few weeks, he had done a great deal of digging.

This morning, there had been new stars in the sky again: more xenos, he had feared, until he had learned the truth. The newcomers were more servants of the Imperium: Adeptus Astartes, humanity's much-vaunted defenders. He had wondered, briefly, if they would defend him too; if they might be the ones to rescue him, after all.

He had chased the thought away: a foolish dream.

He knew there was no saving him now. Kenjari knew how he would likely die; at least, where his mortal remains would come to rest: in a burial pit like this one, unidentified, un-mourned and indistinguishable from all the others.

His future was becoming more certain to him each day. And yet, still it scared him witless.

CHAPTER V

The tanks advanced on Sergeant Lucien's mark.

His Predator Annihilators and Vindicators separated into two columns, grinding their ways around the north and south ends of the Krieg trenches. Their guns had shorter ranges than the static Earthshakers, but would do more damage to their target when they hit it.

Lucien stood outside the command dugout, reluctant to be confined within it. Inside, the Krieg captain and his commissar pored over a tactical hololith, which was constantly updated by tireless aides as voxed field reports were received.

Lucien only had to raise his head to overlook the trenches, to see two lines of bright blue ceramite and plasteel converging upon their objective; as always, the sight spurred a patriotic fervour in his hearts.

'Sergeant, what is our mission?' a slightly slurred voice

rumbled inside his ear. It was Ultracius, voxing him from the surface.

'We are to take the star fort,' he answered.

'An Imperial star fort?' the Dreadnought queried.

'In ork hands,' Lucien reminded him, patiently. When his body was blasted to pieces, Ultracius had lost some of his brain functions too. His long-term memory had survived intact, and he liked to reminisce about campaigns from many centuries past. More recent events, however, often proved elusive to him.

'Have you been briefed on the ork theft of the star fort?' asked Lucien.

There had been a fleet review in the Ultima Segmentum, so the story went. In the midst of a thousand Imperial Navy ships, the *Indestructible* had had its shields down, conserving power, and the orks had swooped on it.

It was whispered that the star fort shouldn't even have been there. It had been brought out of hiding at the insistence of a vainglorious Lord High Admiral, overriding the objections of the tech-priests to whom it had been assigned. The orks had been searching for the *Indestructible* – for the Emperor knew what reason – and now they had known exactly where to find it.

'They towed it away,' recalled Ultracius with an effort.

The orks had been flying hijacked vessels themselves, and had not been detected until it was far too late. They had boarded the star fort and quickly seized control of it. A protective energy bubble had flared around its ramparts and its crew had ceased to respond to urgent hails. The rest of the fleet had reacted too slowly to what was happening in front of them. They had destroyed a handful of the orks' tugs, but not enough to stop them.

The *Indestructible* had plunged into the warp and was lost.

It had not been seen since that fateful day – until now.

'Orks!' cried Ultracius, as if Lucien hadn't just said so. 'Greenskins hijacked the *Indestructible*.'

'Now we're taking it back,' said Lucien. *Now* I'm *taking it back,* he thought. Sicarius had placed him in command of the operation, at least the above-ground part of it. He had reserved the most dangerous assignment for himself, still eager to make his mark. When the story of this incident was told in future, Lucien would be named in it, although his captain would probably be the story's hero.

That alone, he thought, was reason enough to fight this battle. He didn't have to know anything more. It didn't matter why Khargask wanted the *Indestructible*, nor why the Adeptus Mechanicus wanted it back. It only mattered to him that they did.

More voices were breaking over the vox-net now.

He picked out a report from the battle-brother at the head of the northern armour column; he was closing into weapons range of his looming target.

Lucien told him to start firing as soon as he could, and reminded him to aim for the gun emplacements in the star fort's north-west-facing quadrant.

He watched as the tanks, having bypassed the trenches, began to fan out into two lines in front of them. The *Indestructible*'s guns – according to Techmarine Renius – had a long range; once they were close enough to start shelling the star fort, so would it be able to shell them in return.

The Krieg captain voxed Lucien: 'Let me send my men over the top.'

Lucien scowled. 'Not yet.' What was the man thinking of, he wondered?

A rumble of gunfire swelled from the east, like approaching thunder, almost drowning out the rhythmic crumps of the Earthshaker cannons. Staccato flashes lit the sky like lightning. The orks had fired first, the vox-chatter informed Lucien, the gunners behind their walls succumbing to their own impatience. He ordered his tanks to hold their positions, let their enemies waste as much ammunition as they wished.

For twenty seconds or more, the orks obliged. Then, as the thunder died down, Lucien gave the order, 'Armour, advance and fire at will!'

The tanks advanced, their main guns blazing; within seconds, a smoke cloud had descended over no-man's-land and Lucien could see nothing but hazy, slowly-shifting silhouettes through it. He had to rely on the vox-chatter to tell him what was happening. His tank commanders were reporting strike after strike against the *Indestructible*'s ramparts, but little visible damage being done to them.

In contrast, it didn't seem at all long before the first Vindicator took a direct hit which ripped its roof off. Its crew of three survived, thank the Emperor, but were forced to bail out of their burning vehicle. They found themselves in the heart of a veritable firestorm, caught in the crossfire between two inexorable forces. The Ultramarines power armour would do little to protect them from the shells that were whistling around their ears; nor were there any enemies in range of their handheld weapons. The only thing they could do was run for cover.

'My men should be out there.' It was the Krieg captain's voice again.

'No. I'm holding back our infantry,' said Lucien, 'until the biggest guns have been disabled. Then they might stand a chance of actually making it across that killing field to the enemy. That applies to Imperial Guardsmen and Space Marines alike. Right now, there's nothing they can do out there but die.'

There was the briefest of pauses before the captain said, tonelessly: 'That is what the Death Korps of Krieg does best.'

Lucien wasn't sure he had heard correctly; but then, the captain continued, 'Each shell that a Korpsman intercepts is a shell that doesn't hit one of your tanks – which in turn means the tank can keep on firing. I have many hundreds of men and they are easily replaceable. You have only a handful of tanks and we cannot afford to lose them.'

He couldn't argue with that logic.

Lucien remembered what Captain Sicarius had told him. He only had to keep the orks occupied, he had said, while his combat squad dug their way into the star fort from below. The plan seemed risky to him, though, and he could win the battle on the surface, he was sure of it.

Sicarius couldn't be contacted any longer; but anyway, he had left Lucien in command. Lucien knew that, if he agreed to the Krieg captain's suggestion, let the Korpsmen form a human shield for his artillery, then the casualty rate would be horrendous – but then, wasn't that the Krieg captain's call to make?

And wasn't he also right? Human lives – the lives of Krieg men, especially, from what Lucien had heard tell of them – were the Imperium's most expendable commodity. The *Indestructible*'s value, it seemed, was inestimable.

There were hundreds, maybe thousands, of Imperial Guardsmen on this moon, in addition to the Ultramarines themselves, the Emperor's finest – but they couldn't defeat their enemies, nor even keep them occupied, if they were cowering in holes in the ground.

A Predator commander reported a glancing blow that had cracked his vehicle's armour and crippled its engine. Its weaponry, however, was still functional, which, against a static target, was all that mattered.

A moment later, there was rather better news. Two of the enemy's guns had fallen silent. There was too much smoke for anyone to tell for sure, but the assumption had to be that they were damaged or destroyed.

'Target the guns around them,' Lucien ordered.

The star fort's cannons were well-protected, built into its walls as they were, but that meant they had a limited field of fire. If his tanks could take out enough of them in a row, he thought, then they might create a blind spot on the battlefield through which his infantry could advance with relative impunity.

It was a realistic hope, but regrettably one short-lived.

A new sound, an angry scream, sliced through the other sounds; a new light, blinding, white, turned the fog transparent for an instant. The vox-channels were clogged by a dozen voices, each trying to describe what they had just seen: '–beam of energy–' '–from one of the star fort's towers–' '–cut through the *Imperial Thunder* in a–' '–armour plating just melted like–'

The *Indestructible* had a lance, an ultra-powerful energy weapon.

Of course it did. It had a battery of lances; they were right there on the schematics, it was just that Khargask hadn't seen fit to use them until now. Sicarius had hoped that they had been damaged in the crash, or that they simply devoured more energy than the star fort could currently generate.

Lucien tried to contact the *Imperial Thunder*, but received no reply, only a telltale hiss of static. He counted forty-one seconds – of recharging time? – before a second energy beam lashed out; but, thank the Emperor, this one was off-target and only ploughed a new trench into the ground.

In the meantime, two more of the star fort's main guns had been put out of action.

'We could pull the tanks back,' suggested Dast from inside the command dugout. 'We certainly have the orks' attention. If we regroup at the edge of the lance's range and keep up the Earthshaker bombardment, then I'm sure we can hold it.'

Perhaps, thought Lucien.

'No. Send them forward,' said the Krieg captain. 'The lance is mounted inside the star fort's basilica. The closer they get to it, the harder it will be for the orks to target them – until eventually, the angle becomes impossible.'

He was right. The problem with his plan was that the Imperial tanks would find themselves pinned down, at the mercy of the star fort's cannons, though possibly not for very long. If they could just do a little more damage themselves, thought Lucien, knock out a few more of those emplacements...

It could mean the difference between a frustrating stalemate and a glorious victory – or perhaps, he had to admit to himself, a terrible defeat.

It was the captain's next words that convinced him: 'My men are still at your disposal, Sergeant Lucien.'

He set his jaw grimly and gave the order. 'All Imperial forces, full advance. Krieg infantry to take the vanguard and protect our tanks to the best of their ability. Artillery commanders, don't stop until you reach the star fort's walls and break them down. Ultramarines, bring up the rear, and be ready to board the *Indestructible* as soon as you see an opening. The Emperor is with us and, with his strength in our arms and his fury in our weapons, we can vanquish his enemies today and reclaim what is rightfully His. Courage and honour!'

He could do this, he thought. He could visit vengeance upon the upstart xenos, expunge the Imperium's very public shame – and be the hero of the story, after all.

CHAPTER VI

The orks had blocked the mine tunnel with broken props, razor wire, scraps of rusted machinery – and the badly decaying corpses of Death Korpsmen.

Techmarine Renius had been working on the barricade for almost twenty minutes. A krak grenade would have been quicker, but too noisy for Sicarius's liking. The Termite-made tunnel was too narrow for him to join his Techmarine up front and lend his assistance. He had no option but to sit back and let Renius do his job.

Patience was not one of the captain's virtues, and he chafed at every second of enforced inactivity. He wished he could contact Sergeant Lucien – better still, Brother Ultracius – to ask how their part of the operation was proceeding; but he was probably too deep underground, and, anyway, vox silence was advisable.

Renius wrenched the last stinking body from a wire tangle and passed it up the sloping tunnel to get it out of his way. Sicarius noticed that the Korpsman had been stripped of his body armour and weapons – by the orks or by his own comrades?

There was a sizeable gap in the barricade now, which Renius squeezed through feet first. Sicarius followed him eagerly, and lowered himself into a dusty mine tunnel taller than he was and, thankfully, three times as broad. A chain of lumoglobes was strung from the ceiling, but they were inactive.

The darkness was total, and Sicarius could only see in infrared. The mine tunnel ran north-south. To the north, it ended in a blank rock face, while to the south it had collapsed around a broken support. It was approximately four hundred metres long, with two openings in its eastern wall.

The first opening had caved in too and was completely blocked; the second, according to the Krieg captain's information, might lead them to the *Indestructible*. Sicarius detected a faint current of air between the opening and the one through which he had just emerged, which was a promising sign.

'They ought to have posted a sentry here,' he grumbled. 'If I were Khargask, I would have posted sentries.'

'Perhaps he had none to spare,' Brother Lumic suggested, clambering out of the tunnel wall behind his captain. Like the rest of the Ultramarines, he moved with a stealth and precision that belied his considerable bulk. Still, every scrape of his armour against rock, every contact between his boots and the ground, sounded like a crack of thunder in Sicarius's ears; as had his own.

'There are hundreds of kilometres of mine tunnels,' added Renius, 'and no way for the orks to know where we might enter them. If their leader is as smart as we think he is, he'll have set up tremor sensors to detect any digging or drilling.'

'I would still have had these tunnels patrolled,' said Sicarius, obdurately.

The rest of his team had joined him in the tunnel by now. They numbered five in all: the captain, the Techma-rine and three veteran battle-brothers from his command squad. He wished that Ultracius could have joined them. He missed the Dreadnought's pragmatic counsel, not to mention his heavy bolters and power fist.

He cranked his auto-senses up to maximum sensitiv-ity. He could hear tiny insects crawling in the nicks of the walls, but detected no other signs of life, no body heat or exhaled gases, within his range.

Cautiously, he advanced towards the unblocked tunnel entrance, motioning to his brothers to follow at a discreet distance. The tunnel ran eastward, its mine props intact, for as far as he could see. It was an open invitation.

He looked again. There had to be something else, and now he saw it: a metal thread, a fraction colder than the surrounding air. It was stretched across the width of the tun-nel, forty metres in. He pointed it out to Renius: 'A tripwire.'

The Techmarine ventured forwards and crouched in front of it. He followed the wire with his eyes, to a hidden recess in the northern wall. He reached into the hole and teased out a bundle of crudely-constructed stick bombs, holding them by their handles. He lowered the explo-sives carefully to the ground; only then did his servo-arm crane over his head to snip the wire.

Renius stood up, turned back to Sicarius and nodded.

* * *

Another barrier awaited them, further along the tunnel.

This one wasn't constructed as the last one had been; the tunnel roof had simply collapsed, though whether by accident or design was impossible to tell.

Sicarius's auspex revealed a path through, wide enough for an undersized human being to negotiate – or something wirier. It wasn't nearly wide enough to accommodate an armoured Space Marine – and any attempt to broaden it, Renius warned, would likely only bring more earth down on top of them.

Sicarius consulted his uploaded maps to find a way around. He sent two brothers to scout a pair of likely looking tunnels, while he explored a third. Barely had he taken ten strides along his tunnel when he detected another cave-in ahead of him and was forced to turn back, frustrated.

He heard a flurry of movement behind him, from the tunnel he had just left, then a squeal and a sharp snap of bone. He hurried back, to find the Techmarine and Brother Filion standing over a dead gretchin.

'It came crawling through the blockage, captain,' explained Filion. 'We heard it before it could see us and were waiting when it poked its head out of the dirt.'

They listened, all three of them, but heard no more creatures coming after the first. Still, the presence of just this one confirmed that they were drawing close to their objective – and that this area, at least, *was* patrolled.

'If we're lucky,' said Renius, 'there will only be gretchin down here. The orks will be manning the guns up top as we planned. Still, we cannot allow one gretchin to see us and live. It will scuttle straight back to its masters with word of our approach.'

* * *

Brother Gallo's explorations bore more fruit than the others, thank the Emperor. They marched along an ascending, narrowing tunnel, and soon heard noises ahead of them: the capering and screeching of many more gretchin.

The others held back as Sicarius crept to the tunnel's end. It opened onto a precarious stone ledge: it was a gallery, in fact, with a handrail, which circled and over-looked a large natural cavern.

It looked as if the cavern had been used as a storeroom for mining equipment. However, its roof had partially col-lapsed too, and its occupants were busy digging scraps of metal out from under the wreckage. Presumably, Khar-gask had set them to that task – which made Sicarius wonder, once again, what his objectives were. What was he trying to build?

A single lumoglobe had survived the collapse, hanging from a frayed wire. In its flickering white light, Sicar-ius counted twenty gretchin, scampering sure-footedly across treacherous heaps of debris.

He returned to his battle-brothers and appraised them of his findings. 'We have no choice,' he told them. 'We have to go through them.'

He sent Lumic and Filion out onto the gallery first and had them circle left and right respectively. The gretchin heard them almost immediately, of course, their pointed ears twitching as their oversized nostrils sniffed the air.

By then, however, Sicarius had vaulted the balcony rail.

He landed with an unavoidable clang, though the pair of gretchin he had chosen to use as crash mats soft-ened the sound somewhat. One of them died instantly, crushed by his plummeting weight. The other tried to wriggle out from under him, but Sicarius thrust his gladius through it.

He used the short-bladed weapon rather than the Tempest Blade. The hereditary weapon of his family and symbol of his role as Knight of Talassar was his preferred weapon, but the gladius was better for such close quarter fights. It didn't have the reach of the larger blade, but then it hardly needed it. Five, six, seven gretchin piled eagerly on top of Sicarius, clawing and snapping at him viciously. Some of them hacked and bashed at his armour with primitive knives and clubs. At least the orks hadn't armed them with guns, he thought.

It wasn't these gretchin that worried him.

Others of their kind had been wiser, or just more cowardly. They had seen the other intruders up on the gallery and had known they were outmatched. They had scattered, and several of them had made straight for the exits.

Eight tunnels led away from the cavern in all, at various levels. Sicarius's map had indicated that at least two of them could lead to the star fort. Sure enough, the majority of the gretchin were headed towards those tunnels.

Brother Lumic leapt into their midst, his boltgun drawn. He was too late to stop three of them from reaching a tunnel mouth. He clicked his weapon to full auto and sprayed the gretchin from behind, cutting them down.

The others did as Sicarius had expected they would. They scattered. They leapt behind – and, in some cases, under – mounds of debris, or made for the openings on the opposite side of the cavern. It was this latter group that concerned him the most. If they were left wandering the mine tunnels...

It wasn't an issue. The fleeing gretchin found Brother

Filion in their path, and fully half of them shied away from a confrontation with him. The remaining three tried to bull rush him out of their way and swiftly paid for their mistake.

Sicarius had deliberately been fighting a defensive battle, outnumbered by his attackers but wanting to keep them occupied, letting them imagine that they stood a chance against him. The time for that pretence had ended, as Renius and Brother Gallo dropped into the cavern to each side of him.

The gretchin were quick to see that they were beaten, their rabid jabbering giving way to terrified squeals. They dropped away from Sicarius, but found they had nowhere left to run. He caught one as it tried to scrabble away from him; it squirmed and scratched and spat as he crushed its windpipe with one powerful arm.

His brothers employed their gladii where they could. They slashed and stabbed at their enemies' throats and stomachs, until the air was heavy with the stink of xenos blood. Only once did Renius have to loose off an explosive bolt-round, at a gretchin that had almost managed to slip past him and away.

Barely two minutes after it had begun, the skirmish was over.

It took a little longer for the surviving gretchin to be rooted out of their hiding places in the rubble and efficiently executed, usually by a quick slash of a blade across the throat. Sicarius and Filion did the honours, while their brothers stood guard over the exit tunnels. Sicarius was glad to see that no orks or other creatures had appeared in response to the noise they had made.

At last, his auspex detected no more living beings in

the cavern, other than the five Ultramarines themselves. They collected their enemies' bodies, intending to cover them in case something did eventually pass this way. Renius counted the dead and reported that there were nineteen of them.

'There were twenty,' Sicarius growled.

He double-checked the Techmarine's count, but found no fault with it. Behind his concealing helmet, his face folded into a scowl. 'I saw twenty gretchin here,' he reiterated, knowing that all present would understand the import of his words.

'One of them got away.'

CHAPTER VII

In the end, after long weeks of waiting, the inevitable happened suddenly.

Kenjari heard the order through his earpiece, without fully understanding it; perhaps, rather, without wanting to believe it.

The voice of the Krieg captain had been entirely dispassionate, too much so for a man who was sending other men to their deaths.

He bent his knees. He lifted another shell off the pile and onto his shoulder. He straightened up and turned, and his blood turned to ice-cold water.

His crewmates were climbing down from the Earthshaker platform. His sergeant yelled at him and jabbed him in the side with a bayonet. He almost dropped the shell, trying to place it down. His hands were trembling.

He did what he had to do. He followed his sergeant, although it was the last thing his leaden feet wanted. As they hurried through the trenches, they were joined by tens, scores, hundreds of other Krieg soldiers. They could have been as scared as he was, thought Kenjari, but he doubted it; anyway, if they were, it wouldn't show.

He kept an eye on his sergeant's stripes, knowing that if he lost him he would struggle to locate him again. Conversely, he was sure that if he tried to hide himself, the sergeant – worse still, Commissar Dast – would find him.

His four-man Earthshaker crew were joined by six more to form a squad. The other Korpsmen were forming into groups of ten too, and spreading out along a wide, straight trench. They were at the eastern edge of the trench network, Kenjari realised, as close as they could get to the enemy. Emperor, this was really happening!

A blue-armoured giant was wading through the throng, his shoulders squared, his gauntlets clasped behind his back. His face was masked, like the faces of the Korpsmen, with metal rather than cloth but equally impenetrable. Kenjari had never been this close to a Space Marine before, and was daunted by his palpable presence.

He recalled his brief hope of salvation when the blue ships had arrived; it seemed even more absurd to him now than it had then. When first he had set eyes upon a Krieg Korpsman, he had feared him to be an angel of death. The Adeptus Astartes, however, were often given that nickname too.

Kenjari stood in the trench among the others, their bodies pressing in on him, his nostrils filled with the stench of his own terror. He had drawn his lasgun, following his sergeant's lead, but his hands were so sweaty that he thought it might slip out of them. He had tried his best to keep the weapon maintained and to understand its functions; he prayed it would work for him when he needed it. For what it might be worth.

He strained to hear his sergeant's voice over the crashing of manmade thunder. His eyes were distracted by flashes of man-made lightning. His orders were the same as those of the rest of his squad, the rest of his regiment. The Death Korpsmen of Krieg were to rise up out of their trenches into that raging storm. They were to march on the star fort, the fallen castle, and wrest it back from its usurpers.

It didn't sound like much of a plan to Kenjari.

Not that he had a say in it. It seemed like an eternity before a whistle blew, somewhere, and the sound was taken up and amplified by Krieg officers closer to hand; an eternity, and yet the time passed in a heartbeat.

The men of Krieg surged forwards, almost trampling him in their rush to mount the trench wall. If Kenjari thought he could hang back, though, he was mistaken. His sergeant grabbed the scruff of his neck and dragged him bodily up after him. His gloved hands scrabbled to find purchase on the uneven surface and he almost dropped his gun again. He managed to dig a boot into the side of the wall and lever himself upwards, flopping onto his stomach with his legs dangling behind him. The sounds of shelling seemed suddenly much louder and he didn't want to raise his head, but his sergeant was there again, hauling him to his feet, propelling him onwards.

Kenjari found himself running. He couldn't see where he was going. He was following the soldiers ahead of him through the smoke, spurred on by the soldiers – the identical soldiers – at his heels. He spotted a rank insignia on an epaulet and realised that the captain had sent his officers out here to be slaughtered too. He had seen no sign of Dast in the trench, however.

He trampled over coils of razor wire, already demolished, flattened into the hard earth by the tracks of the Space Marines tanks. A monstrous shape emerged from the haze in front of him, then resolved itself into two smaller, angular shapes: a pair of tanks. One of them was dead, a gutted metal corpse, which the other was using for cover. Its main gun belched out fire and more smoke, and blazed a trail towards the Korpsmen's objective like a route marker.

A moment later, fire blossomed among the soldiers to Kenjari's left and only a little way behind him, close enough that his neck was seared by the blast heat; he could smell their burning flesh. They didn't scream; or if they did, he couldn't hear them over the guns. Were the men of Krieg really so stoic, he wondered dimly, or was it just that they hadn't had time to suffer?

Would he suffer, he wondered, when the fire consumed him too?

He didn't know how far he had to go. He couldn't see the star fort through the smoke, and he had lost all sense of time and distance. He felt as if he might have been running forever and might yet be. The thundering of the shells to every side of him – the Imperial tanks were still firing, despite the risk of striking their allies – had merged into a continuous roar; except that sometimes, his ears picked out a louder, closer explosion than the others and he knew that another ten or twenty or thirty masked soldiers had just been wiped out.

This wasn't at all how he had pictured it in his nightmares. He had thought he would see his death coming.

He had lost sight of his sergeant, after all. The soldiers around him may have been his squad-mates or not, Kenjari couldn't tell. It crossed his mind that he could pretend to stumble or to have been hit by shrapnel, just fall to his stomach and let the others pass over him; but he was afraid they might trample him to death or he might be shot by an officer who saw through his deception, so he kept on running.

Then, to his surprise, he saw it: the star fort, or at least its towers looming over him in menacing silhouette. The sight of it lent strength to his weakening legs and bolstered his straining lungs as, for the first time, he thought he might be one of the fortunate few, the ones that actually made it there.

He focused his thoughts on that goal and followed the Korpsmen's stout example. He willed his feet to fall one after another, his chest to rise and fall as he sucked in iron-tasting filtered air in an almost mechanistic rhythm. He lost heart as the towers seemed to grow no larger in his sights. He had misjudged their distance, he realised, deceived by the sheer scale of the construct and the intervening smoke.

He was all too close to the star fort's guns, however.

The next explosion dazzled him and may have burst an eardrum. Its heat wave knocked Kenjari off his feet, and for an instant he thought it could well have been the one. He was caught, unexpectedly, by the Krieg Korpsmen behind him. They saved him from falling; had they not, he wasn't sure he could have picked himself back up.

He was still dazed, disoriented, when they thrust him forwards again.

No soldiers remained ahead of him to follow, none that

Kenjari could see, just the space where they had been – until he felt the soft wetness of their dismembered bodies underfoot and, looking down, saw their blood spattering his fatigues.

A voice, his sergeant's voice, burst over his comm-bead at that moment, with a bluster of hollow encouragement. 'Almost there,' he insisted, 'less than half a kilometre to go.' A moment later, it was four hundred metres, then three hundred...

He could no longer see the star fort's towers, he was too close to it. Instead, he was beginning to make out more intricate details: arched walkways and battlements and decorative mouldings – and a cannon barrel pointed squarely at him. The blank glare of the barrel transfixed him; he knew he was at its mercy. He could only pray for the greater mercy of the Emperor, if only he had had the breath.

He must have been heard, anyway, because the cannon didn't fire. The Imperial tanks must have knocked it out already. Kenjari had survived. He had made it across the killing field. He was footsore, exhausted and only wanted to collapse into a quivering heap, and yet somehow he had made it.

He had made it – all the way to the place of his nightmares.

At least he would be safe from the castle's remaining guns here, too close to their hidey-holes in the walls for them to get an angle on him. He was still in danger from friendly fire, however, as he realised when a shell burst too close over his head, peppering him with hot shrapnel. For the first time, he began to worry about the other perils ahead of him, the ones he hadn't expected to have to face.

New shapes were forming ahead of him through the smoke, hulking figures with stooped postures and arms hanging down to their knees. Kenjari caught a glimpse of wild eyes beneath a heavy brow and tusks jutting out of a drooling mouth. *The orks*, he thought. The orks were coming out of their castle, pouring over its ramparts to greet the would-be invaders, impatient to engage them in physical combat.

He remembered how he had seen them tearing soldiers apart.

He stumbled to a halt and almost fled, momentarily forgetting how afraid he was of the Korpsmen and their leaders behind him; remembering, before he took his first step, how afraid he had been of the star fort's guns, finding himself paralysed between a choice of violent deaths.

'Trooper 3117-Delta,' his sergeant's voice bellowed. 'You have a weapon. Use it!'

At least, against the orks, he could try to defend himself. His fingers had slipped from his lasgun's trigger guard and he fumbled to find it again.

Many of the Korpsmen around him and behind him had dropped to one knee, bracing the butts of their weapons against their shoulders; so, clumsily, he followed their lead. He located his sights and squinted through them with his right eye, but couldn't keep them steady. He saw a mass of green brutes thundering towards him, bearing down on him, swinging axes and crude chainswords.

One of them wielded a cobbled-together automatic weapon, and was spraying out bullets ahead of itself, indiscriminately. The Death Korpsmen had begun to return fire, and Kenjari's sergeant's voice was screaming in his good ear, urging him to do the same.

He screwed his eyes shut and squeezed his trigger.

CHAPTER VIII

The orks were massing ahead of them.

Sicarius could hear their guttural voices, grunting half-formed words in their own crude language. He understood enough to know that they were gathering for battle. They spoke of intruders in the mine tunnels.

The missing gretchin had found its masters, after all; with that, his hopes of reaching the star fort undetected were finally dashed.

'We have a fight on our hands,' he told his combat squad over their shared vox-channel. He saw no point in keeping radio silence now.

The tunnel they were following was narrow, and they had to proceed in single file. Sicarius took the lead, making no attempt to quiet his ringing footsteps. He could hear orks ahead, waiting out of sight, and could smell their xenos stink.

He detected Khargask's hand in their actions again.

It wasn't the way of these brutes to wait patiently in ambush, and he guessed that some of them would be chafing at their orders, as he would have been himself. He decided to test his theory.

He stopped short of the tunnel's end, activated the Talassarian Tempest Blade's energy field and bellowed one of his Chapter's war cries: 'Courage and honour!'

Two greenskins took the bait.

They tumbled out of hiding, jostling with each other to be the first through the tunnel entrance. The winner stampeded towards Sicarius, with bloodlust in its eyes and a blood-caked axe raised over its head. He had time to snap off a single plasma pistol shot before it reached him. The bolt of superheated energy struck the ork in its shoulder, burning through flesh, and it howled in pain but didn't flinch from him.

As it brought its axe head down, Sicarius ducked under it and parried it with his energy-wreathed blade. The blow was strong, but not as strong as he had expected, perhaps weakened by its wielder's injury. He thrust the axe away from him and plunged his blade sideways into the ork's chest. It coughed up blood and the axe fell from its numbed fingers; still, it managed to shift its falling weight onto him. It yanked at his helmet as if trying to dislodge it or snap his neck, and he couldn't break its grip.

Instead, he lowered his head and thrust himself forwards. Surprised, the ork was lifted off its feet and carried along with him. He slammed it into its comrade, coming up the tunnel behind it, and felt its bones being crushed between them.

The ork let out a half-grunt, half-groan and let go of the

Ultramarine's head. It was still on its feet, albeit with support from the second brute behind it, so he tore its torso open with a double-handed, downward stroke.

He stepped back and loosed off a series of plasma bolts at the second ork. It tried to use its dead comrade as a shield, with limited success. It let the body drop to the ground instead, trampling and tripping over it to get to its tormentor. By the time it stumbled within striking range of Sicarius, the second ork was half-dead itself, and his Tempest Blade finished the job.

Two down, and neither of them had landed a blow on him. These narrow confines gave him a distinct advantage, forcing the orks to engage him one by one despite their greater numbers. Sicarius amplified his voice and yelled along the tunnel again: 'Is that the best you can do? Send me your real fighters. I need a challenge!'

He heard a choked splutter from ahead of him. This time, however, no orks responded to his taunt; they had learned the folly of that. Had he had more time, Sicarius might have tried again. As it was, he had no choice. His enemy wouldn't come to him, so he had to go to them – even if it meant marching into a trap.

He fingered a frag grenade on his belt as he stepped forwards. He thought about rolling it ahead of him: it would scatter the waiting orks, at least, and likely injure a few of them. An explosion, however, could have brought down the roof and cost him more time than he could afford to lose. He couldn't risk it.

Nor, however, would he approach his enemy timorously. Sicarius picked up speed along the tunnel, his pistol levelled, his Tempest Blade ready, knowing that the rest of his combat squad would follow him, intending to burst upon the cowering orks like the Emperor's wrath personified.

He was six steps from the tunnel's end when a gretchin popped up in front of him. With a wide-mouthed cackle, it lobbed a small object his way. His Space Marine reflexes kicked in and he shot the creature before it could duck back out of sight. The thrown object, in the meantime, skipped across the tunnel floor between Sicarius's feet, and he shouted a warning to his battle-brothers behind him: 'Grenade!'

It was a stick bomb, like the ones they had seen before.

There wasn't enough space for the Ultramarines to scatter away from it; chances were, their armour would be proof against it, anyway. The danger, once again, was that it might collapse the tunnel and slow them down, even divide their forces.

There was no time for Sicarius to issue an order. Brother Filion acted on his own initiative. He dropped to his hands and knees on top of the bomb, which bounced into his plastron and burst. He hadn't quite smothered the blast, but he did absorb the brunt of it. The tunnel trembled – as did Filion, though his arms remained locked into position – and sweated dirt, but maintained its integrity.

Sicarius never broke his stride.

He erupted from the tunnel mouth like an oncoming tank, swinging his blade and firing his plasma pistol blindly, a war cry in his throat. As he had expected, he was immediately attacked from both sides. At least six orks piled onto him, battering him with clubs and meaty fists. They weren't prepared for the momentum he had built up, however, and he carried them several steps before they wrestled him to a halt.

The short stretch of ground thus gained by him proved crucial, allowing his brothers space to emerge from the tunnel behind him.

Lumic and Gallo fired up their chainswords and laid into the captain's attackers. He felt them beginning to fall away from him and dislodged another himself, with a hefty punch to its stomach, but was borne to the ground all the same. An axe head slammed into his helmet, making it ring, and his blade was knocked out of his hand.

He jabbed his elbow into an ork's throat, and suddenly only one remained.

He managed to turn the tables on the brute, pinning it beneath one knee. He jammed his pistol into its slavering mouth. Its comrade, the one with the fractured larynx, leapt onto his shoulders, gasping and spluttering incoherently, but couldn't stop him from pulling the trigger.

The ork on his back was trying to throttle him. Sicarius reached over his head and seized it by its brawny forearms. It was strong, but its strength was waning quickly. He managed to lever himself to his feet and propel his opponent backwards, slamming it against a rock wall. He felt its fingers losing their hold on him, and threw the ork over his shoulder. It landed on its back and, thanks to its throat injury, couldn't regain its breath. Sicarius saw his Tempest Blade on the ground and snatched it up. He sliced through the ork's neck, so it wouldn't have to worry about breathing again.

For the first time unencumbered, he took a good look at his surroundings.

He was in another cavern, man-made and smaller than the last one, little more in fact than a confluence of several tunnels. It was heaving with green-skinned orks, many more than had initially leapt on him – but his strategy of punching a hole through their ambush had proven effective. His blue-armoured battle-brothers – and one in red – had ploughed right into their midst and were cutting a bloody swathe through them.

Sicarius could see the *Indestructible*: a part of it, at least. The star fort, he recalled, had extra landing pads and gun towers on its underside, the better to defend itself in its natural environment of space where up and down had no meaning. One of those towers had crashed through the roof of one of the tunnels. In the process, it had been reduced to scrap. Beneath its burnished armour plating, the tower was fashioned from something that looked like stone – a super-dense stone, he had learned from the schematics, mined on one particular world – but this too had been shattered.

There had to be a way up through the wreckage, Sicarius thought, and into the Ramilies itself. His gaze strayed upwards, but alighted upon something else instead: the rounded edge of another large structure, relatively intact, welded to the star fort's hull; something that had not been in the plans.

It's an engine pod, he realised. They were fighting almost directly underneath an engine pod! Was it operational, he wondered? If so, then Khargask only had to fire it, only had to operate a series of control runes somewhere, and Sicarius, the other members of his combat squad and their enemies would all be incinerated.

He wondered why a Ramilies-class star fort – never meant to fly under its own power – had been fitted with an engine in the first place, and by whom? Khargask could have been the culprit, of course; Sicarius, however, suspected otherwise. *There would have to be more of them,* he thought. *There would have to be hundreds of engine pods on the hull to stand a chance of lifting such a colossal mass.*

He needed to talk to Techmarine Renius.

These thoughts – and more – raced through his mind in a second. *A second too long,* the captain chided himself inwardly. His brothers appeared to be getting the better of their enemies, but he knew how suddenly the tides of battle could turn.

He saw an ork wielding a huge but primitive-looking blunderbuss, apparently fashioned from a pair of cannon barrels roped together. It brought the weapon to bear on Brother Lumic, and Sicarius shoulder-charged it, throwing off its aim as it fired.

The ork peppered its own allies with explosive pellets. In its blind fury, it turned its gun around and clubbed Sicarius with the butt. The impact did more damage to the blunderbuss than it did to his power armour. An answering blow from his sword to the greenskin's shoulder drew blood.

There was no turning back now, even had he wanted to.

If that engine should fire, then its superheated exhaust fumes would billow out through the surrounding tunnels. There would be no escaping them; not even an Ultramarine would be able to outrun them. The only safe place from the inferno would be inside the star fort itself – and the only way to reach the star fort was through the orks.

Now, then, more than ever, it was imperative that they won this battle quickly.

And with the Emperor's blessing, thought Sicarius as he plunged into the heart of the melee, *Khargask's attention may just be held elsewhere. He may not have understood that he is facing not flesh-and-blood soldiers this time, but something more deadly, more powerful by far – and we may surprise him yet.*

CHAPTER IX

Dast had left the shelter of the command dugout.

He strode through the trenches purposefully. He had never seen them so devoid of life before. He had already passed three abandoned cannon emplacements.

The captain had dismissed him without argument or question, with barely a glance at him. He had been too busy counting the casualty reports.

As a commissar, he had been trained to be dispassionate. Sometimes, however, a feeling took him by surprise. Right now, he was feeling angry. He was keeping it in check, clenching his fists tightly.

He was looking for Sergeant Lucien. He was surprisingly hard to find, considering his size; he moved more quietly than Dast would have imagined.

At last, he caught a glimpse of shiny blue inside one of the enclosures. He stood in the entranceway and cleared his throat, calling attention to himself.

Lucien was lost in thought, or perhaps he was voxing orders inside his helmet. Dast didn't doubt that his presence had been noted, however. He waited impatiently until the Ultramarine deigned to acknowledge him.

'Sergeant,' he said, crisply. 'I hoped we could talk.' What he had to say, he couldn't broadcast, especially not where the captain could overhear him.

Lucien looked at him. His helmet rendered him expressionless, but Dast was more than used to that. 'The battle is going well,' he rumbled finally, as if that meant there could be nothing more to talk about.

'For your Space Marines, perhaps. My regiment has lost a third of its strength, hundreds of men.' Reports were still coming in from Krieg sergeants and quartermasters at the front, an endless litany of bloodshed in his ear.

'Your soldiers fight with exceptional courage,' said Sergeant Lucien.

'They always do,' said Dast, 'even when they are sent to the slaughter.'

Lucien stepped towards him, but the commissar stood his ground. He had never seen a Space Marine up close before today, and it was hard not to feel small and vulnerable in their presence. However, he refused to be intimidated.

'The Ramilies's generators are failing,' said Lucien. 'Its shields have already collapsed in several key areas. We have silenced most of its guns – and all this was made possible by the sacrifice of the Krieg Korpsmen. Had they not drawn the orks' fire as they did, then our tanks would have been–'

'Your tanks could have bided their time,' insisted Dast. 'Your captain, Sicarius, only asked for a distraction.'

'I saw a chance to do more,' Lucien snapped. '*Your* captain offered me that chance. It was he who offered to send his men out there – I did not ask him. If you have a problem with his decision, you should take it up with him.'

He was right. Dast made himself breathe before he answered.

Before he could, there came a renewed peal of thunder from the east, and the vox-net was flooded with fresh incident reports. The orks had got their big guns working again – a whole battery of them – and shells were raining down around the Imperial forces. *Perhaps,* thought Dast, *the guns were never out of action in the first place, and Khargask lured us into a trap.*

His soldiers, those caught in the open, were being eradicated again, by the phalanx. The spiralling numbers of the dead were reported in a flat tone by the voice of a servitor. It was easy to feel detached about those numbers from a distance. Nor was Dast especially concerned about individual Krieg lives. As the captain had said, dying was his people's sole purpose.

'What would you have me do?' asked Lucien, unexpectedly. 'Summon your Guardsmen back here? Have them run the gauntlet of the Ramilies's guns again?'

'No,' said Dast. 'No, I–'

Lucien clenched a fist. 'This is only a temporary setback. Khargask believes he can outthink us, but an ork is still an ork.'

'The Death Korps of Krieg *are* courageous,' insisted Dast. 'To a man, they are fearless, loyal and highly disciplined.' They were the most disciplined soldiers he had encountered; they hardly needed a commissar. 'Any one of them would surrender his life in a heartbeat, for the smallest advantage.'

'And they can be replaced, in as little as nine

months – or even less, if the rumours I hear about Krieg can be believed.'

Vox-chatter told Dast that more Korpsmen had made it to their goal. They were battling orks in the *Indestructible*'s shadow; once again, it appeared, just a handful had spilled out of their fortress against their leader's orders. The Korpsmen outnumbered them and were faring well against them. It was something.

The Ultramarines Predators and Vindicators were advancing too. They were mercilessly firing at the star fort's active battery. Dast grimaced upon hearing that an artillery shell had fallen short, exploding in the midst of the fighting orks and Guardsmen, decimating both forces.

'At least,' he implored, 'send your Space Marines forwards now. Have them and the Korpsmen scale the ramparts together.' Lucien didn't answer him; Dast didn't know if he was considering his suggestion or not.

He waited a moment, then ventured: 'You undervalue them. I did the same when I first joined a Krieg regiment, but the Death Korps is one of the Imperium's finest assets. Individually, yes, each one of them is expendable, yet that is also their greatest strength. En masse, they can be an unstoppable force.'

'You are not of Krieg yourself?' asked Lucien.

'I've never been there.'

Others had made the same assumption – despite the fact that commissars never served with soldiers from their own planets. Dast only wore his facemask and rebreather when he had to – which, in itself, distinguished him from the rest of his regiment – but then, the Death Korps was often sent to worlds with poisonous atmospheres, worlds like their own. He had begun to notice that, when he was wearing the mask, he found it harder to make his voice heard.

Sometimes, his job was to save the Death Korps of Krieg from themselves.

'If the men of Krieg have a failing,' he said calmly, 'it is that they undervalue themselves too. They will die for you gladly, if you tell them they are dying for a reason, any reason. I am asking you, please, do not abuse that trust – and don't squander the resources you have here. That is all I have to say.'

He was talking to Lucien's broad back. The Ultramarine had turned away from him in mid-sentence. Perhaps his helmet vox had distracted him again, Dast thought; perhaps he had more orders that he needed to issue. A moment later, without turning, Lucien said, 'I must join my battle-brothers up on the surface. It is almost time for us to march on the Ramilies ourselves.'

'Thank you,' said Dast, although he wasn't sure he had anything to thank him for. He hesitated for a second, then turned and walked back towards the command dugout. He had said his piece, as his field report would make perfectly plain. By the end of the day, the 319th Krieg Siege Regiment may well no longer exist, but at least he would have done his duty.

The Krieg captain hardly acknowledged Dast's return, any more than he had acknowledged his departure from the dugout.

Hovering between them, the tactical hololith showed a closer view of the combat zone than it had before. The *Indestructible* was a dark shape on its eastern border; arrayed before this were the survivors of the 319th regiment, each squad represented by a black skull with wings and a helmet. There were far fewer skulls to be seen than when the commissar had left.

The orks were represented by skull symbols too, but theirs were green and malformed with tusks and horns, and there were fewer of them still. A vox-caster crackled and buzzed in one corner, a servitor's hands flickered over the holo-projector's runes and a number of the green skulls blinked out.

The captain spoke over his comm-bead: 'Sergeant Lucien. My men have the orks outside the star fort under control. I can have ten squads disengage and begin to scale the walls.' A rare emotion had crept into his voice: a hint of pride.

A long time passed, it seemed to Dast, before the response came: 'Tell your Korpsmen to deal with the orks and then hold their positions.'

The vox-caster buzzed again, as did his comm-bead, each reporting a new presence on the battlefield. This new information was programmed into the holo-projector, and suddenly there they were: the blue stylised-U symbols that denoted the Ultramarines infantry, heading east, past the almost-static markers of their own armour units. One of them had to be Lucien himself.

The star fort's lance stabbed out of its tower again.

Its interruptions had been decreasing in frequency, as if it was becoming ever more reluctant to recharge. Unfortunately, its blasts were still as potent as ever; already, the first of the blue newcomers had to be removed from the board.

The rest of the Ultramarines kept on going.

When the Death Korps of Krieg had advanced, it had

been in a ragged line of black skull icons, through which the enemy guns had punched hole after hole. The line, each time, had reformed, a little thinner than before but relentless. The Ultramarines blue line, in contrast, was thinner to begin with, but it swept across no-man's-land more rapidly and maintained its integrity throughout.

Within minutes, blue icons were mingling with the black and the green in the star fort's shadow, and the green orks were dying more swiftly than ever. Dast picked out one of the many reports in his ear: a Krieg quarter-master, describing how the Ultramarines Dreadnought had ignited his fist and driven it through an ork's chest, shattering its ribcage and its spine and emerging from its back.

'Sergeant Lucien,' the captain voxed. 'My men are ready to scale the walls.'

'Captain,' Dast protested. 'Might it not be, ah, a wiser strategy to allow the Ultramarines to take point here? Their armour will protect them from anything the orks have to throw at us, and, with their superior firepower, we can take the ramparts in a fraction of the time and likely with a fraction of the casualties.'

The captain fixed him with a blank-eyed look.

Dast decided to appeal to his sense of pride. He knew it existed, well-hidden but surfacing from time to time. 'Why don't we show them what the Death Korps of Krieg can do? Show these self-styled angels that we are capable of more than just lying down and dying for the Emperor, if only we are given the chance.'

He couldn't tell if his words were reaching the captain's ears or not.

At that moment, however, the vox-caster spluttered

again, and Lucien's voice rang out of it. He couldn't have heard the commissar's plea, and was responding to the captain's latest broadcast. 'Agreed,' he said curtly. 'Send your men over the walls, and advise them the Space Marines have operational command.'

The captain nodded and turned away from his commissar, abruptly. After a short pause, Sergeant Lucien spoke again, and Dast had no doubt that this postscript was meant for his ears specifically.

'After all,' he said, 'they are your men, captain. You know how best to utilise them.'

CHAPTER X

Sicarius felt as if he had been fighting for hours, though he knew it hadn't been nearly that long.

The orks in the cavern were tenacious, like any of their kind. They battled on after being dealt mortal blows, their bodies fuelled by rage and a primitive, mindless lust for battle. They had landed a few good blows of their own too.

At one point, Lumic had gone down. His brothers had fought their way to him in time, thank the Emperor, and a chainsword blade had severed his attacker's weapon arm before it could complete a killing stroke.

Sicarius was backed up to the cavern wall, duelling with a massive brute with a head too big for its squat body, teeth like neglected gravestones and breath to match. It had a makeshift chainsword of its own, fashioned from real ork teeth, spitting out black gobbets of promethium as it whirred. The ork's technique needed work, but it

wielded the weapon with more than enough force to
compensate.

His own blade parried each of its clumsy thrusts, but
he quickly tired of being on the defensive. He allowed the
ork's next blow to land on his shoulder, the whirring teeth
chewing into his pauldron. Some teeth were blunted or
snapped clean off their chain; still, the cut was deeper
than Sicarius had expected, nicking his flesh.

He thought about the engine pod, hanging over him
like an executioner's axe, and he pressed the advantage
his feint had bought him. He slashed at his opponent,
once, twice, three times, cutting a series of dark red
trenches into its flesh.

The ork was on the back foot, but still struggling.
'Emperor,' Sicarius cursed, 'how do you convince these
things that they're dead?' No longer pinned, however,
he could now bring his plasma pistol to bear, placing a
shot right through the greenskin's body in an eruption
of blood.

The ork joined its comrades, many of them, in a growing heap of bloodied corpses. There were only three
of them left now, outnumbered by their stronger and
better-armed attackers, two of them wounded but fighting on beyond reason.

This was taking too long.

A new sound echoed between the tunnel walls: a deep,
metallic clunk. Sicarius knew where it must have come
from, and his auto-senses confirmed it. He looked up
at the engine pod in the roof. It hadn't ignited yet but a
second clunk came from somewhere inside it, like the
tolling of a death knell.

'Brother Filion,' the captain yelled, 'we don't need you

here. Climb up inside the star fort. Renius, behind him!' The Techmarine was his most vital squad member on this mission, and had to be saved. Filion would go ahead of him to take the brunt of any more ork ambushes or traps.

He took Filion's place in the melee. Another ork, a walking mass of blasted flesh, had finally lost too much blood to remain standing, so only two remained. At that moment, however, the engine pod emitted a third clunk, which was followed this time by a cough and a puff of acrid, white smoke.

Brother Filion voxed Sicarius: 'I'm inside the gun tower, sir. You were right, I think there's a way up through here, through the debris of the internal bulkheads. It's narrow – but wide enough for an ork to squeeze through, after all.'

Techmarine Renius reported that he was having more difficulty. His servo-harness was a definite problem for him, but it also provided a solution. He could cut or tear his way through any blockage, and thus was making slow but steady progress. Sicarius sent Brother Gallo after him, while he and Brother Lumic squared off against a single ork each. He took the biggest and healthiest-looking brute for himself.

The engine pod was spluttering and coughing up more smoke, denser clouds of it, while sparks were beginning to dance around its mouth. The engine was struggling to fire, there could be no doubt of it. Sicarius was alive thanks only to its decrepit state – and any second could bring an abrupt end to his reprieve.

Lumic despatched his wounded opponent with ease and, with the same blade stroke, cleaved into the last remaining greenskin's back. Sicarius bundled his battle-brother ahead of him, towards the gun tower. A bright bolt of energy discharged itself from the engine pod, striking the ground between Sicarius's feet. He followed Lumic through a gash in the star fort's outer wall and began to haul himself upwards, away from the threat, through twisted hunks of stone and metal.

His ankle snagged on something.

Looking down, Sicarius realised that a massive green fist had closed around it. He saw a snarling green face glaring up at him, and recognised the brute with the ork-tooth chainsword, the one he thought he had slain. It was screaming something, but he couldn't make it out because the engine's spluttering had turned into an unrestrained roar. The ork was trying to drag him back down into the tunnels; it didn't have the strength, but then nor could he seem to shake it loose. He wanted to stamp on its crooked gravestone teeth, but his free foot was wedged into a crevice, while his pistol was pinned to his side.

The ork *was* dead, it just hadn't accepted it yet; not while it could still drag its killer down into the inferno behind it.

Superheated exhaust smoke billowed up the inside of the gun tower.

Sicarius saw the ork's flesh stripped from its bones. Its face was little more than a leering skull when he lost sight of it; still, its eyes glared up at him, full of hatred, as intractable as its death grip on his foot. Alarms began to screech and wail and blink inside his helmet, detecting intolerable temperatures without.

He pulled for all he was worth, and finally tore himself free of the clinging fingers. He felt as if his every nerve was afire, but he couldn't allow himself to succumb to the pain. He scrambled for handholds above him, straining every muscle and fibre bundle in his arms to lift himself out of the deadly cloud. He was grateful now for Renius, who had widened the way ahead of him.

He might have blacked out briefly, the conscious part of his mind at least. Like the orks, however, Sicarius didn't know when to die; while, unlike them, he had selfless allies to make sure that he didn't.

He felt Brother Lumic's hands tightening around his wrists, felt himself being lifted when he didn't have the strength to lift himself. He sprawled onto his stomach inside a large, octagonal chamber. Cracks ran through its walls, and its ceiling bulged in the centre and groaned ominously. He felt dizzy. He didn't know if he could stand, but he stood anyway and refused to let his battle-brothers help him.

The alarms in his helmet were quieting one by one, while scrolling displays told him how many painkilling and invigorating drugs had been pumped into him: enough to keep him active and alert, which was all that mattered to him.

His power armour required repairs, when he had the chance to see to it. Its protective layer of ceramite had begun to bubble and crack with the intense heat – though it had maintained its integrity and thus preserved his life. The floor was trembling violently, no doubt because of the engine beneath it – and how many others, Sicarius wondered, attached to other parts of the star fort's hull?

For the first time, he noticed a pattern on one of the chamber's walls, picked out in coloured tiles. It was the icon of the Cult Mechanicus: a half-human, half-machine skull bounded by a cogwheel, representing the perfect fusion of Man with the Machine God.

The Machine God was a minor aspect of the Emperor, in Sicarius's view. Still, it angered him to see that the mosaic had been defaced. Many of the steel-grey and ivory-white tiles that formed the composite skull had been pried loose, while others had been cracked or shattered in the attempt. Someone had spray-painted an ork face, inexpertly, over the image. The insult focused the captain's attention on his mission.

He rounded on his Techmarine. 'No more secrets,' he growled, the throbbing of the engine – the engines – underfoot lending his voice a threatening undercurrent. 'Tell me what the Adeptus Mechanicus were doing aboard the *Indestructible*.'

'I'm sorry, captain,' said Renius, setting his jaw stubbornly.

'I need that information, Techmarine!' Sicarius flared. 'I'm standing in the bowels of the Emperor-damned thing, aren't I?'

The rest of the Ultramarines closed in around Renius, in silent support of their leader. He looked at each of them in turn, then conceded defeat with a nod. 'There was a project,' he confessed. 'The tech-priests were attempting to make a star fort mobile – independently mobile, I mean.'

'By fitting it with engines,' said Sicarius. He wasn't surprised.

'Many engines,' confirmed Renius. 'Thruster engines and warp engines. Think about it. The Ramilies' greatest asset is its ability to traverse the immaterium. It can generate a warp bubble around itself, which allows it to withstand–'

'I already know this,' Sicarius said impatiently.

'But imagine if, instead, the Ramilies could provide its own propulsion. Imagine if it could shift from one star system to another, without having to wait for a fleet of ships to tow it and with negligible risk: a mobile command base with weapons fully charged and fully-stocked repair and resupply facilities.'

He sounded almost evangelical about the prospect.

'Imagine,' Sicarius growled, 'if the *orks* had that capability.'

Renius inclined his head. 'Khargask is attempting to bring the project to fruition, and has clearly come closer than we hoped. I suspect it was a test flight that brought him to the Agides System. Something went wrong. The *Indestructible* came down here, but its engines slowed its descent, at least. The damage to the propulsion systems and plasma generators may have been minimal.'

'And what about the energy flares that the Krieg men saw?'

'Attempts to re-establish the warp bubble,' Renius surmised, 'and to reconfigure it to maintain the Ramilies's integrity, to hold it together against the incredible stresses of take-off.'

The floor and the bulkheads around them were still trembling, but less violently now. The engine below them had ceased its angry protests and settled into a comfortable rhythm, almost a hum. Sicarius asked himself why it was still running at all, now that the five Ultramarines were safely out of the reach of its backwash. He didn't like the answer he came up with. He turned back to the Techmarine.

'Is there a control room?' he asked. 'There must be a control room.'

'The basilica,' said Renius. *Of course.* 'Beneath the Grand Chamber.'

Sicarius pinpointed the location on his schematics. He had already calculated his own position, towards the inner edge of the star fort's south-west-facing quadrant, and he quickly mapped a route from one to the other.

There were narrow, winding, upward-leading staircases in each of the chamber's eight corners. Most of them had partially collapsed, but the one he needed looked to be just about passable. Sicarius hurried towards it, his footsteps crunching on broken mosaic tiles, and his battle-brothers didn't need to be told to follow him. If what he suspected, what he feared, was true, then his mission was more urgent now than ever.

He had to get to that engine control room while there was still time.

CHAPTER XI

The Korpsmen were wheeling siege towers across no-man's-land: tall, teetering wire-frame and canvas constructs, six of them in all. The *Indestructible*'s energy weapon stabbed out at one of them and reduced it to smouldering ashes.

The towers didn't look as if they provided much protection. Most of the Death Korpsmen didn't wait for them to arrive, anyway. The order had come for them to scale the star fort's ramparts, so scale them they did.

Mouldings and gun emplacements provided plentiful handholds, and some Korpsmen were equipped with crampons and grappling hooks, so the climb itself was easy – but for the green-skinned creatures waiting at the end of it. Kenjari could see their brutish faces, peering through crenels above him; then the faces were replaced by guns and rocket launchers, firing downward.

He could almost have admired the men of Krieg, the

way they never flinched nor wavered, just swarmed up those walls as many around them were riddled with bolts and bullets and sent hurtling back to the ground. He could almost have admired them – had he not been expected to follow them.

Kenjari shrugged his rucksack from his shoulders, sifting through it for climbing tools with shaking hands. He found a small hand axe, which would do. As he straightened up, he realised that his sergeant had seen him vacillating and was elbowing his way towards him – through a scrum of waiting Death Korpsmen – with his bayonet poised to deliver his customary encouragement.

Then, a series of warning cries rang out: 'Look out below!'

Two orks had tipped a vat of something over the side. Some of the Korpsmen managed to leap for cover, but those higher on the walls were drenched in a viscous, silver tidal wave that sizzled through their flak armour. Several of them, these normally taciturn warriors, screamed. Kenjari gasped as a maimed body smacked into the ground at his feet, writhing in agony. His sergeant judged that the casualty couldn't be saved and put him out of his misery with a gunshot.

He heard the voice of an officer over his comm-bead: 'Keep climbing. Climb! Climb! The Emperor expects.'

He realised that the guns of both sides had fallen silent; it could only just have happened, because his ears were still ringing from their barks. Blue-armoured figures marched out of the battlefield smoke, and Kenjari was filled with awe at the very sight of them. The Angels of Death didn't mount the ramparts themselves, but they aimed their bolt and flamer weapons up at the defenders and several brutish faces quickly disappeared from sight.

The remaining siege towers crashed into the side of the star fort, and the nearest Korpsmen poured into them at ground level, to emerge a minute later onto platforms at their tops. Kenjari tried to make it to a tower – it seemed like the safest option for him, relatively speaking – but too many others were in his way. He found himself pushed up against the *Indestructible*'s ramparts and, though he had thankfully been separated from his sergeant, he could feel a hundred other blank eyes upon him and he knew what he had to do. He had to climb.

It was like the trek across no-man's-land again, just in a different plain. He was following pairs of booted feet above him, spurred on by the blank-faced men at his own heels when his every muscle only longed to surrender, fearing that he ought to pray for a speedy death because it might be the kindest fate on offer. Time after time, shots rang out above him – despite the efforts of the Space Marines below – and a nearby Korpsman lost his grip on his hand- and footholds and tumbled past him, no longer a human being but merely a sack of flesh and bones and blood.

A body glanced off him and almost took Kenjari down with it. His right hand lost its grip on the wall and that side of his body swung away from it. He hadn't climbed as high as he had imagined; he could have survived a fall, but he would likely have been injured and his sergeant might have euthanised him too. To his relief, the Korpsman at his ankles caught his slipping right foot and boosted him back into position with a growl: 'The Emperor expects.'

He felt light-headed, sweaty and sick, and just wanted to cling to something solid for a moment, but the masked man beneath him was still pushing and he had to climb again. He saw a gun emplacement within reach – no threat because the barrel of its cannon had been shattered – and gratefully utilised the broad, firm ledge it offered. As he pushed off from it, with a little more confidence, a green hand was thrust through the gap above the cannon and grabbed him by the knee.

Kenjari squealed in terror. It was the first time he had ever touched a xenos, and a tiny, irrational part of his brain insisted that he was contaminated now.

When the orks had attacked at the star fort's base, the men of Krieg had saved him, though that hadn't been their objective. They had saved him by getting between Kenjari and the xenos and by fighting them relentlessly, many of them to the death. Three squads of experienced Guardsmen – grenadiers – had charged the orks with bayonets and, though they hadn't been able to match their strength, they had kept them busy while their comrades had sniped at them from the sidelines.

Kenjari had loosed off several shots himself, firing blindly in panic, and he knew that his efforts had amounted to precisely nothing.

No one else could save him this time. His lasgun was slung across his back again, but his hand axe was clamped between his teeth in case of need. He clung to the wall with his left hand, snatched the weapon with his right and struck down with it. He wasn't thinking clearly enough to aim, and his blows made criss-cross patterns of cuts across the ork's flesh instead of slicing through its muscles.

The Emperor was with him, however, and it proved to be enough. The ork's fingers spasmed and let him go; his axe head must have struck a nerve. He dragged himself away from there as quickly as he could, his weariness forgotten.

To his right and above him, a siege tower had extruded a gangplank over the star fort's battlements. Death Korpsmen were teeming across it, though it was only wide enough to accommodate two of them abreast.

He couldn't see, but could imagine, the reception with which they were greeted. He could see the results of it too, as more bodies came hurtling over the parapet. Death Korpsmen were backed all the way along the gangplank, jostling to get forwards. Perhaps Kenjari was better off where he was, after all. Rather here, he thought, than queuing up the steps of one of those fragile towers, waiting for his turn to confront the monsters above...

He was nearing the top of the ramparts. Other Korpsmen had made it ahead of him; most had detached their bayonets and were wielding them like knives, knowing that the orks would quickly close upon them. Perhaps, Kenjari thought, by the time he was able to join them, the combatants on both sides would be occupied and he wouldn't be noticed. Perhaps he could slip past them and find a nook somewhere inside the star fort to hide until the fighting was over.

The structure was shaking.

Kenjari hadn't noticed it at first, with all the sound and motion around him. The vibrations, however, were growing fiercer, and suddenly the air was charged with electrical energy and he could see sparks of it, purple and green, flaring around him. The sparks seemed to be building inside the walls themselves, until they were too powerful to be contained. For a moment, the energy wreathed him, making his nerves tingle and his hair stand on end beneath his helmet, but fortunately doing no worse.

A new sound, far louder than the others, rose from the bowels of the earth: a groaning of tortured machine-spirits.

Kenjari had seen this happening before, but from a distance, standing up on his toes to sneak a glance out of a Krieg trench where no officers could see him. He had heard it suggested that the orks were building and testing a powerful weapon inside the *Indestructible*. Were they about to test their weapon on him?

The Space Marines were finally climbing the walls beneath him. They were climbing faster than any Korpsman could; in some cases climbing right over them. The Korpsmen's handholds weren't strong enough to support them, so they were punching new ones through the star fort's adamantium skin into the metal beneath.

One of them – a blue tank with two legs and a single arm – had been lifted by a gunship right onto the top of the battlements, landing with a thud, squashing countless ork defenders. He managed to swing out of the juggernaut's way, into a space left on the wall beside him by a Korpsman who had taken a stray bullet to the head.

'Follow the Space Marines,' the ever-present voice in Kenjari's ear buzzed. 'They are the Emperor's angels, and it is they who will bring justice to His enemies.'

The star fort was shaking more violently than ever and, suddenly, glancing down as he clung to its mouldings for dear life, Kenjari saw the reason why. The star fort – the castle from the sky – was straining to lift itself off the ground, to return to the heavens from which it had so unceremoniously fallen.

It wasn't going to make it. It wasn't just the gravity of the Agides moon that was holding onto it. The star fort's lower levels were entangled – inextricably so? – with the moon's mine workings and its subterranean tunnels. It had failed to pull itself free of them before, he suddenly realised.

This time, however, was different. This time, the machine-spirits weren't about to give up their struggle. Their groans had steadily increased in pitch and volume until they became full-blooded howls of defiance. The emissions from the star fort's walls were combining to form a bubble around its massive structure, a flickering, flaring energy shield; there were still a few gaps in it, but they were closing up fast.

The *Indestructible* seemed to scream as it wrenched itself free from the grip of the hard, black earth and began to ascend.

It was, for Kenjari, just the latest in a succession of overwhelming terrors; one more than he could bear. He saw some Korpsmen shaken from the ramparts, plummeting towards the ground, and he felt a powerful stab of envy towards them. It occurred to him that he could plausibly fall too. He might break a few bones, or he might find a soft landing on the bodies that were piling up underneath him.

Either way, the xenos would fly their castle away from him, and take the Death Korps of Krieg and the bright blue Space Marines with them. They could carry on their bloody war without him, among the stars. Kenjari would live.

There was no time to think about it, to second-guess himself. The surface of the moon was already beginning to recede beneath his feet, and in a second it would be too late, he would be trapped. He had one chance to save himself, and that chance was now.

Kenjari jumped for his life.

CHAPTER XII

The *Indestructible* was in motion.

Sicarius was hurrying along a curving passageway, fighting to stay upright as the floor bucked like a panicked mount. The walls were getting the worst of it, his pauldrons leaving indentations in the stone and shattering lumoglobes.

Back above ground, he had been able to vox Sergeant Lucien. His second-in-command had been proud to report his progress. He had led their Chapter over the star fort's ramparts and they were fighting its occupiers hand-to-hand. It was more than Sicarius had expected.

So far, as his command squad had journeyed to the star fort's heart, they had met little resistance. A few gretchin had crossed their paths – inadvertently, he suspected – but not for long. Now he knew what was keeping most of the orks busy. Lucien had not seen the big mek himself, however.

Sicarius knew where Khargask would be; and he knew that, no matter the situation outside, he would not be alone.

'These xenos are not so tough,' a welcome voice boomed over an open vox-channel, 'when they have no cannons to hide behind.' Evidently, Brother Ultracius had made it to the Ramilies too.

Sicarius opened a private channel to him. 'What's the situation out there?' he asked. 'How high up from the ground are we?'

'I can't tell from here, Knight of Talassar,' replied Ultracius. 'Much higher, though, and these Guardsmen without faces won't be able to breathe.'

'The Krieg Korpsmen are...?' He stifled the question. He was already mentally putting the pieces together, beginning to see what must have transpired in his absence. He didn't much care for the image that was forming. He had to find that control room; apart from any other reason now, for the sake of hundreds of Imperial soldiers – at least, he hoped there were still so many – about to die by asphyxiation.

'Never thought I would say this,' said Ultracius, 'about anyone, but these Krieg men are too fearless for their own good.' He had, in fact, said the same thing more than once about Captain Sicarius himself, if only he could have remembered it.

A blocked shaft had forced them to take a detour. Sicarius led his battle-brothers up a flight of steps, to what the star fort's schematics called the command level. The engine room was now one floor below them. They followed a covered walkway with armaplas windows along one side, looking out upon the black sky.

The orks came to meet them as they rounded the next corner.

They were in a spacious atrium. Ahead of them, a pair of grand iron doors, inlaid with intricate carvings, stood wide open. Through these, Sicarius could see the *Indestructible*'s Grand Chamber, once a haven for prayer and reflection.

Its rows of seats had been uprooted, its statues had been bludgeoned to pieces, while a row of five patterned windows, ten metres tall, had been defaced by crude ork glyphs. The whole place stank of ork faeces.

A hole had been gouged out of the floor, twenty metres long and about a quarter as wide. Smoke was billowing up through it, along with a sickly green light. 'The engine control room!' Sicarius announced. Now, all they had to do was reach it.

Eight brawny figures stood in their way already, and more were clambering up out of the ragged aperture. They were slobbering at the long-denied prospect of a brawl. The Ultramarines were almost as eager them-selves and, for once, Sicarius sent his brothers into the fray ahead of him.

Two lines of ruthless warriors smashed into each other like opposing tidal waves, and the air was filled with the sounds of revving chainswords, bolts and bullets, the pounding of axes and clubs against plasteel and ceramite. Sicarius's hand twitched on the pommel of his Tempest Blade, but he held himself back.

He had hoped the enemy line might give with that first impact, giving him a gap to slip through. It was no use. He should have known that, this close to their leader and his all-important project, the orks would be more disci-plined than ever.

He raised his sword and plunged into the melee.

The next few minutes were a blur of slicing and shooting and punching, of hate-filled faces coming at him with drooling mouths wide open, of foetid ork breath and ultimately ork blood in his nostrils, the stench strong even through his helmet.

For every enemy that fell, it seemed that two more emerged from the hole in the Grand Chamber's floor to replace it. With no time to strategise, Sicarius placed his trust in his own instincts, enhanced by his armour's auto-senses.

'They're stronger than the orks we faced below,' Lumic grunted, 'as strong as any I've ever encountered.' Clearly, Khargask had held back the best of his mob for his own protection. They parried Sicarius's blows with almost enough force to send the weapon spinning from his hands. Outnumbered, he couldn't block all of their blows in return. A massive iron-headed hammer smashed into his ribs, and his helmet readouts told him that his armour had sustained hairline fractures.

The star fort's violent shaking only added to the Ultramarines woes, though it hampered the greenskins equally. The floor suddenly tipped away from Sicarius, throwing two orks in front of him off-balance; he helped the first of them on its way with a booted foot to its stomach. It reeled into the second and they toppled and rolled, hopelessly entangled, each howling indignantly at the other.

Another ork appeared in front of Sicarius to replace them, but he had expected that and was more than ready for it. For the first time, momentarily, he had only a single opponent, and he took full advantage of that opportunity too. A fusillade of plasma bolts left the greenskin blinded and stunned. A follow-up series of swipes from the captain's Tempest Blade carved it up neatly.

Not all his battle-brothers were faring as well.

Brother Gallo had stumbled when the floor had tipped, landing in the midst of five enormous greenskins. They were battering him mercilessly, cracking open his armour and driving him into the ground. Brothers Filion and Lumic were doing their best to help him, but that meant turning their backs on other opponents, which left them vulnerable. Sicarius had to make a painful decision.

He voxed his squad: 'Leave Gallo to fend for himself. We can't afford to be kept on the defensive. We have to reach that control room.' One life was unimportant, he told himself, when so many more were at stake.

Next, he voxed Ultracius, out on the ramparts, again. 'We need you down here,' he said grimly, knowing that the Dreadnought could lock onto the source of his transmission and find him.

'On my way,' came the immediate reply.

From under the floor, Sicarius heard a series of small explosions, and the sound of orks cursing as they spluttered to draw breath. He heard one voice, deeper and more strident than the others, booming angrily as the floor bucked again beneath his feet. *What are they doing down there?* The background rumble of engines burped and hiccupped, then resumed in a slightly more throaty tone than before.

'Renius?'

'It sounds like... they're actually trying to make a warp jump,' the Techmarine returned his vox. His voice was strained, as well it might be; he was on the back foot against a pair of axe-wielding brutes. He employed his servo-arm as a weapon, clawing at one ork's face, gouging blood out of its eyes as he struggled to hold it at bay. 'If they do, and the energy shield around the Ramilies holds–'

'A warp jump?' repeated Sicarius, horrified. 'While we're still in the atmosphere? It'll tear this moon apart – and we could end up anywhere in the galaxy.' *Most likely, in the heart of ork space*, he thought.

'Those of us that survive the journey,' said Renius, pointedly. 'Our battle-brothers on the ramparts risk being hurled out of the warp bubble and torn apart on the currents of the immaterium. That is, if the warp jump is successful.'

'If it isn't?'

'If the warp jump fails and if Khargask refuses to abort the attempt...'

Renius took a breath as he brought his favoured weapon to bear on his attackers: a power axe, with a ridged blade shaped like half of the Cult Mechanicus's symbol. It crackled and blazed as it bit hungrily into an ork's stomach. 'In that case,' he resumed, 'the reactor will almost certainly explode, with enough force to consume the *Indestructible* and dislodge this moon's flaming remains from orbit.'

The orks, at least, were running out of reinforcements to throw at them. The flow of fresh bodies from below had finally abated, and the battle now had an end in sight. Sicarius continued with his tactic of hammering at one spot on the enemy line until suddenly – as another opponent fell with a gash in its throat, choking on its own blood – most unexpectedly, he found himself stumbling through it.

There was nothing now to keep him from his goal, from diving through the hole in the floor and confronting his true enemy at last. Nothing but the knowledge, which Sicarius accepted grudgingly, that another was needed down in the engine control room more urgently than he was.

Techmarine Renius was fighting three orks at once, one with each of his real and mechanical hands. Sicarius spun on his heel and slashed one of them across the back. Renius's axe felled the second a moment later, while Lumic obligingly stepped in to engage the third. Sicarius yelled, 'Renius, with me. Lumic and Filion, keep us covered.' Seven orks were still fighting and Lumic had been badly bloodied; they were leaving their brothers outnumbered, facing almost certain defeat, but what else could they do? Ultracius would arrive soon, hopefully.

Sicarius and Renius burst through the Grand Chamber's open doors.

A greenskin howled as it saw what they were doing. It hurled a wrench at Sicarius, who deflected it with a backhand swipe. He couldn't see anything through the rectangular hole in the floor – there was too much smoke down there; the hole, he suddenly apprehended, had been dug for ventilation – nor could his auspex give him any definite readings. Whatever was waiting for him down there, however, his duty was to face it. He didn't break his step.

Sicarius pushed off from the edge of the hole and plunged into the unknown. He dropped four metres and crashed down in the centre of a smaller chamber.

Through the smoke haze, he could make out flickering flames, the dark, angular shapes of rune panels around the walls – and the silhouettes of several sturdy inhuman figures in frantic motion.

Renius touched down heavily beside him and took a moment to get his bearings. 'You deal with the engines,' said Sicarius, 'I'll deal with the greenskins.'

A shadow, much larger than the others, came hurtling towards him.

He had a fraction of a second to try to work out what it was. It looked like a machine: an ork machine, haphazardly bolted together, heavier on one side than on the other, with all manner of random protuberances. It looked like a smaller and shabbier version of a Dreadnought – though not much smaller.

It was only when the shadow let out a curdling war cry that Sicarius saw a slobbering mouth and a glaring, blood-crazed eye in among the mechanics and realised that it was a flesh-and-blood creature. That was when he recognised his ill-famed enemy, at last, and knew it for what – and exactly who – it was.

Khargask!

CHAPTER XIII

Commissar Dast stepped out of the Centaur transport vehicle.

He had planned to join the men of Krieg on the front lines of their desperate battle. He was too late. He had felt the ground – the whole moon, it had seemed – trembling as the *Indestructible* had slowly wrenched itself free from its moorings.

He had had his driver bring the Centaur to a stop. Dast stood on the barren surface of the Agides moon; for once he was glad of the facemask that concealed his expression of horror.

He knew what had happened, having picked up the details from the vox-chatter that filled his ear. He ought to have been prepared to face it, and yet to see the massive star fort just hanging in the sky, where it had no possible right, and no reason to be hanging... he wondered how anyone could have been prepared for that.

He lifted a pair of magnoculars to his eyes. Even through their lenses, the Korpsmen clinging to the star fort's walls looked smaller than ever. From this distance, even the Space Marines beside them appeared almost insignificant. Korpsmen and Space Marines alike, however, clung stubbornly to their uncertain handholds. *Why didn't they jump when they had the chance?* Dast thought. *Why didn't their captain order them to jump?*

The commissar had excused himself from the command centre in the dugout, because he had done as much as he could there. Sometimes – more often than not, he had always prided himself – his captain actually heeded his advice; just not today. Today, the Krieg man preferred to listen to Sergeant Lucien.

It wasn't just that the captain was in awe of the Ultramarine. Dast knew that, at heart, he genuinely agreed with his point of view. He agreed that a Space Marine was worth a hundred ordinary men of Krieg. Perhaps he was right. Anyway, the captain had made the decisions he had made. He had given his orders, and that was all that mattered. Dast could better serve his regiment elsewhere now.

The *Indestructible* had stopped climbing. It was shaking and groaning as if the effort of merely staying aloft might tear it apart. A transparent bubble of energy had formed around it, but it flickered and sparked as if it might burst at any moment.

As Dast watched, another Korpsman fell off the side of the star fort, followed in short order by yet another. They tumbled through the energy bubble, and from here he couldn't tell if their bodies had been burned or fried by it. Either way, their next stop was the ground, too far below them.

Some of their comrades were hardier, or had been luckier. They had made it onto the star fort itself, onto the lowest of its stepped surfaces – the tops of its virtual ramparts – where of course they had a mob of eager, baying orks to contend with. Dast could only catch glimpses of the fighting from where he was, and hear breathless snatches of reports from those trapped in the thick of it.

The orks, to begin with, had had the advantages of height and cover over their attackers, not to mention their bestial strength. The arrival of Sicarius's Ultramarines, however, had tipped the balance. A tide of bright blue-armoured warriors were tearing into the green-skinned xenos, eviscerating them with their whirring blades. Dast wished he could have been with them.

In addition, he was hearing – over the Ultramarines vox-channel, to which he had been granted access – that Sicarius's command squad had penetrated the star fort's heart. They were about to take on Khargask himself. He relayed the news to his regiment, to boost their morale. He told them that victory was almost within their grasp. Whether that was true or not, it didn't matter.

He heard the Krieg captain's voice: 'Remember the value of the Adeptus Astartes to the Imperium – they are the Emperor's angels.' He knew he was speaking Sergeant Lucien's words. He gathered that Lucien himself had attained the ramparts too and was leading his men from the front, fighting valiantly.

At the same time, he had had the Krieg Korpsmen form up in front of the Dreadnought, Ultracius. He was their most powerful weapon, according to Lucien, and Dast had certainly heard nothing to gainsay this. He couldn't keep track of every single vox-report – hence the tactical hololith and its attendant servitors in the dugout – but more than once he had heard tell of the Dreadnought's twin-linked heavy bolter, tearing through ork flesh whenever it barked.

Lucien addressed the men of Krieg again: 'The orks are desperate to take our best weapon out of action. So, let them slice and shred their way through you to get to him – because even as you die, you are frustrating them in their efforts.' Dast chose not to dwell on the picture that those words painted.

The star fort gave another violent lurch, and he saw another score of figures – Korpsmen and orks alike, even a couple in blue – flung over the edge. The Space Marines had their armour to protect them, of course, and would survive the landing, perhaps even the passage through the energy bubble; the others had no such hope.

Dast lowered the magnoculars.

Only now did he realise that he had been walking across no-man's-land, though he had no way of reaching his hovering objective. Even if he could, he knew he would be far too late. The *Indestructible* had shaken itself into a veritable frenzy. One way or another, it couldn't endure the stresses being placed upon it much longer. One way or another, this battle – another war – would soon be over.

Had Dast fought alongside his regiment today, he would likely have died alongside them too, and for nothing.

The plain around him was almost eerily silent. The smoke that had smothered it had dispersed on a thin breeze. The Ultramarines artillery guns were biding their time, having done all they could for the present. There was no point in shelling the *Indestructible* any further, in dealing it any more damage than they already had.

Beyond the blue tanks, five siege towers stood in a forlorn row. The star fort's sudden take-off had left them stranded, and though many Krieg Korpsmen had jumped from the tops of the towers to the star fort while they could, others had been left behind. They milled around the bases of the towers, helplessly.

Joining them were the men who had lost their grips on the walls, while the drop to the ground had been survivable. Dast counted roughly sixty figures in all, some of them badly injured. They were the lucky few.

There was little these few survivors could usefully do, little but try to stay alive despite the hunks of debris, pieces of unanchored equipment and bodies that were raining down from the teetering structure above them. Dast lowered his head and hurried to join them. He took charge of them, ordering them to heft their wounded onto improvised stretchers and begin to withdraw from the danger zone.

Above, the carnage showed no signs of abating. The voices of three quartermasters competed in the commissar's ear with their roll calls of the recently deceased. The reports were coming in too fast for the servitors to collate. His guess was that, at most, four hundred Korpsmen remained in the fray, and that number was dwindling by the second.

'Ultracius is withdrawing from the battle.'

'–just ordered the Korpsmen that were protecting him to part and–'

'He caught the orks, the ones in his path, unprepared. He just charged through their line and scattered them around him. He–'

Dast picked out Sergeant Lucien's voice from the

others: 'Our Dreadnought has been summoned to assist Captain Sicarius inside the star fort. Men of Krieg, you follow in the shadow of the Emperor's angels. Let them guide you to glory, let them guide you to salvation, let them be your shield against the alien and the unclean. Obey their orders without question for you serve the greater glory of mankind.'

'Ultracius just shot out a stained-armaplas window,' a quartermaster reported, 'and crashed through its remains into the star fort's inner compound.'

'–left the greenskins reeling, disorganised in his wake. They can't decide whether to follow him or–'

'–paying dearly for their hesitation. The Ultramarines guns are cutting through them like–'

Dast heard the scrape of a boot against the earth, where there should have been no such sound. Instantly, his attention snapped back to his immediate vicinity. He spun around, in time to catch a glimpse of movement out of the corner of his eye. He whipped out his bolt pistol and bellowed a challenge: 'Who goes there?'

There came no answer.

His finger flicked to his ear, silencing his comm-bead. Now, Dast could hear frightened breathing; it was coming from behind the burned-out corpse of a Predator Destructor. He took a step towards it and issued his challenge again, in a sterner tone this time. A wretched-looking figure emerged from behind the ruined tank. He was wearing a Death Korps uniform, facemask and rebreather unit; immediately, however, Dast knew that this was no man of Krieg.

'Identify yourself, trooper,' he demanded. When the figure's response caught in his throat, Dast prompted him, 'You were issued with a number. What is it?'

The trooper had to check his own dog tags before he could answer.

Dast nodded. The number was a recently issued one. He didn't need to tap it into his data-slate to confirm his suspicion: that this was one of the Agides miners who had been found here and pressed into service. He couldn't remember his name, but that was unimportant. He kept his pistol levelled at the trooper's head: he might just have been stupid and desperate enough to think about using his own weapon.

'Why are you hiding, trooper?' barked Dast, knowing the answer.

'I...' the trooper stammered.

'Who ordered you to leave the front lines?' He knew the answer to that too.

The trooper lurched towards him; for an instant, Dast thought he *was* going to attack. Instead, he fell to his knees in front of the commissar and his lasgun slipped from between his fingers, disregarded. 'I... I'm a worker, not a soldier,' he pleaded. 'I was never trained to fight. I was never prepared for... for this.'

'You jumped from the star fort,' Dast guessed, presenting the question as a statement of fact. 'You didn't fall. You chose to jump.'

The trooper's guilty silence was the only answer he needed. The commissar's duty was clear.

This man had disobeyed orders. He didn't need to be told the consequences of that. Dast told him to remove his helmet, which he did, with trembling hands. Dast put his gun to the trooper's temple. He gave him a moment to make his final peace with the Emperor, then he squeezed the trigger.

He beckoned one of the other survivors to him. He had him strip the flak armour, the lasgun, the rucksack and the rebreather mask from the cowardly trooper's body. He averted his eyes from the dead man's face as it was revealed. He never looked at their faces, not the ones who had faltered in their duty. Their lives hadn't mattered and were not worthy of remembrance.

The man's equipment would be passed on to the Death Korps of Krieg's next recruit. Dast hoped that, with the Emperor's grace, this time it might be issued to someone more worthy of it.

CHAPTER XIV

Khargask cannoned into Captain Sicarius, with enough force to bowl him over had he not seen it coming in time to brace himself.

He had stooped to take the impact of the charge on his shoulder, which gave him leverage to thrust his attacker away from him. He swung his Tempest Blade at the massive ork, but a rusty servo-arm blocked it, showering both combatants with furious sparks. Another mechanical limb, with a snapping claw attachment, slithered over Khargask's shoulder and struck for Sicarius's throat. He was forced to surrender a step to wrench himself free from it, before it could tighten its hold on him.

In the meantime, Renius had downed a greenskin mechanic with his power axe, and a bank of rune panels was his now. His voice came over a vox-channel, calm and clear: 'There's a blockage in the hyper-plasmatic energy conduction system and a synchronous vibration in the tertiary warp engine manifold.'

Sicarius had found the orks' guttural language easier to understand. There was no mistaking the Techmarine's next words, however: 'It won't make it.'

In his flesh-and-blood arms, Khargask clutched an oversized shooter. Something flashed inside it and it bucked violently in his grip as it fired with a series of deafening pops. Its bullets sprayed the engine control room almost indiscriminately, but three of them tore through Sicarius's armour. The damage to the unique Mantle of Suzerain would pain the artificers on Macragge.

One of the bullets lodged itself in the muscle of his left leg.

The pain only lasted for an instant before a cocktail of chemicals suppressed it. However, he could feel the bullet shifting, tearing through more tissue, as he twisted to avoid another metal-armed swipe from his opponent. *It's like fighting a giant octopus*, he thought ruefully, *I'm being attacked from every direction at once.*

To Renius, he voxed: 'I don't want to hear that. I want those engines shut off. That's why I included you in this mission, so do your duty!'

Khargask had only one eye, his left, red and rheumy. The other had been replaced by something that looked like a sniper scope, jammed into the socket; it wasn't helping with Khargask's aim. Sicarius suspected that it might serve as a primitive auspex. It looked painful; he hoped it was.

He ducked between the big mek's whirling arms and hacked energetically at the armour that protected its chest. He felt he had dislodged something, but he failed to draw ork blood. He did raise Khargask's ire: he was seething and spitting, hurling insults at the Ultramarines captain.

More than anything else, Khargask seemed affronted. He was more than aware, Sicarius guessed, of his own notoriety. Indeed, he had pulled off quite a coup, stealing the *Indestructible* from under the noses of the massed Imperial Navy. '*Khargask!*' The ork kept bellowing out his own name as if it ought to mean something.

One of Khargask's claw arms fastened onto Sicarius's blade. The machine-spirits in both fought a savage duel of their own, rending and biting at each other's metal flesh, oily black blood spraying from their arteries.

The Tempest Blade, ancient and mighty, emerged as the victor. Sicarius let it rest while he emptied his plasma pistol's charge into Khargask's face. Most of the sun-hot rounds melted intervening servo-arms, but one of them scorched the big mek's eyepiece.

I'll deal with the greenskins, he had assured Renius. He chided himself for his overconfidence. It was almost more than he could do to stand up to a single ork, this ork. *Smart and strong and savage,* he recalled. He had underestimated Khargask, despite warning others against that very mistake.

'Another one coming your way,' the Techmarine warned him.

A greenskin had left its station at the edge of the room and was lurching towards him through the smoke. It was another mek, bristling with bionics but not engulfed by them as Khargask was. Sicarius feinted, luring Khargask into his ally's path as it fired a burst of flame from a welding torch. He howled at the mekboy, sent it scurrying back to its rune panels. The big mek wanted Sicarius for himself: his first mistake.

The other orks were wrestling with levers, fighting fires, too busy to pay much attention to the battle raging behind them. Khargask employed his full complement of mechanical limbs to keep his opponent at bay, and bellowed orders at them that urged them to work faster.

A second ork mek saw what Renius was doing and sprang at him from behind. He didn't turn, but his auto-senses must have seen the ork coming, because his servo-arm met it with a punishing blow. The ork's knees buckled, but it pushed itself back to its feet with a roar of defiance.

It lunged at Renius again, just as a rune panel blew out in front of him and sprayed the pair with white-hot plasma. Renius got the worst of it, but the ork had no armour to protect it. For a second time, it staggered, clutching its hands to its eyes. It was blind and helpless, just awaiting the mercy of a killing blow.

Sicarius returned his focus to his own fight. He blocked the big mek's next swing at him with his Tempest Blade, but shifted too much weight onto his left foot in the process. The bullet in his leg squirmed again, and he all but fell into a mighty, power-assisted punch to his jaw. He rolled with the blow, because it gave him the space he badly needed to reemploy his plasma pistol.

Khargask was panting eagerly, sensing his enemy's weakness. He held himself in check long enough to finger a rune panel on his arm. A pair of pylons strapped to his back burst into ozone-stinking life and projected a luminous, close-fitting aura around him. The way the aura popped and crackled, it surely couldn't endure for long – it had to be a drain on whatever power source he was using – but while it did, the big mek was well-protected.

He bore down on Sicarius, straight through a hail of plasma, which his force field comfortably deflected. He mauled and clawed and even bit at his armoured foe again. He succeeded in breaking the seals on Sicarius's helmet, so the smoke that wreathed the control room seeped into his nose and throat.

Renius's voice broke through the fog: '–can't power down the engines. The only thing I can do is try to starve them of air, make them stall before they–'

A claw arm jabbed through Khargask's force field, and Sicarius caught it. With a laboured grunt of effort, he ripped the arm from its harness and set about the big mek with the sparking end. He hoped that some of the strength of his blows might make it through the field, or that he might be able to overload it.

Khargask shrugged off his efforts and responded with another shooter burst. Sicarius tried to twist out of the way of the bullets, but his injured leg betrayed him – as he had known it eventually would – and he found himself falling. He caught himself, just, on his hands and rolled onto his back, his pistol flaring wildly and in vain. Khargask took a moment to stand astride his downed opponent, with his ugly face twisted into an even uglier sneer, savouring the taste of victory.

Sicarius snarled up at him. 'Enjoy it while you can, you brainless brute, because your schemes have come to nothing. Your engines don't work and we're all about to be blown to bloody–'

Khargask's sneer froze. His eyepiece, even broken, must

have warned him of imminent danger. He dived for cover as a fusillade of explosive bolt-rounds churned up the floor where he had been standing. A mass of solid blue armour came plummeting through the vent hole in the ceiling, landing with an impact that threatened to knock everyone else off their feet.

It was Ultracius, of course; and behind him appeared Brother Filion, his power armour scratched, dented and burned but his chainsword dripping dark ork blood from its teeth and howling for yet more. 'Orders, captain?' he requested.

The remaining ork meks were abandoning their rune panels, realising perhaps that there was nothing more they could do, seeing their enemies among them, and seeing a precious chance for a good fight. 'Brother Filion, deal with them,' Sicarius ordered as he pushed himself to his feet. 'Ultracius, you too. Ensure that Renius's work is not interrupted.' The Dreadnought and the big mek had been squaring up to each other, as the former ignited his power fist. Sicarius was grateful for the respite that Ultracius had given him, but Khargask was his and his alone.

He readied the Tempest Blade.

He hurled himself at his enemy's back and thrust his blade through a gap between the flickering bands of the ork's failing force field. The sword's energy field spluttered and screamed as Sicarius jammed the weapon into a vent in Khargask's makeshift servo-harness. Machine-spirits danced and buzzed around his gauntlets in impotent fury, as the big mek's mechanical arms went limp and the force field sputtered and died.

Khargask pitched forwards and took Sicarius's blade

with him. He was staggering under the dead weight of his useless servo-arms. He made one final attempt to bring his shooter to bear, but Sicarius was waiting for him and fired when he saw the angry red of the ork's remaining eye.

This time, his plasma rounds thudded into green ork flesh and mined wells of viscous ork blood. Still weighed down by his broken accoutrements, Khargask stumbled backwards and flailed into an instrument bank. For the second time, he was wreathed in dancing energy; but this time it was hurting him, scorching his skin. His single eye rolled back into his head, a mixture of blood and snot dribbled from his snout and he crumpled and slid to the floor.

Ultracius was making short work of the remaining meks, with the able but almost unnecessary assistance of Filion. It felt as if the star fort was shaking itself apart, and the greenskins were struggling to stay upright, let alone fight.

Sicarius was fighting to stay on his feet too, and to cross the room to Renius. He was finding it difficult to breathe. His armour was pumping air to his nostrils, but too much of it was escaping through the cracks in his artificer plate. Throwing out his hands, he fell heavily into a rune panel beside his red-armoured brother.

'I'm no Techmarine,' he growled, 'but it seems to me we're out of time. Can you stop those engines or can't you?' If the answer was negative, then he and his brothers – his entire company – were about to die... and the *Indestructible* would be lost too. Sicarius would have failed in his mission.

Renius hesitated for a moment, then made a decision.

He plunged his claw arm through one of the rune panels in front of him. He shattered dials and switches and yanked out bundle after bundle of tangled wires, wrenching them from their roots. Sicarius opened his mouth to yell something at him over the roars of the engines, then realised that, abruptly, the sounds of the engines had ceased. The star fort had stopped trembling too.

Everything seemed preternaturally still, for a moment. Then the floor dropped out from underneath him.

CHAPTER XV

Sicarius woke to a barrage of vox-chatter in his ear.

His chrono told him he had been out for almost eight minutes. His auto-injectors were pumping him full of stimulants. He could feel weight pressing down on top of him. The roof of the control room and much of the Grand Chamber above it had collapsed onto his head. Either that or the floor had rushed up and smashed him into the roof; perhaps both had happened.

The weight that pinned him was shifting, lightening a little. Someone was digging their way towards him. He had fallen on his hands, so he could easily brace himself and start to lever himself upwards. He felt debris sloughing off his back. He heard a booming, mechanical voice, but not through his comm-bead. It was Ultracius, welcoming him back to the land of the living.

'We didn't jump?' Sicarius checked. 'We're still on the Agides moon?'

'Dropped like a stone and landed hard, Knight of Talassar,' the Dreadnought confirmed. 'A lot of Krieg men didn't make it – the impact turned their bones to jelly. No shields to protect the star fort this time, either. The tech-priests won't salvage much from it.'

At least they'd be able to salvage something, Sicarius thought. Their clandestine project had been a failure, anyway, he could certainly tell them that.

Ultracius was working slowly but methodically, with one giant hand. He wrenched a heavy plasteel beam from the wreckage and tossed it over his shoulder, almost casually. Sicarius found that he could stand now. The fires in the engine control room had been extinguished, but the smoke of them lingered. Nearby, an Apothecary in white armour was tending to a pair of casualties. Filion was already trying to sit up; Lumic must have fallen from the floor above and was ominously still.

Sicarius voxed Lucien and asked how many battle-brothers they had lost. He responded with Gallo's name and ten others. Each one was a tragedy, but Sicarius knew the list could have been much longer. He hesitated to ask the next question: 'And what of the Krieg regiment?'

'Still counting their dead,' Lucien told him, gruffly.

Sicarius picked his way across the room to where the body of the ork's big mek lay, half-buried. Khargask's hand twitched, but it must have been a post-mortem spasm or perhaps a shock from his still-sparking servo-harness. Sicarius's auspex detected no breath on his lips, and confirmed that his body heat had all but dissipated.

He turned the body over with his foot and wrestled his sword out of its back. He ignited the energy field, which flared into life. Sicarius smiled. Like his tortured armour, the Tempest Blade had served its purpose well.

He raised the blade and sliced through Khargask's thick neck. He picked up the ork boss's head by one of its tusks.

Sicarius didn't need a trophy. He had, however, heard Khargask's name spoken too often for his liking. He was dangerously close to becoming a legend to some; and legends were difficult, almost impossible, to kill.

The Imperial Navy would want to announce the *Indestructible*'s recapture to the galaxy. They would want all faithful servants of the Emperor and His enemies alike to know that its hijacker, the upstart ork, had paid for his transgressions. The story of the star fort's loss would still be told, but now it would have a new and more apposite ending. A whispered rumour of the Imperium's folly would become a cautionary tale of its bloody and righteous vengeance.

It would behove the Lord High Admiral to have tangible, unequivocal proof of his claims; Sicarius would present him with exactly that. He tied the ork's head to his belt, unceremoniously.

He scaled a mountain of debris, which slipped and shifted beneath him every finger- and toehold of the way. He was having to drag his injured left leg behind him, and more than once he almost suffered a fall that would have been embarrassing if not actually injurious to him. *My body requires repairs,* Sicarius thought ruefully, *as badly as my armour does.*

He clambered up through the wreckage of the Grand Chamber, out through its double doors. The atrium beyond was relatively intact, though cluttered with greenskin corpses. Brother Gallo's body was here too, lying where it had fallen. No lumoglobes had survived the star fort's crash – its second crash – but pale starlight leaked through narrow windows and cracks in the walls.

The slope of the floor was steeper than it had been before. Sicarius had to hold on to the walls to keep his footing. He headed downward and westward, towards the brightest light source. A fading heat trail, detected by his auspex, suggested that someone had recently come this way: the Apothecary, he hoped.

He ducked beneath a half-collapsed archway and emerged into the light.

The *Indestructible*'s basilica towered, battered but defiant, behind him.

Sicarius looked out over the stepped layers of two of its quadrants, towards the labyrinth of Krieg trenches in the near-distance. The star fort's brief flight had taken it right back to where it had started. It was cradled by the same impact crater that its first and more violent crash landing had created.

The damage, this time, was more extensive, as Ultracius had intimated. Many of the star fort's hangars and weapons bays had crumbled into each other. There were bodies, hundreds of bodies, sprawled across them. Many of them belonged to Khargask's brutish followers; more of them, the majority, did not.

He removed his helmet, to feel fresh air on his face again. He remembered that the air of this tiny moon was poisonous, so he couldn't risk breathing it for long, though his genhanced body would filter the worst of it. Sergeant Lucien had already contacted their orbiting battle-barge and had them send the Thunderhawks. Sicarius would welcome their timely arrival.

He heard a skittering of adamantium chips above him.

A squealing, scrabbling something landed heavily on his shoulders. A gretchin, he realised, had concealed itself behind one of the decorative gothic mouldings, waiting for a target to pass beneath it.

He wondered if it had waited especially for him, if it possessed the intellect to identify his captain's insignia. Had it not been for its abominable xenos nature, he might have admired its gall. Its ork masters were dead and their plans, quite literally, in ruins. It could have slinked away and perhaps survived; instead, it was taking one final, desperate chance to do harm to its enemies.

The gretchin stabbed at Sicarius's eyes with a knife.

Having heard it coming, however, he was already in motion. He dropped to his good right knee before it could secure a grip on him. Its blade thrust went awry and the gretchin's feet shot out from underneath it. It bounced off Sicarius's left shoulder and he caught it with his right hand. The wiry creature squirmed fiercely in his grip and slashed at his armoured fingers with its blade. He drove its head into the wall of the basilica behind him, dampening its defiance by cracking its skull.

He tossed the gretchin over an ornamental balustrade. It cleared two of the star fort's outer storeys to end up smeared across the third. Sicarius thanked the Emperor for a fortuitous escape. Small and weak as the creature had been, it might still have blinded him or worse. He could have been the captain who had lost an eye to an imp, an object lesson that no foe should ever be underestimated.

He clambered over the balustrade himself, and lowered himself to the next level and then the next. Beneath him, he saw Death Korpsmen digging through the wreckage to their dead. Did they never rest, he wondered? He thought, at first, that they were trying to extricate their late brothers-in-arms for burial. They seemed more interested, however, in salvaging what they could of their equipment.

Some of his Ultramarines were assisting with that effort, in lieu of further orders, while others had weapons and armour of their own to patch up.

The *Indestructible*'s western-facing ramparts were lower than they had been, thanks to its new and more pronounced list. It was possible to hop from them to the ground; at least, it was for someone wearing power armour. In the star fort's shadow, Sicarius saw a Korpsman – or rather, a Korpsman's peaked cap – that he recognised, and knew that he ought to face its wearer.

Commissar Dast was busy coordinating the recovery effort. Sicarius waited for him to take a breath before he approached him. He congratulated the commissar on his regiment's loyal service. 'Had your men not fought so hard and so well, then Khargask would have had more orks to protect his engine room. This war might have ended very differently, and more tragically for all of us.'

That said, he asked how many Krieg men had been lost.

'Our quartermasters are still counting the bodies,' said Dast. 'I expect the final tally to be close to eighteen hundred.' If he felt any bitterness about that, his tone didn't betray it. *Close to eighteen hundred lives,* thought Sicarius. *Almost ninety per cent of their original strength.* He knew how he would feel were he ever to lose ninety battle-brothers to a single mission.

'The most remarkable thing is,' a voice interjected from

behind him, 'that, while we are screening and conditioning and training and implanting new, raw recruits to replace our fallen battle-brothers, the 319th Krieg Siege Regiment will be back up to full strength and fighting for the Emperor in a matter of months.'

The voice belonged to Sergeant Lucien, who had walked up behind Sicarius as he and Dast conversed. 'Isn't that right, Commissar Dast?' Lucien asked pointedly, though he didn't meet the commissar's blank-eyed gaze. He had noticed the big mek's skull attached to Sicarius's belt and was admiring that instead.

Sicarius detected a brief hesitation before Dast answered. 'That's right,' he agreed. 'The Death Korps of Krieg is, ah, indestructible.'

He turned smartly on his heel and strode away.

'The Astra Militarum has a medal,' Lucien told his captain, 'the Triple Skull. It is awarded to survivors of campaigns where the casualty rate has been extremely high. We ought to recommend the survivors of the Krieg 319th for that honour. Their captain should be awarded the Winged Skull for his inspirational leadership.'

Sicarius nodded, silently.

'Never did a man of them flinch from his duty,' Lucien continued. 'Never did they question what the Emperor would have them do, nor stand back and hope that someone else would offer his life in their stead. I wish you could have seen them as I did, captain, for you would have been as proud of them as I am.'

An approaching scream of engines drew Sicarius's eyes to the sky.

Ultracius and the others had just emerged from inside the *Indestructible*, carrying Gallo and Lumic between them. Sicarius hadn't seen Renius since he had woken. He wasn't listed among the dead, however. He had likely descended to the star fort's buried bowels, to sift through the remnants of the Adeptus Mechanicus's precious engines.

Sicarius set out across the cold, dark plain to meet the first of the arriving Thunderhawk transport ships. There were other battles to be fought, and more glory to be won.

MARNEUS CALGAR: LORD OF ULTRAMAR

GRAHAM McNEILL

The Temple of Correction was quiet. Well into the Veil Watch, Calgar saw only a handful of pilgrims and supplicants walking the slow circuit around the shimmering sepulchre of the Avenging Son.

It wasn't just the late hour that kept the Temple of Correction quiet. Visitors to Macragge were few and far between these days.

The war against the Bloodborn had seen to that. Scattered remnants of M'kar's ruinous host still infested the asteroid belts and the farthest corners of Ultramar, raiding and causing whatever spiteful havoc they could muster.

Lazlo Tiberius had the Chapter fleets rooting the traitors from their every bolthole, but Ultramar was thick with places to hide.

Upon seeing the Chapter Master of the Ultramarines, the pilgrims bowed or fell to their knees in adoration. A few even hesitantly approached, but a warning glance from the axe-bearing warriors of the Honour Guard soon dissuaded them from coming any closer.

Calgar wished Eryx's veterans did not have to be so inflexible, but the Decree of Protection was absolute and unbending. Bloodborn infiltrators had reached the surface of Macragge in the guise of pilgrims, and no-one wanted a repeat of what happened to Fabian of the Third at Evanestus.

Calgar recognised the specific gene-traits of men and women from Espandor and Quintarn. He heard dialects from those worlds closest to Macragge, even a man whispering in the dark vowels characteristic to Konor's eastern cities.

To reach the crown world of Ultramar, these people would have followed the Pilgrim Trail from Iax to Calth, from Calth to Espandor and then to Macragge. Those with means might once have diverted to Talassar to see the ancient walls of Castra Tanagra, but nobody went there now.

Castra Tanagra had seen too much death, too much suffering. Its wounds were too fresh to be gaped at, even respectfully. In time, the pilgrims would return to its high valley, but Ultramar had tears yet to shed before then.

'I like to come here when I need to restore my equilibrium,' said a voice from a recessed reliquary. 'I imagine it is the same for you, my lord.'

'Were you waiting here for me?' asked Calgar, as Varro Tigurius emerged from the reliquary, his skull-topped staff held loosely in his right hand.

'Why would you think I might be?'

Calgar bit back his first response, in no mood for his

Chief Librarian's habit of answering a question with one of his own.

'Because you have petitioned me for the last week with an audience, and you know I often come here when it's quiet.'

'Does it help coming here?' asked Tigurius. 'To lessen the burden upon you, I mean?'

'Sometimes,' admitted Calgar. 'I look up at Lord Guilliman and I think of the times he lived through. It comforts me to know that what we face is a spit in the rain compared to what the Five Hundred Worlds faced then.'

'Then I will pre-emptively offer an apology.'

'For what?'

'For adding to your burden.'

Calgar beckoned Tigurius forward. The Honour Guard parted to allow the Librarian within their armoured shieldwall.

'The last year has been hard, yes?' said Tigurius, taking Calgar's proffered hand.

'I don't have time for this, Varro,' said Calgar, and they set off on a circuit of the mighty primarch's shimmering stasis tomb. 'Just say what you have to say.'

'The past year has been hard,' repeated Tigurius. 'The losses suffered in turning back the Bloodborn were grievous, and all efforts are bent to replenishing the ranks of the fighting companies. Few are the petitions from beyond our borders for aid to which you will grant an audience.'

'Fewer still are those to whom I send my warriors.'

'With good reason,' said Tigurius. He paused as they came to the marble slab marked with the dead of the Veteran Company. 'Our realm is weaker than it has been for centuries and, more and more, the burden of its defence falls to the mortals of Ultramar.'

Calgar's huge gauntlets curled into fists. His temper had been a fraying thing of late, and the obliqueness of Tigurius's approach was only making it worse.

'Did you set this ambush just to depress me further or is there a point to all this?' he asked.

Tigurius nodded and looked up at the list of names rendered in gold leaf on the pale marble. At the head of the list was the name of First Company's greatest hero in living memory, Saul Invictus.

Calgar reached out to touch it as he always did.

'The point, my lord,' continued Tigurius, 'is that a decision must be made concerning Agemman. I know you value his counsel and his sword arm, but this is not the time to allow past glories and a lifetime of honourable service to blind us to the fact that Castra Tanagra has changed him.'

'Severus Agemman is a hero of Ultramar,' said Calgar with a warning tone. 'A hero of the Imperium.'

'That he is,' agreed Tigurius. 'No question. I stood with him on the walls of Castra Tanagra. I watched the two of you face the daemon lord, but he is not the man he once was.'

'None of us are, Varro,' said Calgar, looking at the gaunt, drawn features of the librarian. 'Perhaps you most of all.'

Holding the daemons back from the walls of Castra Tanagra had drained Tigurius in ways Calgar could never know.

Tigurius smiled grimly. 'There's truth in that, my lord, but you know of what I speak. The First Company needs a warrior who can lead them in battle, and Severus has never fully recovered from the daemon lord's blow that struck him down. You know it, and I know it.'

'You would have me replace him?'

'I would,' said Tigurius.

'And who could replace him? Sicarius? Ventris? Galenus?'

'It is not my place to say.'

'Since when has *that* ever stopped you?'

'This decision must be yours and yours alone,' said Tigurius. 'Much depends upon you making the right choice.'

Calgar heard the subtext.

'Is there something I need to know?'

'Many things,' said Tigurius. 'But chief among them is that a new enemy gathers, an inhuman foe whose ancient mind is beyond anything we have faced before.'

Tigurius looked up into the face of the Avenging Son.

'And we must be ready to face it.'

ABOUT THE AUTHORS

Gav Thorpe is the author of the Horus Heresy novel *Deliverance Lost*, as well as the novellas *Corax: Soulforge, Ravenlord* and *The Lion*, which formed part of the *New York Times* bestselling collection *The Primarchs*. He is particularly well-known for his Dark Angels stories, including the Legacy of Caliban series. His Warhammer 40,000 repertoire further includes the Path of the Eldar series, the Horus Heresy audio dramas *Raven's Flight, Honour to the Dead* and *Raptor*, and a multiplicity of short stories. For Warhammer, Gav has penned the End Times novel *The Curse of Khaine*, the Time of Legends trilogy, The Sundering, and much more besides. He lives and works in Nottingham.

Nick Kyme is the author of the Horus Heresy novels *Deathfire* and *Vulkan Lives*, the novellas *Promethean Sun* and *Scorched Earth*, and the audio drama *Censure*. His novella *Feat of Iron* was a *New York Times* bestseller in the Horus Heresy collection, *The Primarchs*. Nick is well known for his popular Salamanders novels, including *Rebirth*, the Space Marine Battles novel *Damnos*, and numerous short stories. He has also written fiction set in the world of Warhammer, most notably the Time of Legends novel *The Great Betrayal*. He lives and works in Nottingham, and has a rabbit.

Graham McNeill has written more Horus Heresy novels than any other Black Library author! His canon of work includes *Vengeful Spirit* and his *New York Times* bestsellers *A Thousand Sons* and the novella *The Reflection Crack'd*, which featured in *The Primarchs* anthology. Graham's Ultramarines series, featuring Captain Uriel Ventris, is now six novels long, and has close links to his Iron Warriors stories, the novel *Storm of Iron* being a perennial favourite with Black Library fans. He has also written a Mars trilogy, featuring the Adeptus Mechanicus. For Warhammer, he has written the Time of Legends trilogy The Legend of Sigmar, the second volume of which won the 2010 David Gemmell Legend Award. Originally hailing from Scotland, Graham now lives and works in Nottingham.

Josh Reynolds is the author of the Blood Angels novel *Deathstorm* and the Warhammer 40,000 novellas *Hunter's Snare* and *Dante's Canyon*, along with the audio drama *Master of the Hunt*, all three featuring the White Scars. In the Warhammer World, he has written The End Times novels *The Return of Nagash* and *The Lord of the End Times*, the Gotrek & Felix tales *Charnel Congress, Road of Skulls* and *The Serpent Queen*, and the novels *Neferata, Master of Death* and *Knight of the Blazing Sun*. He lives and works in Northampton.

Steve Lyons's work in the Warhammer 40,000 universe includes the novellas *Engines of War* and *Angron's Monolith*, the Imperial Guard novels *Ice World* and *Dead Men Walking* – now collected in the omnibus *Honour Imperialis* – and the audio dramas *Waiting Death* and *The Madness Within*. He has also written numerous short stories and is currently working on more tales from the grim darkness of the far future.

WARHAMMER
40,000

LEGENDS OF THE DARK MILLENNIUM

SONS OF CORAX

GEORGE MANN